# *The* **Icing**
## *on*
# *The* **Corpse**

## Mary Jane Maffini

### RENDEZVOUS PRESS

Cover art: Christopher Chuckry

LE CONSEIL DES ARTS DU CANADA DEPUIS 1957 | THE CANADA COUNCIL FOR THE ARTS SINCE 1957

We acknowledge the support of the Canada Council for the Arts for our publishing program

Napoleon Publishing/RendezVous Press
Toronto, Ontario, Canada

2nd printing 2007
Printed in Canada

11 10 09 08 07    5 4 3 2

13-digit ISBN  978-0929141-81-7

Canadian Cataloguing in Publication

Maffini, Mary Jane, date—
    The icing on the corpse: a Camilla MacPhee mystery


ISBN 0-929141-81-4

I. Title.

PS8576.A3385I25 2001          C813'.54          C2001-901970-X
PR9199.3.M3428I25 2001

I owe special thanks to Mary Mackay-Smith, Janet MacEachen and Keary Grace for their generous help with this book. I am also grateful to Dr. Lorne Parent and Kate Jaimet for their time and information.

The Ladies Killing Circle: Joan Boswell, Victoria Cameron, Audrey Jessup, Sue Pike and Linda Wiken continued to supply their eagle eyes, sound judgment and firm friendship. My daughters, Victoria Maffini and Virginia Findlay and my husband, Giulio Maffini, to whom I present an ongoing challenge, have shown endless support.

I am most fortunate to have Sylvia McConnell as my publisher and Allister Thompson as my editor. They never fail to be unflappable and enthusiastic.

*You won't find Mimi Melanson's Bridal Bower, Women Against Violence Everywhere, St. Jim's Parish or the exact location of the Justice for Victims office anywhere in Ottawa. However, you can certainly eat BeaverTails on the canal and skate to work if your timing's right.*

# One

Work is what saves me. It has been four years since that loser chug-a-lugged a six-pack then swallowed a palmful of downers and hurtled his RX-7 into the Toyota Tercel carrying my husband. Now Paul is just a picture above my desk, forever thirty, but the lowlife who killed him still breathes and drives.

Perhaps a time will come when I can forgive.

If I didn't see people much worse off than I am every day, who knows how far down the greased ladder of self-pity I could slide. But I do see them and, when I do my job well, I believe I can make a difference.

When I do it well.

\*     \*     \*

It was still dark when I snapped awake. Lindsay Grace's file was on my mind. This was one case where I had to make that difference. Because with Lindsay, we were talking the difference between life and death. I was prepared to do anything. Depositions. Court appearances. Appeals. Calls to the media. Hunger strikes. Name it.

This one mattered.

I remembered the first day she had come to see me. She was tentative but pumped up by my friend, Elaine Ekstein, the Executive Director of Women Against Violence Everywhere. Elaine had explained that WAVE was committed to assisting women like Lindsay, and I damn well should be too. I listened to Lindsay's story, and Elaine squeezed her hand.

Then it was my turn to talk about legal options. That's why I run Justice for Victims. I talked long and hard. Nearly two hours later, Lindsay began to imagine the possibility of life without the man who could stub his cigarette on the soft skin of her belly after they'd made love.

I found it hard to picture the high-flyer Lindsay Grace had been. Hard to understand why a successful and attractive financial analyst would let herself become the emotional hostage of someone like Benning. It was harder still to keep my personal opinions to myself and concentrate on the job at hand. I bit my tongue.

Somehow, after that session, Lindsay Grace found the strength to testify against Ralph Benning. She stood in court and faced him. She knew, as we all did, that if Ralph Benning ever had the chance, he'd kill her without letting the smile slip from his handsome face.

Convictions weren't enough to keep her safe. During his previous trial for assaulting his wife, twelve jurors took less than an hour to express society's revulsion. The judge expeditiously sentenced Benning to the maximum allowable sentence for the crime. Not soft time in medium or minimum security. Kingston Penitentiary. The real deal. But the law's the law, and it cuts both ways.

Mandatory supervision placed Ralph Benning back on the streets eighteen months later. He'd had long enough to work up a good head of steam against the women who had put him in maximum security. Against Rina Benning, his damaged wife. And the girlfriend he had trusted to perjure herself for him. The woman who had let him down with a little help from her friends.

Lindsay Grace. He hadn't found Lindsay.

Rina Benning hadn't been so lucky. It was a hard six months before she got out of rehab. She hadn't been well enough to testify at his current trial for damn near killing her. Not that it mattered.

No thinking person would believe for a minute Ralph Benning could end up a free man. Not after those photos of his wife's bruises, not after the X-rays showed the damage a baseball bat had done to her ribs, not after the dry, flat tone of the expert witness describing the internal injuries, not after seeing Rina Benning with her jaw still wired, one eye sightless.

What court could fail to find him guilty? It was his twenty-sixth conviction. All that remained was the sentencing. But it would take more than that to put Lindsay Grace's mind at ease.

*   *   *

Peace bonds. Restraining orders. Lindsay Grace knew well enough that you can't count on papers to work with someone who doesn't feel bound by the rule of law. Someone like Ralph Benning.

How many times had Benning made the news for being totally out of control? And how many times had he been on the street in less than a year? Ten years wouldn't be enough to civilize Benning. It was time to put him behind bars and let him rot.

As Benning's sentencing hearing drew closer, the media was paying attention. It was an open secret the Crown was planning to bring an application to have him declared a dangerous offender. Benning was always news in our town. Rina Benning had declined to be interviewed about her husband. Persistent calls from reporters and the flash of cameras outside her Hunt

Club residence wouldn't be doing her nerves much good.

Lindsay Grace was no better off. Even though Elaine Ekstein and I were supposed to be the only people who knew where she lived, she still spent the days in tears and the nights in panic.

Now, in four short hours, after one trial too many, the Crown would apply to launch the long process. I'd done my best to help. I was one hundred per cent certain Ralph Benning would reoffend. The stakes were high enough. If he weren't locked away at the pleasure of the Queen, Lindsay Grace would never have another peaceful moment.

I'd had my kick at the can. I had delivered documents, statements, evidence, addresses, files, you name it, to the Crown Attorney's office. Anything that would help.

They'd have to do it without Lindsay. She was far too frightened to come out of hiding, terrified of facing Benning again in Court. Two years earlier she'd been cool, beautiful, affluent, a rising star. Today, there weren't enough drugs to take the shake out of her hands.

Lindsay's scars might be less visible than Rina's. But they were no less real. The Crown would not be able to rely on her in their bid to toss away the key to Benning's cell. That was too bad. The court doesn't hand out dangerous offender designations with ease. You have to work hard for them.

January 31 would be the first day of a long fight. And with Benning's charm and history of manipulating the law, the odds were against us.

# Two

Some Mondays start badly. When the wind chill factor approaches minus forty, you can count on it. Any day I ran into Mia Reilly started badly too. With the Benning application on my mind, I didn't need the weather or Mia. But she was right in my face as I sniffed the cranberry muffins and waited for a caffeine boost at the Second Cup on Elgin.

I stamped my feet and blew on my fingers.

It wasn't even eight o'clock.

Some of my old law school classmates are quite tolerable, but you couldn't put Mia into that category. She'd always been irritating. Her hundred-dollar haircut was irritating. The nose she'd had restructured after graduation was irritating. The teeth she'd had capped last year were irritating. The same could be said for her cologne: some pricey combination of cedar and bergamot. Mia was on the fast track as an Assistant Crown Attorney, which compounded all the other irritations.

It always bugged my butt to see Mia in my own personal Second Cup, even if it was just a block from the courthouse. If I'd wanted to chat, I would have picked my police reporter buddy, P. J. Lynch, who waved from the bench in the back. P. J.'s one of the world's great talkers, but I wasn't in the mood. On the other hand, this was not the right day to get on the wrong side of the Crown Attorney's office.

"So, Camilla," Mia lifted her expensive nose, "I hear your

sister's getting married again."

Leave it to Smiley Reilly to remind me my favourite sister, Alexa, was about to marry my not-so-favourite Ottawa cop, Detective Sergeant Conn McCracken. Even worse, I'd been fingered as a bridesmaid.

I ignored her and showered an extra thick haze of chocolate powder over my *latte*. I should have remembered it takes more than rudeness to ditch Mia Reilly.

She was in an upbeat mood. "Your sister's what? Fifteen years older than you? Late forties? Fifty? Hope for anyone, I guess."

She leaned in, still smiling expensively, and moved her hand so I couldn't avoid the diamond solitaire. It had to be in the twenty thousand dollar range. One false move and she could knock your eye out with that sucker. "You're right," I said. "There's hope for anyone."

I didn't grow up with three older sisters without learning to be a bitch when the moment requires.

But that was too subtle for Mia. She tossed her head and each strand of the sleek blonde bob fell back into place artfully. "So, Camilla. Are you ever going to try the dating game again?"

I snapped the lid on the *latte*. "When Hell freezes over."

She laughed. Irritatingly. "Bitter, bitter."

"You bet. And speaking of bitter, do you think the Crown will mess up with Benning today?"

"That is so not fair. Of course they won't. He'll get dangerous offender status. It will take a while, but he's going away *forever*."

"About time," I said.

"I wish I'd worked on that file. I ended up with the *drill bandit* instead."

"Who?

"You *know*. That guy who drilled little holes in car doors parked near the canal, then popped the trunks and made off with one credit card from each purse? You haven't heard of that? I mean, he's pulled off hundreds of these. But he slipped up. I'm so glad we got him before Winterlude this year." With a last fond look at her diamond, she slid her hand into a pair of fur-lined black kid gloves.

I was at a loss for words. As if a minor pilferer was even worth talking about on the day of Benning's sentencing. I barely managed not to say "Who gives a rat's ass?"

I picked up my cup and the bag with my chocolate almond *biscotti* and made a serious effort to put as much distance between us as possible. I elbowed my way through the crowd and out the door. Outside the Second Cup, I couldn't resist a sharp intake of breath. Hell had frozen over all right.

I jumped at the tap on my shoulder. P. J. Lynch was shrugging on his coat in the cool way young guys have and sharing his wide grin.

"Big day for you."

"No kidding." You have to love P. J. Maybe it's the carrot-coloured hair. Maybe it's that space between his two front teeth. Maybe it's the way he loves to shoot the shit.

"Fingers crossed, Tiger." He lit a cigarette. He's usually pretty perky, but this morning he was rumpled with dark circles under his eyes. Probably up all night.

"Thanks. What are you doing in the Second Cup, P. J.? I thought you disapproved of fancy coffees."

"Free country. You heading for Court?"

"I have a couple of items to take care of at the office first. Benning's on the docket for 10.00 a.m. today." The truth was I didn't want to spend an hour pacing publicly. It would be hard enough to keep still and shut up during the application. If I showed up early, there was a distinct chance I'd get myself in some trouble while waiting.

"Don't forget about our Winterlude date," he said.

"What?"

"Winterlude. We're taking my sister's kids out on the canal this weekend, remember?"

His sister's kids? I didn't even remember that P.J. had a sister, let alone that we had a date with her kids. The whole Benning thing had been blitzing my brain. "Right," I said.

"You're not going to slither out of it, Camilla."

"I never slither."

"Sunday evening."

"Of course."

"Got a tip for you. There's more to life than work."

"Not today there isn't," I said.

P. J. blew smoke out the side of his mouth and away from my face. The wind blew it back. Lucky for him he was cute. "Don't worry. That creep will get what's coming to him today. It doesn't matter how many cops he has in his pocket."

"Here's hoping."

"Make sure you practice your skating, Camilla. These two little guys are a handful." He turned and headed back into the Second Cup.

That was a relief. P. J. was a helpful colleague, and I knew he believed someone on the local police force had done a lot of favours for Benning in the past. But any quotes from me would have led to grief if they had gotten into print. My family kept reminding me to watch what I said to the media. I tried.

In the few minutes it took to hike the block and a half towards the offices of Justice for Victims, I could feel the welcome heat seep out of my *latte*. With fresh snow on the sidewalk, it was lousy weather for staying on your feet. Everyone was late. People were mad as hell. Drivers peered through golf-ball-sized peepholes in frosted windshields. Just a matter of time until one of them swerved off the street. Perhaps it only looked liked they were aiming for pedestrians.

I was nearing the office when I heard the first sirens shriek. Three police cruisers, roof-lights flashing, edged past the stalled lines of traffic and shot north on Elgin St. I figured it must have been a robbery. Normally, I'd picture a terrorized teller in a big bank on Sparks Street, gaping at the gun pointed at her face. Of course, normally, I wasn't fighting hypothermia and losing.

I caught a glimpse of P. J. rocketing out of the Second Cup, his coat flapping open as he raced along the sidewalk. He might have been up all night, but where there are sirens, there are stories. Life had been a bit harder for police reporters since the Ottawa police acquired their digital system which you couldn't pick up on an ordinary newsroom scanner. So P. J. Lynch didn't pass up stories, even if he'd just worked all night.

I'd almost reached the door of the office when my cellphone rang. I balanced on frozen toes and tried to avoid getting knocked into the street by a slip-sliding man with a briefcase. To hell with it. I let it ring. It would be one of my three sisters and the subject would be Alexa's wedding and why I wasn't more cooperative about it. They all had cellphones and there was no getting away from them.

So hardly worth getting killed over. Another minute and the *latte* would be as cold as my toes and I wasn't even sure they were still attached to my feet. By the time I hit the front door, two more cruisers had flashed past. Must be one hell of a bank job, I thought as I heaved myself up the stairs to the second floor. I figured the *latte* was solid.

The sirens screamed on.

I opened my office door, holding the coffee between my chest and my chin. The bag with my chocolate almond *biscotti* was clutched in my teeth.

"Gotta go, Ma. Camilla's getting in. Don't worry about anything." Alvin, my office assistant, hung up the phone.

"I hope I don't find another batch of collect calls from Sydney on the next phone bill," I said.

"Hey, Camilla. Just fourteen days left before Valentine's Day, *le jour de l'amour.*"

"Do not speak." I kicked the door closed. Valentine's Day is never my favourite occasion. This year my sister had chosen it for her wedding day. Another strike against it.

The bag with the *biscotti* slipped from my mouth and tumbled to the floor. Naturally, the cellphone rang again.

"Gee, I wonder who that is?" Alvin said. "We've already had a couple of calls from your sisters this morning."

I let it ring. "Tell me something I wouldn't already know."

Alvin tossed his ponytail. "This wedding is making you grouchier than usual, although *that* is hard to imagine. Try to chill out."

"I'm chilled, Alvin."

I plunked the *latte* on his desk and started to remove layers. Trusty parka. Wool hat. Thinsulate gloves. Snazzy leather boots. They were just three months old. Too bad they held in the damp and let out the heat. I had to replace them, but it was too cold to shop. I hate when my teeth chatter.

"People carry on about the weather up here, but I think it's all in the mind," Alvin smirked.

"Oh, come on, don't you miss those mild Atlantic winters, Alvin? Soft fog, gentle breezes, mild temperatures?"

"Wet feet," Alvin said, "grey days. Nope. Give me real weather any time. I love this stuff."

Too bad. I always had high hopes I'd stumble on a way to send Alvin back to his loving family in Nova Scotia.

As usual, it was marginally warmer inside the offices of Justice for Victims than outside. I kept on the fleece, the silk long underwear and the red thermal socks—good to thirty below. I figured it wouldn't take more than twenty minutes until my toes rejoined the party.

You get what you pay for in office space. In our case, not much. Justice for Victims is in a lousy financial position at best. It would be a hell of a lot worse if I took a realistic salary. Or if Alvin did.

Was it my imagination or could I see my breath? I put the hat back on.

"Guess you're not expecting anyone to drop in," Alvin said.

I still didn't bite.

"Wind chill factor must be some new record. I can tell because all those little hairs on your upper lip are covered with frost."

My hand shot up to my face.

"What hairs on my upper lip?" The words were out of my mouth before I could stop myself.

Alvin so often wins in the game of gotcha. As if it weren't bad enough being the stubby, dark-haired younger sister to a trio of elegant, willowy blondes, now I had a moustache. This could send my family into crisis. They'd have me waxed and plucked and probed by a dermatologist if they even suspected a hairy upper lip.

Alvin leaned back and flicked his ponytail over his shoulder. Behind the cat's eye glasses, his eyes glittered. He didn't react to the cold other than conversationally. The shirt with the parrot motif was a nice touch. So was the Jimmy Buffett CD. "Margaritaville" blasted out of Alvin's portable player.

But what was different about him? Ah. I spotted the squeeze tube of flash tan on the desk. That explained the coconut scent in the air. It also explained why Alvin's face was an odd shade of rust, as was one of his arms.

"Are you turning orange, Alvin? Perhaps you should seek medical attention before it's too late."

"I'm using the power of positive thinking. You should try it. Decide it's not cold. Let your mind dictate to your body."

"Assuming you have a mind," I muttered. "The jury's still out."

But Alvin wasn't finished. "If your mind dictates to your body, then you don't have to be a prisoner of winter and wear ugly clothes and have frost on your lip which makes you look like W. O. Mitchell. The white moustache, I mean, especially teamed with those red socks. Although, I'm not sure W.O. would have been caught dead in that hat."

I picked up the coffee from his desk, bent down and retrieved the bag with the *biscotti*, and limped over to my own desk. I sat in silence and popped the lid. All the foam was gone. I took my first taste. Slightly better than a cold shower.

"It's not a style for everybody, but you carry it off, Camilla."

Sometimes you have to make the best of adversity. On a typical day, I send Alvin on clusters of low-level yet time-consuming errands all over town: the post office, the dry cleaners, the bank. He finds addresses from the public library, pays traffic tickets at City Hall, and picks out birthday cards for my sisters, although after his last selection I had to stop that. But this could be the morning to send him to the drugstore for panty liners.

I dipped my *biscotti* into the flat cool *latte* and daydreamed about precisely what it would take to carry Alvin out of my life. I was rubbing my socks in an effort to restore feeling to my toes when the phone rang. And rang again.

"Answer the phone, Alvin." I did not swear. I did not indulge in sarcasm. I did not hyperventilate. Not even on the third ring. I didn't want Alvin to press my buttons. This was harder than it sounds. "And take a message if it's one of my sisters."

Midway through the fourth ring, before it flipped over to call answer, Alvin lifted the receiver with a languid hand and produced the kind of upbeat chirp you might expect in a chewing gum commercial.

"Justice for Victims. Good morning! Yes. Yes, it is. What? Oh! All right, certainly, I'll see if she's available. Please hold."

"What? Of course I'm available. I'm right in front of you." I reached over and snatched the receiver from Alvin's hand. "Camilla MacPhee here."

"It's your sister," Alvin said.

"Damn." Too late. I didn't even have time to ask which one.

Edwina's measured tones drifted down the line. "Camilla, you have to get rid of that boy." In a previous life Edwina might have been a head of state, leading the population through war and famine, brooking no opposition, keeping the dungeons full. Of my three sisters, she is the one I am least fond of finding on the end of a phone line.

"Perhaps you're right," I said, "but I'm always afraid they'll bring back the death penalty."

"Why can't he answer the phone like any normal person?"

"He can't, that's all. He just can't, and he'll never be able to. Deal with it and move on, Edwina. Or better yet, back me up the next time I try to tell our mutual father why I need a change of staff."

"Oh, Camilla, you know how Daddy is about helping people. He'd never understand."

Nicely understated. Somewhere back in time, my father had fond memories of Alvin's mother, now the widow of a spectacularly alcoholic shoe salesman. Alvin was number six of seven children and definitely in need of help. Since my father is the only person in the world I've never talked back to, Alvin continues to clog my life in his own special way.

My cellphone rang. This time Alvin answered on ring one.

"You're right, Daddy won't understand," I said to Edwina. "And I'm stuck with the situation. So learn to call me at home."

Alvin tapped my shoulder.

Edwina likes to dish out orders, not receive them. "No need to be snippy, Miss. I need your cooperation to deal with Alexa's wedding. The way it's going, it will drive the whole family crazy."

I swatted at Alvin's hand. "Take a message," I mouthed.

"The whole family's already crazy, Edwina," I said. "And what do you have to complain about, anyway? It's not like you're stuck with being a bridesmaid. Try a little perspective."

"Perspective?" Edwina sounded like she was choking. "Don't tell me to show a little perspective, Little-Miss-I-can't cooperate on any of the arrangements for my own sister's wedding because I was put on this earth to make life difficult for the human race."

Alvin moved over to the front of my desk. He had his hand over the receiver. "I think you'd better take this one."

"Listen, Edwina, if you mean the…"

"You know exactly what I mean."

"No need to be nasty."

I showed Alvin my middle finger.

Edwina sputtered from the receiver.

*14*

"Gotta go, Edwina. We should keep the discussions of the wedding to non-office hours, since you're so emotional."

"What? You listen to me, Camilla MacPhee. You are the biggest problem we have. The point of my call is to tell you to shape up."

Alvin stuck his face six inches from mine. Behind the pointy black spectacles his eyes were slits. He tried to wrap my hand around the receiver.

"*One minute.*"

"Don't you 'one minute' me," Edwina barked. "Your sister has a well-deserved second chance at happiness, and she doesn't need you to act like a spoiled brat and ruin everything. Do I make myself clear?"

"If Alexa's foolish enough to think she can be happy with a pudgy middle-aged police officer…"

It takes more than a loud voice to force the supreme ruler to back down. "Fine. We're having a family dinner," she said. "Wednesday. My place. Six thirty. We'll discuss it then."

Family dinner? I thought fast. Trip out of town? Frostbite? Amnesia? "But."

"No buts. Stan will pick you up." Edwina hung up before I could think of twelve unassailable reasons why I couldn't attend. Trounced again.

Alvin paced in front of my desk. The parrots on his shirt flapped.

"Is it necessary to hound me when I'm on the phone?"

"It's Lindsay Grace," he said. "She says it's an emergency."

I grabbed the receiver.

"Lindsay?"

Nothing.

"Lindsay? It's Camilla. Are you all right?"

Dead air.

"Lindsay!" Shouting didn't help. The dial tone was the last sound I wanted to hear. I sank into my chair. To do Alvin credit, he didn't think it was funny.

"Did she say where she was calling from?"

He shook his head.

"Did she say what happened?"

"No. She said it was urgent, and she needed to talk to you."

"That was it?"

"She kept saying Benning was out."

"Hardly."

"That's what she said. She was practically hysterical."

"Well, she's often hysterical. And he can't be out. That's absurd."

"But what if he is?"

I couldn't bring myself to think about it.

"Not possible. Ralph Benning is a guest of the Regional Detention Centre, and he's not going anywhere."

"But it's *Benning*. Anything could happen. He is going somewhere. They have to move him to the Courthouse." Behind the fake tan, Alvin was pale. Who wouldn't be?

"Look, Alvin. He is behind Plexiglas and bars. When they move him, he'll be shackled and surrounded by big guys with Glocks and nervous twitches."

He turned toward the wall and bit his lip. "He'll murder her. Remember? He's threatened to."

I remembered all right. If anyone could escape, he could. And if Ralph Benning was out, he would find a way to kill Lindsay. No doubt about it. But how could he be out? My hands were shaking as I dialed her number.

But Lindsay Grace didn't answer.

# Three

Stop hyperventilating, Alvin."

"Well, do something. If he's cunning enough to slip out of jail, he can find her too."

"It's obviously some kind of mistake, but if she's upset, she needs help. I'll head right over and see what I can do to reassure her. It's probably the stress of knowing the sentencing hearing's today. She's been overwrought."

"I'll call 911," Alvin said. "She needs help."

I yanked the receiver from his hand. "No. Remember the last time he was on the loose so long? People figured he has some kind of inside contact. Even Lindsay thought so. We don't want some dispatcher blasting out Lindsay's address and the wrong person hearing it and passing the information on to Benning. He could use some of his connections to harass her."

"Lord thundering Jesus."

"Exactly." I stuck my feet into the depths of the icy boots.

"I'm coming with you." Alvin grabbed his studded black leather jacket from the coat rack. I knew his jacket had no winter lining, although it was accessorized with an extensive Mickey Mouse scarf. Oh sure, that was all I needed. To have to explain to my father and Alvin's sainted mother how I'd encouraged him to die of exposure while under my tutelage.

"You must be kidding."

"I'm not kidding." Alvin's black eyes flashed behind the cat's eye glasses.

"You are not coming."

"Yes, I am." Alvin was already zipping up the jacket.

"Get this straight, Alvin. You are staying here."

"Wrong."

I hate that manic glitter in his eyes. Time to change tactics. No point in discussing his lack of suitable winter clothing. I didn't want to bring on another bout of mind over matter. "Your newfound interest in social justice is touching, but it's important for you to be in the office."

"That's quite a change in policy."

He had a point. I spend my energy devising ways to remove him from the office on a permanent basis. He raised one eyebrow over the rim of the cat's eye glasses. It was an effect my sisters would have envied. But I was ready for him. "Lindsay may call here, and if you don't answer, she could panic and put herself at risk. She could go into hiding, and we wouldn't be able to contact her at all. That's why."

Alvin's hand paused on the zipper.

I said, "So, if she does call, keep her calm, find out what happened and call me on my cellphone."

Alvin removed the jacket and slumped back in his seat.

"Okay," he said.

I busied myself with my parka and gloves. I was still wearing the hat, socks and long silk underwear. Alvin busied himself staring at the phone. Jimmy Buffett busied himself singing "Trying to Reason With Hurricane Season".

I snatched the cellphone. "And turn the music off and put the radio on CBC. This is not a holiday camp."

Alvin plunked his feet on the desk and watched me slantily. "Aloha," he called as I headed for the parking garage.

*   *   *

I'd been parked long enough for my recently acquired, pre-enjoyed Honda Civic to chill. The engine turned over on the third try. By that time, the vinyl seats had frozen my behind. Despite the red socks, my feet felt ready for amputation. I sat shivering and prayed the car would warm up before the engine flooded or the battery died. It wouldn't help Lindsay Grace if I joined the long list of people praying to be rescued by the CAA. A one-hour wait on sub-zero vinyl.

Therefore, I wasn't going anywhere until the heat gauge crept from the red into the black zone. The air in the garage was full of exhaust fumes. I gobbled some mints to get the taste out of my mouth. Winter in the nation's capital. No end to the fun.

I kept trying Lindsay's line, but the phone rang on and on. I was about to dial for the tenth time, when my own phone rang. "Hello, Alvin. Did Lindsay call back?"

"Not yet."

"Then why are you tying up the line?"

"Don't you have your radio on?"

"No, I'm warming the car, and I don't want to drain the battery. I also don't want to chat. Hang up."

"It's on the radio. It's confirmed. Benning's escaped."

"What? I can't believe it!"

"Believe it. He was supposed to have had a dental emergency, and when they were moving him somewhere, he overpowered his guard somehow and disappeared."

"Not even possible."

"Possible, and that's not all. The guard who was escorting him? Benning bit off his nose."

"What?"

**19**

"Bit the guard's nose off." Alvin's voice rose.

"Oh, how could that happen? He had only one guard?"

"I don't know how many, but they reported Benning was armed."

"How could he be armed? He was in jail!"

"You tell me."

My heart thundered against my ribs. Lindsay.

Alvin said, "And there's an unconfirmed report an officer was shot."

"*When?*"

"As far as I can figure out, it must have happened about an hour ago. Explains all those sirens."

"Where are their brains? They might have figured out a lunatic like Benning would need a back-up guard. A guy facing an indefinite sentence might be willing to take a real big chance. But how the hell could he have a weapon?"

"Wait a minute. There's an update. Wow, shot at *least* one officer during his escape."

I was thinking fast.

Alvin squeaked, "He must have called Lindsay. No wonder she was so upset."

"No, her phone's unlisted. Only a couple of people have it. He wouldn't know it."

"Oh, right."

"Maybe she caught the news report and called us right away."

"Maybe."

"Has to be," I said.

"You better shift your butt, Camilla."

I let it slide, just that once.

Ralph Benning had nothing to lose going after Lindsay.

"I'm on my way, but we have to get the police there fast

without alerting Benning to the location."

"But you said… Okay, so how do we let them know?"

I fished out my phone book. "You track down Elaine Ekstein. Here's her cell number. She always picks up. Explain what's happened. She'll fix it. She makes a lot of noise as Executive Director of WAVE. She'll tell them to hustle enough officers over to Lindsay's and do it on the QT."

"But Elaine's a civilian. What if they don't listen to her?"

"Trust me. They'll listen. Every cop in this town's scared shitless of Elaine."

\*     \*     \*

My father spent twenty years as a high school principal. The legacy is a nice pension and a collection of useful clichés. His favourite saying has always been when the going gets tough, the tough get going. My sisters prefer to say when the going gets tough, the tough go shopping. In my case, when the going gets tough, the tough get stupid. Which means that I wasn't giving proper respect to Benning's cunning abilities as I eased off the ramp and onto the street.

January's gift to the residents of Ottawa had been snow. Most of it was still piled on the edges of the side streets. That reduced the streets to one car width in many cases. Under the snow was ice. I didn't want to slide off the road, because I already knew I wouldn't find a tow truck in any big hurry.

Well, what did I have to bitch about? Icy vinyl seats? Small potatoes compared to knowing that a man who would slam a wounded woman with a baseball bat was on your trail. Benning would still have the taste of the guard's blood in his mouth. But Lindsay. I couldn't imagine what it would feel like to sit alone and wait for Ralph Benning.

I used the time at red lights to place calls that might yield a bit of new information on the Benning situation. First, I phoned my brother-in-law-to-be in Major Crimes. We didn't see eye to eye on much, but he would be steaming over this. Conn McCracken takes a dim view of domestic assault, to begin with. He'd done the groundwork on Benning's last arrest. He'd seen Rina Benning's broken body in the hospital. He'd know what it meant to have Benning loose. He'd understand what Lindsay Grace was up against.

I left a message after the beep.

You'll never catch me complaining about voice mail. I love it. What's not to love about a technology where no one can avoid your opinions and instructions any time of the day or night?

Next I punched in P. J. Lynch's cell number. That's the best part about having a reporter friend. He'd know what was happening. If I were lucky, he'd fill me in. Speculation and all. He must have been on the line. I left my detailed message after the beep.

Twenty minutes later, six blocks from Lindsay's townhouse, my brain engaged. Benning was smart. I still got chills remembering his cocky smirk when I'd accompanied Lindsay to testify at his trial. He knew I was her legal support. He knew I was connected and in touch. As soon as the word reached her or me, he'd bet I'd head out to protect her.

He would have done his homework, would have had some confederate research all of Lindsay's contacts. He probably had my home address. He'd know where I worked. All he'd have to do was sit and watch my office during the day until I headed out. Then he could follow me. He'd have no trouble waiting. Plenty of practice in Kingston.

I had failed Lindsay once, and I was about to fail her again. I pulled over and sat nudged up against four feet of solid packed snowbank. On the far side of the banks the red vinyl covers on the parking meters told me parking was off limits until the snow clearing had been completed.

A steady stream of cars edged by, most of the drivers shooting reproachful glances. Every second driver blew his horn.

I stared back at each vehicle, expecting to catch Ralph Benning's hard black eyes boring through my soul. The first break in the traffic, I climbed out and pretended to fish a blanket from the trunk. No one was parked behind me. I didn't spot Benning in the straggly line of traffic.

But he was out there. So how the hell could I connect with Lindsay without inviting Benning to the party?

\*     \*     \*

"What?" Alvin said. "Are you out of your tiny mind?"

"Show a little respect. I am, after all, your employer."

"I suppose you are. In the broadest sense of the term."

"I am your employer in every sense of the term. Do I understand that is no longer your heart's desire?"

"Yeah, but this is not an office administration activity. Admit it, Camilla."

"I believe it falls under Other Duties as Required."

"Well, I don't think it's legal to ask someone to pretend to be someone else."

"Alvin, say the word, and I'll put an ad in the paper for a replacement."

"No need to be snotty. You could at least give me one good reason."

"Lindsay Grace is the reason. If Benning follows me, and he's sharp enough to, I'll lead him right to her."

"Well, why didn't you say so? Do you have to be so frigging

mysterious? Give me a minute. And listen, I can't reach Elaine. I left messages at her home, her office, and her cellphone."

"Did you leave my cellphone number?"

"Of course."

"Don't worry. We'll hear from her. And Alvin…"

"On my way." He hung up before I could tell him it would take me a while to negotiate the drive back.

The line was already busy when I dialed again. Oh, well.

"Aloha," I said.

\*   \*   \*

With a one-way street system, you don't get anywhere in a minute. No matter how much you want to. With the clogged streets and cop cruisers everywhere, it took nearly half an hour to reach my parking garage.

I drew some satisfaction from the thought of dragging Benning on a wild goose chase. I tried not to dwell on Alvin in the garage. By the time I edged up the ramp and into my spot, the car was nice and warm. Alvin was neither warm nor nice.

"If you hadn't hung up on me, I would have told you to wait for me in the office."

I couldn't make out what he answered the way his teeth chattered.

"Head back to the office." I clanged after him down the metal stairwell to our level. "We'll talk on the beach at Fort Lauderdale."

"Mmmind over mmmatter." He didn't break stride.

\*   \*   \*

"All right," I said when Alvin showed signs of recovery. "I

**24**

should have made myself clear." It was hard not to feel bad about Alvin's half-frozen state. Especially since I'd been hoping he'd exhibit an unacceptable level of insubordination and I would be forced, despite my kind and gentle nature, to fire him.

"The weather doesn't bother me." He shook like a wet wolfhound.

I was not used to him being polite. "I told you I was sorry."

"And I told you I'm fine. Not cold at all. Don't waste time. That maniac could be on his way to Lindsay's right now."

"I don't see how. She made sure nobody knows where her new place is, except us."

"Us? You mean you," said Alvin.

"Right. Me. None of her friends. None of his friends. Not the police. No one but me and Elaine, of course."

"He could find out."

I shook my head. "I don't think so. Not this quickly."

Alvin took a deep breath, but I wasn't finished.

"I'm his best bet. He'll figure I'll head straight for her. I can't take the chance that he'll follow me there. "

"Lord thundering Jesus, you need to check on her."

"Hold that thought, Alvin. So, to finish up, he can follow me. Only I will be you. You will be me. And you can lead him to think he's on his way to Lindsay's."

On the bright side, at least Alvin would be warm, and I wouldn't have to put his pine-boxed frozen corpse onto a train bound for his weeping mother in Sydney.

No indeedy, Alvin would be real toasty in my parka, my thinsulate-lined gloves, my red hat and my recently-warmed car as he led Ralph Benning on a fool's errand around the second coldest capital city in the world. He even had my cellphone, for what it was worth.

I tried not to dwell on how Alvin would drive without the cat's eye glasses. Sometimes you have to trust in a higher power.

I wanted to give Alvin plenty of time to drive down the ramp of the garage and back out into traffic. I figured after twenty minutes he'd be stuck on Elgin going nowhere fast. Not even Benning could find Lindsay Grace in less than an hour.

I hoped like hell I was right.

# *Four*

M y old friend Merv picked up on the first ring.

"Blessed are those on sick leave," I said, "for they shall be available on weekdays to help their buddies."

"Sorry, wrong number," Merv said.

"Can you pick me up?"

"In this weather? Not if my life depended on it." That Merv. Always one with a snappy comeback.

"Someone's life does depend on it. Pick me up at the library front door in half an hour."

"Forget it, Camilla. I'm busy with daytime TV. And I've learned people have to respect my boundaries."

"You're an active RCMP officer, even if you are malingering. And I know how much you like to save defenceless women at risk from dangerous men."

Merv snorted. "Defenceless women? I love that, Camilla. You're about as defenceless as a grizzly with two cubs."

"Not me. It's a serious and dangerous situation. I'll explain later. And, as an added bonus, I promise to respect your boundaries. You can tell me what they are when you pick me up."

"Aw, c'mon, Camilla." I could tell by his voice he was hooked.

"The library. Laurier entrance. Keep your front passenger door unlocked."

"Don't tease. Tell me what's happening."

"And bring your pajamas."

"What?"

"Twenty-nine minutes, Merv. You're a bud."

I stuck my nose in the Lost and Found section, otherwise known as the bottom drawer of the filing cabinet. It was a great source of mismatched gloves, scarves, a couple of musty cardigans, an Icelandic sweater, four umbrellas, several handkerchiefs, paperbacks, glasses, an old raccoon hat and Alvin's lunch. I filled a bag with all the sweaters, scarves, gloves and the fur hat. I left the umbrellas. I slipped on Alvin's glasses and surrounded myself with his jacket. It was long but tight. I guessed I could learn to live with the coconut smell of the flash tan. At least we were both wearing black pants.

My teal suit would have been a dead giveaway.

*   *   *

The cold was like a blow.

I had kept the silk long underwear and the thermal socks, but the thin skin of Alvin's studded leather jacket and the Mickey Mouse scarf wrapped around my head were definitely too little too late.

I was heftier than Alvin, so slipping on a few sweaters would have thoroughly undermined the disguise, even if there had been room. So what, I decided. When the going gets tough, the tough get the lead out.

I concentrated on Benning, a man filled with hate and anger. A man who would express his emotions physically. Perhaps with an aluminum baseball bat, perhaps with a gun. Those thoughts propelled me down Elgin Street towards the public library, one of Alvin's regular runs.

I told myself Alvin's own mother would be fooled by my appearance. The light snowfall helped to obscure vision. It was supposed to be too cold to snow, but I guess no one told the guy in charge of precipitation. Overhead, blue and white Winterlude flags snapped in the wind.

I kept my head down to keep the sharp blowing snow from my eyes. I checked for ice patches. The leather jacket made the cold colder. How the hell did Alvin survive?

His glasses didn't help. What kind of a wacko prescription was that anyway? Typical of Alvin to have unusual eyes. In spite of the vision problem, I hurtled along the sidewalk. I must have been clocking six miles an hour when I collided with someone solid and stubborn. The impact knocked the breath right out of me. Visions of lawsuit danced in my brain. I could see the headlines: negligent lawyer mows down elderly woman, claims temporary blindness. My ears rang.

"I am so sorry," I blurted. "I hope you aren't hurt."

The person was still standing, although I wasn't sure how. I took off the glasses for a better look. Only after I'd apologized to the parking meter did the full impact of the damn cat's eyes glasses sink in. I glanced around. All I saw were faces half-hidden by parkas, scarves and tuques. No one cared what I did.

I reapplied the glasses, this time pushing them halfway down my nose, and shouldered on down Elgin.

\*     \*     \*

When I hit the Main Branch of the Ottawa Public Library, I scurried through the front door and up to the Reference area. Alvin spends a lot of his time on site, doing errands for Justice for Victims—but I suspect also putting the moves on some of the junior staff. Thanks to my tax dollars hard at work, the library was warm.

I asked for a couple of back issues of magazines. The girl at the counter blinked at me. "Do you have a brother?"

"Weird, people keep asking me." I carried my mags to the table with the best view of the staircase. Ten minutes later, I was convinced Ralph Benning had not followed me to the Reference Department. I headed to the ladies' room.

Five minutes later, Alvin's jacket, scarf and glasses were in the bag, and I was redefined. I had a quick drink at the fountain to rinse the taste of old clothes out of my mouth. But the dusty, musty, bottom of the drawer residue was the least of my problems.

The girl at the desk didn't even blink as I slunk past. She also didn't ask if I was related to the guy in the Mickey Mouse scarf.

\* \* \*

Merv had been under the weather since my friend Robin had headed off to spend a month in Mexico with another man. That's a different story, but I wondered if it were connected to Merv's spell of bad health. It doesn't do to coddle middle-aged heartbroken Mounties, especially not tall, lanky, good-looking ones. I was doing him a favour, I decided, as I wrenched open the door of his car.

"Hey, you, what are you doing? Get the hell out."

"Morning, Merv. Nice to see you too."

"Yeah, yeah. What's going on, Camilla? Make it important."

"What ever happened to 'Good Morning, Camilla, you look lovely today?'"

"First of all, it's not a good morning and second, you look unlovely." He eased into the traffic on Laurier Street. "What's with the get-up? Costume party? Bag lady convention?"

"I have a strategic reason for the disguise. Turn left on O'Connor."

"Who elected you queen, Camilla? What the crap is going on? Didn't you buy a new Civic in the fall?" In all the time I'd known him, Merv had always been crotchety, so I let it roll off. "Start talking."

I might have felt some apprehension if I hadn't known how Merv felt about pale, delicate women who find themselves in desperate situations. You could count on a man who still wore Old Spice after twenty years.

"Do you remember the Benning case?" I said.

"How could I forget it? It was all over the media."

"Do you remember Benning's girlfriend, Lindsay Grace?"

"The one who testified against him? Sure. Why?"

"Have you listened to the news today, Merv?"

"Nah. I'm watching Rosie and Jenny and the other girls."

"Did you hear Benning broke out?"

"Broke out of what? Isn't he some kind of psycho?"

"He's a psycho all right. He was on his way to court, his sentencing hearing. He shot a cop, and he's on the run. And he'll be after her."

"Shot a cop? That explains it."

"Explains what?"

"We must have passed twenty Ottawa cruisers. And plenty of unmarked ones. They'll get him. Wouldn't want to be him when they do."

"He won't be easy to catch. He's not going to hitch a lift in a police cruiser. He doesn't look like a psycho. He has money and connections. He'll have a plan. He'll hide out, and he'll go after her."

"Money and connections?"

"The money's supposed to be from drugs, big-time stuff.

He's a career criminal. People say he's such a loose cannon even the major suppliers and dealers are scared shitless of him."

"Jeez. That's bad. I'll give you a hand, but you know the Ottawa force has jurisdiction. They have communications, backup, they'll call in a tactical team. That's the kind of protection she needs."

"They're not at Lindsay's place, Merv."

"Be serious."

"I am deadly serious. Head right down O'Connor and cross over at the Pretoria Bridge. She's on Echo Drive."

"Holy shit. Why isn't Ottawa covering this Lindsay Grace?"

Good question. "The last time Benning jumped the fence, he had help, and he always was one step ahead of the police. Rumour is he had inside help."

"Crap."

"That's the buzz. Might explain why it's been so hard to keep him behind bars, and why he was able to break loose today."

"Where'd you hear that?"

"P. J. Lynch has been talking about it."

"Oh."

"Right. Not some wacko. P. J.'s a serious guy, and if he believes Benning has an inside man, my money says he's right. Lindsay thinks so too. But Benning never let on who the inside connection was."

"Yeah, yeah. You still need the Ottawa guys."

"I realize that. Elaine Ekstein will hit the police brass. She's probably there already. She'll make sure the address is given out on a need-to-know basis. They'll cooperate with Elaine if they know what's good for them. In the meantime, Lindsay's my client. She's afraid, and I had to respect her wishes. And I'm scared shitless he'll find her."

"And this Benning's been out how long?"

"Couple of hours. You don't know this guy, Merv. He's smart and capable of extreme violence. Totally out of control. We have to protect Lindsay now. We'll sort out jurisdictions after. But are we ever going to move?"

"Aw jeez, someone stalled up ahead on the bridge. It's too late to back up. We're stuck here."

"Mind if I use your phone? Alvin has mine."

"Would it matter if I did mind?"

I dialed Lindsay's number. Still no answer. "I should hop out and run the rest of the way."

"Better let me go. What can you do if this guy shows up?"

"She doesn't know you. She'll never let you in."

"Two women up against this maniac? Your best bet is still the Ottawa Police."

"Watch your blood pressure. I have no choice. I'll get to Lindsay's on foot. You could be stuck here for an hour."

"Wait a minute. We're moving again."

He was right. The tow-truck lights flashed up ahead. Traffic started to inch over the bridge. I leaned back and exhaled. Three more minutes.

"So listen, Camilla. Does the get-up relate to the situation?"

"This? Yes, it does. At this moment, Alvin is on a mission."

Merv snorted. "Alvin? And speaking of blood pressure, that guy's a one-man stroke-inducing machine."

"Sure is. But at this moment he's risking his own life in my car wearing my parka and hat in order to draw Benning away from Lindsay."

"Sounds like a weird plan, even for you, Camilla."

"We think Benning might try to follow me to locate Lindsay. Alvin's laying false trails."

"I like it. Alvin could be in danger. God knows he has it coming."

"I don't think you should be bitter over imagined slights."

"Hey, he could be killed. This Benning's a time bomb, right?" Merv grinned, even when the light turned red. Probably imagining thoughts of Alvin laid out on a bed of blue satin with a wilted lily in his cold, dead paw.

"Let me give him a call." I kept the phone out of Merv's reach.

# Five

"I'm sorry, Ms. Camilla MacPhee is not available at the moment, please leave a message after the long snore."

"Most humorous, Alvin." I could afford to be snarly, since he was not dead.

"I thought you were one of your sisters. Don't they have lives?"

"Don't go there."

"They've all called. Some twice. You need to set *them* straight."

"I'll set them straight after I practice on you."

"Oh, he's alive?" Merv said. "Too bad. Any chance he's been tied up by Benning and is about to be dumped off the Interprovincial Bridge into the frigid but open waters?"

"I'm sure he would have mentioned it. No, not you, Alvin. Merv inquired about your wellbeing. Tell me, any sign of Benning?"

Alvin said, "I'm not a hundred per cent sure it's him, but there's this red Taurus. I can't shake it."

"Who's driving?"

"Can't tell."

"It's not close enough?"

"He's riding on my bumper. But the windows are fogged."

"Try and see if it's Benning."

"I told you, I can't see through the windows."

"Fine. What about the licence plate?"

"Haven't been able to catch it so far. A big chunk of snow is plastered over it. But here he comes again."

"Where are you?"

"On Sussex. I'd better turn around. Don't want to end up on the Eastern Parkway."

"No, you don't. Alvin? What's that screeching sound? Did my car make that noise? Alvin! Answer me."

"Hey, Camilla, keep your shorts on. Just a one-eighty."

"Don't you do one-eighties in my new Civic."

"Lord thundering Jesus!"

"What?"

"Holy crap."

"What happened?"

"He turned too."

At this point I felt the hot blast of Merv's breath on my ear. "I'm happy I can reserve a portion of my communications budget for you to give driving instructions to earring boy, Camilla. Make sure you get the story of his life," Merv said.

"Might not be a long story. This is serious."

"No shit," Alvin said. "Here he comes. He's gunning it."

I yelled. "Floor it to 24 Sussex and drive up to the gates. They have enough Mounties for a musical ride. Do you hear me?" Nothing. "Alvin?" More nothing. Followed by a crash and the sound of tearing metal. Then ragged breathing. "Alvin?" I turned to Merv. "Benning's caught him."

"Camilla?" A squeak on the receiver.

"Yes!"

"You were right. When the security guys ran out, he took off."

"Great. Then?"

"And guess what? I got a partial of the licence plate."

"Excellent. What is it?" I turned to Merv. "He caught some of the licence."

To do Merv credit, he pulled out a notebook and a pen.

"Okay, Alvin, shoot." I strained to hear. Muffled voices buzzed on the line. Then Alvin squawked like he was having his feathers plucked.

"Hey wait," he said. "I don't want to get out of the vehicle. Listen. You can put the guns away. I was being chased by that guy, Benning, the one who just escaped. Don't you guys listen to the radio?"

"Alvin's experienced first hand the high level of security at the PM's residence. Those are your boys, aren't they, Merv?"

"Yes, indeedy. And they will check out Mr. Ponytail dressed in women's clothes, driving a vehicle registered to someone else, and then he'll try to give them his usual level of mouth." Merv chuckled.

While I have no problem with Alvin as the butt of a joke, I didn't want to go to the hoosegow and bail out the boy again. It wouldn't be the first time he'd had his fingerprints taken while in the midst of a Justice for Victims activity. Whenever Alvin gets arrested as a result of some action of mine, I pay for it for a long time. This time, the payment would include bodywork.

"Hey, you can't do that. I have a right to legal advice." Alvin's voice shot well into his higher ranges.

"Alvin," I shouted into the phone.

"Let go of me."

I tried again, "Alvin, Alvin, put the officer on the phone." I turned to Merv. "Can you talk to them and explain?"

Merv made a *moue*. "They have procedures."

"Well, of course, they have procedures, but we both know Alvin wasn't doing anything wrong. It would be most unfair if he's interrogated."

"Hang on, Camilla, we're moving again."

"But you have to speak to them."

"We can't block the bridge."

He had a point besides the one on his head. "Fine, but as soon as we can pull over on Colonel By Drive, you'd better talk to them."

"Sure," Merv said. "But I don't think we can park on Colonel By."

"As soon as you turn onto Echo then."

Merv started to hum, not altogether an auspicious sign. Or a pleasant sound. I stuck a finger in my ear.

"Alvin. Don't argue with the officers."

More squawks.

"Listen to me. Put one of them on the phone immediately or your leather jacket's history."

Merv made the left onto Colonel By Drive this time and proceeded north with unnecessary caution.

"Get the lead out," I said to Merv. And then to Alvin, "Goddamn it, do what you're told, this once. Oh, sorry, officer, I thought I was speaking to my colleague. My name is Camilla MacPhee, and I am a lawyer with Justice for Victims. That deranged creature is in my employ. And I can assure you he was in grave danger. He has a partial licence plate number and a description of the car to be relayed to the Ottawa police. What? Excuse me? I can't believe this. Wait a minute." I turned to Merv. "This guy's a real comedian. You want to speak to him?"

"Not sure I want to be associated with either of you," Merv said.

"I'm glad you think it's funny. I think Alvin's been arrested."

"Again? Couldn't happen to a nicer guy."

But he did take the phone. "Merv Morrison here. Who's talking? Right. Sure. No shit, he's for real, believe it or not. Me? Yeah, I'm on the mend. Couple weeks. What? No, no. I'm with an acquaintance. Right. I know you got procedures. Hey, no problem. Take it easy."

I would have killed him on the spot, but we'd reached the town house Lindsay Grace called home. "Park here," I said.

Merv was still chuckling. I decided not to react. I needed to keep my mind free. On the other hand, I did need to know what to do about Alvin. Plus the usual when, where and how.

"They'll take him to the Leomont Building at Vanier and McArthur. And they'll impound your vehicle. You'll get him out, but they'll need to assure themselves he poses no risk to the Prime Minister or other august bodies."

"I'll have to help him."

"I wouldn't rush. I figure on five different jurisdictions involved in this baby, if you count the Prime Minister's Protection Detachment and National Security Intelligence. He'll be their guest for most of the day. City cops will be the least of his problems."

"Okay, one challenge at a time. This is Lindsay's place."

Alvin would have to wait. Now it was time to deal with Lindsay Grace. Was it possible Benning had found her before he pursued Alvin? Logic said no. But logic and Benning don't mix.

\*    \*    \*

Merv said, "Catch that view of the canal. She must be rolling in cash."

"Do you think that matters when someone wants to kill you, and all you can do is hide out and pray?"

Merv kept his mouth shut, but he checked out the wrought-iron fencing, the solid brass details on the doors and the landscaping designed to look appealing even when covered with snow.

"Even so," he said. He can be the most stubborn person in the world sometimes, despite some serious competition from my relatives. "Must be four hundred thousand minimum for this baby. Echo Drive, two minutes to downtown. Are you kidding, half a million. Did this Benning bankroll this?"

I jabbed the doorbell. "Lindsay Grace was a hotshot financial analyst, a high flyer, when she hooked up with Ralph Benning."

"So not stupid."

"No, that's the tragedy. She's a bright woman who fell into the wrong relationship."

Merv snorted. "How smart could she be if she teamed up with this character? Didn't he serve time for spousal assault?"

I tried again. The bell pealed loud enough for us to hear it outside. It couldn't be missed inside the house. "About as smart as the other women he was with. His wife taught high school physics. Not any more, of course. Her face isn't easy for people to feel comfortable with. And his other women have been smart and assured." I gave the bell one final vicious poke.

Merv shook his head. "Makes you wonder."

It sure did. I took a deep breath. "Time to go in."

"No way. You won't catch me breaking and entering. I have my pension to think of."

"Actually, I thought I'd use the keys."

I unlocked the Yale and the deadbolt and inched the door open. I had thirty seconds to get the jump on Lindsay's alarm system. I punched in the code and felt a flush of relief. Merv and I stepped into the foyer and stamped our boots on the marble floor. I stopped long enough to reset the alarm, then called out. "Lindsay?" I thought I heard a small noise from upstairs. "You hear that?"

Merv tilted his head. "Music."

40

I slipped out of my icy boots. I'd kept my mind off my frozen feet on the ride over. Merv ditched his size thirteens. I stepped into the living room. One small benefit from Alvin's close call: not even Benning could be in two places at one time.

So why had I been so frantic? Because, Benning, as the police now knew, appeared to be able to breeze through walls.

"He can't find her here," I said, trying to convince myself.

"I don't see why not." Merv stepped up right behind me. "How long has she lived here?"

"Since September. But she was discreet. No one knows. Unlisted phone number."

As we checked the living room, Merv said, "If the guy has any kind of connections, he could tap into the hydro service or find the address on her driver's licence through MOT."

I knew that too.

Merv seemed impressed by several bronze sculptures, the rather nice abstracts on the wall and the large arrangement of fresh and fragrant lilies as we passed through the dining area. My sisters would approve. The only whiff in my dining area was from my running shoes.

The kitchen was empty too. On the counter was a plate with a half-eaten slice of toast. A cup with cold coffee. The radio was tuned to CBC's Radio One. I touched the espresso maker on the granite counter. Still lukewarm. So Lindsay had been home that morning, and chances were she'd been alone.

I took a deep breath and retraced my steps. I hesitated at the base of the stairs then hurled myself up. Wimpiness was never one of my problems. But if you've ever stumbled over a dead body, you don't feel the same about closed doors.

"Lindsay?" I called out, in case she was afraid of Benning creeping up the stairs. "It's Camilla and a friend. We want to make sure you're all right."

Upstairs the door to the guestroom stood open, as did the door to the master suite. The bed had been slept in, but the elegant pewter-coloured bedding was merely folded back, no careless jumble of sheets for Lindsay. No sign of a struggle. No blood.

From behind the closed door, we could hear water running. And another sound. Music. Vivaldi. The air was steamy and fragrant with floral and musky and expensive scents.

Abruptly, the water stopped.

"Lindsay?" I don't know what the hell I thought, as I stood at the foot of the enormous bed. I sure didn't expect Lindsay Grace to step from her bathroom to her bedroom, shaking her damp hair behind her.

"You're all right," I blurted. "Thank God. We were so worried."

She whirled, screamed and dropped her towel. She hit the floor on the far side of the enormous bed.

"I'm so sorry," I said quickly. "I guess I panicked after your phone call. When you didn't answer, I drove over here in case. Now, of course, I see you're all right. So I guess I'll leave you alone to get, um, organized." It's not like me to babble, but this time, I couldn't stop. Lindsay scrambled back into the bathroom. Who could blame her? I felt like a fool. "I'll be downstairs."

"All right," she said, in a muffled voice.

"Are you sure you're okay? Didn't mean to scare you. I brought a friend with me. He's a Mountie. He works in security."

"Give me a couple of minutes." The voice was shaky.

"No problem, Lindsay. I'll make some fresh coffee."

I caught sight of Merv. People look healthier after neurosurgery.

"What's the matter?" I whispered. "Haven't you ever seen a naked woman before?"

42

# *Six*

Merv's coffee went down fast. He takes three sugars, but this time he drank it straight. I was still dipping the teaspoon in the sugar bowl when he drained the last drop.

Merv keeps his hair clipped about the length of a five o'clock shadow. His scalp was pink, another measure of his state of mind. I had no choice but to lean across the kitchen table and stare him straight in the eye. "Pull yourself together."

"Holy shit," he said. And not for the first time.

"And try a little conversational variety while you're at it." I twitched the teaspoon dangerously.

Merv poured himself another cup. Before I could dump the three teaspoons of sugar in it, he said "holy shit" again.

"Lindsay might come downstairs. Do you think you can act like a rational human being? Imagine how traumatic it was for her coming across a strange man in her bedroom while she was…"

"Holy…" Merv said.

"…fresh from the bath. And if she does comes down, if you can't say something intelligent, don't say anything at all."

Merv didn't say anything, but I was pretty sure I knew what he was thinking.

I asked myself some tough questions. Why hadn't Lindsay answered the phone after her hysterical call? How could she relax and listen to music in the tub while waiting for Ralph

Benning to kick in the front door? I knew her first steps would have been to the medicine cabinet for an extra boost of the sedatives that helped her get through every day. But even so.

"Merv, let's not sit on our duffs wasting time. We should review the security here. That's your specialty."

That seemed to snap him out of it.

"Okay," I said, "there are bars on the basement windows, top-grade Clear Defence security film on every pane of glass in the house, bars across the patio doors, a first-rate silent alarm system, wired to every door and window, panic button, and double deadbolts on the doors. Do you think she's missing anything?"

I was still talking when Merv bounded off to check the basement and the first floor. It gave me time to think about Benning and how he might try to get in. These security products would discourage a burglar, but not a psycho with nothing to lose.

Twenty minutes later, I was brooding over my third cup of coffee, when Merv returned. "Impressive. Someone did an fine job on this place."

"Anyone else but Benning and she wouldn't have a worry."

"I don't see how anybody could get in," he said, grudgingly.

"Benning could. Even this security won't keep out a hail of bullets or a two-thousand pound vehicle ramming the front door."

"You'll get rapid response with that centrally-monitored system."

"On a normal day, sure. But with every unit after Benning and the roads clogged, the response time will be pathetic."

Merv opened his mouth to speak. I shook my head to silence him as a slight movement in the doorway caught my eye. Lindsay Grace entered the kitchen with the soft, smooth movements of an expensive cat. Elegant and understated in a cream-coloured slim tunic and leggings that looked like cashmere. Her dark chestnut hair was dry and brushed back into a ponytail. That golden olive complexion didn't need makeup, not even the dab of lip-gloss she'd applied. Her only decoration was a tiny pair of gold hoop earrings. As usual, she smelled good. Organza, if I remembered correctly.

Lindsay had the kind of face you'd see on the cover of *Chatelaine*. Except a photo might not capture the soft backlit skin and the fragility. If it wasn't for the lack of focus in her eyes, you would have thought she hadn't a worry in the world.

She didn't match the stereotype of a battered woman. Of course, in my line of work, you learn fast not to rely on those preconceptions. None of Ralph Benning's victims had looked the part.

"Mmmm," she said, "I smell coffee."

"Ready for one?" I asked.

"I'm sorry about the call to the office." She reached for her coffee, her hands steadier than mine.

That took me by surprise. "You're sorry? What do you have to be sorry about?"

"Alarming you. I panicked when I turned on the radio and heard a prisoner had escaped. I don't know why I assumed that the prisoner who had escaped was Ralph. That was stupid of me. I guess I'm strung out because it's the sentencing hearing. That's all I can think about. You didn't have to come all the way over and on such a terrible day too. I wasn't using my head. I had to take an Ativan, well two, and a long bath with some Vivaldi to calm down. I called back to tell you not to bother, but I got the answering machine."

"I wanted to be here."

"Well, I appreciate it, but I'm all right."

I took a deep breath. "Lindsay, have a seat."

She slid onto the attractive light metal chair. "Sorry for screaming, but I didn't recognize you for a minute. I've never seen you dressed quite like that. And I didn't know your friend."

It must have taken at least three Ativans to let Lindsay feel untroubled by the sight of Merv with his jaw around his ankles. I decided not to explain my outfit. I had no choice but to introduce Merv.

"Lindsay, meet Merv Morrison. He's with the RCMP." Out of regard for our longstanding relationship, I didn't mention Merv's sick leave, nor did the words gall or bladder leave my lips.

Merv was already standing. Although maybe not breathing. Lindsay held out her slender hand and allowed it to be swallowed by Merv's. "Thank you for coming," she said. "You must think I'm out of my mind."

I was impressed. Not every woman can handle an introduction to a man after he has had an eyeful of her birthday suit. Of course, it could have been the drugs.

Merv said "holy shit" under his breath.

Someone had to show signs of intelligent life. I tried. "We should work out a plan for what to do until Benning's back behind bars where he belongs."

She blinked. "What do you mean?"

I didn't think I'd been the least bit unclear.

"I mean, we want to make sure you are safe. You should stay somewhere else." I did not mention Merv's theory about Benning being able to find out her address. I did not refer to the inside police connection. I did not describe what I thought Benning might do.

"What do you mean, back behind bars?"

I leaned over and put my hand on her shoulder. "Benning

did escape. It took a while for the name to make the radio news." Before I could add it was lucky she hadn't known that during her hour-long wait for our arrival, Lindsay slipped gracefully from the chair to the floor.

Merv said "holy shit" once more for good luck.

*   *   *

Merv deposited Lindsay on the sofa in the living room. But even after she lifted her head from the butter-soft leather, things continued to go wrong.

"It's okay," I said, "we're here with you. Everything's going to be all right."

"No. Nothing is ever going to be all right. Ever."

"Sure it is. Every cop in town is on the lookout for him."

Lindsay struggled to sit up. She leaned her head back and closed her eyes. "Remember what happened to Rina? Living in that secure building. She thought she was safe. We're talking about a man who broke out of police custody. What could be more secure?"

"They'll get him. In the meantime, we'll stay with you. The police will be here soon, and we can move you to somewhere safer."

"I'll never feel safe."

"Sure you will. Once he's back in custody, they'll take extra measures. This can't last long. And we won't leave you alone."

"Fight or flight, isn't that what they call our two basic reactions to fear? Well, I've had the flight reaction, and you know what, it's hell. I'm his prisoner. As long as he's breathing, my life is not worth living."

"Your life is worth living," Merv said.

"Merv's right, Lindsay. That's just your nerves talking. And

I understand how you feel. But this isn't a typical situation here."

"You do not know how I feel. You're so confident. So sure that things will be all right. You haven't lived in hell like I have. You can't even imagine what it does to your brain."

"I shouldn't have said that. I'm sorry." She was right. Every now and then I give myself away. I know the theory about the effect of abuse on the personality. I just don't feel it in my bones.

"I'm not going on the run. I'll stay in my own home."

"Holy *shit.*"

"Shut up, Merv. Listen, Lindsay, that would make a lot of sense, normally, but this situation is not normal."

"I know. Ever since I met Ralph, my life has not been normal. And as long as he's alive, it won't ever be."

"You won't be away long. This is just temporary. They'll have him back behind bars, and they'll throw away the key."

"I'd give anything to believe that, Camilla. If he can escape from custody here, he can escape from a maximum-security institution. He can escape from anywhere. I'll never be safe. So I have to live my life anyway." The fine chin seemed even more pointed. Her hazel eyes were steady and calm. She reminded me of some sweet sainted virgin, strolling serenely to her martyrdom.

"Fine." I didn't mean fine at all. "But I'm staying with you."

She shook her head. "You should use your time to boost the Crown's case. Plus, two small women, what could we do? Neither one of us will have a chance."

I hate this kind of thinking. But I had to admit Benning had at least one gun. Plus it had been less than nine months since I'd fought for my life with a killer. I wasn't sure how well I'd cope in the same circumstance. But it wasn't like I had a choice.

"Okay, there's safety in numbers. So we need reinforcements.

Merv's here. And we can get other people. I think the danger period, if they don't pick him up first, will be in the night. Elaine will come over, for sure. What about if Alvin joins us until they capture Benning?"

Lindsay opened her mouth, but the strangled sounds came from Merv. "Alvin? That little peckerhead? I don't *think* so, Camilla."

I always find myself defending Alvin from other people. "Alvin thinks the world of Lindsay. He'd lay down his life for her."

"That Alvin is just so sweet," Lindsay said. "But no one should put themselves at risk for me. I created this situation by getting involved with Ralph. I don't want to drag anyone else into it."

Interesting. I thought I caught a glimpse of the woman Lindsay must have been in her pre-Benning life.

"Fair enough." I played for time. "But have you even contemplated..." Before I had time to figure out what she should have contemplated, Merv stretched his long legs and stood.

"You can't defend yourself against someone like Benning. And you don't have to. This is not happening because of anything you did." He looked way down at Lindsay. She tilted up at him. "I'll be here until you're safe," he said.

It didn't matter what I thought. It didn't matter what I did. It didn't matter that I was there.

"All right," Lindsay said.

"So that's settled." I'd like to think they noticed, but I know damn well they didn't.

\*    \*    \*

A few phone calls later, I still hadn't tracked down P. J. That was no great surprise; he'd be chasing the action. I left Merv's cell number. I wasn't giving Lindsay's number to anyone. P. J. might have been my buddy, but he was a reporter first, and I never forgot that.

I had better luck finding out where Alvin was being questioned. I had to get him off the hook, but I had a problem. I could hardly take Merv's car. He'd never let Alvin park his bum in it, and I didn't think I could wrestle the keys from him. It was too goddam cold to walk anywhere with those useless boots. My car would have been impounded after its brush with the gates at 24 Sussex. The taxi dispatcher sneeringly informed me a car would take an hour.

When Lindsay's phone rang, I answered it. Force of habit.

"Camilla? It's Elaine. Holy moly, I'm glad you're there. Alvin left me these hysterical messages. I've been to the police, and I'm on my way. They're sending a couple of cars immediately."

"Glad to hear it."

"Listen, no one answers in your office. I tried your cellphone. Don't you ever pick up your messages? Is Lindsay all right?"

I filled her in on the situation, omitting Merv's reactions. She offered to drive me to the Leomont Building to get Alvin, to resolve any outstanding issues with the Mounties, starting with the Commissioner, and to make sure our lad was not traumatized.

"We have to wait until the police get here," I said.

"That shouldn't take long. Poor Alvin. He has such a hard time."

Once again, I bit my tongue.

I jumped when Merv soundlessly arrived behind me. "Good news item number one: she's sleeping," he whispered.

I raised my eyebrows. Not because Lindsay could fall sleep—that was no surprise with her system clogged with sedatives—but there was just something about Merv tiptoeing around like a nervous auntie.

"Good news item number two: the Ottawa guys are here." I followed him back through the living room to the front window. A cruiser, with two officers, was parked conspicuously in front of the townhouse. "There's another car in the back," Merv said.

"They're taking it seriously. Usually it's one cop per cruiser."

"They're taking it seriously all right. They did everything but run a DNA test on *me*."

"But you're RCMP."

"Jurisdictions, remember? No reason for a member of the force, even one on sick leave, to be here. They don't like weird stuff."

"You'd think they'd be happy to have someone trained in security in the house looking out for Lindsay."

"Yeah, yeah. They're cops, Camilla. They're never happy. But anyway, I passed the test. I don't hold out much hope for you, though."

"Funny."

\*　　\*　　\*

Less than ten minutes later, when Elaine's SUV crested the snow bank in front of Lindsay's place, I forced myself to take a deep breath and head out. Elaine was in fine form, metres of tightly curled red hair sproinging out in all directions from under a fake leopard fez. Not an easy effect to carry off.

"I'll go in and see Lindsay first," she said as I climbed into her SUV.

"She's out cold. Give her an hour or so."

"Holy moly," she said, "out cold. I don't blame her."

"Drugs," I said.

"What else is she going to do? Was she awake when you arrived?"

"Yes. Which reminds me, did she call you this morning and tell you about Benning?"

"No. The first I heard of it was Alvin's message. Who could believe that bastard's loose again?"

I must have had a look on my face.

"Come on, Camilla, don't start feeling guilty."

"I don't know. If I'd done a better job on the brief to the Parole Board last spring, he wouldn't have been paroled and attacked his wife, and we wouldn't have this whole situation."

"Get over it. Remember? You were caught up in a murder investigation. Benning's nothing but trouble and always has been. It's not you. It's not her. It's not the wife. It's him. Plain and simple."

I gasped, less from self-insight than from the SUV spinning toward the canal as we made an illegal U-turn and didn't quite connect with the road.

"Don't be so jumpy," Elaine said. "This guy's making you nuts."

"Of course he is." The little pine-tree deodorizers danced with each swerve Elaine made.

"But Merv will be a match for him."

"I guess so."

"I know so. Who'd argue with him? Didn't you tell me once he had special training when he was doing security stuff?"

"But he's nearly fifty years old, with a wonky gall bladder that acts up when he's under stress."

"So what? Wasn't he a bodyguard for the Prime Minister?"

"That was then. This is now."

"You don't lose that kind of training. Lindsay's in safe hands with Merv. Anyway, the police will pick Benning up any minute. Okay, we need to rescue Alvin." She gunned the engine as we skidded along.

"Let me use your phone. I want to leave another message for P. J. just in case..."

"No problem."

"Thanks, Elaine."

"What's to thank? After all, you've helped me plenty."

I gasped again as the SUV veered intimately close to the side of the road. "I have? Like what?"

"Like working on our sculpture."

"What sculpture?"

Elaine applied the brakes, sending us into a one hundred and eighty-degree spin. I shrieked. I believe the driver in the oncoming lane did too.

I was still jumpy a minute later.

"Don't carry on so much," Elaine said. "You shouldn't say 'what sculpture' if you don't want a reaction."

This definitely wasn't the right time to tell Elaine I had no idea *what* sculpture. "You're right," I said. "It's too important."

"It is."

"So, do you have a plan?" This was a safe bet because Elaine always had a plan.

"Natch," she said.

"Of course. Watch out for the salt truck!" Merging onto the Queensway with Elaine is not something I ever want to repeat. Thank God, we were just one exit away from the Vanier parkway.

"You're not the easiest person to drive with, Camilla. You know that? It's your tendency toward theatricality."

"No doubt you're right." I pulled myself up from where I'd slid under my seat belt. "And so the plan for the sculpture hasn't changed?"

"No. Why should it?"

Why I was so worried? After all, how much of a problem could a sculpture be? A bit of art. A spin to Montreal to some retrospective at the *musée?* No big deal. Especially if *I* drove. Alvin's collision with the wrought-iron gates of Rideau Hall meant my car was out of commission, but I could rent. Problem solved. I felt flooded with relief, in part because we were already off the Queensway.

"Camilla? Are you listening? Why should it?"

"No reason. Just asking. Elaine. Red light. Red light! Oh, well."

"Hey, you don't like it when I slam on the brakes, so you'll have to control yourself if we're in an advanced yellow light stage when we reach an intersection. Okay?"

If we hadn't immediately accelerated to seventy, I would have removed myself from the SUV at this point and finished the conversation by phone.

"Okay?" Elaine is not one to give up.

"I'll try to control myself if you try to stop for red lights."

"You never let go, do you? So anyway, for the sculpture, tonight's the night."

"Great."

"I hope it warms up a bit," she said.

"Well, what difference does it make?"

She gave me a bit of a strange look.

"Please keep your eyes on the road." I watched as a pedestrian dove into a snowbank.

"We'll meet in Confederation Square."

"What?"

"We'll meet in Confederation Square at seven, I guess."

"Call me crazy, but given the winterness of it all, why don't we meet inside?"

"Why would we meet inside?"

"Because it will be cold outside?"

"And where will we build the sculpture?"

Almost blew my cover. "Oh, right."

"Exactly."

"Hmmm."

"Confederation Square, seven o'clock. Bring your own bucket."

I hardly noticed the rapid approach of the bus.

*　　*　　*

"Relax, we owe her big-time. She drove me here to pick you up and waited patiently for the cops to finish with you, hours might I add. Plus she made a few effective phone calls on your behalf, or you might have been spending the night. Aren't you happy to get out of here?" I said as I accompanied Alvin through the foyer of the Leomont Building under the watchful eye of security.

"What? Are you deranged? It doesn't matter whether I'm happy, I won't do it." Alvin's ponytail flipped in protest.

"Alvin, let's settle this here. I don't want to argue in front of Elaine, who is doing you a favour. I thought you liked her."

"I do like her, but this has been a crappy day for me, and I'm not going to spend the night in the park."

"No buts, Alvin."

"Plenty of buts. I have been grilled by the Gestapo. My name will be on file forever. If I drop a candy wrapper on the street, I'll probably serve hard time. Of course, my name was already on file with the Ottawa police. Let's see. Why would that be? Oh yes, that was a result of another one of your great ideas, Camilla. So, I think I've done enough for you and Justice for Victims today. And if Lindsay's safe, I want to relax. I don't need to work overtime."

"You do now."

"It's bad enough I'm still out in public in your clothes. Here, take your stupid hat back. All I want to is to go home and forget all about today." His pointed nose was aimed at the ceiling, always a bad sign. "And what's more, you had no business telling Elaine I would help out with this project."

I couldn't tell Alvin I had no recollection of volunteering either of us to work on an ice sculpture for Winterlude. None. It was hard to explain, but Elaine can have that effect. "Lighten up, Alvin, it should be a lot of fun."

"If it's so much fun, don't let me deprive you of any of it."

"Listen, Alvin…"

"The last time I listened to you I had my nose mashed against the gate at 24 Sussex. Then I met two large Mounties with small brains and big guns. I don't think I'll listen again. Thanks anyway."

I decided it was better not to mention that Alvin's copious nosebleed after the accident had spelled the end of my parka. "Wait a minute. I thought you wanted to help Lindsay."

"I did want to help Lindsay. But I'm not sure how much it helped her to toss me to the wolves."

"I'm sure Lindsay will appreciate what you did. It was your way to combat Benning. And that's what this ice sculpture event is all about. You have to admit it's a worthwhile cause. Women Against Violence Everywhere plans to raise awareness of issues of domestic violence with it."

"Raise this." Alvin lifted his skinny middle finger.

# Seven

It was pushing five thirty and dark again when Elaine dropped me at my apartment building. My lousy mood was compounded by the fact that Elaine and Alvin had sulked all the way to Alvin's place. But that was small potatoes compared to the fact that Ralph Benning remained on the loose.

Since I hadn't eaten all day, my plan was to snatch a bite, take a quick bath, then toss a few essentials into a suitcase. With Benning still at large, Merv and I would take shifts on alert throughout the night at Lindsay's. I didn't see how Benning could get past the police guard, but if he was going to make an attempt, he'd almost certainly do it in the dead of night. Having to do guard duty at Lindsay's relieved me of ice sculpture commitments, but it would take more than that to let me relax.

I skulked into the elevator and headed for the sixteenth floor.

Some people you don't want to run into after a hellish day. My neighbour, Mrs. Parnell, is at the top of the list. Mrs. Parnell had not learned to mind her own business in the first seventy-seven years of her life, and I didn't have much hope she'd start now. I barreled down the long hallway with my head down. I smelled the smoke before I spotted the glowing tip of her cigarette.

"Ah, Ms. MacPhee." Mrs. Parnell leaned forward on her

walker. "What an outfit. I must say, you look even less fashionable than usual. Still, it is nice to see you."

"Nothing is nice," I said.

A waft of Benson and Hedges smoke tickled my nose. "Can't be that bad, Ms. MacPhee." You can always count on Mrs. Parnell to take the opposite point of view.

"Can be and is." My frozen toes contributed to the bitchy tone in my voice. As did the news that the damage to my car would be at least two thousand dollars. Plus, my insurance company thought driving into metal gates to avoid death constituted "at fault" on Alvin's part. And I'd been indiscreet when a newswire reporter caught me on the cellphone in a weak moment on the way home. I did not want to socialize.

But avoiding Mrs. Parnell was one of those camel through the eye of a needle situations. If I hadn't owed my life to the woman, I would have told her to go to hell on the spot.

"Nothing a taste of sherry wouldn't fix," she said evilly.

I know when I'm licked. Bite the bullet, get it over with. If I didn't want to feel Mrs. Parnell's stainless-steel eyes trained on my door for the rest of the evening, I'd have to have a sherry with her and fill her in.

"Sure. Let me ditch these frozen boots, and I'll be right over."

I hobbled into my apartment, peeled off my outer layers and slipped my numb feet out of the boots. Mrs. Parnell's little calico cat followed me. I bent over to give her a stroke. This was one night it would have been nice to come home to a cozy, warm, well-furnished home with curtains on the windows and food in the fridge. But you can't have it all. Mrs. Parnell's calico was sure glad to see me. I'd given the calico to Mrs. Parnell as a demonstration of gratitude, but due to some outstanding issues, I generally fed the cat and offered her a place to sleep on my bed. She spent her days in my apartment and didn't even seem to hold a grudge after I took her to be fixed.

Five minutes later, I pushed open the door to 1608, and Mrs. Parnell's peach-faced love birds shrieked in alarm. I limped over to the capacious leather lounger and sank into it. Might as well have the best seat in the house. I curled up and rubbed my toes. Mrs. Parnell's apartment is furnished in leather, brushed chrome, glass, serious stereo components and, most recently, state-of-the-art computer equipment. It might not be cosy, but the seats are damned comfortable, and I prefer that to doilies and Royal Doulton.

The birds continued shrieking.

"You'd think they'd get used to the puddy tat after eight months," I said.

"Lester and Pierre don't mind the cat. Although they find you quite undesirable."

"Well, they have lots of company."

She seated herself on her black leather sofa and splashed a healthy dose of Harvey's Bristol Cream into a pair of Waterford crystal sherry glasses. The cat hopped up on the glass coffee table and made herself comfortable on Mrs. P.'s open copy of *The War Memoirs of David Lloyd George, Vol. II.*

"Here's what the doctor ordered." Mrs. P. handed me my drink.

"Right. This your largest glass? I think I need to soak my frozen toes in it."

"Sherry's the best medicine for cold feet. Learned that in the trenches. The radio reported Ralph Benning was on the lam."

"Yes."

"Thought so. That why you're such a sour puss?" Mrs. Parnell does not have a long pointed nose for nothing.

"You got it."

"So what is the report, Ms. MacPhee?"

"Not sure what I could tell you, Mrs. Parnell, that you wouldn't have picked up on the radio."

"Radio's fine as far as it goes, but it doesn't give you all the background information." Not enough to keep Mrs. Parnell going. "This Benning, wasn't he the fellow you worked to keep behind bars last spring?"

I nodded. "Unsuccessfully."

Mrs. Parnell drained her glass with a flourish and refilled it. I covered mine in time to prevent a serious overflow. She leaned forward. "Still no sign of him?"

"Right."

"They say the police have deployed a tactical team."

"They did. Because one of their officers was injured. Much more important than some pesky woman being beat up."

"You made the same point in your radio interview. You had a spendid sound bite on the five o'clock news. Won't win you any allies on the police force."

She was right. One of the established ways to ensure the cooperation of agencies is not to trash them as soon as someone thrusts a mike at you. It's one of those life lessons I've never mastered.

"Glorious ineptitude," Mrs. Parnell wheezed. "Nevertheless, it is a very serious matter. What is going on behind the scenes?"

"They're tight with information in order not to alert Benning. Elaine Ekstein made sure of it. According to my sister's fiancé…"

"Ah yes, the delightful Sgt. Conn McCracken."

"I believe you described him as a Labrador retriever at one time, Mrs. P. Anyway, I'm told they have a heavy guard on Rina Benning. The police are also watching Lindsay Grace's place."

"Lindsay Grace? Oh yes, she was your client who testified

against him. Smart and beautiful and yet somehow extremely unwise."

"Which reminds me, may I use your phone? I want to call her, and it's occurred to me Benning could tap into my phone or cell."

"Paranoia, Ms. MacPhee."

"Just because I'm paranoid doesn't mean they're not out to get me."

"Words to live by. Top up your sherry?"

"Thanks, but I need to be ready to head back soon."

I dialed Lindsay's number and reached Merv.

"She's sleeping again," Merv whispered. "She heard an unsettling report on the news and she had to take another sedative."

"Oh, boy."

"They sure made a big deal about how Benning chased Alvin and Alvin crashed into the PM's gates. They've found a stolen car abandoned in a park, and they think that's the one Benning was driving. They figure he got away on foot. The radio made it sound like no one in town is safe."

"Not far from the truth."

"The little lady here has guts though."

"Don't I know it." I remembered Lindsay's testimony at Benning's trial. "Cops still in sight?"

"Yeah."

"Great." I wished I felt confident a trio of officers would be enough. "I have my cellphone back, so will you call me on it if anything strange happens? Or if you need help?"

"Sure. But I think it's fine. I'm on the alert."

"I know, but I can hop in a cab and be over in fifteen minutes. Twenty tops, if you want to sleep. Or need a change of scenery."

"You know what they say, Camilla. You can sleep all you want when you're dead."

I shivered. "Try not to be dead, Merv."

"Who was that?" Mrs. Parnell was never one to disguise her interest in the affairs of others.

"Merv. Looks like he's in love again."

She leaped to her feet. "I approve. Let us make a toast to love!"

"Count me out. I have no desire to encourage love, Mrs. P."

\* \* \*

Back in my apartment, I snatched the last edible piece of cheddar from the fridge and swallowed it in two bites. I made a phone call to P. J. on general principles. This time I suggested I might have valuable tips for him. Not that I planned to let any information slip. I didn't have a twinge of guilt. He'd have done the same to me. I ditched the rest of the clothes, slipped into my old flannel housecoat and turned on the bath. I tossed in one of the fragrant bath bombs Alexa had given me for Christmas and stroked the calico cat. But first I felt the need to apologize. "Sorry I haven't had much time for you, but it's not like you don't have a loving home with Mrs. P. and the boys." The cat's tail twitched.

Three minutes later, I sank into the warm water and sniffed watermelon-scented air. The calico paraded along the edge of the tub. I thought about Lindsay. I told myself she was well protected. The police were watching, Merv was fussing.

Before I could unkink, the pounding started. I flung my housecoat on my sudsy body and raced down the hall. A sudden looming shape took my breath away. Someone had broken into my apartment. I grabbed a dining chair and raised it to fight off the intruder. Until I recognized her.

"Mrs. Parnell," I yelled, "what are you doing here?" She was white as the front of a windshield. "You told me you no longer had a key to this apartment. You assured me you would stop doing this. I'm entitled to privacy, and it's time you learned to respect it."

"No choice, Ms. MacPhee. You didn't answer your phone."

The water must have drowned the ring. "I was in the bath."

"Nevertheless, you must hear about this. They've interrupting regular programming…"

"It's Benning, isn't it?" My knees felt deboned. I leaned over and steadied myself on Mrs. Parnell's walker.

"Yes."

"Has he found Lindsay?"

"He slipped past the police guard and kidnapped his wife."

"Oh, no."

"They don't know yet where the wife is, as far as I can tell."

\*　　\*　　\*

"Yeah, yeah. I heard." Merv couldn't keep the tension from his voice.

"Are the cops still around?"

"Of course they are."

"I'm just making sure. How many?"

"Still three."

"No one can figure out how he sneaked past the police guard to snatch his wife."

"Holy shit. It's like the bastard can walk through walls."

"Told you so. I'm on my way. The more people in the house, the less chance he can get Lindsay."

I hung up and collided with Mrs. Parnell's walker.

"When do we leave?" she said.

"We do not leave at all. *I* leave on the double."

"I am magnificent in an emergency. As I think you know, Ms. MacPhee." She likes to play that card.

"True enough. But this isn't your kind of emergency, Mrs. P. It will be a long night of waiting."

"I'm nearly seventy-eight years old. Do you think I don't know about waiting?"

"I'm sure you do."

"These ears are sharp. I hope you don't think they're for decoration." Mrs. Parnell's ears and the word decoration do not even belong in the same sentence.

"Absolutely not."

"And, consider this, I have a perfectly serviceable vehicle available in our own parking garage which is more than we can say for you. Plus I have a pair of Sorel boots, lined, waterproof, never been worn, which I will give you in return for a piece of the action."

I put up a token argument. "If he does show up, it could get dangerous. Who knows what could happen to you."

"You forget, Ms. MacPhee, that I'm dying."

"*What?*"

"Of boredom. Let's hit the road."

\*     \*     \*

Thirty minutes later, Mrs. Parnell and I pulled up outside Lindsay's place on Echo Drive. Mrs. Parnell's perfectly serviceable vehicle shuddered to a halt. The unmarked cop car still idled across the street.

By the time I had hoisted the walker from the back seat, an officer had ambled over to greet us. Nice as pie, his hand on his holster. The other officer was also out of the cruiser. Maybe they needed a stretch. Maybe they thought we looked suspicious.

Maybe it had been a while since they'd seen a 1975 Ford LTD.

Mrs. Parnell clutched her two metal-pronged back-up canes. She opened her mouth to speak.

"Don't be a smartass," I told her. "Evening," I nodded to the cop. I recognized him from court.

He, on the other hand, did not recognize me.

It took longer to talk our way into Lindsay's town house than to cross town. In part this was because I was dressed in Mrs. Parnell's thirty-year old beaver coat with the matching hat. I looked like her evil twin, although I did think the neon yellow laces and trim on the Sorels were a nice contemporary touch. Both cops squinted at my picture ID for long enough to make a point.

I was glad of the Sorels, because we stood and waited while the officer poked through our overnight cases, sniffed Mrs. Parnell's bottle of Harvey's Bristol Cream, inspected the walker for hidden hazards, and checked out Mrs. Parnell's ID. Then he put me on the phone with my brother-in-law-to-be, Conn McCracken, to make extra sure. I even had to hand the phone to Mrs. Parnell so Conn could confirm her identity.

"Resist the urge to be cute," I told Conn as I handed the receiver back to the officer. "It's cold out here."

It took long enough, but we passed the test and scurried through the door. Merv seemed almost glad to see us, although I wouldn't want to stretch it. He settled Mrs. Parnell into an oversized armchair with a glass of sherry and her David Lloyd George biography. I perched on the ottoman. He continued to pace, long legs stretching out over the distance from kitchen to living room, living room to kitchen. Lindsay didn't even lift her head off the sofa. She lay with her eyes closed, her hair cascading over one of the large cushions.

"I think it's hitting her. He's holding Rina and is totally out of control," Merv said.

We all went quiet. I think Rina's situation was sinking in with everyone.

"I thought he didn't know where this young lady lived," Mrs. Parnell said after a while. "And that is why we took my car and why Ms. MacPhee wore some of my outerwear. To throw him off the scent in case he was tracking her."

Merv met my eyes. The police had placed a heavy guard around Rina too. We both knew Benning would be after Lindsay regardless. Just a matter of time. Question was, would he find her before the police found him? And would we be able to stop him?

*     *     *

The doorbell pealed, loud and musical. Merv snapped to attention. Mrs. Parnell struggled to her feet. Lindsay lifted her head from the sofa. We gawked in the direction of the front door. I ran behind Merv to the foyer.

"You guard the back door in case he tries to distract us and kick his way in," Merv said.

I thought I heard a small cry from Lindsay. I would have chewed Merv out, but he'd heard the cry too, and he was chewing himself out.

"I'll watch the rear door." Mrs. Parnell was already lurching toward the back of the house, moving her walker menacingly.

The doorbell rang again. I don't think anyone in the room had even exhaled at this point.

"Who is it?" Merv pressed the button on the intercom. He didn't sound his tough old Mountie self. Lindsay was weeping softly in the background.

"It's me. Alvin."

"Alvin?" I said.

"That's right, it's *Alvin*."

"No need to be peevish."

"Well, what part of 'Alvin' don't you understand, Camilla?"

"Be civil."

"I'll be civil when I get inside."

"Well, you'd better try before. By the way, it's nice and warm in here."

"I never complain about the cold. You know I like this weather. It's the company I don't care for." At least I think that's what he said. It was hard to tell with his teeth chattering.

"Okay, let him in, Merv."

"How do we know the little peckerhead's alone?"

"What?"

"Benning could be right behind him, using him as a ploy to push his way in."

I thought I heard another gasp from the sofa.

"Nevertheless, I'm ready for him if he does." Mrs. Parnell had made her way back from the back door.

Lindsay raised her head from the cushion. "Press the button on the airphone and you can see who's outside." Sure enough, the small screen showed Alvin. Next to him stood one of the officers from the unmarked car. Behind him, a cab idled.

It took a while for Merv to bite the bullet and open the door. Alvin's image was cool rather than cold. The tip of his nose looked frostbitten, which was too bad since Alvin was no beauty to begin with.

"It's okay," I called to the officer. "He works for me. Although not very hard."

"Hello, Lindsay." Alvin made his icy way into the living room. I was glad I wasn't the one with nine visible earrings and a metal eyebrow ring. No doubt even Alvin's belly button chain was frozen to his skin.

**67**

Lindsay managed to smile at him. I put it down to the parrots on his shirt.

*    *    *

"Listen," I said into my chirping cellphone, "this is not a good time." I could feel everyone's eyes as I tried to disengage Alexa from her theme: my need to pick out a bridesmaid's dress. "I'll go into the kitchen for this. Since it's hard to hold a private conversation here"

Alexa continued to squeak.

"Hold that thought," I said into the phone. "I'll head to the other room so I don't interrupt any of the fascinating conversations in here. Hold your horses, and I'll be right with you."

Two minutes later, I was holed up in the kitchen with a fresh cup of coffee and a grip on myself. I tried to think about what made my sister tick so I could use the information to get her off my back.

"Alexa. I know this wedding thing is important to you."

Squawk.

"As it would be to anybody. Of course…" I took a deep breath. You can try to beat my family or you can join them. But it's a hell of a lot easier to join them, because to the best of my knowledge they've never been beaten. I'll take my chances with politicians and defence lawyers. "What? No. I do *not* intend to demean the ceremony and all it stands for…what an idea… Well, Alexa, that's a lot to read into someone's reaction to shopping for a dress."

This could be dangerous. In an unguarded moment, I might reveal to Alexa where I was and why. Ten minutes later my nearest and dearest would pile into the townhouse to help by

**68**

bossing everyone around. We already had enough bosses, and I didn't want my sisters interfering with the tricky business of keeping Lindsay safe.

"Fine, I will put my money where my mouth is... Sure, I'll make a commitment to shop for the dress. Okay, okay, it doesn't have to be neutral. Yes, I understand black is out of the question. I'll do it... Yes, I know the ceremony's only two weeks away. Yes, I promise... No, not tonight. I'm tied up for the next little while."

Who knew how long it might be before Benning's rampage would end?

"I can't help it. I'll shop with you on Saturday, and we'll find a dress you approve of." Saturday had to be a safe bet. No way Benning could evade the entire focus of the Ottawa police much longer.

"Oh, it is not too late, Alexa. Be serious. That's more than a week before the ceremony. No, that's the absolute earliest. Well, I can't help it. Previous commitments. Yes, I realize being a bridesmaid is a commitment... No, I do not have any reason to want to ruin the ceremony for you. None at all... Alexa, you are out of control. What is it with you? The way you carry on, all this stress and anxiety, perhaps you don't want to go on with this wedding. Could that be it? Second thoughts? Cold feet? Alexa? Alexa?"

\*    \*    \*

I returned to the living room to face a weird tableau. They might have been cast in bronze, statues in a public plaza. Merv stayed in a half crouch, Alvin's mouth hung open wide enough to reveal fillings. Mrs. P. leaned against her walker. I could smell the spilt sherry from her overturned glass. No one moved to wipe it from the pale hardwood floor. The sole sound was the local weather news from the radio.

"What is it? What happened."

No one spoke.

"Will somebody tell me what the hell's going on here?"

"They found her body." Alvin dropped his voice.

"Whose body?"

"Holy shit, keep your voice down," Merv said. "Lindsay will hear." Lindsay lay motionless on the sofa, covered with a mohair throw.

"You're the one yelling, Merv."

"Settle down, troops," Mrs. Parnell whispered. "There was a news bulletin, Camilla. The body of a woman has been dumped in a snowbank off one of the side roads west of Kanata."

Alvin whispered, "Benning's wife."

# Eight

"T hey gave her name on the radio? Before notifying her family?" I couldn't believe it.

Mrs. Parnell nodded. "Someone who was being interviewed blurted it out. Must have been traumatic finding her. She'd been beaten."

From the sofa, Lindsay murmured, "What happened?"

Merv and Alvin broke out of their statue routine. Merv loped over and sat by her side. He picked up her small white hand. "It's okay," he said.

"Is it Ralph?" She rubbed her eyes with her free hand.

"Yes," I said.

Merv gave me a warning look. "No."

Alvin dug an elbow in my ribs. Even Mrs. Parnell shook her head. What was this dopiness? Why would we keep this information from Lindsay?

"Please, what is it?" Lindsay sat up, small and shaky.

Merv said, "Nothing. And nothing will happen to you while I'm alive to prevent it."

From Lindsay's other side, Alvin slid onto the sofa. "Goes double for me."

Lindsay appeared not to have heard them. She leaned forward, head in her hands. "It is Ralph, isn't it? No one can stop him."

"I can stop him," said Merv.

"Me, too," said Alvin.

Lindsay was right, even if she didn't have all the facts yet. I knew it even if those two bozos didn't. Time to set the record straight here. I opened my mouth. Mrs. Parnell motioned me to step aside.

"In a minute," I said.

"It's important." She gripped her walker and headed for the kitchen.

Fine. I followed her.

"Wait until the right time to tell her," she said, when we were out of earshot. "She's a bit shell-shocked. We're not all suitable for life in the trenches."

"Oh, come on. She's not a child. She has a right to know. Do you think she won't hear it on the news? She's shown courage. What's wrong with you people?"

"Not everyone is like you, Ms. MacPhee."

"Maybe not, but she's an intelligent woman, and she…"

"Let us be circumspect."

"Mrs. Parnell, I expect you to be sensible. What is gained by not telling her?"

"She's traumatized. You should wait until she's had a chance to let those pills take effect. I recognize the situation is serious. Nevertheless, we have to be gentle if we want her to get over this."

"Listen, she's the one whose life is in danger. And she's already doped to the ears."

"The police are bound to catch up with him after this. But in the meantime, even if he shows up, she's safe with us here."

"I hope to hell we're up to the task."

Mrs. Parnell straightened up smartly. "Up to it? This will be our finest hour."

Maybe. I'd already found out the hard way I can fend off a

murderer. Mrs. P. was equal to any emergency, although you'd never guess it. Merv had the security training. He and Alvin were prepared to lay down their lives for Lindsay if they had to.

On the other hand, how many officers were searching for Ralph Benning and had failed? How had he managed to evade them? I hoped Mrs. P. was right. I couldn't let myself think about Rina Benning's last moments. We would mourn her once Lindsay was safe.

Until Benning made his next move, there didn't seem to be a goddam thing we could do.

*   *   *

I swallowed my pride and put in another call to my brother-in-law to be. Not that he answered or that anyone in her right mind would expect him to during this emergency. But I can't stand sitting around.

I stalked through the house. Up to the second floor and then down. Opened every door. Tried each window. Stepped out on both balconies. Stretched my neck into the attic crawl space. Crawled under the beds. Snooped around the walk-in clothes cupboards. Reached behind the coats and the out-of-season wardrobe. Stuck my nose past the shower curtain. Poked around in the front entrance closet, behind Lindsay's fur coat and ski gear. Peered in behind suitcases and packing boxes in the basement. Checked inside the movers' boxes still stacked three high. Inspected the gas furnace. Merv had done pretty much the same thing a couple of hours earlier.

The two musketeers were still huddled around Lindsay when I arrived back in the living room. Mrs. Parnell hulked in her chair looking vigilant and more than a little dangerous.

I cleaned up the spilled sherry. Then I slipped on my Sorels and the beaver coat, pulled on the hat and stuck my nose out the door. The cruiser was still parked in front of the building.

"Keep an eye on me," I said to Mrs. Parnell.

Once she'd lurched across the room, I stepped through the door. I stood on the front steps and scanned the street. Intermittent traffic inched along the smooth curve of Colonel By Drive. Across the road, a lone jogger, face covered by a balaclava, puffed along the canal footpath. From the vantage point of the steps, I could see small packs of resolute skaters glide along the ice of the canal, scarves fluttering. No need to worry this year about melting ice or rain. Just the clink of falling fingers and noses. You don't have to be crazy to live in Ottawa in the winter, but it helps.

We had a new police shift parked in front of the house. The driver looked vaguely familiar. The two officers watched the jogger head around the bend and under the Queensway. They probably figured a jogger, wearing black, could get real close to Lindsay's place in the dark. And all joggers look alike. When the runner puffed out of sight, one of the cops turned to watch the skaters and the other scanned the condo front and sides. He spotted me, looking nothing short of dangerous in my get-up. He climbed out of the cruiser and placed his hand near his holster. Oh good, my tax dollars hard at work yet again.

Still, was it enough?

"Heard the news?" I asked. The other officer was female, although it was hard to tell with her police-issue winter hat. At least she didn't have the fur flap down, *Fargo*-style. She was sipping Tim Hortons coffee, the cup held in her leather-gloved hands. The two of them exchanged glances.

"What's he got to lose?" I said.

"Do I know you?" The driver squinted at me.

"Camilla MacPhee. Justice for Victims, Constable James. And you know damn well who I am and why I'm here."

I'd seen him in court often enough, and he had an easy name to remember.

"Oh right. I heard you were here."

I just smiled. Even if the Ottawa force hadn't sent Mr. Congeniality, I was glad they'd sent two officers, and they were awake and suspicious. Suspicious was just what we needed.

I was suspicious too. Not to mention worried about just how secure Lindsay's building really was. If Ralph Benning had nothing to lose before, now he had less than nothing. Getting shot by the cops was the best he could hope for. If the laws of physics permitted it, Benning would do it.

So did the laws of physics permit Benning to get into Lindsay's house? Only one way to find out. "You want to let the guy in the back know I'm coming around to check things out?" No point in getting shot myself.

Lindsay's place was an end unit. Pricey, an extra wall of windows with a panoramic view down the frozen canal. Glamorous. Security was well thought out. Floodlights eliminated most shadows. I pussyfooted along the side of the unit, feeling the eyes of the two officers on me. Motion detectors picked up my movements, and more lights flicked on. A shadowy Mrs. Parnell dogged my footsteps from window to window. I nodded. She waved her Benson and Hedges.

The back was an open courtyard with visitor parking. I peered under the small deck at Lindsay's utility entrance, but it was a *pro forma* exercise. I couldn't imagine Benning holed up on the petrified ground letting himself freeze to death. Although one could always hope.

In the back of the condo, I crunched in the snow, which was near the top of my Sorels. In the dark kitchen window, the tip of Mrs. Parnell's cigarette glowed.

If it hadn't been for the fog of breath on the window, I might not even have spotted the officer in the unmarked car, out of view. He'd spotted me though. I ambled over to the driver's side. He opened the window. I was glad the police were covering the house so well, even if he didn't look pleased to see me.

"Did you hear Benning killed his wife?" I said.

He nodded.

"We don't want another tragedy. You tracking the cars coming in and out? You have to inform us if you see anything suspicious. Here's a cell number." I gave him Merv's.

"I think *you're* suspicious." He wrinkled his nose. Might have been from residual mothballs on the beaver coat.

"Funny." I turned and headed back. I stopped at the cruiser out front first.

"Can I do something else for you?" Officer James asked.

"Sure, you can make sure we all stay off the major media by keeping my client alive." You can always tell when people bite their tongues. "Let's not forget Benning slipped past a bunch of your boys at his wife's place."

The faces hardened.

"He has the same grudge against Lindsay Grace," I said. "Make sure you keep her alive."

"We have round-the-clock surveillance. We know what he's capable of. He shot an officer, remember? We want him just as badly as you do."

"What about the roof? How do you know he won't come across the roof, rappel down the side or back of the house and cut his way into one of the windows? Or cut a hole through the roof itself?"

Their eyes met again. I thought the second officer mouthed the word "crackpot."

76

"Trust me," I said, "Nothing's too farfetched in this case."

"We're on the job here. You head back inside and let us do it."

"Make sure you're up to it. One woman dead in a day is more than enough. You people didn't keep him away from her." I figured making them mad would keep their adrenaline up nicely, make them more alert.

The driver blurted, "She gave them the slip." His colleague's coffee slopped as she reached over to touch his arm. A gentle way of saying, shut up you fool.

If I'd had coffee, I would have slopped it too. "*She* gave them the slip? No way she would have wanted to elude her police protection. I don't believe it."

The woman officer spoke as she mopped up her coffee. "Believe what you want. If you want news updates, turn on your radio. That's not our job." She reached over and the window slid up.

I stomped back to the condo, trying to imagine why Rina Benning would flee from safety straight into the arms of death.

*    *    *

Mrs. Parnell was the only person in the motley crew guarding Lindsay who made any sense. I had to admire her. But even so, by eight-thirty that evening I was tired of her company. There's a limited amount of time you want to spend in someone else's kitchen while your neighbour expounds on her hobby, the allied leaders of World War II.

On the other hand, Churchill and Rommel were fascinating compared to Alvin and Merv, still fawning over Lindsay in the living room. I did my damnedest to tune out their voices. At least I didn't have to listen to their stomachs growl as the traditional meal hour came and went. I'd already checked Lindsay's cupboards, fridge and freezer. Except for the quality coffee, they were enough to give empty a good name. Unless you counted the two slices of bread still left in the bag and the pat of butter on a pretty plate on the dairy shelf. Under the circumstances, take-out seemed ill advised. It seemed wiser to get some food into the house, to keep up Lindsay's strength.

I felt a moment's twinge about having gotten my sisters in such a snit. Otherwise I might have been able to call one of them to bring over provisions without revealing why. Oh well. Mrs. Parnell never appeared to eat anyway. I resigned myself to a gurgling stomach until the morning arrived or Benning was captured. Perhaps we could arrange for the next shift of cops to bring us some doughnuts.

In the meantime, Mrs. Parnell and I sat in the kitchen and busied ourselves trying to find out more about Rina Benning. With the portable TV relocated and a pair of radios set to different stations, we had been able to determine a body had indeed been found, apparently bludgeoned. Despite the early blurting of her name, we had no official confirmation. The police and the Coroner have procedures.

The media are inventive at skirting procedures, but P. J. was still incommunicado. The evening dragged on. Mrs. Parnell found herself out of sherry. I found myself pacing.

She checked every cupboard in the kitchen and came up empty. It seemed to make her critical. "You know your problem, Ms. MacPhee?"

"I'm too polite?"

"You are too driven. You have to learn to focus more and relax."

"Thanks."

"Focus is the first principle of effective surveillance."

Not for the first time, I gawked at her. The long, elderly body, the sharp nose, the startling ears, the perpetual cigarette, tip glowing. The wispy hair disappearing into a bun, the gnarled knuckles. "It is?"

"Of course, Ms. MacPhee. Check any basic surveillance manual." I didn't have a basic surveillance manual. And I was surprised to hear Mrs. Parnell did. Although it wasn't the strangest thing about her by a long shot.

"You have a manual on surveillance?"

"Covert operations. You could learn a lot from them, Ms. MacPhee. A bit of patience would do wonders for you."

"I don't have time for it."

"Blood, sweat and tears," she said, "but no sherry. I will try the dining room. I think I saw a cabinet there. You keep your ears open for breaking news."

"You should stay put. If Benning shows up, we'd be better off cold sober."

"Speak for yourself. I am always ready to fight."

*   *   *

"Right, Elaine." I held Merv's cellphone away from my ear. "I'm glad it's going well. Yep. I'm sorry to miss out on that sculpture activity, and I'm glad you understand that this is where I have to be. Lindsay's safety has to take priority. I'm sure building an ice sculpture is a great way to solidify relationships. Really wish I could be with you, but I'll help WAVE some other time. And Alvin will too." I ignored the look I got from him. "I know he was keen to take part in the ice sculpture contest. And as I said before, we would love to be with you, enjoying the outdoors, instead of cooped up here without a bite to eat."

Both Merv and Mrs. Parnell listened with amusement. I didn't appreciate the smirks. Elaine was the most single-minded, stubborn person I knew. Even worse than my sisters. Let them try to deal with her sometime, I thought.

"In fact," I added, "if you are looking for volunteers, next time, don't forget to ask Merv and Mrs. Parnell. They're both extremely good-humoured. Don't thank me. Stay in touch."

Merv's phone rang so quickly I thought it was Elaine again. P. J.'s voice was a relief.

"Well, well, Clark Kent. Great to hear from you. At last."

"I'm short on time, Tiger. Whatcha got?"

"Interesting stuff but first, tell me, what the hell is going on? We heard Rina Benning has been murdered. How could Benning get her?"

"Don't have official confirmation yet on that, but it looks like she went out to meet him. Christ, can you believe that?" I could picture P. J. running his fingers through his wiry red curls.

"Not even possible. I can't believe they'd let her go," I said.

"You and me both, but apparently she distracted the guard and drove off to meet him. So what's the scoop?"

"It can't be true."

"It is. They found a message from him on her answering machine. He asked her to meet him in the usual place. Told her he loved her and he wouldn't hurt her and he had to see her before he died."

"Oh my God. And she actually went? Do they know where he is?"

"They have no goddam idea. So what do you have for me? Where's Lindsay Grace hiding out?"

"What? I can hardly hear you. The batteries must be running low on this thing."

"You mentioned you had some information. Hey, come on, Tiger."

"P. J.? Are you there? Hello? Hello? Damn it, Merv. It's time you bought a decent cellphone."

I hung up.

*   *   *

We had spent a long and jumpy evening irritating each other and listening to stomachs growl, when the doorbell sent us all skyward at nine forty-five. A couple of Alvin's earrings scratched the ceiling.

"Lights out," Mrs. Parnell yelled. "Hit the floor belly first and keep moving till you are in the trench."

I reached the front door before Merv and grabbed an umbrella for protection. I pressed the button on the airphone. Elaine Ekstein's cheerful voice came as a surprise.

"Elaine?"

"Holy moly, open up, the pizza's getting cold."

Elaine stood like Nanook of the North with a pile of boxes. Over her shoulder Officer James loomed, carrying a cardboard box. Behind him the cruiser idled, with the female officer in view.

Elaine kicked off her furry boots. They careened across the marble entrance floor. The heel from the left one left a jaunty little scuffmark on the fresh taupe paint on the wall. "I decided to take the high road. The WAVE sculpture team seems to have everything under control. I decided you need me more than they do. Justice is well served. So I put my money where my mouth is and headed to the Colonnade."

"And not a moment too soon," I said.

"Pizza?" Merv took his eyes off Lindsay in the heat of the

moment. The moment didn't last long. Merv resumed the lovesick schtick before you could say pepperoni and anchovies.

"That's the best." Alvin stood and flicked his ponytail in approval. It's always hard to tell when Alvin's excited, but the parrots on his shirt seemed to be engaged in some hula activity.

Merv pressed his advantage and gave Lindsay a soothing stroke on the shoulder.

"Elaine, you are now my favourite person," I said, "because you have four boxes of pizza. Is one of them mushroom and bacon?"

"For sure. I know your taste. If you can call it taste."

I decided she'd better be careful, or I'd have to mention she looked four feet wide in her lime-green quilted parka. But at least she wasn't wearing the faux leopard outfit.

The officer followed Elaine into the condo.

"Gotta take care of our boys and girls in blue." Elaine headed for the kitchen. "Come on down gang. First, Lindsay, I'd like you to meet Constable James. He and his partner are watching the front of the building. Another officer's stationed in back. You're in good hands."

Lindsay's face said it all. She wanted to be in good hands. She wanted to believe three officers outside and five people inside would be enough to ward off Benning. But she couldn't quite believe it.

I didn't believe it either. Rina Benning had been in good hands too, until she had voluntarily gone to meet her death. Now we had nothing to do but wait and hope the cops wouldn't screw up again. So for the moment, pizza was exactly what we needed to take our minds off Benning.

The cardboard box held two thermoses of coffee. "That should do you." Elaine flipped open the first top. "It's still hot, despite the ridiculous amount of time you kept me waiting outside."

"You can't be too careful in a pindown situation," Mrs. Parnell said.

"I hope that's not the bacon and mushroom you're sticking your hands in, Elaine," I said.

"How about Hawaiian?" Alvin positioned himself.

"Your favourite." Elaine flung open the second box, to reveal the lethal combination of ham and pineapple. Alvin's earrings twinkled.

Would this little feast leave us in a more vulnerable position than before? But how could it? Still, the primitive part of my brain kept repeating, eat first, think later. I ate mine with my hands.

Mrs. Parnell pronounced that the combination was splendid. Merv swooped in close enough to cut a delicate piece, which he placed on a plate. He added a knife and fork to the plate, folded one of the napkins into a crisp edged triangle and headed back to Lindsay on the sofa. You can count on too much pizza to help you get a grip on a tough situation.

Five minutes later, Elaine took off her lime green coat. I slugged back a large mug of coffee and tried not to sulk when she snatched the entire thermos from me and handed it to Constable James.

"Stop bitching, Camilla," she said, opening the second thermos. "There's plenty to go around." Constable James headed back to the cruisers with a couple of slices from each pizza for his colleagues. I caught his sneer.

We all washed down the rest of the pizza with the remaining coffee and tried not to burp. Except for Lindsay, who sipped her coffee but left her little plate on her lap, the neat slice of pizza untouched.

Elaine whispered in my ear. "I picked up some interesting rumours from one of the crown attorneys about how the bastard escaped."

"Really?"

"Yes. It looks like he must have had an accomplice. You're right about one thing. They're convinced it was someone on the police force."

"So P. J.'s right after all."

When Merv's cellphone rang again, we all jumped. Conn McCracken. "We think we have him cornered. Thought you'd like to know. It should be over soon. Hang in. And while you're at it, do you think you could be a bit nicer to your sister?"

As usual, he hung up before I could ask him what, when, where and how.

"Great news," I said. "That was the police. They think they have him. They expect to have him back in custody soon or…" I watched Lindsay's face for signs of emotion. I didn't suggest Benning would probably be killed. I knew she had loved him and perhaps still did. Just like Rina Benning. "I don't have any details."

"I'll get back to my post and monitor the situation." Mrs. P. heaved herself to her feet and wobbled back to the kitchen.

For once, everyone fell silent, until Lindsay began to talk. "He'll be killed."

No one else said a word.

She was crying softly again. "I know you don't understand how easy it was to love him."

She had that right. I scanned the sympathetic faces. Merv squeezed Lindsay's hand. Okay. So everyone else understood how a highly educated, beautiful, accomplished, financially successful woman could hand over her self-respect and autonomy to a guy who belonged under a rock. Why did I have so much goddam trouble with the whole idea?

Of course, my opinion was coloured because the only two men I'd ever fallen for were dead. And my sisters always told me any man in his right mind would walk a mile to avoid my black moods. I couldn't even imagine having an agreeable relationship with an attractive, presentable, engaging living man with ginger hair and a gap between his front teeth.

"It's a syndrome, Lindsay," Elaine said. "They have a technique, these creeps. They make you think you have the love affair of the century, then they gradually erode your self-esteem, they isolate you from your friends and colleagues, they play with your brain, they make you think everything wrong is all your fault. If you were better, smarter, cleaner, nicer, more something, they wouldn't have to hit you. That's how it works. Don't blame yourself." There was something in Elaine's voice I'd never heard. Maybe I didn't know everything about her.

"He told me no one ever loved him as much as I did," Lindsay said. The napkin was in bits. "His life wasn't easy. He knew I would always love him." She didn't say he was right. She didn't have to.

Mrs. Parnell spoke from the kitchen door. "We cannot always choose whom we will love and how."

True enough.

*   *   *

Elaine cornered me in the kitchen where I was engaged in breaking up the pizza boxes and hunting for the recycling container. I needed to keep busy to stay awake. Despite the coffee and the large amount of pizza I had wolfed, I was feeling groggy.

"Having a little trouble understanding Lindsay's situation?" Elaine said.

"Why do you ask?"

"I don't know. Your expression maybe. Don't be too superior in this area, Camilla. It's easy for this to happen to any woman."

"I know."

"I don't think you do. You think it couldn't happen to you."

She was right, but damned if I wanted to admit it. "You're forgetting I run an agency for victims, Elaine."

"Not for a minute, Camilla. But you might ask yourself who you are to judge whether a person is a victim or not."

\*   \*   \*

I was worried about Mrs. Parnell's cat. Mrs. Parnell was worried about Lester and Pierre. Elaine was worried about potential disaster for the ice sculpture contest. Merv and Alvin were worried the other one would get in some extra shoulder pats. These were nice distractions from the real worry.

Every creak in the building had us all on full alert. At thirty below, the ceiling joists can make some startling sounds. We had been leaping out of our chairs regularly, then looking around, feeling silly. When Conn McCracken's call came in at eleven fifteen, I felt a flood of relief. I wasn't alone. All eyes were on the phone. We needed to hear the word that Benning was secured and Lindsay was safe.

"So," I said, "is it over?"

"Bad news, Camilla. The son of a bitch got away."

They were all looking at me when I hung up.

"Lord thundering Jesus, Camilla, you're dead white," Alvin said.

"My dear Ms. MacPhee, you certainly are."

Merv looked up. "I've seen flour with better colour than that."

"What's wrong?" Elaine asked.

Lindsay buried her head in her hands.

*   *   *

Okay, looking at the team guarding Lindsay, I would be the first to admit the whole thing was like a bad sitcom. Cast of quirky characters in high-tension situation unlikely to occur in real life. Half an hour of snappy dialogue and rigged up conflicts and then a nice neat resolution. Canned laughter and then cut to commercial. Then nothing to do but wait for next week's show.

Except that in real life a little sitcom goes a long way. And no one was laughing.

With the threat to Lindsay, it's hard to believe we were all dozy. I smothered a yawn. So did Elaine. Alvin didn't even bother smothering his. Merv let out a little snore. Mrs. Parnell's head jerked a tad. Lindsay was horizontal on the sofa, unmoving. The arm of the cream tunic sweater peeked from under the blanket Merv had placed gently over her.

"Okay, listen up," I said. "We can't let down our guard. That means staying awake."

"As a rule," Mrs. Parnell said, "you take turns keeping watch." Merv and Alvin turned their attention to her. "Since we are five," she continued, "let us have two keep watch, and three sleep. Four hour shifts work best. Then three will be fresh at about three in the morning, when, if I were Benning, I'd be making my entrance."

"Right." Exactly what he would do. But where did she get this stuff?

"So," I added, "who gets the first sleep shift?"

Of course, Lindsay was actually already asleep, her

**87**

cashmere arm covering her face. That's tranks for you.

"You go first," Merv said, without taking his eyes off Lindsay. "I don't need to sleep. That way there will be three of us at all times."

"I don't actually sleep either," Mrs. Parnell said. "Never close an eye in the average night."

"Me neither," Alvin said.

Elaine crossed her arms. "I certainly don't want to miss anything. I skipped the ice sculpture competition for this. I don't intend to snooze through it."

"Fine," I said, "we'll all stay awake all night, the whole bunch of us. No one closes an eye."

That's the last thing I remembered.

# Nine

I opened my eyes to see something black, vile and smelly. It took a while to recognize Alvin's sock, still containing Alvin's foot. How many times had I heard Alvin say kiss my foot? But I'd never thought it would happen. I pushed the sock away. It banged, vigorously. Leave it to Alvin.

But the noise came from somewhere else. Oh, the front door. Strange. Not my front door. Where was I? And why was I anywhere with Alvin's foot? It took a minute to recognize Lindsay's place.

Lindsay's place, where I had apparently chosen to bunk down on the gleaming maple floor for a long winter's nap. Every bone in my body complained as I stumbled to my feet. To make matters worse, Alvin continued to snore. No wait, that wasn't Alvin. Merv, his face mashed up against the leg of the sofa, issued a thunderous *largo* roar. In a pleasant counterpoint, Elaine emitted high-pitched flutelike trills. She lay with her head under the end table.

The banging continued. My heart thundered. Who was at the door? Would Benning have the nerve to knock? No way. He'd never make it past the cops. It must be the cops checking up on us. Bang. Bang.

"Coming," I bellowed.

You'd have thought it would be loud enough to wake the others.

Not so. Even Mrs. Violet "I never close an eye" Parnell continued to snooze intently, bent over in her chair at a forty-five degree angle, her head cushioned by the stainless steel handles of her walker.

I was the only one awake but we were all there, as far as I could see.

Everyone but Lindsay.

*     *     *

"I don't know," I said to Conn McCracken, once he had stopped stomping, blowing on his hands and swearing.

"What do you mean, you don't know?"

McCracken, his ratty little partner, Leonard Momberquette, and their cold bulky coats crowded the front entrance. Someone had left a pair of leather boots where I could trip on them. I skidded on a muddy puddle marring the elegant marble tile. My head buzzed.

"Just woke up. She must be here. Let me check upstairs. She's probably in the bathroom."

I started on the stairs, two at a time. McCracken thudded behind me. Images of injuries and death flooded my brain. I heard the sound of my own voice: "Oh God, we were all asleep. What if Benning got in?"

As my foot hit the top stair, I lurched sideways into the banister when something rushed by me. Merv shot toward the closed door of Lindsay's bedroom. McCracken's voice boomed behind us, "Stop. Don't open that door."

Merv yanked the door open. I was glued to his heels as he exploded into the bedroom. We both stopped. I hardly noticed the pain in my foot as McCracken stepped on it.

Lindsay lay on the bed, on top of the pewter silk spread,

unmoving in the dim morning light. She glowed, pale as dust, her red sweater sleeve like a slash of blood. Her hand stretched out toward the window. Eyes closed. Merv flung himself at the bed. He sounded like he was strangling.

I exhaled with relief. I knew she couldn't be dead. Benning would never leave her so undamaged. As I reached the bed and bent over, I saw her chest rise. She was breathing. Tears stung my eyes. She was all right.

I whirled on Conn McCracken. "You scared the shit out of us."

"You ain't seen nothing yet," came a voice from behind him. Leonard Mombourquette. The man we're all better off without.

"*Lennie,*" McCracken said. I heard the warning whether or not Mombourquette did.

Merv reached down and stroked Lindsay's limp hand. "Thank God, thank God."

I tuned into the racket coming from the staircase. Footsteps. Voices. Alvin led the second wave. He squinted without his glasses, his ponytail hung loose. "Is...?"

Elaine appeared behind him, pink and panting, her wild red curls beyond all hope. She edged into the room, banging her hip on the edge of the dresser. "Is...? "

A strange metallic thumping filled the air.

"What the hell's that?" McCracken moved toward the door. "Lennie, get on it."

Mombourquette's hand shot towards his holster just as Mrs. Parnell lurched over the top stair clutching her metal cane for balance. "You better put your hand down, sonny," she said, "before you get into trouble."

"For Christ's sake, Lennie," McCracken said.

Mrs. Parnell pushed past Mombourquette. "Is...?"

"She's alive," I scurried to the bed and insinuated myself around Merv, "and she hasn't been beaten. But no one could sleep through this, so something's not quite normal." I bent over and tried her pulse. Slow but sure. I brushed against a small vial near a round cut-velvet pillow.

"We'd better see if she's …" Merv reached for the vial.

"Don't touch that, Merv," I said.

"Okay, everybody out." McCracken pointed to the door as he called for medical assistance.

Nobody moved.

"Everybody out."

I could have told him it would take more than that to get this crowd to abandon ship.

"Your problem. Stay here, people, if you want to get charged." Mombourquette can always manage a sneer.

But Mrs. Parnell can sneer with the best of them. "I shall not abandon my post for the likes of you, young man."

"This is not the time to get huffy, Mrs. P. We need to find out what happened here and see if Lindsay requires medical attention. I think she's okay, but it's better for her if you all wait downstairs."

Mombourquette likes to give the orders. He opened his mouth.

"Keep in mind, it's best for Lindsay," I told the crowd.

"Get these people out of here, Camilla," he said.

I chose not to argue with him. I had my own reasons for wanting them out of the room.

"She's probably fine. My guess is she took a couple of sleeping pills to get her through the night, and she's in a deep sleep. But we'd better find out. We won't do her any good here. She might even panic if she wakes up to a scene from *Lethal Weapon*."

"Right." Merv wasn't moving. I figured he meant everyone else could leave.

"Why doesn't somebody put on coffee? We can all use it," I said.

"I'll do that." Elaine whacked her knee on the door on her way out.

"Alvin, can you give her a hand?"

Lindsay's eyelids fluttered but remained closed. "Merv, can you help Mrs. Parnell down the stairs?"

"I'm staying here."

"Don't argue. And that goes double for you, Mrs. P."

I reached over and checked Lindsay's pulse again. It gave me something to do. Lindsay issued a small hopeful sigh. Her colour seemed healthy. Cream, not white.

"So what's happening?" I whispered to McCracken. "Any leads on Benning?"

Mombourquette raised an eyebrow at McCracken. McCracken shook his head. I studied them.

"Don't worry about me, boys, I have all the time in the world. I wish I could say the same for Lindsay here. But take your time, no need to get off your butts and put Benning back where you should have kept him in the first place."

Okay, so I couldn't really blame them for Benning's rampage. But when you wake up kissing Alvin's foot, it gets your day off to a bad start.

"You haven't heard?" Mombourquette snorted, and McCracken fired him a warning glance.

"Heard what?"

"We found him."

"And he's back where he belongs?"

"You could say that." Even at the best of times, I find Mombourquette's smirk hard to take.

"Lennie," McCracken growled.

"You might say we have him on ice." Light twinkled off Mombourquette's pointed incisors.

"Careful, Len."

"High time, if you don't mind me saying so. I hope you can keep him behind bars this time."

"Camilla." McCracken doesn't usually call me by name, but this wedding thing had softened his brain.

"Forever would not be too long."

"He'll have forever." Mombourquette's tail twitched with amusement. A slight movement from the bed distracted me. Lindsay's eyes opened wide. "And then some," Mombourquette said.

"I guess you haven't turned on your radio," McCracken said.

\*   \*   \*

They all thundered back up the stairs and crowded into her room as soon as Lindsay began to sob.

"C'mon, folks, give the lady some air." McCracken pushed us all back into the hallway, closed the bedroom door and stood guard.

I thought Merv would punch him out, with Alvin's assistance. I hoped this unholy alliance would not endure past the immediate emotional situation.

"What have you done to that girl?" Mrs. Parnell pulled herself up to her full height, slightly more than Mombourquette's. She raised her steel-tipped cane, to steady herself I suppose, and accidentally brought it down on his instep.

Lucky for us the paramedics arrived.

# Ten

Elaine screamed. When she stopped screaming, she said, "No, I refuse to believe it."

"Please." I put a soothing hand on her shoulder. "We don't all have to get hysterical." She jumped away.

It had taken the better part of an hour to get the paramedics out of the house, to make sure Lindsay was safe and sleeping and to get the rest of the circus downstairs where it belonged. Mombourquette stayed, but you can't have everything.

And Elaine, of all the unlikely people, kept screaming. "Easy for you, Camilla, you didn't even work on it. Holy moly. It's not possible. It couldn't happen."

"Well, it did."

"Listen, I was there," she said. "I worked on that sculpture. There's no way Benning's body could have been in it. Ice is translucent, you couldn't fail to notice a dead body. It was a stunning figure of Justice, by the way, for those of you who were too wimpy to make it to the volunteer team because of inclement weather."

I put out my hand to steady Alvin. "Let it go, Elaine. You know exactly where we were."

"Wicked," Alvin said. "I sure would have liked to have seen that body. Is it still there?"

"Alvin." I tried to inject a fearsome warning note into my voice. As much as I'd hated and feared Benning, I didn't feel comfortable with his body as a spectacle.

Merv liked the idea too. "Frozen solid, serves the bastard right."

"What is wrong with you people? I was *there!* I saw the block of ice. With absolutely no dead body in it. Nothing but ice, ice, ice. Ice all the way. You can see through ice, you know." Elaine banged on the kitchen table.

"There's a body in it now." Since there were people in the room who didn't hate Mombourquette, he'd have to keep being himself until they did. Wouldn't take long.

"But there wasn't last night." Elaine had trouble with the central idea of the body in the sculpture.

"Nevertheless, transport would have been the issue," Mrs. Parnell said. She jammed another Benson and Hedges into her ebony holder and flicked her silver lighter.

"Transport? Do you think we would have transported him?" Elaine gripped the side of the table and shrieked.

"Takes a certain amount of strength to lift a man, unconscious or dead, never mind encased in ice. Of course, a dolly could make it possible, even for a woman." Mrs. Parnell let out a two-foot curl of smoke that tickled my nostrils. "Could do it myself on a good day."

Elaine issued a strangled sound. "Unconscious? No, not unconscious. Oh, God. No, that's too awful."

I gave Mrs. Parnell a look she shouldn't have recovered from. Not that she noticed. "I'm sure he was already dead," I said.

"Oh, wow," Alvin said. "He would have died from exposure. He had that coming."

"Shut up," I said.

Elaine started to hyperventilate.

"Sit down and put your head between your knees," I said. "And listen to me. He would not have died of exposure." I don't know why I felt such utter certainty. The pathologist probably hadn't even laid his latex pinky on Benning yet.

"Consider this," Mrs. Parnell said. "If he were unconscious, that would make it murder."

"But." Elaine paused for breath between each word. "It's. Not. Possible. Not in our ice sculpture. It must have been some other one."

"Trust me, it was your sculpture. There's no doubt about that," McCracken said. "We won't know what happened to him for a while yet. It takes time for the results of the PM to come back. Then we'll see."

"PM. That's a Post Mortem," Mrs. Parnell said with an air of authority. "You can learn a lot from those things."

"I think I'm going to be sick," Elaine said.

"You are going to be fine." I turned so my back blocked Mrs. Parnell from Elaine's view. "This is a ghastly end to a terrible series of events. Unfortunately, it ended in murder, however…"

"However, it couldn't have happened to a nicer guy."

"Alvin! This is no laughing matter."

"Look, Elaine, don't pay any attention to them." Deep down, I agreed with Alvin, but that was not my official stand on potential murder victims, no matter how deserving of retribution they were.

"Don't get me wrong," Elaine said, "I'm not sorry he's dead either. It's the politics of it. People will think we did it."

I jumped in before Mrs. Parnell and Alvin could volley another series of inappropriate remarks. "No one would ever suspect Women Against Violence Everywhere of murder."

As the words left my tongue, I wanted to bite them back. I could think of no other group in town who would have more reason to want to put Benning on ice. But my platitudes drew quite a reaction from Elaine. "The hell they wouldn't. *Everyone* will think WAVE did it. They'll say we conspired as a board of directors. This is not a tragedy. This is a bloody public relations disaster!"

"Not necessarily," Mrs. Parnell said. "Could be seen as a wake-up call in certain quarters."

"Frigging right," Alvin said. "The time has come for domestic batterers to chill out."

Usually, I was the most insensitive and outrageous person in any given room. That day, I ran well back in the pack.

"Yes," Elaine said. "Of course we'll deny it, but who'll believe us?"

"Plenty of people will be under scrutiny, not the least of which will be Ottawa's finest." I gestured to Mombourquette.

McCracken shrugged. Mombourquette grinned, although the grin slipped as Mrs. Parnell shot a stream of smoke into his face.

"Well," McCracken said, "while we're here, why don't we have a little talk with Ms. Ekstein?"

\* \* \*

Okay, I felt sorry for Elaine. But she had stamina. And anyway, I knew she had nothing to do with Benning's death. I could imagine circumstances under which she might have killed him, but she would never let it reflect badly on WAVE. But I had other things on my mind. Someone else to worry about.

I was glad the crowd in the kitchen was so distracted. I had to think. Who needed to kill Benning? Not out of philosophical distaste or moral outrage, but from the standpoint of staying alive. It was too late for Benning's wife.

The only other person with as much to lose was upstairs,

sleeping. Being gazed on with adoration by Merv, hard-edged RCMP officer and all-round cynical guy. Lindsay. Lindsay, who could now rest, her long nightmare with Benning over. Lindsay, who had fallen asleep before any of us. Lindsay, who had succumbed to Benning's psychotic brand of charm. Lindsay, who could have been lured into meeting him the night before.

Lindsay Grace had needed Benning dead.

*　　*　　*

"Give Elaine a break," I said to McCracken.

"No, you give me a break. I can't believe you would stick your nose in another murder investigation days before your sister's wedding. Even for you, Camilla, this is inconsiderate."

Inconsiderate? He hadn't seen anything yet. And what the hell did the wedding have to do with it?

"Look. We don't need to be on opposite sides. After all, we both want the guilty person locked up for this. Anyway, the wedding's two weeks away."

He flashed me one of his looks.

"Well, nearly," I said. "Whoever killed Benning would have a strong defence."

"Murder's still murder in my book."

"That's sweet and old-fashioned, McCracken. But the fact is it could turn out to be one of your own."

"It won't be a cop."

"I love it when you get all steely-eyed. No wonder Alexa wants to marry you."

"Stop playing games, Camilla. Stay away from this one. I'm serious."

"Oh, so am I. Everyone knows Benning had a contact on the

inside. Someone who would want him out of the way now that the heat is on. Means, motivation and opportunity. Who better than the cops? And, you may want to remember the last time the police tried to railroad an innocent woman, I was on the job."

"I remember you came close to death."

"Well, that's the downside. But with Benning on ice, what can I say? I feel lucky."

Elaine was not so lucky. Or maybe she was luckier. It depends on how you react to getting trotted to the cop shop and grilled. It would bother some people. Elaine wasn't one of them.

That Elaine. She was known for turning every cloud into a chunk of gold bullion. Her enthusiasm, as they say, knew no bounds. She made you want to hibernate from sheer exhaustion after five minutes in her presence.

WAVE was her life and, unlike me, she didn't have a ton of personal baggage dragging her down. She loved to make a difference. I figured she would make a real difference to the officers who drew the short straw and had to question her about Ralph Benning's death. Good cop. Bad cop. Elaine would reduce them to crazy cop in a few short minutes.

Even so, I wanted to get over to the Elgin Street station as soon as I could. In order to avoid a laugh riot among the people I know on the force, I left Mrs. Parnell's beaver coat behind and borrowed a parka from Lindsay from her extensive winter outerwear collection. With the sleeves rolled up, it did the trick. I stuffed my red hat in the pocket.

Lindsay leaned wanly against the door as I headed out. Merv and Alvin buzzed around her like deranged deerflies. She didn't seem to notice them. "Keep the jacket as long as you want, Camilla. I feel responsible for what happened."

* * *

By the time I showed up, Elaine had the cops on the ropes. I ran into McCracken in the hallway outside the interview room at police headquarters on Elgin Street. He was about to exceed the recommended dosage of Tylenol Extra Strength.

"That's what you get for trying to play in the big leagues," I whispered.

Four tablets spilled from his hand and danced across the grey tile floor. "We're doing our job. And you know it. Why not help instead of making things worse?"

"Try to help the police question clients? Oh yes. It's all flooding back to me. That's the defence lawyer's official motto, isn't it? Learned it in law school."

"Funny. But you're not Ms. Ekstein's defence lawyer." He quivered a bit when the word "Ekstein" crossed his lips.

"News flash, McCracken."

Even Mombourquette appeared subdued. Excellent. Maybe he'd need stress leave. Elaine, on the other hand, had never looked better. Her eyes shone with the light of battle, her chin glowed.

"This is an outrage. I need to speak to my client alone." I prepared to fight.

Mombourquette's ratty face brightened. "Take your time," he said, scooting out of the interrogation room.

"Don't get your tail caught in the door," I said.

As soon as it slammed shut, I turned to my alleged client. "You're enjoying this."

"Well, it is an opportunity. Think of the profile for WAVE. You know, Camilla, at first I thought we had a disaster but on sober second thought, I realize this will give us some major media coverage."

"Forget that, Elaine."

"So it's a positve story. Which reminds me, why are you here? I thought you'd be out fielding interviews."

"I'm your lawyer."

"No, you're not."

"I am now."

"I thought you gave up your practice."

"I'm a licensed Member of the Bar. Ready to go at a moment's notice."

"Do you think I'll need a lawyer?"

"Yeah, right. Maybe a psychiatrist would be better."

"No seriously, I mean, you can't buy this kind of publicity." She gripped my arm. "It's great."

"Trust me, it's a lot of things, but great isn't one of them."

"C'mon, what can go wrong?"

"To begin with, you could get charged with murder in the first degree, go to trial, get convicted and because of the bizarre, premeditated aspects of the case, you could get the full weight of the law—twenty-five years. Of course, reformers are trying to get that extended so...who knows."

"Camilla. You know perfectly well that won't happen. And you have to admit this presents such a wonderful opportunity to highlight the plight of battered women and to show the world people like Benning do exist and they can be stopped."

"Please do not say that or you may be highlighting this very plight from a correctional facility. Might be another wonderful opportunity for you. You'll find many situations need fixing in the slammer. What a terrific outlet for your energy. Congratulations."

"Don't be silly, Camilla. After all, it's not like I'm guilty."

"It's so cute the way you think only the guilty go to jail."

"Oh, come on."

"No, you come on. Why do you think the system needs two sides, prosecution and defence?"

"Okay, sure, but let's face it. Most murderers get caught and they're fairly convicted."

"Four little words for you: Marshall, Morin, Milgaard, Sophonow."

This did not have the desired effect on Elaine. "You're right. I should get involved. There's only so many hours in the day but, I guess I should give the Elizabeth Fry Society a call. Maybe John Howard too. And what's the group that works with the falsely convicted? I feel a bit ashamed of myself that I've never done a thing for those people. Isn't there another organization that works to reopen hopeless cases? What's it called? Yes, I lose perspective sometimes."

"Like right now, for instance. Look, forget your crusade. Just tell me what they asked and what you answered. And then don't say one word to anyone under any circumstances. Not to the police and especially not to the media."

"Are you kidding? This is my chance. Nothing will shut me up."

\* \* \*

"Don't be like that, Conn. We're family. And besides, non-disclosure of pertinent information to the defence can get your carefully constructed case tossed out of court." I didn't like the stubborn way McCracken's jaw jutted out. "You hear me? I said *tossed out of court*."

He shrugged.

"Hey, your call. No hard feelings," I said. "Wonder if it's too late today to get a court order."

McCracken turned his head and stared at the empty wall.

I said, "That is an exceptional wall. I wonder if we should get a camera and get a couple of shots of it, send them to the media."

"Funny. You want to know what happened?"

"I want to know what she said."

"No problem." He reached into his rumpled suit pocket and yanked out a small white notebook.

"That's more like it."

"Let's see, where are we? Oh, yeah," He flipped the pages. Lucky he hadn't called my bluff about the judge, because I prefer to reserve court orders until my back is to the wall. "Okay, Camilla, here's what your client said."

I held my breath.

"All right. To the first question, name and address, she refused to answer. Then she gave us the following responses:

"I don't believe I can answer that question.

"No, officer, I don't remember.

"Seems to have slipped my mind.

"I have no idea.

"Hard to say.

"Are you sure? I don't recall.

"It could be, but I'm not certain.

"I prefer not to comment.

"My mind is blank there.

"I must have been asleep.

"My apologies, officer, but what can I say?

"Gosh, I wish I could help but..."

McCracken smirked when he snapped the notebook closed. "Lucky you, your client has no recollection of leaving the property on Echo Drive last night during the key hours when Benning would have been dumped in Confederation Square."

I pursed my lips.

"She'll be a big hit with a judge. Can't wait to see that."

That Elaine. There's no one in the world quite like her. "You have to admit she is polite."

"She's the only person I can think of who's more irritating than you, Camilla."

"Oh, come on, she's not trying to irritate you. She wants to protect WAVE."

"Don't be so sure."

"But I am sure. Elaine Ekstein has a heart as big as the world. She might have hated Benning for what he stood for and what he did to women, but she would be totally unable to commit a murder. I know that the way I know my own sister's name."

"Well, that's great, Camilla."

"What are you smirking about?" I asked.

"Might it be the video surveillance footage of the big-hearted Elaine Ekstein as she wheels a box out of a parked van and down into the centre of an ice sculpture? Nice thing about this video camera: it recorded the time and the date."

I tried to keep my jaw from hitting the floor.

McCracken smiled. "Ain't technology grand?"

"I think I'd better see this video."

# *Eleven*

W ell." I stared at the grainy video footage of a woman, muffled to the ears with a thick scarf, hair hidden by a slouchy hat as she struggled to wheel a large wooden box on a dolly down the loading ramp of a white van.

"Well, indeed," McCracken said.

"I don't know. Could be anybody all bundled up with a scarf."

"You think so?" he said.

I chose not to mention that I recognized the slouchy hat as Elaine's favourite faux leopard number, the ugliest and most recognizable article of her clothing. If you didn't count the matching coat. Moonlight lit the sky behind Elaine. Great. Maybe I could incorporate the full moon as part of a diminished capacity defence for her.

"Nice attention to detail," McCracken said. "See how she sets it up at just the right angle, right in front of the original ice sculpture of Justice. Smooths it out. Adjusts the sign and all. She's a pro. And yet, she doesn't remember any of it."

"You know, Conn, I'm not sure that's her in the video. In fact, I'm almost certain it's not. But, even in the unlikely event that it were, she'd have to be psycho to move a body in front of a surveillance camera. I'll make sure she gets a proper psychological evaluation."

Mombourquette leaned forward and gazed at the screen.

Elaine stood, apparently admiring the unboxed sculpture, her face turned away from the camera. She ran her hand over the smooth surface of the ice.

Mombourquette's pointy little teeth showed. "Spunky little gal, though, isn't she?"

* * *

Okay, so here's what I believe. Sometimes life can treat us roughly. Then we need a bit of help to cope with some of the slings and arrows. Big deal. I do my bit through Justice for Victims. I've seen what big bureaucracies, small minds and bad breaks can do. I'm happy to line up on the side of the angels and toss a few punches.

But that's where it ends. I do not believe victims have the right to make every one else miserable. I do not believe it gives you special privileges or absolves you from the responsibility of looking after yourself and just getting over whatever shit happened to you. And except in clear and immediate self-defence, I sure as hell don't believe it gives you the right to kill another human being. *Period.*

Despite years in the law, I was foolish enough to believe in justice. I bored myself with my personal philosophy as I drove Mrs. Parnell's LTD back to Lindsay's place on Echo Drive. Elaine might be happy, locked in a cell in the Elgin Street station, waiting for her bail hearing, but I was not.

Her wacky perception of the public relations benefits for WAVE didn't do it for me. But something bothered me even more. All I needed to put my mind at rest was a couple of minutes upstairs at Lindsay's without anyone watching.

* * *

"Nothing, Merv. I'll tidy things up a bit. Take care of a bit of girl stuff."

"You? Tidy up? Girl stuff? Holy shit, what can I expect next? A rain of red frogs?"

"There are thousands of comedians out of work," I said. "Several of them are slumped on their butts in the kitchen. I wouldn't try to change jobs if I were you, Bucko.

"Some things scream for commentary, Camilla."

"Right, and here's one. The cops are grilling Elaine about the discovery of Benning's body. They gave me the boot. I need to keep busy. But, as one of the brotherhood, you might be able to ferret out some information from the Ottawa police. I'll keep an eye on Lindsay."

Merv stood and looked way, way down at me. "What are you up to?"

"Nothing."

"Don't upset Lindsay."

"Why would you even suggest that, Merv? For one thing, she's sound asleep and sedated up the ying yang. And why would I want to upset her? I'm here to help my client, remember? I brought you here. Does that ring a bell? Who looked after Lindsay's interest while you bitched about driving over?"

"Yeah, yeah, you know what you're like."

Tricky. What could I say? No, I don't know what I'm like? Or I'm not like anything? Neither served as a snappy comeback. After Merv reluctantly headed downstairs, I muttered, "I'm the good guy here."

I said it to Lindsay. In fact, I leaned over and whispered it into her ear as she slept. Not so much as a twitch. Excellent. That gave me some time.

The funny thing about Lindsay was, no matter how terrifying her life became, her home and her bedroom remained pristine. So I found no piles of underwear, no rumpled clothes heaped over a chair, no shoes kicked in the corner. No brushes or makeup tumbled on the dresser tops. No stockings slung on the brushed metal doorknobs. No magazines open. I spotted the golden swirl of her bottle of Organza on the bathroom vanity counter. Her slippers were parked by the bed, waiting for her. That was the extent of the disorder.

First, I lifted the lid of the laundry hamper. I'd never seen anyone's dirty clothes folded before. Not even in a fashionable bleached cotton mobile hamper. For a bizarre second, I thought Merv might have done it, in a peculiar form of homage to Lindsay. But then I remembered Merv's living quarters. Merv didn't even fold clean laundry. Possibly Merv didn't even have clean laundry.

Fine. The folded laundry made it easy to check. But I didn't find what I was looking for.

The customized walk-in closet was the next hot spot. It equalled the size of my Grade Eight classroom at Saint Jim's but with a lot more mirrored surface. I hoped my sisters never got a look at this closet, or serious renovations could replace weddings as the next family obsession. Maybe Lindsay was fussy or a careful spender, but there weren't many clothes in the closet to check. She could have increased her wardrobe tenfold and not filled the hangers, drawers, shelves and shoe holders. I glanced over the jackets, dresses, blouses and slacks hung in colour order. I checked the drawers.

I returned to the bedroom and dropped to my knees to peer under the bed. Next I tried the laundry room. Someone that meticulous could run a load of laundry even when faced with immediate death. It made as much sense as folding your soiled bra. The laundry room was discreetly out of sight on the bedroom level. The one basket sat empty. So did the washer and dryer. Nothing hung on the little stainless racks.

I wasn't happy. I headed back to the bedroom and poked behind the shantung silk pillow shams and four pewter-coloured pillows. Lindsay had turned over. I checked the spot where she had been lying, but I didn't find what I was looking for.

Bad news. Or perhaps I was overreacting. After all, it hadn't been the most relaxed twenty-four hours in my life. So where the hell was the cream cashmere outfit Lindsay had worn the previous day and evening?

I sure as hell hoped it turned up. In the meantime, Lindsay had been through plenty already. I didn't plan to mention the tunic and pants. And if someone tipped the police that Lindsay's leather boots were sitting in a salty puddle by the front door, it damn well wouldn't be me.

She was a victim. In my book, she needed protection, not persecution. So I'd have to find out what happened to that tunic before some snoopy cop did. But of course, they had their hands full with Elaine.

\* \* \*

"Thirty-two messages saved for you on the Justice for Victims voice mail," Alvin said.

"Great."

"You might want to listen to them."

"We have enough on our plate here, Alvin. I'll listen to them when I get back to the office."

"Let me suggest…"

"No, Alvin, let me suggest I'll get to them in my own sweet time. Just because you can phone in and get messages doesn't mean you have to. I'm not a slave to this goddam technology."

Alvin shrugged. "Your choice, Camilla."

"Yes, it is." Everything always had to be an argument with that boy.

"There's something you should know."

"Put a sock in it."

"No problemo." Alvin leapt out of his chair in Lindsay's kitchen and headed into the living room. Merv sipped his coffee and watched his retreating back. Alvin's bony shoulders were held high. I'd be paying for that "put a sock in it" remark, but I held my ground. Maybe sleeping on the living room floor and facing that particular sock at the crack of dawn had brought out the worst in me.

"Why the hell doesn't the little jerk get his mangy butt over to your office and open it up?" Merv said.

"We're off to a slow start today. It can wait. In case you didn't notice."

"You never gonna get rid of that guy?"

"Give me time. At the moment, I have a full agenda."

"Yeah, yeah, maybe you should show a little spine, Camilla."

I put my own coffee cup on the table and stood up. "I'd better go up and talk to Lindsay."

"She's asleep."

"Well, time for her to wake up."

\* \* \*

She raised her head and opened her eyes.

"Be straight with me, Lindsay," I said. "I have a question and I want you to tell me the truth."

"Of course. Why wouldn't I tell you the truth?"

"Where are the clothes you wore last night."

She blinked. "What?"

"Your long cream sweater. The one you wore yesterday."

She puckered her forehead. "Well, it's in the hamper."

"No."

"But it must be."

"Listen to me. It. Is. Not."

"Perhaps I hung it up." Her hands clenched and unclenched. I shook my head.

"Oh. I guess I must have tossed it somewhere."

"Where?"

"I don't know. I'd have to look."

"I've already looked."

"Maybe I hung something on top of it. Maybe it slipped behind a chair."

I glanced around. "Somehow I don't see you tossing things. Or letting your cashmere sweaters slip onto the floor."

"Not usually. But this isn't usually."

"So where's the sweater?"

She met my eyes. "What difference does it make?"

"What difference? Because Ralph Benning was murdered. Because you had a damn good reason to want him dead. Because we all fell asleep and you could have left the house. Because Elaine Ekstein will be charged with his murder. And because..."

"Elaine?"

"That sweater is not in this house. It is nowhere. Ditto the leggings."

"Elaine couldn't murder anyone."

"True."

"How could she be charged?"

"Easy. The police think she could have done it."

"But that's silly. Elaine? What an idea."

"Where's the sweater, Lindsay."

She raised her elegant chin. "I don't know where it is."

"Did you leave the house last night?"

"Of course not."

I spotted the little flash of anger behind her words. Interesting. Anger was a change from Lindsay's usual grace and fragility. Maybe I'd been treated to a glimpse of the real person. "Then where's your sweater?"

Merv loomed into the room and stood between Lindsay and me. "She's already told you she doesn't know."

"Thank you, but I'm not finished here."

"Yes, you are."

"Goddam it, Merv, let go of my arm."

I found myself staring at the closed door of Lindsay's bedroom. Of course, it takes more than that to stop one of the MacPhee girls. I turned the handle. Locked. I rattled the handle. Nothing.

I knocked on the door. Still nothing. I poised to give it a nice solid kick when I felt Alvin's hot breath.

"I can't believe even you would do this, Camilla." Reproach oozed out of his pores.

"Do you believe Elaine will spend the night in the slammer?"

"No, she won't. And even if she did, Elaine's tough as old rope. There's no reason for you to terrorize Lindsay."

"Terrorize? I'll terrorize you, you little twerp."

Alvin managed a certain bony dignity. "You have to pull yourself together, Camilla. I can't allow you to upset Lindsay."

While I sputtered "You? What do you mean *you* can't allow *me?*" I lost my advantage. Alvin insinuated himself between the door and me. The only way to knock would be to push him down the stairs first. I thought about it.

Unlike the others, Mrs. Parnell did not treat me like a pariah. She poured my cup of coffee and issued her stream of smoke away from my face, always a sign of affection on her part.

"Quite the discussion."

"You heard it from down here?"

"I heard you."

"Well, I had a legitimate question and I didn't get any kind of a legitimate answer."

Mrs. Parnell issued one of her long wheezy chuckles that always tempt me to call 911. "So I gathered."

"Maybe I lost it a bit."

"Who doesn't get caught up in the heat of battle from time to time? And the question remains not only legitimate but delicate. We shall have to be most strategic in this matter."

"But Alvin and Merv don't share your opinion."

"Nevertheless," Mrs. Parnell said. "Ain't love grand?

\*　　\*　　\*

"I can't believe you didn't tell me you were protecting Lindsay Grace. I'm your buddy, Tiger. You could trust me with your life."

I lounged at the table at Dunn's and watched P. J. fiddle with his fried eggs. Dunn's has an all-day breakfast, which was handy because P. J. was late, even by his standards. I could tell his mind was on the Benning story and how I might have information to improve it.

"You're a reporter. I wouldn't even trust *you* with your life. And don't bother pouting. It'll give you wrinkles."

P. J. poked at the home fries. "Don't hold back on me. What's the dope on Elaine Ekstein? Cops slapped her into interrogation fast enough. Did she know this Benning?"

I didn't have the heart to tell him I wanted information from him. There was no plan to give him any.

"It's a mistake, P. J. They're grasping at straws."

"Got a tip for you. Cops are confident she did it. They're closing the book on it." He waited.

"That's crap and you know it. Elaine couldn't kill someone. Three officers staked out Lindsay's place. How could she or anyone else get out without them noticing? Incompetence? Or railroading? Your call."

"Point taken."

"Your turn to trust me. If you find out how Elaine was supposed to have slipped by them, let me know. Maybe she can make herself invisible at will."

P. J. slipped from the booth, tossed a ten on the table and ran like hell for the door. "Will do."

Well, that was one way to find out what happened to Benning. Wait and read it in the paper.

\*   \*   \*

"We have no comment at this time." I tried to push past a circus of journalists, mikes and cameras outside the Elgin Street Courthouse on the way to Elaine's bail hearing.

Elaine took a different approach. "I'd like to take this opportunity to say…"

I stuck myself in between her and the brace of microphones. "My client has no comment."

I thought I saw P. J. Lynch well back in the crowd. Of course, unlike the guys with the television cameras, he could head on in and hear for himself. Mind you, that crossed the border between police reporter and court reporter, but maybe it was time for P. J. to make the switch and get the occasional night's sleep.

"Elaine! Did you do it?" An anonymous voice attached to a mike.

"No comment."

"Elaine, do you have any words for battered women?"

"We have no comment."

Elaine said, "Well, I certainly do."

I stood up taller, the better to block her face from the flashes. "My client has no comment on that issue." I turned to her and whispered, "You have no goddam comment. Now move your butt through the door on the double."

"*No* comment," I called back over my shoulder as we swung into the Courthouse.

*     *     *

We were all the way into Courtroom Number Five before I finished Elaine's short refresher on how to behave before the media and in the court. I pulled no punches.

The Superior Court judge had a crisp new perm and manicured short nails lacquered in a classic red. She also had a rep for not suffering fools gladly. I hoped to hell we weren't about to be fools. Although with Alvin along as my able assistant, the possibility was real.

The Crown was represented by Mia Reilly, profoundly irritating in her black robe and expensive cologne. But so what? We were in an excellent position. The Crown might not think Elaine should get bail, but I didn't expect to have any trouble showing cause.

"Your honour, my client is a professional social worker, a tireless volunteer, a member of the boards of directors of numerous charities and social agencies in the city. She is highly regarded." I felt no need to spotlight the small matter of picketing and protesting and even less reason to mention traffic violations and parking tickets. Let alone that awkward occasion when guards had ejected her from the visitors' gallery of the House of Commons.

"She is a respectable member of society, fully supported by her family and friends. We ask that she be released on her own recognizance. There is absolutely no danger of flight, nor is she a threat to the community."

"I wouldn't go that far." Elaine had a voice that carried.

"Be quiet," I said, as softly as I could.

Elaine beamed at the judge. One judgely eyebrow rose.

"Ms. MacPhee, are you responsible for your client?"

"Of course, Your Honour."

"Keep that in mind."

"I certainly will, Your Honour."

"There is no likelihood your client would fail to appear?

"No, Your Honour."

"Could happen," said Elaine.

"Absolutely not, Your Honour," I paused long enough to give Elaine a sharp kick in the ankle.

The judge's eyebrow hit her hairline. And the shit hit the fan. "Bail denied. The accused will be held in the Regional Detention Centre until preliminary hearing."

Of course, that could be six months.

The irritating Mia Reilly smiled and bobbed her sleek blonde head in approval. No one in court had a problem with Elaine being slapped behind bars. Except me and Alvin. Unless you counted Mombourquette. I spotted him in the back row, his mouth a tense line.

"I hope you're happy," I whispered in his greyish pointed ear as I walked past. "An innocent creature like Elaine, think she'll survive in the RDC? Lots of guys in there are serial batterers she helped put behind bars. Something to think about."

Even though we both knew men and women were well-segregated at the RDC, I took some pleasure as his pale olive face turned to putty.

*    *    *

Another thing bothered me. I could understand how I could fall asleep at Lindsay Grace's place, ditto Alvin, Mrs. Parnell, Elaine and even Merv. We'd been lulled by hot carbohydrates and general winter laziness. But what about the two officers watching the front of the house and the one guarding the rear entrance? Shouldn't they have been shot for dereliction of duty? Since when were our tax dollars supposed to be asleep at the wheel? Funny. P. J. knew nothing about them.

I had no choice but to cozy up to McCracken and find out what had happened to the three officers outside Lindsay's place. I gave him a call and tried to cushion the blow by suggesting we meet at the Second Cup near the police station.

He was all business. "Sorry, Camilla. No time."

I cut to the chase. "So, Conn, what's happening with the investigation? No word? Cops got your tongue?"

"I think you have to try to cooperate with Alexa about the wedding. This ceremony means a lot to her."

"This is more immediate. After all, Elaine is in the slammer. You would have checked out security. You know there was no surveillance camera in the Crystal Garden. You will naturally have concluded, as I did, that the video is a fraud. So tell me, what are your esteemed colleagues turning up?"

"Hard for me to say, I'm a bit distracted by Alexa's concerns, as I'm sure most people would understand. Oops, I think that's her on the other line. See you, Camilla."

"Okay, you win. I'll give her a call. Then we'll talk."

"No problem," he said. "Let me know when you've done it."

118

# Twelve

Sooner or later, even I have to cave and attend a family dinner. I had no excuse. Benning was dead, and therefore Lindsay Grace was out of danger. Elaine remained locked up in the Regional Detention Centre for the protection of society at large, and I'd run out of options to get her out. Even though I wanted to crash into bed and sleep off the whole nightmare, I had no choice but to enter the lion's den of MacPhees. The festivities always begin with Edwina's husband, Stan, picking me up.

My sisters are formidable. My two brothers-in-law are merely weird. Donalda's husband, Joe, lives in a dream world filled with fishing trips and golf tournaments. I guess he's harmless. Then there's Stan, the man with the world's best collection of whoopee cushions, plastic dog turds, dribble glasses and press-on cockroaches.

I have to work hard to find something to like about my brother-in-law, Stan. But when he picked me up for dinner, I had to admit his new Buick felt toasty warm. The icy wind whipping along the driveway of my apartment building blew my red hat off my head and almost pulled my hair out by the roots. It was almost enough to make me appreciate Stan.

Almost.

I knew better than to argue with Edwina about having Stan collect me for family gatherings. Shooing him out of the house while she's getting ready for any social event plays an important part in her mental health, not that she'd ever admit it. And with the MacPhees, you have to pick your battles. Especially as this wedding loomed. I would need my strength.

I slid onto the Buick's leather passenger seat after checking it for fake vomit. You don't let your guard down with Stan. Of course, I had threatened him with bodily harm after the last little skirmish. He acted innocent enough. No doubt Edwina had laid down the law before she sent him out to get me.

The new car had a cushioned glide which I enjoyed as we drove along the Ottawa River Parkway in the blue winter light. The steam rose from the river, eerie and beautiful. The dark-shadowed snow covering the ground and dusting the evergreens could have been a painting. The sight of a raised hood and the flash of a tow-truck on the other side of the divided parkway reminded me of reality. Still, I relaxed.

But when my bum started to get warm, I turned to Stan.

"What the hell are you playing at now?"

He simulated one of his special hurt looks. "What do you mean?"

"You know what I mean."

"I don't," he whined.

"You do. This seat is getting hot. And it better not get any hotter, since it is too cold outside for me to get out of the car, so if it gets any hotter I will push you out and drive myself. They'll find your body when the snow melts in the spring."

"Of course the seats are heating up. They're heated seats. It's a feature in new cars. I turned yours on so you would be comfortable."

"Oh."

Hurt silence radiated from the driver's side. Anyone else but Stan and I might have been tempted to apologize.

Given the kind of day it had been, I was grateful for the bit of quiet until we pulled into Edwina and Stan's driveway. As usual, it looked as though Edwina had buffed it with a toothbrush.

*   *   *

My sisters were waiting.

I hate that. I pictured three ash-blonde heads together, plotting in Edwina's new maple and granite kitchen before my arrival. It is always three to one. Always has been. I was the accident, born fifteen years after Alexa. It's not easy to be the short, dark one pitted against a coven of beautiful blondes. My sisters might be well on the road to fifty but they look like a bunch of goddam models.

"Camilla." Alexa came forward to plant a kiss on my cheek.

I had to admit it, her forthcoming marriage to Conn McCracken seemed to be good for her. Her face shone with health. Her makeup was youthful yet appropriate. Her new hairstyle, long yet layered, perfect for the ash-coloured hair.

Too bad I hated the idea. But as Donalda had pointed out, it didn't matter a toot what I thought of Conn. I wasn't marrying him.

"Go see Daddy," Edwina said.

My father held court in the wingback chair in Edwina's brocade and mahogany living room. He's a tall, fair man. My sisters got their elegant bones from him. He still maintains the look of authority developed in his years as principal of St. Jim's High.

I rated the usual look of surprise.

Just once in thirty-three years, I would have liked to have seen him without that expression.

"It's me, Daddy. Camilla." I don't know why I always feel I

have to introduce myself. After all, it was my mother's name, and I'm suppposed to take after her.

"Of course. Um, Camilla."

It's hard to tell what he's thinking. A career school principal learns to play his cards close to his chest. I thought I detected the same look that had been on his face the summer I had hot-wired our next door neighbour's new Lincoln Town Car and took it for a midnight spin down the Queensway. I was fifteen. It had seemed like a fine idea at the time. All three of my sisters did a lot of talking in their smooth musical voices, or I wouldn't have been out of the house again before Christmas. I can remember Alexa saying, "Oh Daddy, girls will be girls."

Not one of them ever rated the look of surprise.

"So, um, Camilla. How is our young man, Alvin, making out in your office?"

"Making out? That's the only thing he hasn't tried. Otherwise, he's rude, abrasive, weird, intrusive, and his feet smell."

"Now, dear, try to remember he lacked your wonderful advantages."

Lucky for me my father is hard of hearing, because I couldn't prevent myself from snorting.

Alexa said, "Oh, Camilla."

My father said, "It couldn't have been easy for his mother living all those years with an alcoholic. Poor Mary raised those children on her own. And every single one of them made it through university, too."

Well, Alvin scraped through art school.

"I spoke to Mary the other day. I was happy to be able to tell her Alvin is flourishing under your wing."

"My what?"

"Camilla." I heard the warning note in Edwina's voice.

"You know," my father said, "February in Ottawa is a lot tougher than in Nova Scotia. Mary's worried he won't be dressed properly. The poor lad's prone to bronchitis. Can you make sure he's bundled up?"

I guess no one heard me choking. All eyes were on my father.

"I assured his mother you were more than glad to do anything you could for him, since he saved your life during that terrible business last spring."

"That's not quite my recollection of Alvin's participation, Daddy. If memory serves, Alvin was nothing but a pain in the butt."

The doorbell rang before any of my sisters could say oh, Camilla. Alexa's hands were a blur fluffing her hair, smoothing her skirt, adjusting her sweater. She finished topping up her lipstick and gave herself a quick spray of L'Air du temps before Conn McCracken strolled into the room. It was enough to make you sick.

Dinner at my sister Edwina's features Minton china, damask table cloths, roses in silver vases and the chime of fine crystal. She has not yet heard we've entered a more casual age.

Not surprisingly, the food is first-rate. The conversation, lively and frequently dangerous. And the main course is always gossip.

As usual, the men were quiet. Stan because his practical jokes were off limits until after the wedding. Donalda's husband, Joe, because he lives in his own internal world of golf courses and fishing camps. McCracken because he was new to the crew. My father wades into a conversation if someone veers too far from traditional Catholic theology. Or swears. That's usually me. Tonight was no different.

"Well," Edwina passed a gold-rimmed plate with pear,

walnut and gorgonzola salad, "am I the only one who's shocked about Elaine Ekstein?"

Donalda looked up from serving pork tenderloin in orange soy sauce. "Who would have thought she had such a vivid imagination?"

"Indeed," Edwina said.

"Pass the can of worms," I said.

"Excuse me?" Edwina narrowed her eyes at me.

"Oh, Camilla." Alexa gave me a look.

McCracken's lips twitched. I decided to concentrate on the rice. Edwina makes the best rice in the family. Firm, fluffy, safe.

"Well," said Alexa, "don't you think something needed to be done? Imagine what those women suffered. And that poor officer who was shot. It's a miracle he's going to live. That Benning was an absolute monster."

The girls never let go of a topic quickly.

"You bet," Edwina said. "It's time we women started to fight back when bullies and wife-beaters get their own way with a spineless and craven justice system that dumps them back on the streets with a slap on the wrist. Or less."

Conn McCracken hunched miserably over his plate.

"Of course, but I would never have thought Elaine Ekstein could kill somebody," Donalda said.

"Didn't you?" said Edwina, "Elaine has spine. I'm glad she took the law into her own hands. No one else was prepared to do it."

"Wait a minute." I made an attempt to wrestle back the conversation.

"Oh, Camilla, there's no need to get defensive," Edwina said. "I know you wanted to, but you weren't as effective as you could have been. The situation got beyond your control. But no one blames you."

"It's not true," I said.

Donalda said, "Well, not you alone, dear, society at large. When you come down to it, how did the man get loose?"

I slammed my silver fork on the table. "Goddam it, I mean, Elaine didn't do it."

Everyone's eyes slid to my father's face. Waiting for the reprimand. His mind appeared to be elsewhere. Playing golf with Joe maybe.

"Of course she did it," Edwina said.

"Don't be silly, Camilla." Donalda moved a few serving pieces out of my reach.

"What do you mean?" Alexa said.

"I mean she didn't do it. What do you think I mean?" I barked. I caught Conn McCracken staring at me. I refrained from tossing food at him.

"Well, she confessed, didn't she?" Edwina said. "That's enough for me. And what's more, I think she has support from the community, and she'll get off on a self-defence."

"Self-defence?" Conn didn't quite catch himself in time.

It surprised me too. Freezing someone in a block of ice? Quite a challenge to portray that as self-defence.

"I don't understand you, Camilla," Alexa said. "Elaine is your friend. Why don't you want to help her? She'll suffer through a long, terrible trial, and for what?"

"She'll get off," Edwina said. "She did what she had to."

"Except she didn't do it!" I might as well have screamed into the wind.

"Fine, Camilla, be like that. Even I know if she pleads Not Guilty she's more likely to get a prison sentence, and then who benefits?"

"No one benefits. Either way. It's still murder, and Elaine still didn't do it."

Stan said, "Any more of that pear stuff?"

"Oh, sure, call it murder. After what Benning did," Donalda said. "What's the matter with you, Camilla? You've abandoned poor Elaine."

"How is Violet?" my father asked.

"What?"

"Your neighbour, Violet."

"Oh. You mean Mrs. Parnell, Daddy. She's fine, I guess."

"Remarkable person, Violet. Lovely. We should see more of her."

"Oh, dear, maybe Camilla's right," said Alexa. "Killing him in such a gruesome way, I'm sure that's not..."

"Legal? Moral? Ethical?" I said. "And speaking of legal, I would like to make the point that Elaine is innocent until proven guilty in this country and even in this house."

"But, Camilla," Donalda said, "she admitted she killed him. We saw it on the news. You stood next to her with your mouth hanging open like a guppy. She told the reporters she did it, that must mean *something*."

"It means it's goddam lucky we don't have capital punishment."

"*Camilla.*" This time my father paid attention.

"And I'll tell you something else," I ignored him for the first time in thirty-three years. "I don't know who killed Ralph Benning. And I don't know why. But someone will get away with murder while Elaine goes up the river."

"River? What river?" Donalda's husband Joe opened his eyes, hoping for a fishing story, I guess.

"I think she's sort of a heroine," Edwina said. "Maybe we should get out and help her. Raise some money for her."

Disappointed, Joe closed his eyes again.

"Well, whether she did it or not, there's not much we can do for her until after the wedding," Alexa said.

                              *    *    *

After dinner, I managed a quick word with McCracken while
Stan warmed up the Buick.

"See? I'm being nice to my sister."

"You call that nice?"

"I'm a MacPhee. It's as nice as we get."

"Christ."

"So, any word on the results of the blood tests?"

"What blood tests?"

Some people shouldn't try to lie. But I would have thought
after a career in the police force, McCracken could handle a
fib. Of course, dinner with my family can leave the most
capable person vulnerable.

"I assume the surveillance officers must have conked out.
I'm sure you would have checked that."

"I can't talk about it. That case is under internal review."

"Three officers snoring like hibernating bears when there's a
crazed killer on the loose? I should damn well hope it's under
review. High time, too. Let's hope they find the internal
connection to Benning while they're investigating."

Sometimes you have to touch a nerve.

"You're too much. You know that, Camilla?"

Sure I knew it.

# Thirteen

I lay on my comforter, feeling the results of too much pork tenderloin and too many fresh rolls. Not to mention too much chocolate raspberry mousse. It was well past midnight, and it would take more than sheep to get me to sleep.

This wedding was making my sisters crazy if they gave it a higher priority than Elaine's incarceration. Their reaction to Benning's demise might be understandable, but I couldn't think of a single judge who would let sentiment justify such a nasty bit of vigilante justice.

Of course, Elaine's situation took the heat off Lindsay, which was one thing to feel better about. Not that my feelings had anything to do with anything. I snapped upright in bed. Mrs. Parnell's little calico cat went flying. That's what was wrong. I was letting the way I felt about Elaine cloud my judgement. It wouldn't be the first time I'd been betrayed by feelings. But in my line of work, justice must be the guiding principle, no matter what the outcome.

Time to get my priorities straight and to use a little logic. Logic told me Elaine could have killed Benning, but she wouldn't sneak around in the middle of the night to do it. For my own peace of mind, I needed to eliminate Lindsay as a suspect. I needed to squish any sympathy. To save Elaine, I needed to identify the real killer.

I think best on paper. I headed for my desk and fished out a notepad and pen, just as the doorbell rang. Mrs. Parnell stood, leaning on her walker and wrapped in a cloud of smoke. "Good evening, Ms. MacPhee. I thought you might want some company."

"It's the middle of the night, Mrs. P. Why would I want company?"

"I could not help but notice the light on in your apartment."

"With all due respect, we are on the sixteenth floor and you live on the opposite side of the building. You can't see my lights. And anyway, it's time you stopped lurking in the corridor half the night. It's unsettling for the neighbours, especially me."

"Step with me into the hallway and close the door, and you will clearly observe light through the frame."

Stepping into the hallway in my chenille robe in the wee small hours was not the smartest thing I'd ever done. The new pneumatic door swung shut behind me and the automatic double lock clicked firmly.

"Consider this. Since you're locked out. Let us pop over and have a quick nightcap."

"I believe you have a key."

"Ah, yes. Where did I put it? Let us put our heads together and think where I might have put it for safekeeping."

I followed her back to 1608 and accepted a small glass of Harvey's Bristol Cream. "But you'd better find the key soon, Mrs. P."

"Oh, absolutely. Absolutely. But first, I must conclude you are troubled, or else you would have been sleeping. Why not use this time to discuss the situation?"

Why not indeed? Mrs. Parnell was smarter than anyone else I knew and far less likely to let foolish feelings overwhelm her common sense.

"Perhaps you could use a bit of help from an old soldier?"

"I don't need help, Mrs. P., Elaine does."

"Ms. Ekstein is not a woman I've ever cared for greatly."

"Lots of people feel that way. But all the same, she never could have murdered anyone, even Benning."

"Tell me, Ms. MacPhee, can you be certain?"

"I am absolutely convinced."

"Be that as it may, it's not as though she didn't bring all this trouble on herself."

I couldn't agree, at least not out loud. "Neither here nor there. Anyway, someone's definitely trying to frame her. The information hasn't been released to the media yet, but the police have a videotape of an unidentified person wearing Elaine's fake leopard coat and hat depositing the body in the Crystal Garden."

"Ah ha! Videotaped proof. And she says she did it. No wonder you are convinced of her innocence, Ms. MacPhee."

"No need to be sarcastic. The person in Elaine's hat and coat kept his or her face turned away. And if it had been Elaine, she'd have stopped to thumb her nose at the camera."

Mrs. Parnell sipped her sherry. When she came up for air she said, "Perhaps she didn't see the camera."

"No. She's been involved in so many women's committees on safety and security, she'd know where there were cameras, security guards, emergency phones in a downtown area in the night. Plus I am sure you realize, she couldn't kill someone in cold blood."

"Nevertheless, I expect it will do her a bit of good being locked up."

"Let me say this one more time. Elaine did not commit this crime. She might be her own worst enemy, but she does not belong in jail."

"I concede, Ms. MacPhee. I suppose we should rise to the

occasion. So what is our plan of attack?"

I plunked my glass on the table. "I think someone made fools of all of us. We're too emotionally involved with Elaine…"

"Speak for yourself."

"…and Lindsay."

"Ah, yes. Lindsay."

"We need to figure out what's really going on here. I'll talk, you react. "

"Splendid. Let us begin with the big question: if not Ms. Ekstein, then who?"

"*I'll* do the talking. Okay, in a typical murder, the guilty party is likely either a spouse, lover, family member or close friend, or a business associate with serious cash to gain or lose, or some drugged-out thug who meets the victim in the wrong place at the wrong time."

She nodded. She loved this kind of thing.

"Call me sentimental," I said, "but I figure you, Alvin, and Merv are not the perpetrators."

"Excellent. I will assume the same for you, Ms. MacPhee. And surely you can eliminate the random mugger. Whoever did this was organized, mobile and had done all the proper reconnaissance work."

"Never mind reconnaisance work, the killer must have known Elaine well in order to set her up by wearing her clothes. Otherwise that video didn't make sense."

"It is not necessary to keep banging your glass on the table."

"If you'll give me a chance to talk, I won't have to. Let's see, the spouse is usually the most likely suspect. But Rina was dead long before Benning's body rolled into the Crystal Garden."

"Someone in the late Ms. Benning's family might have the motivation," Mrs. P. said.

"I thought of that, but how could they have framed Elaine?"

Mrs. P. wasn't giving up. "Nevertheless, let us leave no stone unturned."

Lucky me, I had my pen and paper. I started a TO DO list for Alvin and wrote "leave no stone unturned" on it.

"Lovers are right up there with spouses," I said.

"Well, Ms. MacPhee, Lindsay is the most obvious of the lovers. Let us speculate that she exited the house in the night while we conveniently slept, slipped into Elaine's hat and coat and wheeled Benning's body into the Crystal Garden, all the while keeping her lovely face averted from the cameras. She certainly had the means and opportunity to drug us. And presumably him. He would not have been afraid of her."

I hated this version.

"And what if Lindsay did kill him? She had reason enough. I quite like the girl," Mrs. Parnell said.

"You think I don't? Lindsay definitely had means, opportunity and big-time motive. The police wouldn't have to work hard to convince the Crown about that. She feared for her life and rightly so. She was much better off with him dead. She said it was time she opted for fight over flight."

"High time she did, too. Good for her."

"If he contacted her, she could easily have lured him to meet her. But it's still murder and premeditated. And may I remind you, if Lindsay did do it, that means she's deliberately framed Elaine."

Mrs. Parnell topped up her sherry. Lester and Pierre cheeped.

I rubbed my forehead. "On the other hand, let's use our brains. Lindsay's so delicate, she'd never have the strength to move a body."

"Nonsense, Ms. MacPhee, were you truant during all your high school physics classes?"

So I'd skipped a few of them, but how did she know? "What?"

"Pulleys, wheels, incline planes, winches and other contrivances. Don't forget the pyramids, Ms. MacPhee. Moving the body wouldn't be the big problem. No, in favour of Lindsay's innocence, I would say she loved Ralph Benning."

"I'm with you there, but we have to think it through. There's something else troubling me. When we saw her in the morning, she was not wearing the same outfit she fell asleep in. Remember that cream-coloured cashmere ensemble? It should be in her home somewhere. It's not. I was searching for it when I got into that dust-up with Merv and Alvin."

"Another indication that she'd gone out," she said.

"What do you mean, another one?"

"Did you notice her boots lying in a puddle in the foyer in the morning?"

"Yes." I hadn't realized Mrs. P. had spotted them too.

"But how would she have eluded the officers outside?" Mrs. Parnell sipped her sherry speculatively.

"They were obviously drugged too. I'm certain of that."

"Ah! The pizza or the coffee?"

"Well, Lindsay didn't touch her pizza."

"Everyone else tore into theirs."

"That's the bad news. And everybody drank coffee. Even the cops, although we didn't actually see them drink it. Everybody except Lindsay."

"Troubling. But how would Lindsay have known where to find Elaine's coat?" A stream of smoke wafted by my face.

"She didn't need to know in advance. She could have nipped the keys to the SUV, spotted the coat and hat and used them to throw suspicion onto Elaine."

"To cast suspicion on a friend, that is not in the least bit sporting. If she did that, she'll get no sympathy from these quarters."

"Wait a minute, this is all conjecture. I still don't think it was either Elaine or Lindsay. Elaine's nutty, but not cruel, and this was a cruel crime. I can't imagine Lindsay carrying out such a calculated scheme. Never mind showing enough imagination to encase the bastard in ice. But if the police or the Crown get wind of the fact Lindsay left the house, they might even decide Elaine and Lindsay colluded to kill Benning."

"They could both end up in the hoosegow. We will have to get busy, Ms. MacPhee." She leaned over and refilled my glass before I could protest.

"You bet. And while we're busy, we should ask ourselves why they're both lying. You can stay up and do that. This sherry is messing up my brain, and I need a good night's sleep so I can think clearly in the morning. So hand over my key."

"Young people. Personally, I believe sleep is highly overrated."

*   *   *

I had a faint post-sherry throb in my temple when Alexa showed up at my door, in full make-up, at eight-thirty the next morning.

"No can do. I have a full slate today. And I'm already way behind schedule."

"This will take a minute."

"Look, Alexa, I see the light of madness in your eyes. But even so, we both know it will not take a minute for me to pick out a bridesmaid's dress. I don't have a spare couple of hours today. So forget it."

"Not a chance. I'll be in your face until you get that dress, so get with the program."

*In your face? Get with the program?* What had happened to my warm-hearted favourite sister? I headed for the kitchen.

"You know, Alexa," I said as the coffee worked its slow, slow way through the drip, "this wedding has eaten your brain. You know, Paul and I just eloped, if you remember…"

Talk about a reaction. "Of course I remember."

"Why are you yelling?"

"Maybe you and Paul were happy, but no one else was."

"What?"

"Who do you think dealt with Daddy, Little Miss Totally Utterly Selfish?"

My next door neighbour banged on the wall.

"Fine, maybe my elopement wasn't such a big hit with the family. So what?"

"So what? So what? The *elopement*, as you so casually call it, was the worst calamity ever in our family."

"Be serious."

"How do you think Daddy reacted when his youngest daughter married outside the Church? It almost killed him."

"Keep your voice down. Do you think I want to get evicted?"

"Easy for you. Daddy thought you were going to hell and you were *boinking* on a beach somewhere…

"Boinking?" That was hardly fair. Paul and I had had an ideal honeymoon, nibbling *beignets*, moving to the street music of New Orleans, making love. Not that I ever let myself think about that.

"Who do you think calmed Daddy down? I respected your choice. I didn't have the choice of a beautiful wedding the first time, and I want one."

"Fine. But I have to get Elaine out of jail."

"My *wedding* is more important."

"Elaine is more important than some outdated mating ritual." Oh, dirty trick. She started to cry. "Come on, Alexa. Calm down."

"I will not. You're miserable because you have no one in your life, and you're so grouchy you'll never have anybody either and you want everyone else to suffer too."

"Fine. I'll go get the goddam dress. Just stop blubbering."

*      *      *

Alexa fixed her makeup yet again, this time using the rearview mirror as we waited at a red light. She kept talking while she fluffed her hair. "Promise me you'll behave."

"Of course I'll behave."

"Of course, nothing. You know what you're like."

"Fine. Don't cry."

"If you promise to behave I'll give you a nice bit of gossip."

"Like I care about gossip."

"It's not gossip. It's more like information. You'll care about this. I guarantee it."

"What is it?"

"Say, I promise to behave like a normal human being."

"This better be good."

"It's good. Promise."

"Okay, what's the poop?"

"When we're finished shopping."

Some things are easier said than done. "That could be a while. We're in the Market in the winter. We'll never get a parking space."

"There's a car pulling out." A Saab driven by a man with a competitive look positioned itself to nose in ahead of her.

Alexa gunned her Volvo. Mr. Saab took one look at Alexa's face and reversed hastily. Alexa shot into the spot.

"I liked you more before you morphed into the *Überbride*."

Alexa snatched her purse and opened the door. "Hop to it."

When we reached the shop, she grabbed my arm. "Listen to me. You're going to be polite to the sales staff and you're going to find a dress and then you can go do your so-called important items. And in the meantime, I don't want any bullshit from you. Do I make myself clear?" She brushed a snowflake from her nose.

"Oh, yes."

The minute they opened for business, I followed her through the door of doom into Mimi Melanson's Bridal Bower.

"It's an emergency," Alexa told the assembled sales force.

To do them credit, no one remarked on my red wool hat, although I noticed one sales clerk had trouble taking her eyes off it. I smiled at her and stroked the hairs on my upper lip.

The woman blanched. "Well," she said, "we'll give it a shot."

Go ahead, I thought, let's see you cope with the long underwear, the thermal socks and the fleece. The conversation dragged a bit from that point, because I found myself silenced by the acres of peau de soie and tons of seed pearls.

An hour and a half later we headed out, still dressless. The entire staff looked ready to bolt for the back room in search of a bracing snort of brandy.

Alexa got into the car and slammed the door behind her. I opened the passenger side and slid in. "It's not my fault every single dress looked awful on me."

"I wouldn't say *awful*."

"Revolting then. Let's have that information."

"You don't deserve it."

"Yes, I do. And you'd better keep your end of the bargain if you want me to behave the next time we shop."

"All right. Tomorrow. Holt Renfrew."

"No problem."

"Well, all right. It's about the police officers stationed outside Lindsay Grace's home the night of the murder."

I held my breath.

"I overhead another detective talking to Conn. Don't let on I told you. Apparently, they were drugged."

"Of course they were drugged."

"You knew?"

"Not hard to figure out. Did all of them show evidence of drugs?"

Alexa pursed her lips. "I overheard a conversation. I didn't read a *report.*"

"No need to be crabby."

"I am not crabby. Anyway, Miss-Know-It-All, the guy told Conn they had the results back from the lab and it sounded like Row-something. Maybe in their coffee."

Rohypnol. Better known on the street as roofies. The date rape drug.

"Well, Elaine sure wouldn't drug anyone. Who knows, one of us could have polished off two or three cups of coffee and then what?"

"They're convinced she did it."

"Where would Elaine get Rohypnol, for God's sake?"

"Stop snapping at me. He didn't say how she got it, but he did mention she gave a pot of coffee to the officers. The row-something showed up in their urine."

True. "Rats."

"You're Elaine's lawyer. Wouldn't they have to give you this information anyway?"

"Sure. In time."

"That's why I could tell you with a clear conscience. So you have a head start. And tomorrow we'll get your dress."

I closed my eyes and replayed the scene in the kitchen. I'd slugged down a large mug of coffee from the same thermos Constable James had carried to the cruiser. Elaine had poured hers from the same thermos the others did. It was damned unlikely she'd dosed herself with Rohypnol.

Too bad so much time had passed. There'd be no way to get reliable results from urine tests of the rest of us at this stage, so that wouldn't help us pinpoint anyone. Why the hell hadn't I thought of roofies? Plenty of my clients had been undone by them. The whole thing made me irritable.

I got some of it out of my system by giving my sister a bit of advice. "You're about to marry a cop. You can't go around telling people what he says about the job."

"I'd never do that."

"You just did."

"No. Conn didn't say anything. The other fellow did. And it wasn't official police business, I joined them when they were socializing over a beer."

"Even so, you have to be careful not to repeat things. Except with me, of course."

"I thought you'd be pleased to have the inside story."

"Indeed, I'm thrilled. And since we're sharing inside information, do you have Leonard Mombourquette's cellphone number?"

In my family, you press your advantage whenever you have one. As Alexa copied out the number and handed it to me, I looked straight ahead. "Is that a parking ticket on your windshield, Alexa?"

# *Fourteen*

I prefer not to break bread with Det. Sgt. Leonard Mombourquette. But I found myself between a rock and a rat. Even though it was nearly noon and I hadn't set foot in the office, Elaine had to be my priority.

Mombourquette surprised me and agreed to meet at The Mayflower. He didn't even hesitate. When I arrived, on foot and out of breath, he was already waiting in a booth.

"Nice hat," he said.

"Nice ears," I said.

It was lunchtime, and we opted for the Winterlude Specials. I had chicken pot pie. Mombourquette took the *tourtière*. We followed it up with carrot cake with cream cheese icing. "Gotta get all your food groups," Mombourquette said.

I agreed. I was glad to eat whenever I had the chance, since I had kissed regular meals goodbye.

It was a long time to spend in Mombourquette's company, but I reminded myself Elaine merited serious sacrifice. On the up side, I figured he'd be as emotionally distanced from weddings as I was.

"So," I said, "this wedding fuss. Giving you a headache?"

"What do you mean?"

"You know all this hassle about the perfect flowers, they *have* to be calla lilies and they *have* to be the precise shade of cream. I mean, do you believe there are dozens of shades of cream, and then the *lights* matter a lot and the type of deckle on the edge of the invitations…"

He shrugged.

"Not to mention the hysteria about the music."

"Well…"

"And the candles, for God's sake, they have to be special too."

"It's all…"

"Exactly. Especially the business with the dresses. It's enough to make you nuts. Do I look like I want to wear a butt-ugly bridesmaid's dress at my age?"

"What's eating you? I think the wedding will be beautiful. Two nice people happen to be very much in love and deserve some happiness. Why shouldn't they celebrate it?"

I spilled a bit of coffee. *Very much in love?*

"Sorry, call me crazy, but I remember you gave McCracken a hard time about getting involved with a member of my family."

"But now I understand the difference relationships can make in the quality of a person's life."

"Sorry? I missed that."

Mombourquette squirmed a bit on the banquette. "You know. Love."

"Love?" I'd never suspected Mombourquette was aware of the concept.

He narrowed his beady little eyes. "Problem with that?"

No matter what kind of situation you find yourself in with Mombourquette, you always have to be careful not to corner him. "I never expected you to believe in love."

"What do you mean? Of course I believe in love—I'm human."

"Well, hey, *I'm* certainly human."

"Good thing you told me, Camilla. It sure doesn't show."

I felt like reaching out my icy Sorel and stepping on his tail.

"Okay, Leonard, forget the wedding. I'm on another project. Saving Elaine Ekstein from a life sentence."

Did I imagine his pale gray complexion turned a soft dusty rose? I wasn't about to let up. "So. You think she did it? I mean Elaine is an extraordinarily bad driver. She does have a serious record of traffic tickets, even though she pays them, and this criminal life is a slippery slope. It doesn't take much to move on from parking under a No Parking sign in front of City Hall to fast-freezing the bodies of your enemies and plunking them in parks as part of a ceremonial display."

Sure, I talked smart, but he had me worried. If the evil wedding spirits could get to Mombourquette, no one was safe. But I had other fish to fry. "My calculations tell me you didn't have that surveillance tape in your hot little hands before you rousted us at Lindsay's."

I liked the way he couldn't quite meet my eye.

"Right, so what made you and McCracken focus on Elaine?"

He stared down at the table.

"Hmm?"

He fiddled with a package of sugar.

"Intuition, maybe?"

He shook his head.

"Let me guess, you consulted a psychic?"

The sugar packet ripped. "We got a call."

"How convenient. It didn't occur to anyone the caller might want to put Elaine in the frame?" I did not suggest Elaine was wacky enough to place the call herself. Why buy trouble?

"Of course it occurred to us," he said.

"The rest of your colleagues seem happy to think Elaine did it. And tickled pink to charge her."

He shook his head. "Pressure from up the line."

"Maybe it's the same place up the line that made sure the

evidence against Benning didn't hold up in all those earlier charges?"

He shrugged. I took it as a maybe.

"What's the grudge against Elaine, anyway?"

"I think she made our lives miserable about a lot of cases. Particularly in spousal abuse cases where charges were dropped against batterers because of evidence problems. And she was always agitating for public inquiries and demanding official apologies."

I nodded. "That's our girl."

Mombourquette said, "Anyway, she made plenty of enemies. Inside the force and out."

I had to agree. "Any names?"

"Be serious."

"What about the officers outside the house? You think one of them was involved with Benning in some way?" I was careful not to get Alexa into the soup.

"They weren't in on it."

"How can you be sure?"

"Trust me."

"Yeah, right."

"Look, this will come out eventually, but those three officers were drugged. They were still knocked out when we arrived."

"All of them?"

"What? Yes, all of them."

"How do you know one of them wasn't left awake?"

"If one had been awake, don't you think they would have reported the others passed out?"

"Not if that was part of the plan to get rid of Benning. Maybe he left his sleeping colleagues, stole Elaine's clothes, lifted her keys when we were out cold, then killed Benning and dumped him."

Mombourquette was on his feet. Red as a fresh bottle of ketchup.

I said, "That Constable James, he's a wiry little guy, not much bigger than Elaine, with a collar up over that mustache, he could pass. He could have slipped out while the others were knocked out. A cop could probably get his mitts on Rohypnol easily."

"Rohypnol? Who said anything about that?"

Oops.

"How'd you hear about the Rohypnol?"

"Just speculation. Why? Did I get it in one?"

"Get this, Camilla—"

"You might want to be careful raising that finger, Leonard. You could find it gets caught in a trap." That was going nowhere. I tried another tactic. "So, I'm about to head over to the Regional Detention Centre. Hell of a place, although I don't expect you law enforcement officers to agree. It's great to keep the streets safe, but it's sure not the best environment for Elaine."

"I know. She's way too gentle to be locked up there with those animals."

Gentle? "Yes, I would hate to have anything happen to her because you guys fingered her to cover someone a little closer to home." Double gotcha.

"We didn't."

"Then why would anyone even try to press charges? No matter how they feel about her personally."

"Earth to Camilla. Didn't Elaine tell the world she did it?"

True enough. "So what?" If I didn't know better, I'd have said that Mombourquette's face was wracked with anguish. "You got gas, Leonard?"

Mombourquette shrugged into his jacket. "I got something else. I got news for you. You let your innocent client speak for herself in front of television cameras, and she'll end up convicted. They won't even have to go to trial."

"Tell me something I don't know." But I was speaking to his retreating back. I noticed he'd stuck me with the check.

*   *   *

When the going gets tough, the tough get going. So the tough were getting going, but first the tough had better mobilize a few ground soldiers.

"Alvin," I said, when I pushed open the door to Justice for Victims. The fragrance of coconut suntan lotion filled the air.

"Weather is here, wish you were beautiful," he sang.

My tolerance for Jimmy Buffett songs was slight at the best of times, which this was not. But I smiled brightly anyway.

"Your decor is really starting to make a difference." I referred to the small palm tree on my desk chair as well as the beach scene painted on the window of Justice for Victims.

Common sense told me I should have a close look at the painting before any clients showed up. But where did common sense ever get me in dealing with Alvin?

"Welcome back to Margaritaville," he said.

"This approach will certainly make the long winter days fly by."

"No," he said.

"No what?" I wished it could be no palm trees, no window paintings, no Jimmy Buffett, no eau de coconut.

"No. No, nay, never, nein, nyet, nada, non, nix, ixnay."

I moved the palm from my chair to his and sat down. "Right, so that's settled. Here's what I'd like you to do."

"What part of ixnay don't you understand, Camilla?"

"Here's the drill, Alvin."

"Not for me." Rays from the paper sun taped over my desk

lamp glinted off his cat's eye sunglasses.

"We're going to find out who set up Elaine."

"You won't get me involved in a plan to implicate Lindsay, if that's what you're up to. Forget it."

I was a jump ahead of him this time. "You're right, Alvin. And you will remember that Lindsay is a client of mine. Mine, Alvin. Mine. All mine. And that I care about what happens to her and care deeply too. You will also remember that I arranged for Merv to watch over her and keep her safe from Benning."

Alvin's thin lips pursed. "Merv. He thinks he's God's gift."

"You said it, Alvin."

"He's keeping Lindsay away from everyone else."

"Ah, well, it's Merv's disposition to be a boil on the backside of humanity." I needed to give Alvin his marching orders and get the show on the road. "As soon as we get this mess cleared up, Lindsay's life will be back to normal, and I'll remind her of everything you did."

Alvin frowned.

I added, "By which I mean, let's find out who killed Benning mondo quicko."

"No way, Camilla. You think Lindsay did it, and you want me to be a party to getting her arrested and I won't do it."

My fingers twitched. "Of course you won't, Alvin. And I'm not asking you to. You and Merv are both right. Lindsay is a victim, and of course she couldn't have killed Benning. But surely you don't think Elaine is guilty."

He turned his head. "I guess not. Although she did say she was. But that's Elaine, right?"

"Right. So if she didn't kill Benning, then who did?"

"Not..."

"Don't worry, not Lindsay." I put my hand to my nose in case it was getting longer.

"But you were going on about that sweater and insinuating that she was guilty."

"Look, Lindsay left the house that night while we slept. Some of her clothes are missing, plus her wet boots were in the entrance in the morning. I need to know why."

"I won't do anything to harm her."

"That's the point, Alvin. Benning must have enticed her somehow, and we need to know who and what she saw. If Lindsay is a witness to any part of what happened, then she's in danger herself."

"You mean someone could try to hurt her?"

"Think about it. We've been so worried about Benning, and now that he's dead we figure it's all over. But somebody killed him, and if it wasn't Elaine or Lindsay, who was it? And what will he do next?"

Alvin nodded. "I never thought Elaine did it, but she's a lot tougher than Lindsay."

"Don't go there, Alvin. If Elaine actually gets to trial, as her lawyer, I have an obligation to throw suspicion on others. I'll have to subpoena Lindsay. She'll be on trial even if she's never charged."

"I guess you're right."

"Yup. So, since the police and the Crown are being their usual obstructionist selves, here's what we do. You chase down Rina Benning's relatives and see if any of them might have been in a position to finish off Benning. While you're at it, check out Lindsay's family."

"They've never given her a moment's support. They cut her off when she took up with Benning. You know that."

"Maybe something happened to change that situation."

"Hey, where will you be while I'm doing all the work?"

"I'll be checking out the police, my dear Watson."

# Fifteen

ook. I just called to apologize, Conn. I guess I've been a bit hard-nosed lately. But I *am* going to pick out a dress. Probably later today. Check with Alexa, she'll confirm we've already made a start. We're heading to Holt's in a handbasket. I'm being held up a bit because I have to research the exact timing of the arrival of the late Mr. Benning in Confederation Park on the night of his demise."

"You'll get all the information you're entitled to in plenty of time to prepare for the preliminary hearing, unless of course, your client continues to plead guilty, and then you won't need it at all. I hope you aren't asking me for information outside the normal channels. Again." Conn McCracken's voice had an edge, but then it so often does.

"Certainly not. I don't know how you can even suggest such a thing. I would like your special day to go perfectly. But until I get the timing of the murder nailed down, I'm not free to shop, even though I know how important it is. I'm sure, you, as a seasoned investigator, will understand my priorities."

"You must think I'm stupid," Conn said. "You get off your arse and stop upsetting your sister and get that dress before I start dusting off your files. Might find unpaid parking tickets, information on cases in the dead files, attempts to extort information from an officer of the law. Get my drift?"

I got it.

*　　*　　*

I figured Mombourquette might take a different view.

"No can do," he said, when I phoned.

"Hey, no hard feelings. I was hoping I could find out the time Benning was deposited in the Crystal Garden, then I could make a better case to help Elaine. It must be torment for her in the RDC, but what the hey, she brought it on herself by confessing. I think I'll give the case a rest until after the wedding. I should be out buying an outfit to wear anyway."

"The wedding's not until the 14th. You mean you're going to let Elaine wait until then?"

"What can I do? My family's on my back. You don't know what that's like. But trust me, no options here."

"I'm beginning to learn about that," he said mysteriously. "But even so, I don't think you can let your client just hang."

"Oh, she won't *hang*, Leonard," I chuckled. "Twenty-five years without parole's the worst that can happen to our girl."

I swear to God he gasped before he said, "Just after two. Off the record, of course."

"Of course."

*　　*　　*

Okay, so I was stopped. I couldn't proceed to build any defence without key information: for instance, what exactly did the police know about the state of Benning's body when it was found. On the videotape, you could clearly see the kneeling figure of Benning encased in ice.

But a body wouldn't freeze solid in a few minutes. These things take time. Plus they take facilities. Benning had been over six feet tall and at least one-eighty. It would take a full chest freezer to do a number on him. I figured it had been somewhere around eleven p.m. when the gang at Lindsay's, and the cops guarding us, had conked out.

Three hours. I can't get ice cubes to freeze that fast.

Unless Benning's body had lost all its warmth, would a coating of ice even stay frozen? In order to make the case against Elaine, the cops would have to demonstrate that three hours was enough time to find Benning, kill him, decorate him for the ice sculpture, load the van, assuming she had one in the first place, and drop the body off at the WAVE section of the Crystal Garden.

What's more, if Lindsay had gone out to meet someone, it couldn't have been Benning. So something didn't make sense.

I wouldn't expect much luck getting McCracken to give me the info I needed. I might do okay with Mombourquette, but I'd need to play my cards right. In the meantime, I needed to know how long it would take to get a body to freeze like that and under what conditions. Then I had to work back in time to demonstrate that Elaine couldn't have killed him. Piece of cake, you'd think. But until I lucked into that info, I was stopped.

I don't like being stopped. I put a call in to the pathology department of the Ottawa Hospital and asked for Dr. Harry Varty. Just my luck, Dr. Varty was down with bronchitis. Apparently, the latest strain of the flu had decimated the staff.

"It's a horrible winter," the assistant at the path lab said.

"Tell me about it."

"I'll leave him the message, but we don't expect him to be on his feet before next week."

For some reason, she didn't want to give me his home number. What the hell, I figured, another brick wall.

Speaking of brick walls, I gave P. J. a call. He was always plugged into what was happening. If I could reach him and stay on the ball, there was a small chance I could get a bit more information about the case than I'd reveal. I left a message on his voice mail asking if we were still supposed to go skating with his sister's kids. Or was it too damn cold?

I also left a message for Alvin suggesting he check the medical sciences library for information on the effects of freezing on humans. I also wanted to have a look at exactly what else might have been going on at the site where the videotape captured the deposit of Benning's body. While I was at it, maybe I could clear up who'd had access to the coffee and the pizza and who could have lifted Elaine's coat and hat.

*　　*　　*

"What hat?" The look of utter serenity on Elaine's heart-shaped face didn't match the small stark legal interview room at the RDC. She had also said "what coat?"

The session would have been a write-off if she hadn't slipped and answered one of my questions. Turned out the coffee had been left, in the thermoses, in the SUV, outside the Colonnade, while she picked up the pizzas. Of course, the SUV was locked. Did I think she was demented?

"Look," I said, "don't push me on this. Do you think I have nothing better to do with my life than to watch my friends get saddled with murder charges?"

"Do you?"

"Well, yes I do, Elaine. Lots."

"Like what? You have no life at all outside of Justice for Victims. Since last spring, you're grouchier than ever."

"*I* have no life? This is not about me. It's about you, Elaine."

"Well, then why did you ask me if I thought you had nothing better to do?"

"I was making the point that you are wasting time. Yours. Mine. The justice system's. Everybody's time is getting seriously squandered here. If you leave out the media field day, the only person who benefits is the guilty party."

"But I have explained to you that I am the guilty party."

"Put a sock in it, Elaine. Someone killed that asshole and with good cause. And we both know it wasn't you."

"Well, holy moly, if it wasn't me, I certainly couldn't tell you who it was." She gazed up at the ceiling.

I watched my hands, afraid if I took my eyes off them they'd wrap themselves around her neck and squeeze.

"I'm not suggesting you know who killed him. But since someone who looked a lot like you wheeled a body out of a van and into the Crystal Garden on a dolly, I have to ask questions, and since the someone was wearing what looked a lot like your faux fur hat and coat, I have to ask myself if you are protecting someone. Say someone who had access to your clothing. My question is, are you? And if so, who?"

She looked surprised. "My leopard hat and coat? Why? They were locked in the SUV."

"Listen, you were wearing your parka at Lindsay's. It was still there in the morning. Yet the video shows you wearing the coat and hat. You claim they were locked in the SUV. So tell me, did you change outside when it was minus thirty-five? And then change back again? And why?"

She didn't miss a beat. "Sure I did. They don't call me The Ice Queen for nothing."

She was enjoying this far too much, especially the media habit of calling her the Ice Queen. I had a half-baked theory she might be protecting someone else at WAVE, but the more

I looked at her grin, the more I wondered if I'd ever extract the truth from her.

"Don't be such a turkey. Who has a key to the SUV?"

"No one. I wish you'd believe me that I killed him, Camilla. Alone and without any help. It would save everyone a lot of trouble. We could plead guilty with justification, and we'd be away to the races."

"If that's how you want to refer to maximum security, sure. We'd be away all right. I don't know how much trouble it would save, though."

"I can take it."

"I'm sure you'll love prison. Especially with the new regional arrangements for women. Plenty of social projects to keep you busy for the next twenty-five years."

"Couldn't you try to understand, Camilla?"

Was everybody in the entire world demented? "All right. Let me be fair. Maybe you did do it. Who's to say? Why not?"

"I'm glad you're coming around, Camilla."

I leaned in until I was about a half inch from her face. "Look, I'm willing to try to think that you might have done it, but you're going to have to work with me here. How did you drive the van?"

"Van?" Elaine frowned.

"You know what a van is, Elaine. You've almost collided with enough of them. So a van arrived and a person looking like you wheeled out a large box using a dolly and that box contained the body of Ralph Benning encased in ice."

Her eyes widened. "Really? I mean, yes, that's what happened."

"We're getting somewhere. So tell me, since when are you strong enough to load a box containing the body of a large man onto a dolly and wheel that dolly off the van you think you drove?"

"In an emergency, you find strength you didn't know you had."

"And the Valium you drugged us all with? Where did you get that?"

"Valium? It's everywhere. The whole thing was just too easy."

Bingo. She had no clue about the Rohypnol. I knew she hadn't done it. "It's frigging amazing all right. So who were your accomplices?"

She leaned back against the bare wall and smiled again. "I acted alone. And I'm proud of it."

"I want to tell you something, Elaine."

"No, it's time for me to tell you something."

*   *   *

I was steaming when I checked out through the elaborate security and passed through the tall gate with the razor-wire top at the Regional Detention Centre. I kicked the tire of Mrs. Parnell's LTD. It seemed better than kicking the next human being I encountered.

I sat in the car and tried breathing normally for three minutes. Enough time to fog the windows. It took another five minutes with the defrost going full blast before I could see to ease out onto Innis Road and begin the fifteen minute drive downtown.

It would take a lot longer to get over being fired by Elaine.

# *Sixteen*

I left another voice mail message for P.J., and he left one for me. A bracing round of telephone tag followed until I left my final shot. "Sure, you can play games, but remember the guys at *The Sun* are happy to return my calls."

I figured that should get him.

*     *     *

The Crystal Garden site was lovely. Even though the morning sun beat down on the ice sculptures, they were holding up well. Happy tourists took pictures in front of transparent whales, ships and symbols. Lots of scarves, lots of smiles. I found no indication the sculpture of Justice with Benning inside of it had ever been there. I checked and rechecked for the location of the security camera.

Surprise, surprise.

There wasn't one.

*     *     *

When the going gets tough, the tough get nasty.

That's what caused me to trot across to the Elgin Street Courthouse later in the morning. Nastiness laced with a dose of desperation. It brought me face to face with Mia Reilly. She strode along the second floor corridor in a sleek black suit with a touch of Lycra. The whole effect made her long legs seem longer and her blonde hair blonder. She made a fine poster girl for the benefits of physical fitness.

"Mia." I showed my teeth. "Good morning."

She glanced at me without breaking stride. "What do you want?"

"Want? Me? Nothing." I wanted a chance to pump her for inside dope she might have on the police connection to Benning.

"Good, because I'm busy."

"I can tell by your cruising speed. I'm glad I ran into you. Maybe we could do lunch today."

"Lunch? I don't eat lunch. That's my time to run."

It was my time to stretch the truth. "Gee, bad day for running. It's warming up out there. Snow's melting and the sidewalks will be a mess soon. They're saying the canal will be unusable by the weekend. The paths alongside it haven't been plowed yet. Why don't you take a break at noon and join me at the Mayflower? My treat."

"I don't need a weather forecast from you. I run no matter what."

I believe the best defence is a good offence. Even so, I resisted the urge to yawn in her face. "Well, Mia, I am offended."

"Your problem." She flashed her engagement ring, in case I had managed to forget about it.

"Can't I run into you and say hello?" Can't I run after you would have been more accurate. I had to break into a gallop to keep up.

"I notice you never wanted to do lunch before I was assigned to prosecute your client."

"Well, Mia, I'm glad you mentioned that."

"Sure you are." She made a sharp right and zipped into the

156

reception area of the Office of the Crown Attorney. The plum furniture matched her blouse perfectly.

"I am. I didn't realize you had the case. That's terrific. It saves me calling your office."

"And that is so like you."

"Since we're talking girltalk, what makes you think you want to proceed with this ridiculous charge?"

This time she stopped. Two clerks glanced up with interest as I almost hit the wall to avoid bumping into her.

"Ridiculous? Your friend Elaine confessed. She killed Ralph Benning to make a political point. She's an extremist, as you well know. High on her own rhetoric. Pretty cold-blooded, wouldn't you say? It was clearly premeditated. If you have any brains, you'll have her plead down to manslaughter."

"What?"

"Because if you don't, we'll get her for murder in the first and clang-clang the door closed for twenty-five years, no parole. Of course, there's always The Faint Hope clause."

"Are you out of your mind? You have people sashaying out of this Court House with suspended sentences after they murdered their mothers. Why would you go after Elaine this way?" I wanted to reach out and slap the self-satisfied smile off her face.

"Because it was a horrific murder. Because we know we'll get her. Because it's high-profile. And because it will be a feather in my cap when we do."

Oh, right. I'd forgotten how irritatingly ambitious she was.

I found myself sputtering. "Listen, aren't you the people who couldn't keep Benning behind bars for repeated injuries to his wife? Don't you wonder why? Don't you realize someone in the police force messed with that mountain of evidence? Didn't it occur to you the same person would have framed Elaine? Take a trip to the ice sculpture site. There's no security camera there. Someone set that video up to draw attention to Elaine. You're dreaming in colour if you think this won't come out in court."

I could see she didn't believe me. "If you practiced law instead of taking the easy way out with that pathetic agency of yours, Camilla, you'd remember we get the results we want here."

"Forget the feather in your cap. You'll come off looking like a fool. She's not guilty, and that's the plea we'll enter."

"And what does your client want?"

I stopped myself from saying, "who cares what my client wants," since, in fact, I didn't have a client anymore. This didn't seem like the time to mention it.

"Remember: guilty plea or twenty-five." She flashed the rock once more before she disappeared behind the plum-coloured door, leaving her lingering scent of spice, cedar and bergamot.

Okay, so that hadn't gone too well either. I was down but not out. And Mia was not the only game in town.

\*　　\*　　\*

Don't ask me why the sound of Lindsay Grace weeping bothered me so much. She hadn't forfeited all emotional rights when she took up with Benning. She'd lost her position, her mental stability, her reputation, her ability to sleep through the night and her health. Her tears unsettled me. I thought the death of Ralph Benning constituted grounds for celebration. Cakes, sparklers, voices raised in song. I knew she wouldn't feel the same, but I found her swollen eyes a bit more than I could take. It must have showed.

"I'm sorry." She blew her nose.

Merv gave me a glare that would have reduced a lesser woman to a grease spot on the maple floor.

"Don't worry about it." I handed Lindsay a tissue. "I understand how you must feel."

Merv snorted.

"That's a most unattractive sound, Merv."

"And a well-deserved one," Merv said.

"I do understand, Lindsay. But I need to talk to you about who might have killed Ben…Ralph."

"You're too frigging much, Camilla." Merv snatched the box of tissues.

"It's all right," Lindsay said.

"No, it isn't," Merv said. "She's way out of line, and she has no right to hassle you."

Lindsay reached over and patted his hand. "She has to do this."

"Correct," I said. "Lindsay, Elaine has been a good friend to you. You know the Crown Attorney is prepared to throw the book at her unless we find out who actually did it."

"I know."

"You understand why I need to ask you questions."

She smiled a pale smile. "There's no good time."

"Right." I tried not to concentrate on Merv looming largely in the background.

"Think about who might have wanted to kill Ralph Benning."

"I don't know. I didn't want to kill him myself, and yet he threatened my life over and over again. Don't ask me to explain it."

"Fine, anyone else you can think of?"

"Even though I know I'm better off with him dead." She stopped to blow her nose again. "I know it, but I'll never feel it."

"Right. Let me rephrase the question. Could anyone else be better off with him dead?"

"Well, Rina, of course, but she couldn't have done it."

I tried not to think about Rina Benning's tragedy. Time to

steer the conversation back to Lindsay. "Did anyone who cared for you want him out of the way?"

Merv grunted.

"Present company included." I added.

"No. My family washed their hands of me after Ralph's cases started to make the news. To tell the truth, we were estranged before then. I guess they felt disgraced. Their daughter living in sin was bad enough, shacked up with a convicted criminal and a married criminal to boot was too much. In retrospect, I suppose they had a point." I caught the pale echo of a smile again.

"But even so they must have hated him, not you. Maybe they held him responsible."

"No. They held me responsible. And they would never use physical violence. Too gritty. Too likely to make the papers. It would bring even more shame on the family."

"Maybe one of them snapped."

"I wouldn't expect them to kill Ralph for me. I would have been happy if my parents could even give me the time of day."

There's something to be said for sisters who are fighters, I thought. "Who else? Friends? Former lovers?"

"No one. I've been cut off from everyone in my former life. He made it happen. I guess I let him. At first, my friends and colleagues were concerned, very worried. Then over time, they lost interest. I wouldn't listen. I had excuses for bruises, excuses for broken dates with friends, excuses for sudden changes in plans. Eventually people got fed up and drifted away. Then, one day, he was all I had."

"But there must be someone." The emotion in Merv's voice would have been enough to make another woman blush. But Lindsay remained in her own world.

"No. People get angry. They don't understand how an abusive person traps you. They think you can choose to leave and simply close the door and get on with your life. But Ralph would never release me. They blamed me for staying."

"Until Elaine."

"Yes. It took her a long time and a lot of talk, but she finally gave me the strength to make the break."

"That's why you're alive. Without Elaine, you might have arranged to meet him that last night. You might have helped him escape. You wouldn't have been able to resist." I looked her straight in the eye and waited for the truth.

She didn't fall for it. "You're right. I wouldn't have been able to survive without her. She felt passionate about my need to break free. She never stopped working on me. She kept insisting that understanding had to come first. And later, I would be able to get over the emotional damage. She tried to get me to respect myself."

"Elaine's behind bars, and, because of her desire to save people like you, she'll get convicted of murder."

"They'll never convict her."

"Why are you badgering Lindsay? Elaine fired you."

"Shut up, Merv. What is this talk? Of course they'll goddam well convict her. She'll plead guilty. If, and that's a big if, she gets a conditional sentence, the Crown will appeal. It'll be years before it's all resolved. And once she testifies she did it, even if she changes her mind, there could be mischief charges or worse. Perjury's a big deal. The system doesn't like to be made foolish. She'll serve jail time anyway."

Lindsay bit her lip.

"Think about who you know who could have been involved. Think about Benning's business associates. Think about how he might have been connected with the police. And with whom. Elaine helped you. You have to help her."

Lindsay turned those luminous honey-coloured eyes on me.

Even swollen and red-rimmed, they were beautiful. "I'll try to think if there could be anybody else capable of such a thing. I'll use my imagination. But…"

"But what?"

"Oh, Camilla, how can you believe Elaine didn't kill him?"

Merv stood up. "Okay. Show's over."

It seemed like a good time to leave anyway. I'd reached Lindsay. Now all I had to do was wait.

*    *    *

Don't ask me what librarians see in Alvin. I don't want to know how he gets them to eat out of his hand. There's very little he can't find out in a reference department. Even when he shouldn't be able to.

As soon as I get within sniffing distance of a reference desk, new rules spring out of the ground like tulips. Eyebrows shoot up. Questions are asked. Tempers flare. And I have never ripped covers from periodicals or removed entire volumes from tax-supported institutions without authorization.

But I don't want to complain.

"Present for you," Alvin said, on his return to Justice for Victims.

He dropped a batch of magazines on the desk in front of me and flicked the light layer of snow from his Day-Glo orange lei onto the floor. "I think you'll find these interesting."

"What are they?"

"They're scientific journals. That's what you asked for."

"Do I see the stamp of the University of Ottawa Science Library?"

"So?"

"Stealing journals from a library is pretty low, Alvin."

**162**

"Like you wouldn't do it."

"Take them back."

"Relax, Camilla, just read these articles. They're about the effects of temperature on human tissue. They detail how long it would take a body to freeze under the ice at a given external temperature. I believe you sent me to find out. Am I wrong?"

"No, you're not. But why did you have to steal the articles, Alvin?"

His nose quivered. "What do you mean, *steal?* I don't steal. I borrowed them. Lord thundering Jesus, they're from a library."

"I don't know why you couldn't just photocopy them. You're not even a student there."

"Do you want this stuff or not?"

"Why can't you just search on the internet like everybody else?"

Alvin snorted. "Thanks, Camilla, there's lots of great stuff on the net, but I like my info vetted by an expert who can show me the scientifically sound research. Lot of nutcases post so-called information out there. My way saves time and gets a quality product. We have high stakes here."

I hate to let him win. Especially if he's right. I eyed the stack with distaste.

"Camilla, just read these. Then if it makes you happy, I'll slip them back into the stacks again when I go to see Angela."

Angela. That would be the latest librarian.

What could I say? I needed to know when Ralph Benning had been iced before I could begin to clear Elaine. I'd also need to find an expert witness on the effect of freezing on bodies if the case ever came to trial.

"Alvin, I have places to go and people to pester, so here's the drill. You, that means *you* by way of clarification, can sit here and go through these articles and then when you finish, *you,*

you remember who that is, can tell *me* what you find out. And then *you* can get back to the library ASAP. With the files the cops have on you, if they get wind of this latest caper, it could be the final straw."

I didn't look back as I left the office.

*     *     *

Lucky me. Alexa had a floral emergency, which meant our shopping trip to Holt's could wait until the next day. I headed home.

My luck held in the corridor of the 16th floor when Mrs. Parnell stuck her nose out the door, blew a stream of Benson and Hedges exhaust in my direction and claimed to be too busy to chat. "Lots of fine stuff on the web, Ms. MacPhee, most intriguing. We'll get Benning's cohorts pinned down, and then we will pick them off, one by one."

"Good. But you can't use the internet to tell you if he had a pile of cash stashed or if he pushed a high-level criminal too far." Of course, I was talking to her door.

Never mind. Mrs. Parnell's little calico cat was waiting optimistically in my apartment. She made no demands. She was always happy to curl up on the sofa and purr along with a friend. She didn't mind if the friend made a few phone calls.

I left a message for P.J., a reminder message to Dr. Varty, the pathologist at the hospital, followed by a call to Conn McCracken. I tried to get a message to Elaine at the RDC. Finally, I called my sisters to say I'd be out all evening and not to bother phoning.

Then I flicked on the television, ate a can of mushroom soup and crashed on the sofa until the sun came up.

There's no life like it.

# Seventeen

I woke up in a good mood, which doesn't happen often. In honour of the occasion, I made three resolutions. First, not to let the wedding preparations annoy me; second, to keep a cool head about the Elaine situation, and third, to relax a bit until it was time to resume the hunt for the elusive bridesmaid's dress. I shared a pleasant breakfast with Mrs. Parnell's cat and felt quite mellow by the time I had finished my toast and she had polished off her tuna.

I checked the thermometer on my balcony and was surprised to see the temperature had shot up to plus three. Five minutes later, I realized it was probably as a result of heat generated by the headline in the City section of the *Ottawa Citizen*. It's always a mistake to read the paper before leaving the house.

This time P. J. answered his cellphone on the first ring. "Took you long enough, Tiger."

"You little creep, what kind of friend are you?"

"Hey, what's your problem? I'm doing my job. Same as you. Nothing to do with friendship."

"What friendship? Your nasty headline today. *Ice Queen puts chill on hotheaded defence lawyer*. What kind of crap is that?"

"Hey, I just file the stories, I don't write the headlines, although I did think that one was cool."

"Enough with the jokes. You think this is funny for Elaine?"

"Here's another tip for you. You might not think it's funny,

165

but Elaine will be having the time of her life. You know she hired Berelson. Then she had him call a press conference to announce she'd fired you. And you're wondering what kind of friend I am."

"What a shitty sight to start the day."

"Of course it was. Don't take it personally; it's what I do, as the scorpion said to the frog. So tell me, froggie, ready to go skating on Sunday? Two little guys will be heartbroken if you don't."

Why do I always have to be the bad guy? "I wouldn't disappoint the kids. But you better watch your back."

\* \* \*

"It's good news," Alexa said. "Elaine was always difficult. Being fired frees you for better activities, like skating with your friend's nephews."

She dabbed a little L'air du temps behind her ears and smiled out the window. Alexa's not the most subtle person in the world. I knew she meant it freed me to be more cooperative about the wedding. And I intended to be. We headed off for Holt's at around ten in a mood of cautious optimism.

\* \* \*

"Well, of course, poor Elaine is an absolute *saint*. She was horrified by this man, and she knew she had to stop him before he killed anyone else." Vanessa Gross-Davies might have been Chair of the Board of WAVE and a half-dozen other key groups, but she managed to look like she stepped from the pages of a fashion magazine. That's one of the advantages of marrying the CEO of a leading high-tech company.

It didn't make it any more of a treat running into her in the handbag section of Holt Renfrew. I can't say she was glad to see me. "Great," I said. "I sure would want to have you in my corner, Vanessa, if push came to shove."

Vanessa curved her lips into an expression that, on someone else, might have been a smile. A layer of frost formed on the tip of my nose. Alexa appeared to be fascinated by a display of Italian leather bags.

"Well, Camilla, I am in Elaine's corner. I'm there for her whenever she needs me. Which I understand from the news last night and today is more than we can say for you."

"Right. As you said, Elaine has snapped. She won't talk to me, but if you're her friend, you must ask her to change her plea."

"Jack says Elaine played this one like a pro. The media spin is fabulous. It draws attention to the plight of battered women and the need for the rest of society to fight back."

"Tell Jack volunteering to be the defendant at a murder trial is more perilous than floating your first IPO. It's one thing to lose your shirt, it's another to lose your freedom. She needs people to talk sense into her, not encourage her in this ill-advised behaviour."

"That may be, but she doesn't need *you*. WAVE has arranged *competent* representation for her."

I didn't bite. "Don't get me wrong—I'm glad you and Jack and the board at WAVE are there for Elaine. She needs all the support she can get here. What did you think of her terrible situation at the Regional Detention Centre? Did you try to talk to her through the shield? They put in the Plexiglas after one of the visitors broke down the bars with a sledgehammer. Still, it breaks your heart, doesn't it?"

The eyes hardened. "I haven't been able to visit her yet."

I bet you haven't, I thought. Ms. Gross-Davies would never

park her cashmere bum next to a bunch of strung-out girlfriends and runny-nosed toddlers screaming for the old man behind the unbreakable window.

"Ah, well, the pressures of a full schedule, I'm sure."

"*We* are having a fundraiser dinner for Elaine tonight, and that has taken a good deal of my time. And now if you'll excuse me, I am busy."

"Great, I'm so relieved. A new handbag is exactly what Elaine needs."

"We will do our best for Elaine. She has the finest legal representation, and she'll be out in no time."

"You're funding her legal expenses?"

"We have secured Mr. Sam Berelson as her defence lawyer."

I already knew that. I also knew Berelson didn't make the front pages regularly by being second-rate. He didn't come free either.

"Great. Elaine would never divert funds from WAVE to cover her own legal expenses, so it's wonderful you're paying for Berelson." I reached over and clasped her hand. "Most generous. I am impressed."

She did her best to yank herself free, but I held tight. "Thank you. Thank you," I said.

"Someone call security!"

On the other side of the counter, an elegant saleswoman reached for the phone.

"Let go of me. And leave me alone. Elaine wants you to stay away from her and her friends too."

"Ah, yes," I gave her one final squeeze, "I bet she does."

After that, I did my best to find a dress.

For some reason, Alexa kept checking over her shoulder the entire time we spent in the store. We both found it hard to concentrate. When we left, still dressless, she didn't even whimper. I suggested, "Tomorrow will be better."

No argument.

*   *   *

When the going gets tough, the tough get sneaky. Daddy would have been proud of me. In late afternoon, I hit police headquarters. "I'm here to see Conn McCracken in Major Crimes." I told the officer at the second floor desk outside the Criminal Investigation Division. "He's about to become my brother-in-law."

The officer yawned. I guess that didn't impress him much. Two minutes later, after a quick call from the desk, McCracken lumbered through the door and looked at me in a sadder but wiser way.

"Good time of the year to work indoors," I said as we hiked back down a narrow hall.

I thought I heard a grunt. After that, I kept my mouth shut until I had plunked on the plastic visitor's chair in front of his desk. I smiled at him over the stacks of files in buff folders. I had to hand it to him, he kept an orderly workspace, which couldn't have been easy in an office that made Justice for Victims look spacious. An orderly desk was sign of a good mind, if you believed my father. I always hoped it wasn't true.

An 8 x 10 photo of Alexa smiled down at us from on top of the four-drawer filing cabinet. McCracken settled his big body into his chair. "I'm glad you came by, Camilla."

"What?" I had to stop sounding like a dope, but every sentence I heard lately sounded more peculiar than the last. "There's a switch. Most people seem to remember pressing business elsewhere as soon as they see my face."

"I wonder why."

"No idea."

"Anyway. I needed to talk to you."

"Excellent, because I needed to talk to you too."

"Me first."

"Hey, go ahead. It's your turf."

"Okay." He leaned forward. "Alexa is a wonderful person."

"Yes."

"She'd never hurt anyone."

"Right."

"She cares a lot about you."

"Is there a point?"

"Please try to stop making her crazy. This wedding ceremony is so important to her. It would make a big difference if you would cooperate and not fight with the entire world. Just get the dress and be pleasant. Just ten days, Camilla, then the ceremony's over and you can be your miserable self."

I'd never heard McCracken talk so much in the eight months since I'd first met him. Maybe the shock had brought it on.

"I'm doing my best. In fact, we've already been shopping today."

I didn't like the expression on his face. "Don't try shitting me, Camilla. I heard about that experience. Alexa doesn't need that kind of stress every step of the way. The least you could do is cooperate."

"Not a problem."

His eyes narrowed. "I wish I could believe you."

I looked around. "Where's Mombourquette?"

"Finished for the day. He's headed for a workout."

"So, what's new on the Benning investigation? Did you find the van Benning was transported in? Forensic would be able to confirm pretty quickly if it was the one."

"Maybe you don't know it, Camilla, but we're short of resources. We can't waste time. Do you think we pursue cases that are solved?"

"Solved? By solved do you mean arresting a wacky woman with a lot more heart than brains when she pretends to have committed a crime? When you find that van you won't find any trace of Elaine in it. I know it and so do you."

"I'll tell you something you should know. Word has come down you're persona non grata and members of the force are to watch out for you."

"Persona non grata? Why?"

"Because you've been a pain in the ass of the brass."

"Well, I don't know, Conn, it seems to me I'm the same as always. Except for you and Mombourquette, I'm not in touch with any cops. So whose ass have I pained?"

"I don't know. But the message has been clear. Whoever felt the pain, really felt it."

"So why talk to me?"

"Why not? I got my thirty years in. I can retire any time, take it easy, and enjoy my new life. If I get suspended or disciplined, it won't matter much. Give me a bit more time for the wedding. But you won't find other officers feel the same way."

"Tell me, Conn, this so-called 'word' you're prepared to ignore, you don't find it revealing?"

"What do you mean?"

"I mean Benning obviously had a well-placed contact who helped him get off more than once. Do you think he broke out this last time without inside backing? It's not possible. It had to be a connection in the police. When Benning went right over the edge, he became an incredible liability for his inside man. I thought it was some undercover cop but this message points up the ladder to someone with clout. Someone who would need to get Ralph Benning out of the way before word about the relationship leaked out. The rest of you are dancing to his tune. So who's behind the message, Conn?"

*   *   *

I was almost in the elevator before I caught my breath. I guess you can push Conn McCracken only so far. If I'd been a good little girl I would have kept going and headed out the door and onto Elgin Street.

Instead, I stayed on the second floor and zipped down the hall towards the police gym. What the hell, it was the last chance I'd get to visit, what with directives and all. I peered through the glass slot in the door, and sure enough, caught sight of Mombourquette.

I ditched my jacket and boots in the empty office around the corner and headed in. The police gym smelled just like any other. Mombourquette was working with the free weights. Developing his pecs, I figured. And not a moment too soon. From the far end of the gym came the steady thunk of basketballs.

"Hey, Leonard!" I said.

"What are you doing here?" Mombourquette didn't break his routine for a second.

"I need to see you."

"We're not supposed to talk to you."

"I don't understand that. Maybe you can explain it to me. But first, I wanted to know if you'd heard the latest about Elaine."

"I'm serious, Camilla. Get out of here."

"Sheesh. What a welcome. I was heading in to see Conn about family matters, and I heard you were here, and I dropped in to say hi."

"Hi. Goodbye."

"Hey. Sorry to interrupt your workout. But when would be a good time to talk?"

"Never." I noticed a couple of officers in the far corner glance over.

"Never?"

"We have orders not to give you information. But I bet you already know that."

"I don't need information. I'm giving it out."

"I'm not going to bite."

I refrained from saying "and what a waste of pointy incisors that is." Although I'd kept my voice down, we'd been noticed. One of his colleagues stepped off the treadmill and stared at us.

"No problem. I wanted to let you know the Crown plans to throw the book at Elaine."

He pushed the weights up with his arms. "Get out of here."

"It's true. Mia Reilly told me."

"Now."

"Fine." I turned to leave.

"They won't get a conviction. And even if they do, she won't serve time. She'll get a suspended sentence. At the worst it will be conditional." He kept his voice low.

"You wish. Mia Reilly says she can get murder in the first. It's a good career move for her. They'll pull out all the stops and prove Elaine stood to gain personally from his death. Don't count on a light sentence, because it won't happen."

"We all know she fired you. You have no authority whatsoever. Hit the road." Mombourquette's muscles were getting a workout they wouldn't soon forget.

"She did fire me. Because she wants to be a martyr. And now I hear the cops are not allowed to talk to big, big, bad, bad Camilla MacPhee. Makes you wonder about a cover-up."

"Scram, Camilla."

I couldn't believe it. "Listen, Leonard, I thought you cared about Elaine, and if you do, you'd better be prepared to talk to me, because she needs all the friends she can get."

"You'll need all the friends you can get if you're not out of here in thirty seconds. You want to get charged, keep talking."

"Problem, Lennie?"

The basketballs had stopped thunking. A tall female officer with spiky ash blond hair unbent from a rowing machine and loped over.

"The problem's on her way out." Mombourquette hadn't stopped hoisting those weights. Maybe that's why he turned such a funny colour.

"Think about that, serious time." I hate to let someone else have the last word.

A trickle of sweat worked its way down Mombourquette's neck. "You think about *this*. If you don't want to find yourself in deep shit, don't make any stops on your way out. That includes badgering McCracken."

I turned and pushed open the door. "Good-bye, Lennie. Nice to see you sweat."

The female officer followed me out of the room. She leaned against the wall, crossed her arms and waited while I retrieved my parka and tied up the neon yellow laces of my Sorels. She smelled a bit of linament. No surprise. She didn't look like the type to wear perfume. She followed me down the hall and into the elevator, and she didn't say a word. Must have read that memo.

I kept my mouth shut on the ride down and didn't look back until I hit the front doors. When I did glance over my shoulder, I saw her deep in conversation with the Commissionaire at the info desk. They were both pointing at me.

# Eighteen

Back in Justice for Victims, Alvin had vanished for the day. A stack of pink messages remained, all but one from my sisters. The remaining one said my car would be unavailable for an extra ten days.

I couldn't keep riding around in Mrs. Parnell's LTD for another ten days. Not the way the defrost worked on it. I made a call and managed to snag a rental car. Then I spent a couple of hours catching up on some grant proposals to keep the wolf from the door. It was boring enough to keep my mind off things for a while. But only for a while. Then it was time to get back to the matter most on my mind.

I tried to call Mrs. Parnell for an update, but she didn't answer her phone. Neither did Merv. Neither did Lindsay. I couldn't call Elaine. The Crown Attorney's office would be closed for the day. Ditto the WAVE office, not that I could expect help there. I couldn't talk to the police. I couldn't talk to my best friend, Robin, because she was out of reach in the Yucatan. I didn't want to talk to my sisters. If I didn't get the frustration out of my system, I'd have to scream.

If you can't beat them, join them.

Okay, it's not my motto. My motto is more like, if you can't beat them, run over them with a truck. But I was in enough trouble already. A skate on the canal seemed like the right antidote to my poisonous mood. I figured it would help me to think clearly while I waited for Alvin and Mrs. P. to report back. Plus I needed the practice before I hit the ice with P. J.'s nephews.

I had a pair of skates in the bottom drawer of the second filing cabinet, along with a pair of emergency running shoes.

Sure enough, they were nestled between the single leather glove and the Tupperware containers.

*   *   *

Ten minutes later, I plunked on a bench by the edge of the canal, slipped into the skates and tightened the Velcro fasteners. I tucked my boots into my backpack and headed out to join the Winterlude crowds. Since the temperature held at a balmy zero Celsius, everyone in Ottawa seemed to be out. It felt like a heat wave to me. I stuffed my red hat in my pocket and let myself enjoy the breeze for the first time in two months. The sky was clear and starry already. The three-quarter moon offered natural light in addition to the lamp standards along the canal.

It was after eight on a weeknight, but clouds of kids darted around. The combination of the warm temperature and the number of people made the ice slooshy, but who cared? All you had to do was watch out for the gouges and cracks in the ice surface, relax and have a good time.

I'd forgotten how it felt. It doesn't matter how broke you are, you can always get your mitts on a pair of second-hand skates. Paul and I had spent many hours on the canal, holding hands, laughing. The year we lived in Old Ottawa South, we'd skated to work every morning the canal was open and home again late in the evening, full of cases and news from our respective law firms. I wondered where

Paul's skates were, then I stopped that thought. Fast.

It was the kind of night that Winterlude is all about. Throngs of skaters laughed and spun. Ahead of me a young couple each guided a toddler, the whole family sporting handknit red scarves.

If Paul had lived, would we have had a child? Would we have worn matching red scarves? Enough of that. I had real trouble without making myself miserable with might-have-beens. I let myself get caught up in the good mood. What the hell.

I figured a trip down to the Pretoria Bridge and back would be far enough. I threaded my way in and out of skaters moving in random patterns, passing the University of Ottawa buildings on my left, the Golden Triangle on my right. My ankles ached from the unfamiliar skates. But that was good. It would take my mind off my Elaine problem and would be enough to clear my head and let the unconscious part of my brain deal with all my tricky issues.

I was having fun. I found out I could still twirl. Looking back down the canal, I could see the top of the Peace Tower just visible behind the Laurier Street Bridge.

What the heck, since I was out having fun, I decided to eat. I knew what I wanted. I careened up to the green wooden cabin with the gold letters. Luckily, I remembered how to use my blades to stop. I waited in line and bought a BeaverTail, cinnamon and sugar. I nibbled as I skated along and turned to head back at the Pretoria Bridge.

I tried to concentrate on who might have killed Benning and tried not to get sidetracked by Elaine and her bizarre choice. In the end things always worked out for Elaine. She pulled crazy stunts and got away with them. Everyone remembered her hunger strike over subsidies for better low-income housing, the sit-ins in front of Foreign Affairs, and, of course, the legendary visit to the House of Commons. If there were Stubborn Olympics, Elaine would have medals.

I peered over and up at the town houses on Echo Drive and thought of Lindsay. Then it hit me. Elaine had sandbagged me. I hadn't used my brain for proper analysis. I'd probably missed leads pointing toward the real murderer.

Ralph Benning had been a thug and a villain, a wife beater and a drug dealer and who knew what else. It stood to reason he would have ticked off scarier folks than the Executive Director of WAVE.

Even though I couldn't believe Lindsay might have killed Benning, missing sweaters or not, and most likely her family and friends hadn't either, it still made sense she'd have an idea who would. After all, before she'd been his victim, she'd been his lover. She'd spent her time with him. It didn't cross my mind Benning would have been open with her or anybody, but even so, she would have met his cronies, and business acquaintances. More important, she might know whom he dealt with on the police force.

Pillow talk.

She hadn't told me. But then, I hadn't asked her the right questions. Maybe she had a good reason. Did Lindsay know someone worse than Benning?

I had a purpose for skating besides letting off steam. I was right across the canal from Lindsay's place. There was a convenient set of steps leading up to Colonel By. It was clogged with slow-moving families lifting children right at that moment.

I waited by the side of the canal and tapped the blades of my skates irritably against the ice. At least I had the BeaverTail to keep me busy. I licked a bit of the sugar from my gloves. I had to start to remember to eat more often.

I sniffed the air. I caught a whiff of a familiar scent. What was it? Hard to tell. The cinnamon overwhelmed it.

I was halfway through my BeaverTail when I felt a powerful blow to the back of my legs. Had a kid skidded out of control? Before I could check, I was hit again.

My knees crumbled, and I shot forward. The BeaverTail dropped as I put my hands out to break my fall. I tumbled towards the bank of snow at the side of the canal. My yell was swallowed up by the music. The banked snow rose up to meet my face. Someone grabbed my shoulders as I plunged forward. Thank God. But the hands pushed instead of pulling. A blow to my back propelled me head first into the crusty snow. The hard surface scraped my face as I slammed through it.

I tried to yell but my mouth filled with snow. Somebody's knees dug in my back and strong hands pushed my face further into the soft icy interior of the bank. My arms and hands pressed ahead, trapped by the snow, useless.

I struggled and found more snow in my mouth. I saw exploding pinpricks of light. The person forcing me down was no child. An adult's weight on my back shoved me into a cold, white death.

I struggled to catch my breath. The pain in my chest took over my mind. I could feel my body spasm. My hands jerked against the snow and found only resistance.

*Is this how it ends?*

Nothing but black.

\* \* \*

Who was slapping me? *Don't do that.* I tried to beat them back. To my surprise, I could move my hands. "Stop it."

"She's coming around."

"Are you okay?"

"What happened?"

I opened my eyes to a ring of round-eyed watchers. Court jesters? No, people in tuques, bending over me.

"Can you move your leg?"

I couldn't think. What was going on? A small face inserted itself close to me. A freckled boy grinned, showing two missing front teeth.

"I found you," he said. "I told them and they pulled you out. It was me."

The snowbank, the pressure, the knees in my back. Everything flooded back.

"Don't move. You might have broken bones."

"Here, have a bit of coffee."

"Try to sit up."

"Is she a homeless person?"

"Don't try to sit up."

"Maybe lie down."

"Do you think she's been drinking?"

"No, I don't think she should lie down."

"I found her. I bet I'll get a big reward."

The ring of people must have been five deep by this time. I was obviously entertaining.

A woman in iridescent blue leaned in and held out a cup. "Hot chocolate. Cures every ill."

"Don't move."

"Be careful, you don't want to do yourself a permanent injury. Stay quiet until the skate patrol gets here."

"There's what I need." My teeth chattered as I reached out and grabbed the cup of hot chocolate.

"Or maybe I'll get a medal," the little boy said.

New faces joined the crowd and people pushed forward to get a gander at the action.

"What happened?" a woman asked.

"I might even be on TV," the little boy said.

I wanted the whole damn crowd to disappear.

"Fine, I'm okay," Not true, but that was my business, not theirs.

Since they continued to stand around feigning concern, I asked if anyone had seen the person who'd pushed me into the snow bank. That was enough to make the crowd melt away.

A nice young man from the Rideau Canal Skate Patrol asked me a lot of questions. I guess I answered them all right. It looked like an ambulance wouldn't be necessary, which was good, because I had no intention of going in one. On the down side, my cellphone was out of juice. But the nice young man called a cab for me. For once, I didn't have to wait long. The cab driver didn't have much to say. That was good. I didn't feel like talking to him. I kept my eyes closed in case he changed his mind and decided to chat. But my mind kept racing. Who had pushed me into the snowbank? Was it a coincidence it happened right in front of Lindsay's place? And right after I'd irritated everyone in the Ottawa police force? Which reminded me. Who had tugged on the police chain of command?

Vanessa Gross-Davies and the board of directors of WAVE? Her know-it-all husband Jack? Elaine herself, not wanting me to impede her conviction? Or someone I hadn't even thought of? What the hell were the connections?

Mrs. Parnell was not in her usual sentry spot in the corridor. For once I could have done with a sherry, but she didn't answer her door even after eight or nine vigorous thumps. Never mind, Mrs. P.'s cat and my sofa were all I needed.

*   *   *

I admit there are issues involved in pretending to be someone's lawyer when you are their ex-lawyer or perhaps even their never-was lawyer. These issues can come back to haunt you if you're not careful. I hadn't been careful.

I don't know why I picked up the phone at eleven o'clock that evening. Maybe because it jerked me awake. Maybe because I ached too much to think. Maybe because I didn't recognize the phone number. But since it wasn't a member of my family, it seemed safe enough.

Alvin was breathing hard. "You'd better turn on your radio."

"What for?"

"Never mind. Make sure you catch the next local news."

"Does it have to do with bridesmaid's dresses?"

"No."

"Winterlude and goddam skating?"

"No."

"Good, I'll listen then."

Maybe I should have done that. Instead I rolled over on the sofa and snored open-mouthed to a rerun of *Due South*.

"Camilla!"

Damn. I knew I shouldn't have answered. But Edwina's call came in the middle of a dream and I reached out for Paul Gross and picked up the receiver.

"Hello?"

"How could you?"

"How could I what?"

"I think you know."

"I don't know."

"It's hardly fair."

"I'm sure it isn't."

"What a disgrace. How will Daddy hold his head up in St. Jim's Parish if you get disbarred?"

"What?"

"Can't you say anything more intelligent than *what*? When I think about all your education, well, it makes me wonder. I can imagine how embarrassed Alexa and Conn will be with you in the spotlight right before the wedding."

"What?"

"Oh, Camilla, for God's sake." She slammed down the receiver. It saved me from saying "what" again.

Which was good.

I brushed my teeth, splashed cold water on my scratched face, fed Mrs. P.'s pet and turned on CBC radio in time to get the local highlights.

"In the latest bizarre twist in the Ralph Benning murder case, suspect Elaine Ekstein told reporters she has dismissed her defence lawyer. Ekstein alleges she never engaged the services of Camilla MacPhee, controversial Ottawa legal activist. According to Ekstein, MacPhee, Executive Director of the advocacy group, Justice for Victims, has misrepresented the relationship between them. Ekstein, who is refusing to submit to psychiatric testing, has been denied bail and has yet to undergo a preliminary hearing in the macabre death of Ralph Benning earlier this week, is now represented by Sam Berelson. Assistant Crown Attorney Mia Reilly confirmed that her office plans to lodge a formal complaint against MacPhee with the Law Society of Upper Canada tomorrow."

"What?" I said.

# Nineteen

Even though it was Saturday, Alvin and I both found ourselves at our desks in the office by mid-morning. I was doing my best to be in a good mood despite the cost of the rental car I'd picked up. Alvin was doing his best to be Alvin, with the help of Jimmy Buffett and some Pina Colada mix.

"Of course, I haven't forgotten," I told P. J. when he called. "I've already been practicing."

"Excellent. The little guys are bouncing they're so excited."

"Oh, good."

"And they don't even realize how newsworthy you are."

"So this outing won't compromise your journalistic integrity?"

"Nope. I'm excited. I figure it should be worth a couple of first-rate quotes."

I planned to give him a couple of quotes all right.

Alvin managed to mind his own business at his own desk throughout that conversation. To do him credit, he hadn't mentioned my swollen nose and scraped face that morning either.

"Well," I said, after I hung up, "what did you find out?"

Of course, with Alvin, you have to cool your jets while he gets to the point. That's the price you pay for service. He twirled the little umbrella in his drink. "Well, it's not that easy."

"No, I suppose it isn't." I tried to keep the edge out of my voice, which wasn't that easy either. Since the incident in the snowbank, every part of my body that didn't ache or sting, throbbed.

"A lot of this information is not in the public domain."

"Right."

"I think you'll be pleased."

"Excellent. As long as I'm pleased in this lifetime."

Mistake. I bit my tongue. After nearly a year, I should know certain types of remarks merely slow him down.

"You could have done it yourself. Would have been a lot quicker."

"Okay, Alvin, I'll say 'uncle' at this point. We both know it wouldn't have been faster if I'd done it. Mainly because I tend not to remove materials from libraries without authorization and...what?"

Someone screamed. Alvin screamed too. I whirled around, expecting a lunatic with a raised axe.

"Sorry." Alvin pointed at Alexa. "She startled me."

"She startled *you*? The two of you nearly gave me a stroke. Alexa, do you think it's a good idea to show up here and start screaming?"

"My God, your face."

Alexa was framed in the door, clutching her heart and breathing fast. Behind her loomed Conn McCracken.

"Yes, well. You should see the other guy."

She pursed her lips. "I wasn't expecting...what happened?"

I pointed to McCracken. "Why don't you ask him?"

"What do you mean, ask me?"

"What *does* she mean, Conn?"

"I don't know what she means."

Oh, good. McCracken got to experience one of those dangerous looks.

Alvin said, "She means he knows what happened."

"What do you know about Camilla's facial injuries, Connor?"

Ooh. *Con-nor.* That sounded ominous.

"I don't know anything about them."

"If you say so," Alvin said.

"I *do* say so." McCracken seemed even closer to a stroke than I had been. All in all, a bad health day for both of us.

I was feeling big-hearted. "Give him the benefit of the doubt."

McCracken's face deepened from red to purple, not a good sign.

"Why would you need the benefit of the doubt, Connor?"

"I don't. I didn't ask for the benefit of the doubt. Christ, I have no idea how Camilla got her face messed up."

Alexa stiffened.

"I'm sorry," McCracken said.

"Fine."

"Sorry, lamb chop. I didn't mean to swear. And I wasn't swearing at you anyway. They took me by surprise. And..."

"No problem," Alexa said.

As far as I could tell, there was a problem all right. And it was McCracken's. Alexa had her back to him now. And a nice straight back it was too. "Camilla, what happened to you?"

"Someone attacked me on the canal last night."

She gasped. You have to hand it to my sisters, they gasp beautifully, which adds drama to any situation.

"Who did?"

"I don't know."

"What happened?"

"Someone tripped me and knocked me into a snowbank. Then they made sure my head was buried nice and deep untilI lost consciousness."

"What did the police say? Conn didn't even mention it." She didn't look at him.

"I didn't know. First I heard about it. Do you think I wouldn't tell you, lamb chop?"

"I didn't report it." What the hell, why not bail the guy out.

"What? Why not?" My turn to get the look from Alexa.

"Because I'm persona non grata there, and I've been told to stay away from them. They wouldn't believe me."

"Persona not grata? Why? That doesn't make sense. They're the police and you're a citizen, even if you are remarkably difficult. They have to be available to you. Don't they?"

"You'll have to ask *them*, Alexa."

"I can't believe Connor wouldn't have mentioned you were persona non grata. Perhaps he didn't know."

I heard him say something naughty under his breath.

"It's not possible, is it, Connor?" I think she could tell by his expression it was possible all right. And Conn McCracken was about to find out first hand about persona non grata.

*       *       *

"Oh." Lindsay turned white as soon as she opened the door. But I was getting used to the effect I had on people.

"It's not what you think." I stepped past her into the marble foyer. Lucky for me, there was no sign of Merv.

She looked worse than I did. But her bruises were of the mind. Her eyes seemed sunken and dull, her skin more like putty than silk. For once, she wasn't wearing perfume.

"What's wrong?" One look told me I'd put my foot in it.

"His memorial service will be tomorrow."

His memorial service. That knocked the breath out of me. There was bound to be a public ceremony for Rina Benning and I would plan to attend that. But who in their right mind would go to a memorial service for a monster like Ralph

Benning? His own mother would probably boycott it. If he ever had a mother. Which reminded me, where was Mrs. P. with the information about the people in Benning's life?

I waited for an invitation to come into the living room. It didn't come. I took my boots off anyway.

"What happened to you?" Lindsay asked.

I slipped my parka into the closet. "An accident."

She smiled, turned and headed into the living room, "That's what we all say. Did you walk into a door? Trip on the stairs?"

I followed. "I shot head first into a snowbank."

"Oh yes, happens a lot." She sank into the sofa and stared at me.

I flushed. "This time it did."

"Who am I to argue?" she said.

"Well, I guess you're right. It was a form of battering."

"I wouldn't have taken you for the type. But Elaine says there's no type. We're all vulnerable."

"Yes, well, I didn't do anything to…" I bit my tongue.

She raised an eyebrow. "Cause it?"

"No. Yes. I mean, it wasn't personal."

"Um-humm."

This time I didn't have a snappy comeback. Of course it was personal. No wonder she had that sad little smile. If a person pushes you into a snowbank, sticks their knees into your back and makes sure you can't get your face out, what else could it be but personal?

"You're right. Pretty goddam personal all right."

"Yes." Her dreamy expression returned. The one the boys seem to be susceptible to.

"You look tired. Can I make us a pot of coffee? I know my way around here."

She frowned. "Coffee? Go ahead. You really think I look tired?"

Oops. Hadn't my sisters always told me you never tell a woman she looks tired unless you want to ruin her day? I did not want to ruin Lindsay's day. "Not tired, just oh, I don't know, distracted, perhaps. I'll put the coffee on. Be right back."

Distracted? More like devastated. Anemic. Or even haunted. I had a better cover when I popped back in with two mugs of coffee five minutes later. "Maybe you're worried about that memorial service."

"A person doesn't get over a bad relationship just because the partner dies, you know."

Lindsay was susceptible to Benning. She had to deal with the death of hope, and the survival of love, fascination and desire. And I still looked with longing at Paul's photo on the wall of Justice for Victims. "Don't I know it."

And Benning, what a residue of slime. Even dead, he sparked powerful emotions. I hated him. If I felt his presence, imagine what it would be like for Lindsay who had loved and feared him.

"Here's what happened to me. I was minding my own business, skating on the canal, on my way over to see you when a guy hit me behind the knees and knocked me into a snowbank. Then he knelt on my back and pushed me into the snow and waited until I lost consciousness. I assume at that point he left."

"My God, you don't know who?"

"No idea. But logic tells me he's connected with this situation."

"But who? Do you think it's because you were coming here?"

"No."

"What if it was? How do you know?"

"No one knew where I was headed. I didn't know myself until I put on my skates and headed down the canal."

"That's one thing to be thankful for, I guess."

"But it had to do with my investigation. I rattled a few cages."

"You must have rattled the wrong one."

"Or the right one. I made someone nervous."

She nibbled a polished nail. "Camilla, maybe you should be the one who's nervous."

"Not my style."

"You could have died."

"Probably not. Thousands of people throng the canal. It would be hard to miss a pair of legs sticking out of a snowbank for any length of time."

"But it wouldn't take long. He was prepared to let you die."

I don't know why this was such a shock to me. I hadn't thought it through logically. I'd thought about being attacked but not about being murdered. Lindsay was right. This upped the ante. Whoever slammed me into that snowbank had been prepared to let me die. And I knew it had to be the same person who killed Benning.

"You're right," I said, after a minute, feeling stupid.

"Did you see anyone?"

I closed my eyes and tried to remember the moment just before my headlong plunge. There had been something familiar. Someone I recognized? Or something. But what?

"No, I didn't see anyone. I think I know who was behind it in general terms, and you can help."

"What do you mean, in general terms?"

"I seem to have created a real buzz with the police. I think that's the secret. I dropped in and made waves before the attack and I think that triggered it. I need to know who might have been Ralph Benning's police contact."

She hesitated. "We don't know for sure that anyone helped him."

"Fair enough. But I need to know who he dealt with."

"Well, he'd been arrested so many times. He knew all the cops."

I was getting impatient, and I let it show.

"Come on, Lindsay, get off the pot. There must have been one in particular. I need to know his name."

I didn't expect her to laugh. "What's so funny?"

"I don't know the name. Ralph never told me. But based on what he implied, you're not searching for *his* name. You're looking for *hers*."

# Twenty

Okay, so my week wasn't going well. I told myself things could have been worse and, sure enough, before long they were.

I figured I'd put in a normal day at work just to show the world. The fact that it was Sunday was no big deal. I opened the JFV door before nine, loaded with Tylenol and ready to fight back. I encountered my first setback. Alvin already occupied the office. The lamplight shone through the paper sun, the scent of coconut suntan lotion filled the air, and Jimmy Buffett was singing about sharks.

"It's Sunday. Why are you here, Alvin?"

"I have a present for you," he said.

"Not a good time, Alvin." Some of the aches and pains were breaking through the Tylenol barrier. Alvin was lucky I didn't make him eat that Jimmy Buffett boxed CD set.

"Listen, Camilla, did you or did you not send me to crawl through the transcripts of trials and newspaper reports of Benning's court appearances to find out which cops had the most dealings with him?"

"Yes."

"And did I not spend huge quantities of my valuable evenings finding facts for you? I am an artist, not a detective, and it's taking away from my time for creative projects."

"Get to the point, Alvin. I don't know what you've been

doing, because you haven't told me."

He turned his pointed nose to the wall.

"And don't sulk."

"Who wouldn't sulk working with you?"

"Fine. Alvin? I'm all ears. I can't wait to get the details."

His arms were folded, one eyebrow was raised and he concentrated on the phone as if it held untold fascination.

Time to bite the bullet.

"Okay. I was rude. I'm sorry, Alvin. I am under a certain amount of stress, and perhaps it's making me a bit testy."

He snorted.

"Maybe more than a bit. But, go ahead, tell me what you found out."

He obviously found the phone mesmerizing.

"Please," I added.

"Fine. After I waded through tons of stuff for hours and hours and hours…"

I bit my tongue.

"…I came up with a few names. But the same names over and over again."

"And?"

He whirled at me.

"Sorry," I said. "It slipped out."

Silence.

"Please continue."

"Well, patterns started to emerge."

I nodded encouragingly.

"You want to see them?"

"Please."

"Then tell why you're always taking things out on me."

"I don't know. I *am* sorry. I mean it." I guess I did, too.

"Okay." He jumped out of the chair and started taping up

large sheets of flip chart paper on the wall. No one loves flip chart paper more than Alvin. His eyes glittered. "Have a gander. Impressive or what?"

The papers, with Alvin's meticulous neon highlighting, were as colourful as quilts. The sheets outlined Benning's arrests, complete with dates, arresting officers, subsequent charges, trial dates, pleas, court rulings and sentences when applicable. The sentences didn't appear often enough to suit me.

"Thoroughly impressive."

He lowered his eyes modestly. "Check the highlighted names."

Two names showed up with far more frequency than any others. You couldn't miss them. Particularly with that hot pink highlighter.

One was Sgt. Leonard Mombourquette.

Well. Well. Well.

The other was Constable Randy Cousins.

"You'll see the pattern," Alvin said.

"Oh yes."

"I did some analysis on the others and there are a few also-rans. Bridesmaids, I guess you could call them."

"Don't use that word."

"Some of these people had four or five encounters. I figured it was worthwhile noting the ones who had more contact with him than you'd expect."

"Those would be the green highlighter?"

"Yipper."

"And those with the blue, have two each. I guess that could happen."

I read the array of incidents, encounters with the law, court dates. Lots of bad stuff there. Incident reports, even those calls that never turned into charges, well, it gave quite a picture.

"Hell of a guy, our Benning," I said."

"Yeah."

"I wish I'd had this information before."

"Think it would have made a difference?"

"You never know."

"Hmmm."

"My point is, Alvin, you found a lot of stuff I didn't encounter in the course of my research into Benning. And it's not like I didn't care deeply about the outcome."

"Well, last spring, you remember, was not a normal time. We had the Mitzi Brochu affair on our minds."

"Remember? I'm not likely to forget."

"It's natural you wouldn't have done as thorough a job."

"Kind of you to put it that way, Alvin, but the fact remains that you, using perfectly legal means, put together a far better collection of information about Benning than I did."

Alvin lowered his eyes.

"Much as it pains me, I must congratulate you," I said. "I'm surprised the courts and the police would be open with you."

Alvin met my eyes. "Well, I wouldn't say *perfectly* legal means."

Ah. "Mombourquette shows up a number of times."

"Ten separate incidents. Possibly I may find a few more of the barely-in-the-picture kind if I keep going back."

"Bit more than you'd expect by chance."

"How many did Conn McCracken have?"

"Didn't find any. I checked wherever Mombourquette showed up. No sign of McCracken's name in any of the encounters."

"That's a relief."

"Oh, yeah," said Alvin.

"But on the other hand, it makes you wonder. McCracken and Mombourquette have been working together for years. Why would Mombourquette be on his own for these incidents with Benning?"

"Crossed my mind too," Alvin said.

"Our friend Lennie might have a long twitchy tail after all."

"Bet he does," said Alvin, "but he's not the most interesting development on these charts."

"I see that." Randy Cousins was number one by a long shot. I wondered if by any strange chance Cousins was one of the guys in the police gym.

"That Randy Cousins, if he'd spent any more time with Benning they'd have been Siamese twins."

"Ugly thought, but spot on, Alvin."

"Natch."

"This Cousins. I guess I'll be tracking him down."

"Maybe I should, Camilla. The police are on to you."

"They're probably on to you too, Alvin."

He looked insulted. "I'm subtle."

"Maybe, but you're not my only secret weapon."

"But, Camilla."

"Excellent work, Alvin. Tell you what, why don't you take the rest of the day off. Take a well-earned break. Enjoy winter."

He opened his mouth. But I had already reached to answer the telephone.

The second setback came when Alvin opened the door of Justice for Victims to an early caller. Sunboy had an extra lei in his hands as a gesture of welcome. Normally I would nip this behaviour early and sharply, but I was busy chewing my nails over current developments. Plus, I was on the phone.

"Sure, Edwina," I was saying. "I do understand. It does not reflect well on the MacPhee family to have one of its members making the news for being in hot water with the Law Society. Don't be silly. Of course I couldn't end up disbarred. And might I remind you, Daddy raised us to fight for what we believe and not to let bullies knock us down and win the day.

Am I correct? This media stuff flap won't kill him, even if he is eighty years old."

When Edwina gets her teeth into you, she never forgets that old rule about chew something forty times and you'll be able to digest it. I wasn't out of the woods yet. "Nearly eighty-one. And how do you know it won't kill him? Are you a doctor now?"

"No, but I could use one after talking to any member of my family for even the shortest time." I ran a hand over my brow as I glanced toward the door where Alvin continued to prevent a large and sombre individual from entering. This person did not appear to be taking kindly to the Day-Glo pink lei gaily hanging from his shoulders. Perhaps it clashed with his police uniform.

A fuss seemed to be developing at the door. But with Edwina blasting in my ear I could only hear one side of it. "No," Alvin protested loudly, "she's not here."

"Are you listening to me, Camilla?" Edwina said.

"I am."

"No, I have no idea where she is." Alvin's chin rode high the way it always does when he lies.

"You'd better be," Edwina said.

"No, she never tells me where she is going. However, she does enjoy this kind of weather, so most likely she's headed out for a bracing hike in the Gatineaus. You might try the trail around Black Lake."

"Yes." No point in arguing with Edwina.

"No, I have no idea when she'll be back."

"I have to get off the phone," I said, before she could launch into another tirade. "Alvin's being naughty."

"Ms. Camilla MacPhee?" The officer deked past Alvin into the office.

"Yes." I carefully disconnected, cutting off a stream of

muffled instruction from Edwina.

Alvin whirled and glared at me. I'm always amazed when eyes can be slanted and yet bulging at the same time. "Oh, you *are* there. Sorry. I didn't see you."

The officer smiled and held out his hand. "Constable Michael Perkins," he said cheerfully.

Like a fool, I took the envelope from him and read the contents.

\* \* \*

"Well, how did I know it was a goddam summons?" I said to Alvin five minutes later as I struggled into my Sorels. "I've never had one before."

"You could have trusted me for once."

"Fine. I should have trusted you." I was speaking to Alvin's bony back.

Constable Perkins waited patiently in the corner. He appeared to be inordinately interested in Alvin's window painting.

"But you didn't believe me, and look what happened. Maybe you'll understand how *I* feel always getting arrested unfairly."

Constable Perkins glanced at Alvin with interest.

"Twice, Alvin, not *always*. Don't exaggerate. And didn't I get you out of it both times?"

"Who dragged me into it both times?"

"But with the best of intentions."

"It always happens."

"Not always. Certainly not always."

"Fine, name one time when it didn't."

"People change, Alvin."

"And also, haven't I ended up in the hospital after following your orders?"

"Well, yes."

"And even in spite of this, when I try to help, you treat me like a jerk."

"But it's purely unintentional. Anyway, you have to admit, Alvin, you've never actually been charged. And they've never kept you in the hospital overnight either."

He opened his mouth. I held up my hand. "Don't argue. Do what I say. Close the office. Don't answer any phone calls. Go home. Don't answer your own phone, because the media will track you down. Wait for me there. If I need you, I'll call here and leave a message. You phone in here every twenty minutes and check the voice mails."

It wasn't much. But I enjoyed issuing a few orders. Because I didn't know how the hell to get over this latest hurdle.

*   *   *

I kept my scratched nose in the air as Constable Perkins marched me into the Elgin Street police station. I noticed more than a few familiar police faces smirking. What a joke. It seemed like forever before I found myself nose to nose with a Justice of the Peace to discuss bail. I'd never met this JP before. He didn't grin. Neither did I.

Criminal harassment charges were no laughing matter. I was damned lucky to get released on my own recognizance pending my preliminary hearing. I noticed the JP eyeing my battered face, and I could almost see the thoughts forming in his head. I did my best not to look like the kind of person who gets into bar fights.

My experience with JPs hadn't been great until this point. I decided against using any legal pyrotechnics until I appeared before a judge who actually had a law degree. I kept my nose clean and my mouth closed.

Naturally, I agreed to the restrictions ordered by the court.

I would stay away from Elaine Ekstein and from WAVE. I definitely would not initiate contact with either Elaine or her staff. No problem.

I know when I'm licked.

*   *   *

On my way out, I whirled as Mombourquette scurried up behind me.

"Section 264, Camilla. Heavy. Even for you."

"Very funny, Lennie."

"At least I can laugh," he said. "I bet your sister won't."

I didn't give him the satisfaction of responding.

"Speaking of funny, Leonard, your colleague, a Constable Randy Cousins? Little too close to Benning for mere coincidence. Care to comment?"

His whiskers twitched.

"Since we're chatting, who was that female officer who came over when we were in the gym yesterday? Tall girl, spiky blonde hair? The one working the rowing machine."

"Forget it."

"Do you have some reason for not answering, Leonard? Like maybe she was Ralph Benning's girlfriend?"

"You'd better get out of here, Camilla, before you get hit with a second charge. You won't be strutting around with a sneer next time."

I wanted to stay and argue about the sneer, but reason prevailed, and I left. There were less bothersome ways of finding out who's who and where in the police.

# Twenty-One

Half an hour later, I pulled my rental car in front of a scruffy building in the heart of old Hull. The Château Alvin. He didn't answer his phone, doing what I told him for once. I didn't feel like waiting until he picked up my latest voice mail message.

I followed a child in a bulky snowsuit and a tuque in through the supposedly locked front door and sniffed the illicit substances in the air. Alvin was home and probably still sulking. After two minutes of steady knocking, the door opened a finger's width.

Alvin said, "What, out of the slammer already?"

"I want to come in. I'll explain what's happening and you can decide whether or not you want to help me or whether you want to continue to bitch about perceived slights."

The child, who had been watching our exchange like it was a game, lost interest when I took a step through the door. Just in time, I remembered my last visit, and I gripped the door frame to keep from falling into darkness.

"You don't have to do that any more," Alvin said. "I've redecorated."

Jimmy Buffett should have been my first clue. Alvin's bathing suit with the watermelon motif should have been the second. The floors of the apartment had disappeared under a warm carpet of sand. Where there had been walls, an endless aqua ocean flowed, converging with clear blue sky up toward the ceiling.

"Where did you get the sand?"

"Here and there," Alvin said obliquely. "Artists have to be resourceful."

If I had to count my blessings, I'd put not being Alvin's landlord close to the top of the list.

Within a minute, beads of sweat had formed on my forehead. I slipped out of my parka and boots. I draped the parka over the nearest palm tree and propped the boots in front of the beer cooler. I slumped into a striped beach chair.

The only familiar landmarks were Alvin's big old fridge in the middle of the living room and the toilet with the plant growing out of it. The last time I'd been here it had been an ivy. This was bougainvillea.

It might kill me being nice to Alvin, but I knew there was no other way. I needed a big-time payoff, so I made the first investment. "I'm sorry, Alvin, for the bad things that have happened to you. I realize I'm not always the easiest person to deal with."

His bony shoulders relaxed. "I guess you had a bad day, getting charged. Hey, how about a margarita?"

I shook my head. All I needed was a snootful of tequila to scramble my brain. "I need a cup of tea."

"Hibiscus tea?"

"No thanks."

"Papaya-mango tea?"

I didn't believe there was any such thing, but I wanted to be on the safe side. "Regular, please. Like your mother would make."

Alvin loped across the sand dune and into the clear blue sea to the kitchen. He is one of those people who can talk and lope at the same time.

I made myself comfortable, peeled off my red socks and wiggled my toes in the sand while Alvin made the tea. I spent the next few minutes speculating about how he managed to warm the sand.

Alvin finally showed up bearing a silver tray and the pink flowered tea pot and matching cups and saucers I knew had belonged to his grandmother. This time I was impressed to note he had sugar cubes with a small silver set of tongs to serve them. It might have been a bit formal for the beach if it hadn't been for the little umbrella in each cup.

I put four sugar cubes in my tea, which was hot, strong and black in the best Cape Breton tradition. Then I filled him in on the scene at the police station.

"Wow. Elaine contacted the police to have a harassment charge laid against you?"

"Yep. And they took her seriously."

"Is it serious?"

"You bet. If it gets past the preliminary hearing and goes to trial, it will be."

"They couldn't convict you."

"Life has been full of surprises these past few days, Alvin. The usual couldn'ts don't apply."

Alvin scratched his head. "Why wouldn't the other people at WAVE try to talk sense to her?"

"You tell me, Alvin. None of it makes any sense. It's a high price to pay for some media profile. Most people draw the line at murder as a tactic."

"For once, you might be right."

"Even more troubling is the issue of the police and what they have to hide. Who they want to protect. They're willing to let an innocent person get sent to jail to protect someone. Listen to this, I haven't had a chance to tell you yet, but

Lindsay says Benning's police contact was a woman."

Most gratifying. Alvin came close to dropping his heirloom cup.

I continued. "I wonder if it might not be the same female cop who followed me to the door of the cop shop less than an hour before I was attacked. Maybe she has some connection to this Randy Cousins. Maybe they work together, or they're partners."

"Uh-oh. I can see where you're headed."

"Yep. If I do what I have to and help Elaine help herself, I'm headed for jail, same as her."

"What do you need me to do? Go out to the RDC and talk to her?"

I didn't give this a thought. "Too dangerous, Alvin. As my employee, you are bound by the *no contact* conditions. I'd get clapped in the slammer and you'd be right behind me."

Alvin kicked at the sand. "I don't want to get arrested again."

"Can't say I blame you. But what I have in mind won't lead to any problems for you."

He lifted his sunglasses and stared at me, unblinking. "Are you sure this time?"

"Trust me."

He rolled his eyes. "Fine, Camilla. Tell me what you want me to do."

"Find me Randy Cousins and get a name for our female officer. Priority One. I'm beginning to ask myself if they're in it together."

Alvin said, "I'll call in the reserves."

Mrs. P. would like that.

\* \* \*

With Alvin on the job, I was able to prepare for my skating date with P. J. and the kids. This involved taking a warm bath and the maximum dose of Tylenol.

I knew Alvin would be leaving no stone unturned while he found out which one Randy Cousins had crawled out from under. Even though I'd be back on the canal where someone had nearly killed me the night before, I was reasonably relaxed when P. J. rang my doorbell.

I was glad to see him. But then I always am. He showed his reporter side, asking questions immediately about my injuries. I made sure my answers were the type that wouldn't show up in the next day's paper.

"It's rude to ask a woman about her facial abrasions."

"Thank you, Miss Manners. But I got a tip for you. Maybe you shouldn't be out on your own until they find whoever killed Benning. You know where I am, when you have trouble. No questions asked."

"Yeah, right."

The kids were tiny genetic replicas of their uncle from the red curly hair to the gaps between the front teeth. I found I was glad to see them too. They looked so much like him, I felt I already knew them. Plus they both gave the impression they'd stop at nothing to get what they wanted. Apparently another family trait. Luckily, they were five and six years old, so what they wanted was to eat a lot of junk food and skate around in circles making war whoops.

P. J. leaned over and whispered: "Don't ask them about their family life. Things are iffy. We don't want to set them off."

I certainly didn't want to set them off. I understand how a person wouldn't want to be reminded of family life. The younger one was intrigued by my face.

"Did it bleed a lot?" he asked.

"No," I said.

"Oh." There was no mistaking the disappointment in his voice.

"Hey, with any luck I'll fall down again."

P. J. laughed. I like that in a man. "I don't want you spoiling them, Tiger."

It was a pleasant evening for all of us. I didn't make anyone mad, and no one made me mad. The kids snacked on BeaverTails and hot chocolate and got a lot of exercise. I'm not sure what P. J. got out of it, but since we didn't talk about Benning, Elaine, my latest charges or related matters, it couldn't have been a story.

The kids had a fairly elastic bedtime, it seemed, but by eight-thirty they were ready to drop. So was I.

P. J. and I slipped off our skates on the bench. "I had an okay time, Tiger."

"Me, too. Didn't even make me sick." Two small bodies snuggled up. We wiggled their skates off and slid their little feet into their boots. P. J. warmed the inside of the boots first with his hands. "We should do it again."

"Too late for skating. The forecast calls for more warm weather. This is probably the last decent night to skate on the canal."

"No problem. The kids like to swim."

It was safe to say that. They were asleep.

I stood guard over them while P. J. trotted off to get his car. Five minutes later, we slung them over our shoulders and settled them onto the blanket on the back seat. My shoulder ached like hell, but I figured it was worth it.

P. J. dropped me off first. I yawned. "Thanks for not taking advantage of my weakened state to get a sensational item for the howling masses."

He checked his watch. "That reminds me. Gotta file by ten."

As much as I liked the guy, I knew I'd feel more comfortable when tomorrow came and there was no exposé of the innermost thoughts of arch-criminal Camilla MacPhee by crusading crime reporter, P.J. Lynch.

*　　*　　*

My first clue was the glowing tip of a cigarette in the gloom of my hallway on the sixteenth floor. A small tendril of smoke escaped from the open door on the right.

"Ah, Mrs. Parnell. How are you?"

"Excellent, Ms. MacPhee."

I had a pleasant afterglow from the skating experience, so I decided not to whine about her line being busy all the time and the fact she never answered her door anymore.

"You may be interested in the results of the latest research."

"Actually, I'm interested in collapsing into bed."

"My colleague has filled me in on your recent misadventures, the near-disaster on the canal and the unfortunate encounter with the constabulary. Nevertheless, you are always a trooper. May I suggest you soldier on a bit longer, Ms. MacPhee. You will find what I have to show you well worth the effort."

I decided to save time and get it over with. I followed Mrs. P. into her apartment where the speakers were booming Holst's *The Planets*, "Mars" specifically. The lovebirds shrieked even more than usual, and Alvin was curled up on the leather lounger.

"Make yourself at home," Mrs. Parnell lurched toward the bottle of Harvey's. "How about a drink?"

Alvin shook his head. "That stuff will rot your brain."

I said, "And I'll need my brain to deal with you."

I had to negotiate my way around a laptop computer. Mrs. Parnell splashed healthy doses into two tallish glasses. "Sit down, Ms. MacPhee, and don't hound the boy. I am grateful he included me in this operation."

I sat. A quick slug of the Harvey's seemed like a practical idea.

"Lights," Mrs. Parnell said.

Alvin lifted a languid arm and flicked off the lamp.

"Let 'er roll," Mrs. P. said.

Alvin moved over to the computer.

"We thought you'd like to see the officer who was most often associated with Ralph Benning in recent years."

Oh great. A nice shot of Randy Cousins. Even in the dark, I could feel the two of them smiling. A large image projected itself onto the far wall. It was someone I recognized. The woman from the gym.

"Get to the point. I need to see what Randy Cousins looks like."

"Allow me, Ms. MacPhee, to introduce you to Constable Miranda Cousins. Better known as Randy."

# Twenty-Two

Lucky me. The first person who spoke to me the next morning was Mia Reilly in the Second Cup. First, she furrowed her perfect brow. For once, I smiled at her. Running into Mia without even trying would save me the task of tracking her down at the Office of the Crown Attorney. Information flows both ways. This encounter would allow me to slip a few hints into the conversation. As much as I looked forward to tossing Randy Cousins in Mia's face, I didn't want to give away the surprise. We didn't have any firm proof yet that Cousins was implicated in the Benning situation. You don't want to play your hand too soon.

"Camilla." She tossed the artful blonde hair for punctuation.

"Mia."

"What happened to you?"

"Me? Nothing."

"But you look as if you had some kind of terrible accident."

"A little tumble on the canal. Not serious."

"Oh." I sensed disappointment. "No broken bones?"

"Listen, Mia, I wanted to say I have no hard feelings about that complaint to the Law Society. Excellent PR for the Crown."

"You have no hard feelings? Our office is about to lodge a formal complaint against you to the Law Society because you've been misrepresenting yourself as Elaine Ekstein's lawyer. She's the one who should have hard feelings. Not smart, Camilla."

I turned away long enough to order a large latte and a couple of *biscotti*. As convenient as this meeting was, I would require a wee bit of soothing afterwards. "That's just the kind of reminder I needed to regain perspective. Stop and enjoy life."

"Well, it certainly seems serious to me. I'd be *suicidal.*"

She sure couldn't feign sympathy with any semblance of believability.

"Not me." I picked up my *latte* and headed to the service area to put extra chocolate sprinkles on it. Why not? I was earning them.

"Did you hear me? A *complaint.* That would be so damaging to your career. You have totally upset some important people. You could end up being disbarred. But you don't care much about your career, do you?"

"Bingo, Mia. I couldn't care less. I care about justice, but that's not the same."

"Oh, you are so hard to figure."

"Hey. There's a table. And it's early. Eight-fifteen. Feel like having a chat?"

She straightened. "I can't be giving you information about the case. Especially after you've been charged with criminal harassment."

"That case will get tossed out of court, as we both well know."

"Even so…"

"Trust me, I'm abiding by the court-ordered restrictions, I'm off the case. Remember? I'm getting on with life. Catching up with my social life and touching base with friends. I wanted to hear all about your engagement. And for once it would be nice to drink a *latte* before it's cold. But hey, don't worry about it. Some other time."

"Oh. If it's personal stuff and nothing to do with Elaine Ekstein or our complaint, I guess that would be above board."

Lucky again. The corner of the banquette was available for once. My favourite spot if I actually have time to sit in the Second Cup. I hoped spending a few minutes with Mia Reilly wouldn't ruin it for me.

"Well, Mia." I squeezed behind the table and picked up my *latte*. "Lot's happening, I bet."

"Oh, yes," she said, flashing her gonzo diamond again.

Okay, my girl, it's false sense of security time. "That's quite the engagement ring. Tell about your fiancé. What's his name?"

"Jay. Jay Blackwell. He's great. He's just made partner at Harrington, Lawson and Bly."

Like I cared. I did my best not to yawn. "Golly. Partner. At Harrington Lawson. Big guns. What an achievement for someone in their thirties."

The smile slipped. "Yes, well, he's not exactly in his thirties."

"Oh. Even forties. I mean, it's still a big deal." I may not be the most sensitive person in the world, but I did notice her lips pursing. Since the idea was to keep her in a good mood, I decided to nip that discussion before she had to reveal lover boy was already collecting CPP.

"Age doesn't matter, partner in a big firm, that's terrific." She relaxed a bit. I would have loved to have given her a hard time, but I had to worry about Elaine's wellbeing. "And what about you?" I knew Mia wouldn't want to talk about me unless it was to reiterate my more embarrassing offences and complaints. "I heard a rumour you're in line for a promotion."

"Oh that," she trilled. "Well, yes, they want me, but I have a fabulous opportunity coming up."

"Really?" I tried again not to yawn.

"Yes." She leaned forward, ready to indulge a girlish conspiracy. "What is it?"

"I have been offered a position at Reid Lalonde. Corporate and property law. Serious stuff. What I want to do. Not this crap about getting fifteen-year-old car thieves to write essays on The Young Offenders' Act."

"Mmmm."

"I start next month."

"Fabulous, Mia. You'll be great in Real Estate law. A chance to make a difference."

"Corporate and property, but yes, it's so exciting. And what about you, Camilla? What's new in your life?"

"Let's see. No ring, no promotions, no new jobs, and not even the old job I was on with Elaine. But I did go skating with P. J. Lynch and his two nephews last night. Real neat little guys. Hey, that's three new men."

"You don't have to lie to me, Camilla. It's okay not to have dates. You can expect a dry spell every now and then."

"What? I'm not lying."

"You said you went skating with P. J. and his nephews."

"And I did. Why would I lie about that? If I tell a whopper, at least I make it interesting."

She wagged her manicured nail at me. "Maybe it's not interesting, but it *is* a lie. You should at least get your facts straight if you're going to prevaricate."

"What do you mean, get my facts straight?"

"This is Ottawa, remember. Everyone knows everyone. I grew up in Westboro with P. J. He lived half a block away, and I even used to babysit for him. He's an only child. He doesn't have any nephews. You'll have to do better, Camilla."

I could feel my heart thumping. Had P. J. lied to me? Set me up? She had to be wrong. But what if she were right?

Mia wrinkled her forehead and ran her fingers through her blonde bob. As an attempt to appear concerned, it might earn her two out of five points. "Camilla, shouldn't you get a serious job? I remember when you were ambitious. When Paul was alive. Now you're always in trouble. I don't want to tell you how to live your life, but why do you want to bang your head against another wall? That is so non-productive."

"Silly me. But back to your career move. Maybe we can get together more often now that you won't have to worry about conflict of interest because of my involvement with controversial cases like Elaine Ekstein's."

You could practically hear her alarm bells. "I thought you weren't involved with the case any more."

"Well, I'm not. But people keep giving me information despite this. Who'll be taking over the case after you leave?"

"I don't even have this case. I'm assisting. But you have to pass on information. You know the rules, Camilla. You can't keep relevant details to yourself."

"You see my problem, I'm supposed to keep my nose out of the case. I could get my bail revoked. This information is tricky."

She checked her attractive gold watch and stood up. "Oops, time to go. What do you want from me, Camilla? Do you want to give me the details and have me pass it on in the form of rumour?"

"Excellent, Mia. Thank you."

"Don't thank me. I'm not planning to join you in Deadendsville."

"Here's the deal. You decide what to do. The Crown should be taking a close look at a particular police officer with a surprisingly high number of encounters with Benning. Way more than could happen by chance. Do you get my drift here, Mia? My anonymous phone caller tells me there's fire behind the smoke."

"That old rumour. We're well aware of it, believe me. I don't think there's much there. And we had hopes of finding something solid, but it didn't pan out. But I will pass it on to be on the safe side. Take some advice, Camilla. Pull yourself together and get back into practice. I hate to see you in these situations."

Nice bit of subterfuge. But I knew I had her attention. "Tell them it's worth looking at the relationship with Benning and an officer called Randy Cousins."

She slipped into her coat and wound a silk-lined paisley scarf around her neck. Her fur-lined leather gloves matched the rich green in the scarf. She fixed me with a strange look. "You should get your hair done, Camilla. Even without the scraped cheeks, you used to look a lot better. Why not join a fitness club and get a makeover, and then you might not have to invent imaginary dates."

Well, that was one way to react to news on a potential killer, but, of course, Mia was enough of a bitch to make up that story about P. J. being an only child. She knew it would get under my skin. She waltzed out the door before I had stopped biting my tongue. I reminded myself some things are worse than a cold coffee.

It wasn't long before I encountered a few of them.

\*   \*   \*

"No, I cannot accept a collect call for Mr. Alvin Ferguson." I slammed down the phone. As if I weren't already in a bad enough mood over P. J.

Alvin's head shot up at his desk where he'd been stuck in what looked like an elderly edition of *Canadian Gardening*.

"Oh, nice. I open up my home to you, I knock myself out getting information, I spend my time trying to get you out of bad situations, I get half-killed being a decoy for you, putting my life in danger tracking cops, and what do you do? You hang up on my mother."

"We've had this conversation before, Alvin. I did not hang up on your mother. I hung up on the automated collect call request system. Justice for Victims does not accept personal collect calls. Get used to it. And your life was not in danger finding out about Randy Cousins."

He flicked his ponytail over his shoulder and didn't say a word. I hate it when he gives in so easily. Then I have to wait.

"Well," he said, with unexpected pleasantness, "Mrs. Parnell would like you to give her a dingle."

"As soon as I get home. I have a lot to talk to her about."

"Your decision," Alvin said.

"And speaking of decisions, remember we decided you would check out the medical literature and determine how long a body would take to freeze."

"Done. It's hard to be one hundred per cent sure, but it looks like your first guess was right. It would have taken Benning a lot longer than that to freeze. Based on what I read, you shouldn't have any trouble getting some pathologist to back you up."

"Hmm. Great news. Too bad we're off the case."

"Oh well, maybe you could leak that information to the *Citizen*."

I opened my mouth but found I couldn't bring myself to tell Alvin that my buddy P. J. might turn out to be a lying snake.

"That it?" I said, instead.

"Not quite. Alexa called. Apparently her kids have arrived for the wedding. I wasn't even aware Alexa had children."

"No reason you would be, Alvin. She has two boys, both older than you. My nephews have been out of the nest for years. Great guys."

He let it slide. "Your sisters are having a shindig for Alexa and Conn tonight at the National Arts Centre Panorama Room. Like a shower, only it's a fundraiser."

"Fundraiser? Alexa and Conn don't need funds raised."

"Not for them. Instead of gifts, people make donations to their favourite charity. Which happens to be the Boys and Girls Club."

It's hard to argue with the Boys and Girls Club.

"A great cause," Alvin said. "Promises to be a snazzy affair. Family and special guests. How come you never mentioned it?"

"I didn't know."

"You didn't know? I knew. Why wouldn't you know?"

"I don't know why I don't know and I don't know why you do." Was I losing my mind? I had no recollection of this latest event. I wasn't sure what I could wear to it. Which reminded me Alexa had been awfully quiet about that bridesmaid's dress. I wondered if this alleged shower was some elaborate ploy to get me into a dress shop. Nah. Far-fetched, even for my family. Whether it was or wasn't, maybe I could wiggle out of it since I was nothing but an embarrassment anyway.

"Too late," Alvin said.

"What?"

"Forget what you're thinking. And you do have to go. I took the liberty of telling Edwina you'd been saying how much you were hoping to get together *en famille* again. Stan will pick you up at six-thirty."

"Maybe you'd better call her back and tell her you were hallucinating at the time."

"Well, I would, of course, but, she's gone out for the day. Wedding preparations for Alexa's big event."

"You have a lot of nerve, interfering with my family."

"That's exactly the way I see it with you, Camilla. I guess we're birds of a feather."

"Flock off then."

"Very funny. I'm looking forward to the big event," said Alvin.

"What?"

"It sounds great."

"It sounds hellish, but you will have to take my word for it, because you will not be there. And before you stick your head back in that magazine, here's a task for you."

*   *   *

Okay. I was limited in what I could do. My support systems were in the toilet. A lot of doors had closed. But nothing in my bail restrictions prevented me from talking to a pathologist.

I made a beeline for the Ottawa Hospital and hotfooted down the hallway to the pathology department. Dr. Harry Varty had a puzzled look when I finally tracked him down in a cold green hallway.

"Glad you're feeling better." I seized his hand and shook it. I tried not to dwell on where that hand might have been. "Camilla MacPhee. Nice of you to make time for me."

"I don't believe I…"

"This won't hurt a bit."

"Wait a minute. Camilla MacPhee? Why do I know that name. Have you been in the news? Aren't you the lawyer who was just disbarred?"

This was hardly fair. "I have not been disbarred. Any

complaint will probably be dismissed since it's without foundation."

"And weren't you charged with assault?"

"Assault? Certainly not. There is a misinterpretation of some of my activities. A bit of grandstanding by certain interested parties."

"What happened to your face?"

"Not relevant."

"At any rate, I don't believe you have an appointment."

None of his clients would have appointments, but it wasn't the time to mention that. But he wasn't finished. "And after what I read, I won't see you without checking with the police first."

"It's just a few questions, for God's sake," I said. "Don't be afraid to stand on your own two feet."

But he was already on the other side of his office door.

*   *   *

So that didn't go well either. Never mind. He wasn't the only pathologist in the world. Benning must have died earlier in the afternoon or early evening. It was just a matter of time until I confirmed it.

And that would be great news. Elaine was always overbooked for every minute of the day. Once a time of death was established it would be easy to poke holes in her story. Another positive: Lindsay had been in our sight all day and into the late evening.

Neither one of them could have killed him.

I felt like dancing, although not necessarily at a family party, even though a number of bothersome questions remained. Why did Lindsay lie about her missing sweater? Who wore Elaine's coat and hat in the Crystal Garden at two in the morning? And more to the point, how?

But first, time to nail Elaine's activities. It would help to get a gander at her agenda for the day. How the hell could I find out without visiting the WAVE office or talking to Elaine? Big no-nos.

Until I figured out what P. J. was up to, I couldn't trust him either. My sisters were tied up until after the wedding. The WAVE staff and Elaine knew Alvin. Breaking into the WAVE office under cover of darkness seemed out of the question, mainly because of Alexa's shower. I surprised myself at how easily I pondered a little B and E. It showed how the system creates criminals.

I could have enlisted Mrs. Parnell, but I had other plans for her. Anyway, I had one more item of business to take care of myself.

\*　　\*　　\*

"Hello," I chirped into the phone. "I represent JFV Research Associates. We're doing a survey about the satisfactions of grandparenting. Do you have a minute to answer a few questions."

"I have the minute, but I don't have the grandchildren."

"Sorry to hear that," I said to Mrs. Hector Lynch. She had no idea how sorry. "Could you answer a few questions, anyway? It would help others."

"Sure, why not." P. J.'s mom said.

"Wonderful. How many children do you have?"

"One."

"And how old is he or she?"

"He's twenty-nine, and since you mention it, it's high time he settled down and produced a few grandchildren."

"Hmmm. No daughters, then?"

"No."

"Stepdaughters?"

"No, just the one boy."

"I see. Nieces?"

"No."

"Nephews?"

"Sorry."

I took a deep breath. "Are there any small children in your life?"

"Not really."

"Little red-haired neighbour kids?"

"Pardon me? Exactly what kind of a survey is this again?"

"Thank you, you've been very helpful."

\*　　\*　　\*

"No problem, Ms. MacPhee." Mrs. Parnell beamed.

"Glad to hear it." I accepted a refill of Harvey's Bristol Cream. I felt like grabbing the bottle and chug-a-lugging.

I was sitting on her black leather sofa listening to big sounds from her massive stereo system and wishing her lovebirds didn't have quite such loud and unappealing calls.

"Exactly the kind of challenge I've been needing. Get me away from the computer and the phone."

"I thought it might be."

Mrs. Parnell raised her glass in a toast. "Yes, here's to being back in the swing of things. I have felt a sense of failure since my web searches and calls failed to produce the desired results. Many interesting tidbits though, fascinating, but false steps."

"Don't worry about it. Benning's relationships would be clandestine anyway, not likely to be publicly available."

"Still, I thought I would turn up something, if not on

Benning's criminal connections or family, then at least on Rina Benning's relatives. Nothing but dead ends."

"It's probably good news, Mrs. P. If there are no other significant leads, we can focus on Randy Cousins. You and Alvin did one hell of a job there."

"Nevertheless, I feel like a fool, leading the troops astray, wasting time."

"Something wrong with those love birds, Mrs. P.?"

"The last time they were terribly agitated, I believe it had to do with your cat, Ms. MacPhee."

"*Your* cat. So you're ready to take on the challenge?"

"With pleasure. I'm tied up this evening, but tomorrow's clear. I'll be in the trenches."

\* \* \*

Back in my own apartment, soaking in the tub and making plans for the next bit of investigating, I had a moment's niggle about what kind of trouble Mrs. P. could get into. But the task seemed straightforward.

Her challenge did not extend to the real battlefield. She was an innocent-looking old lady most people would not associate with me. What could go wrong? I relaxed, smiled and splashed a few bubbles in the direction of the calico cat.

We were getting somewhere on the Randy Cousins front, and Mrs. P. would move that forward nicely. As soon as I found confirmation about freezing times, we'd get Elaine back on the street, where she could continue her life's work of annoying everyone she met.

No matter what the evening held, tomorrow looked promising.

# Twenty-Three

The ride to the NAC would have been tense even if Alvin and Mrs. Parnell hadn't been in the Buick along with Edwina, Stan and me. On the up side, in deference to her bad legs, Mrs. Parnell was installed in the front seat, leaving me to stew in the back with Edwina. On the down side, Alvin was also in the back seat, giving me one more thing to stew about.

"Should be a great evening," he said.

I kept my mouth shut.

"Fine food, desserts, nice view. Hmmm."

I bit my tongue.

"I bet it cost a bundle."

"It will be worth it," Edwina said.

"It better be." And I'd thought Stan was asleep at the wheel.

"Lively family conversations." Alvin just wouldn't shut up.

"And the wedding," Mrs. Parnell boomed from the front seat. "Looking forward to an update."

Stan snickered. "Oh, you'll hear about the big wedding."

I turned to Edwina and whispered. "It's only a week until the wedding. Why do we have another social event? I have things to do."

"Smarten up, Camilla. Everyone's busy. Stan and I planned this evening in place of the traditional dinner after the rehearsal."

"Wait a minute, I thought it was a shower."

"It's in place of both. People are thrilled for Alexa and Conn. They want to show it. But, of course, they're trying to combine two households, so they don't need anything. And anyway, it's a nice surprise, which is why we didn't tell you until today, in case you…"

At least I hadn't forgotten it. For some reason, I had been kept in the dark. I thought that was a nice change with my family. "All these parties are too much for Daddy."

"Exactly why we're doing it. We're spreading out the celebrations. We don't want him getting exhausted, and he wanted us together. He's excited about the boys being home."

I gave up. I stared out the window up the hill as we whipped past the Parliament Buildings on Wellington until I felt Edwina's sharp elbow in my ribs. "As for you, Camilla, nobody will mention the mess you made of your face or the trouble with the Law Society and the police. You can reciprocate by behaving like a functioning member of the family. No buts. No smart remarks. Just do it."

"Okay."

"And if that's what I think it is on your upper lip, you'd damn well better get waxed before the wedding, missy."

\*   \*   \*

A little of my sisters goes a long way. This would be a lot of my sisters. They made a big show of cooing over Alexa's tall blonde boys, Scott and Andy. The boys were full of news about their careers. Promotions, transfers, Silicon Valley acronyms. Edwina and Donalda pressed them for information about girlfriends.

Mrs. Parnell and Alvin also received the visiting royalty treatment. As for me, I was conscious of ice crystals forming on the tips of my ears. To say nothing of my upper lip.

"Mrs. Parnell, we're very pleased you could join us," Donalda said, helping to steady the walker and guide Mrs. P. to our table.

"Any time," Mrs. P. said. "All I ever need is an invitation."

"Of course, you have a standing invitation to any of our family dinners," Edwina said, lifting one powerful eyebrow. "Surely Camilla must have mentioned it."

Damn.

"I'm sure she must have, but the old memory's not what it used to be."

"Alvin! What a lovely shirt," Donalda said. "So vibrant. Just what we need to lift our spirits."

I was beginning to think he could blush on demand.

My father was already seated along with Donalda and Joe at a long table with a view of the canal. "Violet," he said, standing and adjusting his tie.

Mrs. Parnell gave as close as you could come to a girlish pirouette while clutching the handle of an aluminum walker.

As a special treat, Alvin had brought Day-Glo leis for everyone. We looked most festive as we waited with the lights low to surprise the bejesus out of Alexa and Conn.

It promised to be a long, long night.

*   *   *

"Gee." Alvin swallowed one more chocolate truffle. "It's getting late, and I haven't heard the latest about the wedding plans."

"Yes," said Mrs. Parnell, "I'd love to have the details."

Oh, nice. From the frying pan into the fire.

"You have your invitation, I hope," my father said.

"Oh, yes," Mrs. P. said. "I can't wait."

"Me neither," said Alvin.

What?

"One week from tonight," Donalda said with a glance in my direction.

"Under control," Edwina said, firmly.

Alexa fixed me with a look. A dress shop would have been a palatable alternative to this shindig, but it seemed better not to mention it.

"We're ready. Even the problem with Camilla's dress is solved," Alexa said.

"I don't believe I've ever been to a candlelight wedding on Valentine's Day," said Mrs. Parnell. "It sounds romantic."

My father said, "Very romantic."

When your parents hit eighty, you'd think you could count on them to settle down and not be making cow eyes at the neighbours.

"Let's see." Edwina ticked items off on her fingers. "The flowers have been selected, cream-coloured roses and callas, the colour scheme's worked out, the favours are ready, the seating arrangements are done, the music's been chosen, the caterer's been whipped into shape. St. Jim's is booked. The men have their tuxes ready. Andy and Scott are here, ready to waltz Alexa down the aisle. Except Camilla has shown not the slightest interest in any of the preparations…"

"What do you mean, the problem with Camilla's dress is solved?" I said.

Alexa said: "Edwina selected one for you. It's being shortened. Ready tomorrow. You don't even have to pick it up."

They do say be careful what you wish for. Having my bail revoked started to look like a better prospect than wearing a bridemaid's dress selected by the Starch Queen.

"What kind of music?" Alvin said. "I have a superb Jimmy Buffett collection. I'd be glad to let you have it."

I would owe him one for the attempt at deflection.

"Then," Edwina said, with just the tiniest flicker in Alvin's direction, "there's just the rehearsal."

"Rehearsal?" I blurted.

"Oh, Camilla."

I hate it when they all speak at once. "Okay, okay, of course, the wedding's a big deal. But aren't they all the same? It's not like we haven't done it before." Everyone was looking at me. "I thought this was in place of the rehearsal. What?"

Edwina narrowed her eyes, "Of course, there's a rehearsal. It's a time-honoured tradition. Although you appear to be unaware of it."

I thought I heard Alexa sniffle.

Edwina crossed her arms. "For my peace of mind, Camilla, tell us where the rehearsal is and when."

Mrs. Parnell leaned forward and whispered to me, "She brings to mind Churchill at his finest hour."

I can think on my feet. Where would it be? Daddy always says when your back's to the wall, use your brain.

"St. Jim's, of course. Sunday night."

Edwina's eyebrow remained raised.

"Saturday," I amended. You probably can't have a rehearsal on a Sunday.

Edwina's nostrils flared. I was running out of options.

"Friday evening then." I detected a sigh of relief around the table. "What are you worried about? I'll be there."

That did the trick. Conversation turned to the wonderful view of the canal.

"Terribly romantic," Mrs. Parnell said. "With those twinkly lights and the fresh snow and skaters."

My father smiled. "We must come here again."

Alexa leaned over and whispered, "Let's go to the ladies', Camilla."

"I don't need to go."

"Yes, you do."

"What? Ouch. Okay."

Once we were through the door, she let me have it. "I want you to promise on your honour to be nice to the best man. Is that clear?"

The best man. Maybe I *was* underinvolved in this wedding. I tried to remember who the best man was. One of Alexa's boys? But hadn't Edwina just said they were walking her down the aisle? Of course, they could do both. I couldn't remember anyone mentioning it. I racked my brain, but it was full of Benning and Lindsay and Elaine Ekstein. No matter what, I knew better than to let on I had no idea who the best man was.

"Why wouldn't I be nice to the best man?"

Alexa leaned over and whispered, "Promise you won't make those horrible remarks about his tail getting caught in the door."

When we returned to the table, Leonard Mombourquette lifted his champagne glass to toast Alexa. His whiskers twitched.

# Twenty-Four

It's hard to believe a twisted creep like Benning could have a following. But if you judged by his funeral service, he did.

My bail conditions said nothing about staying away from Benning family and friends. So that was good. I didn't have to put a bag over my head. I slipped into the back row as the ceremony was starting.

The forces of good were well represented. At the opposite side of the church was Alvin, wearing black, perfect for a requiem if you didn't count the crimson sneakers. I assumed he was scanning the mourners from behind his sunglasses.

Mrs. Parnell had parked herself off to the side. Not in disguise but, as she likes to say, nobody gives old war horses a second look. A smattering of people huddled here and there. I was disturbed by the ordinary appearance of this small gathering. Somehow you'd expect Ralph Benning's enormous evil to leave behind mourners with a twisted, bizarre look.

I wasn't surprised to see Lindsay or Benning's lawyer. But Conn McCracken and Mombourquette knocked me for a loop. And Constable Miranda Cousins was a bonus. I'd heard the cops like to check out funerals for suspects, but talk about overkill. Especially since the state had slapped Elaine behind Plexiglas and steel.

I found myself calculating their average hourly salaries and adding travel time for good measure. I factored in the cost for the legal aid lawyer who was gamely keeping up the pretence that Benning had been worth defending. Quite a tidy sum. Benning had been a one-man growth industry for the local legal eagles.

Wouldn't the local newspapers love to get their mitts on that idea? I decided to mention it to my questionable friend, P. J. Lynch, since I spotted his tousled red head on the far side of the church. He'd probably include the cost of the assistant crown attorney. Of course, Mia was no doubt pretending that poor murdered Ralph Benning was the victim of a horrible crime, the better to build a case against Elaine. On the other hand, she wouldn't get many excuses to wear that dramatic black hat. And I had to admit, she looked damned good in it.

Mia would count on a prime photo op after this funeral. That hadn't mattered to Lindsay, who was the only person in the church crying steadily. She couldn't have looked worse.

The service was one-size-fits-all. How many times had I been told we celebrate God and not the deceased. The bereaved are supposed to take comfort in the future life. This one was no different. Standard funeral with a sermon on God's will and a few brief mentions of Benning. It must say "Fill in name of deceased here."

The officiating clergyman appeared never to have met Benning. That was fine with me. Maybe Benning hadn't deserved to be murdered, but he sure didn't merit tears and hankies. I was thankful I'd bucked the family trend and had Paul's memorial at the Unitarian Church. I'd written the eulogy myself. I had stood in front of the friends, family and colleagues and delivered it. Plenty of time to cry afterwards.

My father  had recovered eventually.

But it's never good to dwell on Paul in public. There were other targets for my attention. I took another gander at

Lindsay in the front of the church. Was she crazy? How could she cry over the man who had reduced her to a tranquillized shadow of herself? A man who would have killed her if he'd had the chance.

She was elegant as always. The deep red of her coat was perfect for her colouring. She projected that touching air of vulnerability. Men would continue to fall at her feet. Merv was already stuck to her side. Sworn to serve and protect. There was something about Lindsay in her red coat. Something nibbled at my memory, but I couldn't quite figure it out.

I turned my attention to Randy Cousins. What the hell was her connection with Benning? A lover? If Lindsay seemed unlikely in that role, how much less plausible was Constable Cousins? At six feet, she would have been taller than him. Her short, spiky hair didn't seem calculated to attract a man. She didn't strike me as the kind of woman he preferred. Rina Benning had once been reedlike and lovely. Lindsay was graceful and petite. Randy looked like she could beat the guys at arm wrestling as a warm-up for a triathlon.

Randy Cousins was strong, confident and attractive. But I didn't think she'd been Benning's lover. But what? Mrs. P. and Alvin were working hard to find out. Time to turn up the burner on my investigation. Especially since my bruised back still ached, and I figured I owed those bruises to Randy Cousins's knees. She had the strength to toss a person into a snowbank and probably the disposition to finish the job.

When people began filing out of church, I leaned back out of the way but not quite far enough to avoid Conn McCracken's eye. Ditto Mombourquette's. And Randy Cousins spotted me. No doubt about it, she knew who I was all right. And she didn't like me much either.

I gave her a merry little wave. From the look on her face, I thought she might pull out her Glock and shoot me for the fun of it. Mombourquette put a steadying hand on her arm as they left the church.

Alvin would find out where she went afterwards and with whom. I stayed in the back of the church until the congregation, the highly paid public servants, the photographers and the reporters cleared away.

The ceremony left me feeling empty. Nothing would undo the damage Benning had done. To the dead, to the living, to himself and to others.

When was it going to end?

On the bright side, I'd figured out where I'd seen Randy Cousins before and why that was important. All I had to do was prove it.

But first, a word with my alleged friend, P. J.

\*     \*     \*

His gap-toothed smile faded as soon as I opened my mouth.

"Don't say a word, P. J. I want to know who those kids were."

"Kids?"

"Yes. The nephews you managed to collect without having a sister. Or a brother."

"Okay, Tiger, so they're not *exactly* nephews. They're close friends of the family."

"Nope."

"Not *really* close friends of the family. I think of them as nephews but, to tell the absolute truth, they're kids from the neighbourhood."

The little bastard.

"Wrong."

"I can explain," he said.

"Explain this," I said, showing my middle finger. I didn't bother to give him my neat story idea.

*    *    *

"For God's sake, Camilla. Are you out of your mind?"

"Hi, Conn."

"What the hell were you doing at Benning's funeral?"

"Last time I looked, it wasn't against the law to go to a religious service. Even for Benning. And, although the forces of law and justice were there in their splendour, you must have noticed I didn't approach any of them."

"Watch it."

"And, for the record, WAVE will be having a memorial service next week for Rina Benning. I'll be there too. Count on it."

"Be careful where else you go. We hear the Crown Attorney's office is howling for your blood. I can't always bail you out."

"When have you ever bailed me out? Don't bother to answer that. But I would like to know what half the force was doing at Benning's funeral anyway, since that case is supposed to be solved."

There was a pause long enough to bake a cake. "Where are you?"

"Does it matter?"

"It does if you're violating your bail restrictions by sticking your nose into this Ekstein case."

"Oh, great. Now it's the Ekstein case. Like she's been tried and convicted. What was the matter with the Benning case?"

"She did confess."

"What is this obsession you people have with confessions? How many false confessions do you get? A ballpark figure will be fine."

"Of course, we get lots of them. Most of them are from nutbars."

"I rest my case."

"Don't rest your case too early. Ekstein's a major pain in the butt, but she's definitely in her right mind."

"I'm beginning to wonder. How can she be if she confessed to a murder she didn't commit?"

"Okay, we've done that one to death. Where did you say you were?"

"Why?"

"Because I want to make sure you're not about to get yourself in a bit more trouble. Not that you couldn't get yourself into all the trouble you want. That's fine with me, except it upsets Alexa."

"Ah."

"So where are you?"

"Where am I?" This was beginning to be fun.

"Yes."

"I'm picking up girl stuff."

"Oh." Apparently McCracken wasn't devious enough to ask if picking up girl stuff meant I was heading off to confirm a few new details about his colleague, Randy Cousins. So I didn't have to lie.

"Hey, no problem. I sure don't want Alexa in a snit. By the way, Conn, do you have any idea if Elaine Ekstein's SUV is still impounded?"

"Yeah. Still impounded. And don't get any ideas."

"I think I left some of my stuff in it. Can I check it out?"

"How stupid do you think I am?" I'm sure he didn't want me to answer. He added, "Don't even contemplate trying to see it. The judge would include Elaine Ekstein's vehicle in those bail conditions. And then slam, slam."

"Yikes," I said, "Alexa would go out of her mind."

"That's right. So start behaving like an adult."

"I'd like to, but I have this huge problem. I need some information from the SUV. If I'm right, and I believe I am, it could show how the killer set her up. It's worth a bit of hassle."

"Forget it."

"You don't even know what it is."

"Are you out of your mind?"

"I have no choice."

"For Chrissake, it will kill your sister if you're banged into the RDC for the wedding."

"Nice talking to you, Conn." I hung up.

McCracken held out for ten minutes. I had to hand it to him. He was getting better. This time next year, I'd probably have to refine my strategies. On the other hand, maybe he'd just needed a private spot before continuing our conversation.

"One question," he said.

"Go for it."

"Just curious. What were you willing to risk losing your bail and wrecking your sister's wedding for?"

I told him.

\* \* \*

The atmosphere in Mrs. Parnell's apartment had changed from my last visit. And it wasn't subtle.

"Hey, Camilla," Alvin said from the sofa where he was hand-rolling a cigarette. I was a bit worried when I saw the parrot shirt; I thought a big dose of Jimmy Buffett was about to follow, but Mrs. Parnell had *The Siege of Leningrad* on. The volume was enough to shake the sherry glasses. Lester and Pierre screeched steadily from their cage. We were not talking tranquil.

"What is that smell?" I asked.

Alvin issued a thin stream of smoke. He crinkled his brow. I could tell he was thinking hard.

I said, "Look, this is an apartment building with paper-thin walls and a door you can practically crawl under. Is it a good idea to smoke weed in the home of a respectable senior citizen? Do you think no one will smell it?"

"Don't get your shorts in a twist, Camilla."

"And as for you, Mrs. P., if you don't want the neighbours dashing down the hall to see if the building's under siege and getting a whiff of Alvin's silly cigarettes, turn the stereo down."

"Alvin's right. You should learn to relax a bit, Ms. MacPhee."

"What? Don't tell me you're doing it too."

"Maybe I should," she said. "From time to time life seems a little dull." I hate it when she gets that wistful note in her voice.

"Better the devil you know, Mrs. P."

"Perhaps you're right. A tiny bit of Harvey's?"

"No, thanks. Look, can we get down to business?"

"You're the boss." Somehow Alvin conveyed a look of wide-eyed innocence through the haze.

"Last call," said Mrs. Parnell.

Alvin cheerfully blew smoke.

"What is the matter with you two? Do you want to get tossed into the Regional Detention Centre on charges of possession? Keep in mind it's probably too late for a bail hearing today. On the upside, you might get a chance to cosy up to Elaine and find out what she's planning."

"What an outmoded, undemocratic and unpalatable piece of legislation anyway," said Alvin. "Absolutely needs to be challenged."

"Ms. MacPhee, you must learn to pick your battles."

"Right. And the battle I'm picking is to get Elaine out of the tank before she engineers a return to capital punishment."

"Wow," said Alvin, "capital punishment. Could that happen?"

"Not in this country." Mrs. Parnell drained her glass of Harvey's. "Nevertheless, Ms. MacPhee's right. We must soldier on in the fight to save Ms. Ekstein from ignoble incarceration."

"No problem," said Alvin.

"I'm beginning to despair of both…" I stopped mid-speech. Was Edwina's tone beginning to creep into my voice? Not that it mattered, since neither of them was paying any attention. "Fine." I started again. "Mrs. P., did you have any luck finding out what I asked?"

"Direct hit to the target," Mrs. Parnell said.

"Ah."

Alvin giggled. Mrs. Parnell rammed a fresh cigarette into the holder. Alvin smirked. "We have her."

"That's confirmed. We have been able to verify Constable Miranda Cousins was one of three officers on duty outside Lindsay Grace's house the night of the murder." Mrs. Parnell loved this game.

"You were right, Camilla," Alvin said. "Those police issue hats sure do make for instant ugly. She hassled me when I showed up, and I didn't even realize she was a she."

"Well, I knew we'd had a woman officer on guard. This is good news," I said. "It's another link between Randy Cousins and our case."

"Calls for a toast," said Mrs. P.

"Let's keep our heads clear and analyze this. First, a cop would be in a good position to get access to a street drug, like Rohypnol. Our gal Randy was on duty outside Lindsay's house the night the murder took place. Did she have access to the coffee? Could she have slipped the drug into it? If she felt confident we were out cold and her partner was drugged too, she would have been free to do the dirty deed and let the suspicion fall on Elaine."

"Way to go," said Alvin.

"Of course, on the down side, she was never alone with the coffee," I said, "but who cares? It muddies the waters, and it's a good start on a defence."

"But we're not Ms. Ekstein's defence team any more." Mrs. Parnell consoled herself with a tiny top up.

Defence *team?* "Perhaps not at the moment. We'll have to wait until Elaine changes her plea, then we'll pass on this information to Berelson. Even if it is full of holes, he'll make the most of it."

"Full of holes, Ms. MacPhee?"

"The crown will claim Constable Cousins couldn't have known about the coffee in advance. Therefore she couldn't have planned to drug it. They'll figure out she wasn't alone with the thermoses. Think back."

"What will you say to that?"

"Nothing, since I've been dismissed from the case, but Berelson could insinuate Constable Cousins would have been looking for opportunities. Even so…"

"Maybe the pizzas," Alvin piped up.

"We've already established the drug must have been in the coffee," Mrs. Parnell said.

"Bummer," said Alvin.

"Nevertheless, we believe Randy Cousins did take advantage of the situation," Mrs. P. said.

"The reason's clear," I said.

"Definitely," said Mrs. P.

"Okay," Alvin said, "I'll play. What was her reason?"

"Things were getting too hot to handle. Benning was…"

"A loose cannon," said Mrs. Parnell.

"That's right. Her involvement in Benning's cases was a matter of record. When Benning escaped and shot a cop, she knew the brass would start to take rumours seriously. They'd flush her out fast. It didn't take us long, and we don't have access to the same information the police and the Crown had."

Mrs. Parnell smiled.

"She had to kill him," Alvin said.

"That's right."

"To keep him from dragging her deeper into the situation."

"She would have been exposed. Her career ruined. Disgrace. Resignation. Humiliation," Mrs. P. said mistily.

"Never mind that, she'd be charged and convicted. She'd be a pariah on the force and in the community. They'd throw the book at her if they could find any complicity. And as a police officer, she'd be extremely vulnerable if she had to serve time."

"Would she serve time?"

"Good bet."

"Could she plead one of those battered lover cases?" Alvin said.

I still couldn't see Randy Cousins as one of Benning's lovers.

"She doesn't look the type," Mrs. Parnell said.

"You can never tell," Alvin said. "The weirdest people fall for each other."

"I'm betting on plain old self-preservation. We just need to bolster our case before we go public," I said.

"Let us do a little more digging, troops," Mrs. P. said.

"Friends, school, previous jobs, the works," I added. "We'll need a home address for her in order to talk to her neighbours."

She drew herself up. "I know the drill, Ms. MacPhee. I've assembled my kit for the occasion and I'm ready to roll out."

"And I can't be seen to be associated with your investigation."

"Of course. And we don't want you lurking around revealing our position to the enemy. Do we, Alvin?"

"For sure." Alvin emitted yet another cloud. "You know, Violet, those lovebirds make an awful racket, but they sure have excellent colours."

Lester and Pierre shrieked on cue.

"Where do lovebirds come from?" Alvin said.

"Not Florida," I said. "Not Hawaii either."

"Lovebirds. They're like the official bird of Valentine's week."

I leaned over to Mrs. Parnell and whispered, "Do not allow him to redecorate your apartment when he's in this state."

"Tackle the task at hand, Ms. MacPhee. That's always been my motto."

"Don't worry," Alvin giggled from the sofa. "We'll get her."

"Yes, I'm sure you will."

"Shouldn't take long." Mrs. Parnell hummed along with Shostakovitch as she set up a flip chart in the corner and popped the top off a black marker. "I'll plan our offensive strategy."

"Good. I'll slip over to my place and feed your cat."

# Twenty-Five

I hate it when I'm stuck. And I was stuck again. Alvin and Mrs. Parnell were having all the fun. I had nothing better to do than sit around and wait for someone to try and kill me. They were still at their research the next morning. I wasn't sure if they'd slept the night before. It seemed better not to ask.

I decided to leave them to it and enjoy an Alvin-free morning at the office. It just wasn't as pleasant as I'd expected. Every single activity at Justice for Victims was boring. Letters to be written, signed and photocopied. Filing. Briefs to be read. Briefs to be written. Plans for fundraising to be thought through.

Not to mention the kind of stuff Alvin puts off.

It would have been a good day to shop for a bridesmaid's dress, but apparently that was already taken care of.

I cleaned out the voice mail, including a breathless message from P. J. saying he thought I'd understand about the non-nephews if he could spend a bit of time explaining it to me. He had a tip for me too.

Delete.

I thought about the case instead. The biggest problem was obviously Elaine. The longer she stayed in jail issuing self-incriminating statements to the press, the more likely she'd get a hefty sentence. Elaine was stubborn, short-sighted and maybe even crazy, but there are worse traits, and, anyway, she'd always been there for me whenever I'd needed help. Trouble was, unless we could prove Randy Cousins' involvement, Elaine's neck would stay on the line. The cops would protect their own, and I had less than no pull with the Crown. There was nothing I could do without making the situation worse.

Or was there?

After an hour of pacing and muttering out loud, I had an idea. And a good way to kill two birds.

\*     \*     \*

"Hey!" I said, "it's Camilla."

Complete and utter silence.

"Hello?"

Not even the sound of breathing.

"Leonard, are you there?"

"What do you want?"

"Is that anyway to talk to a friend? I need to discuss a few of the wedding arrangements with you. Do we have to fight?"

"Wedding arrangements?"

"Exactly."

"Let's see if I understand. You want to talk about the wedding arrangements with *me*. Do I have that right?"

"You do."

"Pull the other one, Camilla."

"No, really. You know what my sisters are like."

"What is your point? I have work to do here."

"The whole is so much greater than the sum of the parts when it comes to the MacPhee girls. They are formidable when they're together. Surely you've noticed."

"Okay, I'll concede they're..."

"You got it. They're a force of nature at the best of times. And Alexa is right over the top about this wedding."

"Well, maybe."

"So, it's difficult for me to ask simple questions or make little suggestions without causing a blow-up."

"I don't have all day."

"Leonard, we're in the wedding party together, remember. I need to know what's going to happen when. I thought we could talk over coffee. But, look, don't worry about it. I understand you can't be seen with me because of this directive. I shouldn't have bothered you. Forget it happened, okay? I'll see you at the rehearsal."

"Look, sorry. I guess it would be okay. You're not going to hound me about the Ekstein case, right?"

"Absolutely not. Well, you're the one with the time constraint. How about the Colonnade for lunch? Say one o'clock? You've gotta eat."

He grunted before he hung up. I took that as a yes.

*   *   *

"Weather's warming up." Mombourquette shook the slush off his boots.

"Terrific." I was happy because he'd actually shown up. "At this rate the snow will soon be completely melted. They don't call it Waterlude for nothing."

I could tell he was checking for signs of sarcasm. I reminded myself to cut it out.

"My treat. Name your poison," I added.

Minutes later we were tucked into a table for two at the Colonnade, sipping hot coffee and waiting for our personal-size pizzas. I love the chicken, mushroom and green pepper version, so I might have been smiling.

"What happened to your face?"

"Came off second best in a fight with a snowbank. You can see why I don't mind if it warms up."

"What…?"

"Never mind. Now, Leonard, the wedding. I thought we could strike a truce until it's over."

"We'll both live longer if we do."

"My point exactly." I slapped a large wedding planner I'd picked up from Mags and Fags onto the table. "As members of the wedding party, we have obligations. I thought we could check them out."

"I already know what to do."

"You do?"

"Yes, Conn gave me a written list of instructions. It had my responsibilities laid out in point form with time frames and a place to check off each activity as it's completed. Came with a little pen."

"Ah. That would be Edwina's doing."

"I assumed all instructions would have come from Alexa." Mombourquette picked up the Wedding Planner.

"Nope. It's Edwina's style."

"Whoever. They're clear-cut, easy to follow. It's just one day, and Conn has been my partner for a lot of years." He started leafing through the pages of the planner.

"So Conn gave you a sheet. But I don't have the equivalent sheet for the maid of honour? I wonder why?"

"I bet it's because you wouldn't follow any of the instructions, no matter who they were from. They probably farmed out your chores to other people." Mombourquette stopped flipping and pointed out a sizeable checklist. "Did you help address the invitations?"

"Is that a joke?"

"Did you arrange the shower?"

"Of course not, Edwina and Donalda did all that. They'd never leave me in charge of something like that. Is there more?"

"Lots of stuff on the wedding day. Help the bride to get dressed. Ensure the other attendants are presentable. Witness the wedding certificate. Remind the bride of the reception time table. Help the bride get ready…"

"This is the first I've heard about any of this. Except maybe the witnessing."

"It's all standard stuff. I guess your family doesn't believe you'll do it. Or they don't believe you'll get it right."

"I'm glad we're having this talk. What happens at this rehearsal?"

"Use your brain."

"Listen, Leonard. It's on Friday, three days before the wedding. I just need to know is there a reason for that timing?"

"Not that I'm aware of. Just a scheduling thing. You should know all this."

"No need to be snippy, Leonard. I guess we're expected to dress up?"

"I'd say we should look respectable. And you should make an effort to be polite."

"I guess I can do that, since the damn thing means so much to Alexa. Even though it's obviously brought her to the brink of psychosis. But hey."

"Good."

"On a related topic, Officer Randy Cousins. You've worked with her quite a bit. Did she ever have a relationship with Ralph Benning?"

His cup hit the table with a bang. "What?"

"You heard me. Is that what the police are trying to keep secret?"

"Did you get me here to talk about that? You are reprehensible."

Big word for a little rodent. "Hey, don't get me wrong. I

needed to talk to you about the wedding stuff. I seem to have the wrong effect on people over the phone for some reason. Since I can't go to police HQ, I figured you wouldn't mind. We're practically family."

"You're barking up the wrong tree about Randy, Camilla."

"Am I?"

"Yes, you're also full of shit."

"Could be. But you might want to check and see how many times she was involved with Benning's arrests, charges and other stuff."

"No, I don't want to. Randy is one of the finest officers I ever met, and I can tell you she has never been involved with Ralph Benning in any inappropriate way."

"She was on guard at Lindsay's house the night Benning was killed. Kind of a coincidence. She a friend of yours?"

"She's someone I have a tremendous amount of respect for."

"We hate it, don't we, when it looks like our friends are unjustly accused. I found out the hard way. Give it a bit of thought."

"You're a real bitch, Camilla." He pushed back his chair.

"You know something, Leonard? I checked the Confederation Park site and guess what, there's no video surveillance there. I mentioned it to Conn and to Mia Reilly. Neither of them deny it." I had him.

"I know," he said.

"How did you get the tape?"

"It was dropped off in the police station."

"Oh, great. Speaking of security, did anyone catch sight of the person who dropped it?"

"It was just left in the second floor hall." He wasn't meeting my eyes.

"That's interesting. Someone who had access to the police station without being noticed. Someone like, let's say for the sake of argument, a police officer? So, Leonard, who do you suppose took that video footage?"

I could tell by the way he shrugged that he'd been asking the same question.

"If you're about to suggest she did it herself to get media attention, then why was she so careful not to show her face? We both know why. Because it wasn't her. It was someone else. And your job should be to find out who. Here's another question for you. Why did you head for Lindsay's house the morning after Benning died? Did Officer Cousins suggest it?"

"No, she didn't. An anonymous tip." Mombourquette was on his feet, gripping the table.

"Was your anonymous tip from a police cruiser?"

"No, it wasn't."

"Where was it from?"

"A phone booth. Not that it's your business." We had the attention of everyone at the neighbouring tables by this time.

"It is my business. You know what I think?"

"I don't give a rat's ass."

It was hard to let that pass, but I stuck to my guns. "Officer Randy Cousins was in Benning's pocket, and Benning was getting too hot to handle. Maybe she helped him to escape, killed him and then decided to frame Lindsay Grace. She was in a position to do it."

Mombourquette's incisors gleamed. "Listen to me. And listen good. The first domestic Randy pulled, the husband murdered the wife. Stabbed her with the carving knife. Thirty-one times. Randy held her hand while she died. She was covered in the victim's blood by the time the back-up showed. The perp pleaded down and got out in eighteen months. Randy hates wife-beaters. She's a big supporter of WAVE and all those other groups. There's no fucking way she had anything going with Benning."

That was loud enough to get everyone's attention, even the crowd waiting for take-out at the other end of the café.

"Her name turns up in connection with his dozens of times."

"There's a good reason. She pulled out all the stops to get him. She was out to nail the bastard."

"Maybe you shouldn't shout, Leonard."

"Maybe you should learn to listen."

"Okay, I get it. Randy Cousins couldn't have killed Benning because she was out to nail him."

"You got this assbackwards, Camilla. Every member of the force will go out of his way to stop you from hassling Randy."

"I understand why she attended his funeral. I'm not letting this one go, Leonard."

"You'd better. And stay away from Randy."

"Oh, and you asked about my face. I picked up my new look in an attack right after I left you in the police gym. Who followed me out of the gym, Leonard? Think back. Whose raised knees would match up with my kidneys, right here? "

He headed for the door and turned, "Get a rabies shot, Camilla, unless it's too late."

Every eye in the Colonnade followed him as he stormed out the door. I felt the heads swivel back to me.

"See you Friday, sweetie." I blew him a kiss.

I kept my chin up until the two personal-sized pizzas arrived. Then I smiled. Watching the take-out section had given me an answer.

Everyone's coffee must have been drugged at the same time. The pizza had never been alone. Elaine had brought the coffee from the WAVE office. Someone who knew where she was headed must have fiddled with the thermoses.

For sure she'd been to the Colonnade. She would have

waited at least a few minutes. With the snow banks on Metcalfe and the side streets as high as they were, even Elaine wouldn't have been able to park right in view. She would have tucked the SUV into the back parking lot of the Colonnade. She'd probably left the thermoses there while she picked up the pizza. I checked the lot as soon as I left. Busy as the Colonnade is, a suitably devious person could have tampered with that coffee without attracting attention.

Who better than a police officer in uniform? And I knew just the one. I was certain I had it figured out. I just had to wait for an answer from Conn McCracken to confirm how she got into the SUV. Which reminded me, Randy Cousins was still out there. Tall, strong and carrying a gun.

It gave another meaning to the need for police protection.

\* \* \*

While I waited for various well-stirred pots to boil over, I had areas where nothing was cooking. Mainly I needed to find out whom Elaine had seen or talked to from the time she picked up the coffee from the WAVE office until she showed up at Lindsay's place. Given the limitations of my bail restrictions, this was proving tricky.

But I knew one person I didn't have to stay away from, and I was smiling as I rang her doorbell.

"Merv take the day off?" I said when Lindsay peered through the glass. She opened the door and gave a weak grin.

Good start. Not everyone liked my jokes.

"Actually, he took the day on."

"You mean, he's here?"

"I mean he's back at work. He seems to be getting better, and his doctor said he could go back to work part-time."

"Great news." Great because he and his gall-bladder wouldn't be there to run interference.

"You're looking better yourself, Lindsay." I don't know why I said it, since it wasn't true.

"Am I? Well, as they say, life goes on."

She sank wearily onto the sofa, and I took the chair.

"I need to talk to you about Elaine and the murder. I know it's tough for you, but I'm trying to understand what goes through the mind of a woman under Benning's spell."

She blinked. "Elaine wasn't under his spell."

"Right. And she didn't kill him either. But somebody did. I need to figure out what would have pushed that person to murder him. But I don't want to upset you any more."

I had worked up that piece of dialogue and practiced it on my way over. The truth was I felt like shaking her. It was obvious at the funeral she was grieving for Benning. But she took me by surprise.

"I like you better when you're yourself, Camilla. Nobody is going to fall for the phony sympathy."

My turn to blink. "That obvious, am I? Good to know. Let me start again. You were genuinely grieving at the funeral."

"It's not impossible to love someone who's dead."

"I learned that the hard way. But it's not the issue. When he was alive, he terrorized you. He made you an emotional hostage. You broke free with a lot of help from Elaine, and yet he kept his hold on you. He had the same hold on Rina. She went out to meet him despite the danger. What compelled her?"

She gazed out the window. "I don't know why anyone would do that."

"Yes, you do. Because you did it too."

Her back stiffened. Bingo.

"No."

"The night he was killed, you left the house."

"I didn't."

"You did. And you'd better tell me about it. I am not the enemy, Lindsay."

"It isn't true."

"You planned to meet him that night, and something terrible happened. Is that why your cream cashmere tunic and pants were missing in the morning?"

"They're here somewhere.

"If they're here, let's see them."

"You can't. I gave them away."

"Okay. Who did you give them to?"

"I dropped them in one of those boxes for the Sally Ann."

"Which one?"

"I don't remember."

"People are weird. When they give away this season's latest style in cashmere, they don't drop them into boxes and forget about them."

She was crying. I felt like a shit. But that didn't matter, because I feel like a shit half the time, and we were getting somewhere. It took another minute before the fight went out of her. "He called."

"What did he say?" I felt a little rush of blood to my head. "Why in God's name would you go?"

She held up her hand. "Look, this is hard for me to admit. But I don't need you to yell at me."

I took a deep breath. "Right. Sorry. But you're an intelligent woman. And you took such a risk."

"It didn't seem dangerous to me."

"After what happened to his wife? After he beat her to death?"

She raised her chin.

I tried to calm myself. No point in shouting at the victim. It wasn't up to me to decide whether she should have had more sense, which she should have. Lindsay still wasn't the bad guy.

"I hadn't heard about Rina." She had a little resistance left.

"Don't get mad. I'm trying to understand. You were hiding out."

"Yes."

"Terrified he would come after you."

"Yes."

"We were there to protect you."

"Yes."

"What could he have said to make you…" I took a breath.

"Stupid?" she said.

"Well, you went to meet him. In spite of everything you knew."

"I'm not sure I understand it myself. He contacted me."

"How?"

"By phone."

"But we were sitting right in this room all evening."

"Everyone had flaked out when I woke up at about eleven-thirty. I crawled up to bed. He called on my cellphone. I keep it next to my bed."

"Okay. So he phoned."

"Yes, and I spoke to him."

"You didn't try to wake us up?"

"I was half-asleep when I answered. I don't know what I thought."

"Or if."

"He said he was hurt. He sounded faint."

It took a lot of effort not to scream that he couldn't have called. He would have been dead long before.

"He said he had been hit by a police bullet during the escape. He had lost a lot of blood. A lot."

"Go on."

"He had been hurt again when he chased Alvin, I guess."

"He said that?"

"He didn't mention Alvin in particular, but he told me he'd bumped someone with a car and then hit his head and he wasn't feeling right."

"Okay."

"He thought he was going to die. I pleaded with him to turn himself in. He believed the police would kill him. He'd never even stand trial. I tried to reason with him, but it was no use."

I asked myself if I could fall for such a stupid setup.

"I'm sure you find this unbelievable."

"Who am I to talk? I made the wrong move after a phone call once and two people died as a result."

"Someone died as a result of this."

"But that wasn't your fault."

"Maybe. I didn't kill him. I just did what I thought I had to."

"What happened?"

"I tried to convince him he'd be better off with medical attention. He was getting upset. He was almost incoherent. His answers didn't make sense. He wanted to say goodbye to me. He said he loved me, and he was going to die. I believed him."

I had a hard time with the pleading look in her eyes. "So then what did you do?"

"I went back downstairs. Everyone was snoring."

"Where was he?"

"I believed him. I took my cellphone. I thought I could get close enough to see what was happening and then call for an ambulance."

"The cops didn't see you?"

"No, I left from the basement parking."

"What? This house was surrounded. Two cops in the front.

One in the back. You couldn't get out of parking without being seen."

"My neighbour's in Florida for the winter. I have her keys. I took her car. I wore a scarf on my head and a pair of glasses. It's what I've been doing since I've been here, every time I left the house. I thought I'd nod at the cops and then…"

"They could have stopped you."

"Yes. I was ready. I would say I was feeling panicked. What could they do? I didn't have to tell them about Ralph."

"Words fail me."

"I realize how stupid it was. But anyway, it didn't matter, because they were asleep."

"All three of them?"

"The one in the back of the house had his nose squished right up against the window."

"Did you see the officers in the front?"

"The one with the mustache had his head back against the headrest."

"And the other one?"

"I didn't notice. I didn't hang around to see. I floored it and headed out."

I was so caught up in Lindsay's story I didn't even hear the front door open.

# Twenty-Six

What the hell are you doing, Camilla?

I whirled. "Merv. I didn't hear you come in."

"I guess not." In one leggy move he reached the sofa.

"Lindsay's telling me what happened the night Benning died."

"It's time for you to hit the road, Camilla. Lindsay's been through enough."

"We're almost done."

"No, you are done."

"Merv, it's me now or the police in fifteen minutes." In twenty years, I've never seen him look at me like that. "Go ahead, Lindsay. Where did you meet him?"

"In the park by the Rideau River in Sandy Hill."

"What?" said Merv.

"Shut up, Merv," I said.

"Listen, Camilla…"

"Why there?"

"Strathcona Park. We used to spend time there in the summer. Stroll along the river. Watch the swans."

"Thirty below. And you met him outside."

"I had no choice. I had to convince him to get to a hospital. I thought if I told the media he was afraid the police would kill him that would be enough to keep him safe. In protective custody."

"Go on."

"I parked the car in that lot at the end of Mann Avenue and I ran along to the area between the upper and lower park. No one can see you there."

"You weren't afraid?"

"In a deserted area on the coldest night of the year, I didn't expect to find many bad guys." One of her tiny smiles flickered.

I felt like saying there'd been at least two bad guys. Benning and whoever killed him.

"The path was trampled down a bit. I thought I'd see him."

She started to cry.

"He wasn't there?"

"No."

"No one was there?"

"No."

"There was a lot of blood on the snow. A lot. Frozen. I shouldn't have touched the area. But I thought he might be under it, so I started digging. A lot of the bloody snow got on my sweater."

"Your sweater? You weren't wearing a coat? It was thirty below."

"I was, of course, but it wasn't zippered. I left in such a hurry. I was in a state and my medication didn't help my thinking."

"At least that would make some sense. So you dug through the snow. And you didn't find anything?"

"Nothing. I made sure. I looked everywhere. I checked the bushes by the side of the river, and I called his name. I was half out of my mind."

"How long were you there?"

"A long time. I was ready to pass out from the cold."

"And did you call the police?"

She shook her head.

"Okay, let me recap. You left us zonked, passed two police

cars, with sleeping occupants, and drove in the middle of the night to meet the man who'd threatened your life, shot a police officer, bit off someone's nose and beat his wife to death while she was under protective custody. That it?"

Merv was whiter than a snow bank.

"Yes," she said in a small voice.

"Okay. And then you found what you thought was his blood, and you got some of it on you."

"It was crazy."

"Sure was crazy. Lucky for you, Ralph Benning would have been long dead when he called you."

"What?"

"He was already dead."

"He…couldn't have been dead."

"He was."

"Take it easy, Camilla," Merv said.

I was taking it easy. I didn't say Benning would have been nine-tenths of the way frozen by the time Lindsay's cellphone had even rung.

"He talked to me."

"Someone talked to you."

"But…no, it was Ralph. It must have been. No one else knew about our spot."

"He was dead, Lindsay. We know that."

"I don't understand."

"You said his voice seemed different, and you attributed it to his injuries and perhaps the cold."

"Yes."

"Maybe his voice was different because it was someone else pretending to be Ralph. You took a lot of medication that day, and you were under serious stress. Someone was banking on it."

"But why?"

"Most likely to implicate you in the crime. Getting the blood on yourself was a good start. You may have left footprints."

Merv towered over me. "She doesn't need this conversation."

"Oh yes, she does, Merv. She needed to have it before. Elaine is going to be prosecuted, and she didn't do it."

"Yeah, yeah. Elaine wants to be in the media spotlight. She has a political agenda, and you know it."

"That's not the point. Someone killed Benning. Not a woman trying to protect herself from him. Not self-defence, but what looks like cold-blooded murder. Planned. Executed with a certain flair."

"You're not going to badger Lindsay anymore."

"Take a hike, Merv. Or sit here and keep quiet. Because Lindsay talks to me or I call McCracken."

"No."

"The choice is not yours. Lindsay. What will it be?"

"Merv, maybe you could get us some coffee or tea. I knew I would have to talk about this. I prefer Camilla, even though…"

I thought I heard Merv say "even though she's one cold bitch" as he stomped toward the kitchen.

"Okay, we have to work on the voice, Lindsay."

She was back to twisting her hands. "Not just the voice. It was the words he used."

"Like what?"

"My special name and expressions. No one else knew them. Even the place. It was ours." I kept my mouth shut. "He wouldn't tell anyone."

"Someone must have found out and used it to entrap you. Look, this is hard. Let's get through it. Then I can leave you alone."

"I'll do my best."

I tried not to react to her look of defeat. "You arrived there, you found the blood."

"Snow, bloody snow."

"Okay, you dug through the snow and you got it on your clothes."

"I thought he might be under it. I was digging with my bare hands, and it got on my sweater. Some splattered on my coat, but it's red and it didn't show the same way. I was able to clean it off. Then I took it to the cleaners."

Of course. The red coat that I'd noticed at the funeral. It had been hanging in a different spot on the morning after Benning's death. I'd missed that detail. What else had I missed? "But the sweater? That wasn't here when the police came the next day."

"No."

"Where was it?"

"In the car, I turned on the heater and the snow started to melt on my sweater and stain it…"

Red.

"I couldn't stand it. I took it off, I stuffed it in a plastic bag. The leggings were stained too. I threw them in a garbage can on the way home."

"Okay. And that's why they weren't here."

"Yes."

"Somebody set you up."

Merv slid back on the sofa with a tray of coffee cups.

"It must have been someone who knew your secrets and Ralph's and knew how you would behave. That someone tipped the police."

Lindsay choked out her next sentence. "*Little Girl*. He always called me Little Girl. He wouldn't tell anyone that. He couldn't."

Merv said, "Maybe he didn't mean to."

"How...?"

"Drugs can make you say things you don't want to. Maybe he'd been drugged by his killer. How else would he have been vulnerable?"

"Sure," I said. Lindsay wanted to delude herself about the man she'd loved. But I knew there had been no good in Benning. He wouldn't have needed to be drugged to share intimate details with a confederate. Or another lover. Whichever Randy Cousins turned out to be. "There could be many reasons. The point is you were fooled. You were intended to be fooled. The killer set you up. An excellent diversion."

"Yes," she said. "I see that."

Good. "If Elaine hadn't confessed in full view of the world, the police would have received another phone call telling them to check your clothing for bloodstains."

"Maybe the killer will still try to implicate me."

"I don't think so. This tells me the killer didn't have it in for you in particular, otherwise the call would have come already."

She didn't seem to be paying attention. She frowned. "There was something wrong about that place."

"What?"

"Well, it was the way the snow was crushed."

"Crushed?"

"Yes, near the river. The little spot where we used to meet." Her voice broke. "A special place. The snow was broken down to the edge of the river where we used to go. Like something had been dragged."

I kept quiet. What could I say to make this any less painful for her? I could tell Lindsay was making an effort to steel herself.

"Something heavy," she said.

I nodded. I was beginning to figure out what might have happened to Benning.

"Perhaps a body." Her lip trembled. I gave her hand a squeeze. "It looked like someone dragged him to the river and dumped him."

"That would explain a lot."

"You mean how he froze so quickly?"

"Yes."

"Oh, God. I can't think about it."

"Okay, we're almost done. Okay. You saw tracks in the snow."

"Yes. But they'll be gone. The snow's melted."

"There may be something underneath. Can you show me where it was?"

"Yes."

"We'll have to call the police about this."

"I know."

"You could have a problem about messing with the evidence at a crime site and not calling the police. But we can cross that bridge when we come to it."

"I can't deal with it."

"You're going to have to deal with it soon. But let's go back to the voice. It wasn't Ralph's. Could it have been someone else you knew?"

"No. It didn't sound familiar."

"Okay. Could it have been a woman?"

"A woman? No. How could it be a woman?"

"A woman with a low voice, pretending to be an injured man."

The silence was louder than anything we'd heard all afternoon. Finally she spoke. "No, it was Ralph."

I waited a minute. I didn't suggest Ralph could have called

another woman Little Girl, could have taken her to the same secret romantic spots, could have had the same sick relationship with her.

Merv loomed behind me at the door. His jaw was knotted, his knuckles white. The sound of Lindsay sobbing echoed in the marble foyer.

"You're turning into a real little shit, Camilla."

"Nice to see you too, Merv," I said as I left.

\* \* \*

My cellphone rang before I reached the office. McCracken, working late. He said. "I checked what you wanted. You were right. There's a small hole, by the driver's lock. No question about it."

"Great. Keep that under your hat until we need it."

"Oh, sure," he said. "That'll happen."

"And listen, Conn. When you find the van that the killer used to move Benning, check it for drill holes too." I had nothing to worry about. McCracken wasn't going to broadcast the news of the telltale sign of the drillbit bandit right on Elaine's SUV. That perpetrator had been apprehended months earlier, and the case was before the courts. He would have already checked the records and discovered that there was no record of Elaine's vehicle being robbed. McCracken would be scratching his head over what that little hole actually meant.

I was left with two big questions. I hoped Alvin's next round of research would reveal Randy Cousins had been the arresting officer in the drillbit bandit case. Plus, since Randy was supposed to be so active in the war against domestic violence, I was betting she knew our favourite activist at WAVE. I just needed to prove Elaine had been in touch with Randy Cousins on her way over to Lindsay's place on the night that changed her life.

*　　*　　*

I hightailed it back to Lindsay's. It took ten minutes of arguing at the door with Merv before I heard Lindsay's voice and Merv stepped back to let me in.

Lindsay looked worse every time I saw her.

"I won't keep you long. I just need to know if Elaine's SUV was still parked in front when you left the house to meet Benning."

"I don't know. I wasn't looking for it."

"This is important. Think back. Relive it in your mind."

She closed her eyes.

I said, "You drove up out of the garage in your neighbour's car on your way to find Benning. You saw the police officers were sleeping. What else did you see?"

Her eyes opened. "It wasn't. It wasn't there. You were all inside asleep. Elaine too. She was snoring. Her SUV was gone."

"Holy shit. Who the hell could have taken it?" Merv said.

I had my own ideas about that. "A lady with a lot of connections."

# Twenty-Seven

Thursday morning, I hit Justice for Victims in time to find my so-called office assistant stirring a pitcher of orangy-pink liquid, serenaded by Jimmy Buffett. The fumes of citrus combined with high-octane booze nearly overwhelmed the familiar odour of Alvin's freshly applied fake tan.

"Did you get my message? You didn't return my call," I said.

"Changes in attitude, changes in latitude," Alvin sang. "Try some of this punch. It's low-fat and full of the sunshine vitamin." In Alvin's life that would be rum.

"I asked you to do something, Alvin. Can you do it or not?"

"It's a simple photo of a policewoman, Camilla. Have you no faith in my ability?"

"Right. Can you dig that photo fast?"

"Take a gander at your desk."

I checked my desk. The brown envelope labeled Camilla seemed a good start. I ignored the cartoon image of me wearing mouse ears.

Alvin hummed "A Cuban Crime of Passion" while I ripped open the envelope. Inside I found clippings of Randy Cousins in full uniform. Plus a university graduation photo. I flipped through some human-interest stuff from community papers. I tried not to fret about the loss to the local library and instead concentrated on a couple of Polaroid shots of the good officer emerging from a police cruiser in front of Tim Hortons.

Judging from the depleted state of the snow banks, I took the photos to be less than a day old.

"Pick one," he said. "It's a Valentine from me."

"Thanks, Alvin." I might have been more effusive if Jimmy Buffett hadn't been ringing in my ears. "Lucky you didn't get caught."

He smiled enigmatically. Just one more thing I was better off not knowing about.

"I saved a message from Lindsay for you," he said, remembering for a fleeting moment that he was an office assistant.

The message from Lindsay was crisp and to the point. "Camilla? I'm thinking about what we discussed last night. I'm going to need a lawyer. I hope you will be willing to represent me. Please call me."

I bet Merv wasn't going to be tickled. It pleased me because I needed a bit more help from Lindsay, and she'd just given me the means to get it. I called her and said I'd be over to talk to her soon.

*   *   *

P. J. was lying in wait for me on Elgin Street when I emerged from the JFV office late in the morning. The rain had turned his wiry red hair dark and plastered it against his scalp. Good, I thought.

"Thank God you're here. This cold rain's running down inside my collar."

"Couldn't happen to a nicer guy."

"Aw c'mon, Tiger. Let's go have lunch and a brew at the Manx, and I can explain everything."

"Forget it. Anyway, it's too early for lunch."

"Or we can stand here and get soaked. Your choice. Free country."

"I choose to leave you here while *I* go somewhere warm and dry."

"Not an option, because then you'll never learn the truth, and I'll have to keep bothering you, and it's just a matter of time until one of us gets pneumonia." It didn't sound quite that good when he said it, because his nose was obviously stuffed up.

"Fine. Let's get it over with."

By the time we were settled in the Manx, we were wet enough for both of us to get pneumonia. We had the soup of the day then each polished off a pint of Smithwick's for preventive medicine.

"My problem was," P. J. said, as he started on his second one, "every time I asked you to go anywhere, you always said no. I thought if it wasn't a date, you might not turn me down. I knew you liked kids, and I figured you wouldn't want to hurt their feelings."

"I see. Could this be why I didn't remember making the arrangements in the first place?"

He avoided my eyes. "It seemed less likely to fail that way."

"And the rent-a-relatives? Were they in on this complex plot?"

"They're a couple of kids I met doing a bit of volunteer work. Everyone says how much they look like me."

"That has to be the stupidest scheme I've ever heard of."

"Point taken. You'll be happy to hear I've joined a twelve step program for recovering stupid people." He stopped talking to sneeze.

"I hope the first step is to stay out of the rain."

He couldn't have heard me, the way he blew his nose.

I didn't plan to let him off the hook quite so soon. "It didn't occur to you I would find out about the kids sooner or later?"

He sniffled. "Of course, I was planning to tell you. They're such cute little guys, I thought you'd overlook the ploy once you met them."

"Tell you what, P. J. Don't go picking out houses with white picket fences until you get some of the finer points of dating."

I found it hard to stay pissed off with P.J., and I wasn't sure why. After all, I didn't like being deceived, and the guy lied like a rug. Was it because he was so damn cute? Was it that redheaded innocence or the gap between his front teeth? Who the hell knew. Maybe it was just hard to maintain a decent argument with a person who kept sneezing. Maybe I was just too caught up in the problem with Elaine.

P. J. was getting off easy.

I cut my losses, declined a second Smithwick's, left him smelling of wet wool and imported beer and headed home. Lindsay would have to wait.

\* \* \*

She leaned into the hallway, one eye half-closed to avoid the thin stream of her own cigarette smoke. Lester and Pierre screeched in the background.

"Ms. MacPhee, what a pleasant surprise to see you in the middle of the day. Allow me to offer you a hair dryer."

"I need your help, Mrs. P."

"At your service."

"You might want to hear what it is first." I edged into her apartment and slooshed out of my soggy Sorels.

"A little nip of Harvey's to take the edge off the weather?" she said.

"No, thanks, I need a clear head." I didn't mention the Smithwick's.

"I look forward to any task you have in mind."

"Well, let me tell you what I want, and then you can decide. It does involve leaving this warm, dry apartment. I would understand if you didn't want to. And I'd have a different assignment for you."

"Regardless, Ms. MacPhee. I will have done much worse and faced more than a bit of icy water in my career. Don't underestimate me."

"I wouldn't dream of underestimating you, Mrs. P. I learned that lesson last spring."

"All in the line of duty," she said. "Peach-faced lovebirds and Russian composers only go so far in diverting one from the ultimate boredom of growing old alone."

"Right."

"Consider this: you are surrounded by four walls all winter long, staring out at everyone else having a good time leaping into the trenches."

"Leaping into the trenches isn't my idea of a good time."

"A little self-knowledge is always useful, Ms. MacPhee. The front-line battles are exactly your idea of a good time."

"Maybe you're right." I didn't want to get into an argument with my last hope. "But I can think of worse things than being bored."

"You think so? First, give yourself a pair of wobbly legs. And a touch of arthritis. Accept that no one believes you have anything to offer any more. Add a covering of sleet and slippery sidewalks and see how restricted your life gets."

"I take your point," I said.

"Splendid. As they say, old age is not for sissies."

"Okay, here's what I want you to do."

She leaned forward, happy as a bride on a photo shoot. I handed her the photos and clippings Alvin had collected.

"Aha. The attractive yet highly-suspect Constable Miranda Cousins."

"I need someone who will not excite the least bit of anxiety when asking a few innocent questions of her neighbours."

"Allow me to offer my services as a wobbly and confused old lady, utterly unremarkable."

That's not how I would have put it, but I kept my mouth closed.

"I am having a new set of speakers delivered sometime between four and six. As long as I'm back by then. Otherwise, I am completely at your disposal."

"Perfect. Alvin didn't give me her address. But once I find out where she lives, I need you to speak to her neighbours or friends in a way that won't draw any attention and find out if Benning spent any time at her apartment or in her company. You can imagine why I can't send Alvin. He's too…"

"Don't be hard on young Ferguson, Ms. MacPhee. He's a lad of great talent."

"Yes, well, in this case, the talented operative needs to be subtle and believable."

"I'll get my coat," Mrs. P. said.

"Don't step outside until I find the address. I'm thinking maybe I can lean on Merv for this one."

"But I already have the address. It's right here," she said, pointing to a note on her glass table. "Apparently our quarry moved to a new infill town house not far from the University of Ottawa just six months ago. Police officers might keep their home addresses private, but they need Hydro and phone service. Young Ferguson had plenty to do. Tracking down this information only took me a couple of minutes. I've learned a lot about this internet business. I must make up for my past defeats while searching for Benning's connections."

"I hope we're talking legal activities," I said as I copied the information.

"What you don't know can't hurt you, Ms. MacPhee."

No wonder she gets along with Alvin.

I made tracks toward my own apartment for a warm tub with a watermelon-scented bath bomb and a pleasant visit with Mrs. Parnell's purring cat.

"And if you don't mind me saying," she called out, "I'll not be showing the photos of Randy to the neighbours, but rather some respectable shot of Ralph Benning, my grandson. I'm having a hell of a time tracking down that boy. Don't worry about a thing."

Right. I kept going.

*　　*　　*

Maybe it was being called a bitch and a shit on the same day. More likely I preferred to avoid the dress Edwina had picked out for me. If I knew her, it would require serious engineering in the undergarment department. Anyway, I didn't have a lot to do except wait, since Mrs. Parnell had embarked on her reconnaissance mission, and I figured Alvin and Jimmy were still singing in the office.

Since I was warm and dry and had freshly shampooed hair, I did decide to bite the bullet on an alternative bridesmaid's dress before it was too late. Three o'clock found me standing in front of a rack of dresses in a small boutique in the Byward Market.

"May I help you?" Unlike most of the stores, this saleswoman did not imply, after taking in my parka, height and general lack of girlish good looks, that I lay beyond fashion help.

"Yes," I said, "it's an emergency. My sister's having a big wedding, and I need a dress. It has to go with a whole lot of shades of cream. It has to suit her need for elegance and my need not to look like a complete and utter idiot. Any ideas?"

"Is that all?" she said.

"Other requirements are no frills, no slits, no sequins, no pink, nothing long, nothing that adds pounds or restricts movement, nothing you can't wear in front of your eighty-year old father."

"Ooh. I do love a challenge," she said.

"Good, then maybe you can turn up something suitable for a traditional rehearsal while you're at it."

The girl in the boutique delivered, and big-time. I left with two dresses and a serious dent in my savings account. The dead simple taupe silk would go with any shade of cream and the cut was snazzy enough to satisfy the fussiest sister. It didn't look unduly happy. Plus the feel of the fabric was nothing short of soothing. The black wool knit with the square neckline and three-quarter sleeves would do for the rehearsal and every cool-weather social event I'd have for years. I might never have to shop again. The next time my cellphone trilled, I would be able to keep a clear head.

\*     \*     \*

I got home to a flashing message light. My hand hovered. Maybe Alvin had turned up some new lead. But it was Alexa. Flushed with shopping success, I returned her call.

"Listen," Alexa said, "and don't interrupt. I don't want to hear a word until I'm finished. Is that clear?"

I kept my mouth shut.

"Well?" she said.

"Is it safe to say yes?"

"Don't push me, Camilla."

It didn't seem like a good time to ask when whoever had possessed Alexa would be returning her.

"I have your dress," she said.

"What!"

"I said not a word."

"Okay," I said, hoping the tightrope held.

"Edwina knocked herself out to get this dress. It's not like we have all the time in the world."

I made a strangled noise that wasn't technically a word.

She said, "It's perfect, a deep pink, ankle-length and it has a slit up the side and a nice shawl with a ruffle and it's your size, nicely fitted and it should look great on you."

I kept quiet.

"Well, don't you have anything to say?"

"Sounds great, Alexa. Thanks." Sometimes you have to cut your losses.

"The wedding is almost here. Do you realize that? We have no time left, and she had to make a choice and she made it. Of course, I would prefer to have you wear a dress you liked, but I have begun to doubt that's possible, so it's out of your hands, like it or lump it."

"Fine. Where is the dress?"

"Why?"

"So I can go pick it up."

"Oh, ha ha ha."

"Alexa?"

"Oh, sure. You're not going to pull that one. And you're not getting away with it or with anything else from this point on."

"Okay."

"I'm tired of you acting like a brat and trying to ruin my wedding. I don't know what's the matter with you. Don't say it's this business with Elaine Ekstein, because it's more than that. Edwina says you're jealous. I can't stand it."

Maybe she was right. I probably was behaving like a brat. Which might be better than a shit or bitch. Was I jealous? Because I still longed for Paul four years after his death? Because my sole post-Paul attempt at romance had been a disaster?

But Alexa wasn't finished. "Honestly, who cares about your reason at this point? Behave yourself until after the wedding or else."

I was curious. "Or else what?"

"Or I'll fill Daddy in on everything."

Talk about dirty pool. My father is the one person in the world I never want to stand up to.

"You don't have to, Alexa. I will wear the dress. I won't complain about it. I'll behave."

"Well, okay."

"I'll come and get it."

"No. Conn will drop it off at your apartment. That way we'll know you have it, and you won't be able to stall or fib or anything. Will you be in? If not, he'll leave it across the hall with Mrs. Parnell."

"Wait a minute."

"No more wait a minutes. That's it. And, Camilla."

"Yes?"

"Daddy's coming with Conn to keep him company."

"The roads are bad. Maybe they should forget about it today."

"He wants to drop in and say hello to Mrs. What's-her-name. Don't be difficult about that either."

As Mrs. P. would say, sometimes discretion is the better part of valour.

\*    \*    \*

Except for that one night when she didn't answer, I couldn't remember ringing Mrs. Parnell's doorbell. She's always parked in the open door with the tip of her cigarette glowing in the dim light. Now when I needed to warn her about my father and Conn's visit and to recommend discretion, meaning not to mention she'd been checking on Randy Cousins, she didn't answer.

This time I had to ring. After ringing, I tried knocking. Then I switched to banging. Then I switched to thinking.

What was going on? It was just past five o'clock. Mrs. P. had planned to be home by four to wait for her new speakers to be delivered. Had they been delivered and then she'd headed out again? I knew her, she'd have hooked them up and would be happily blasting out some Russian symphonic piece loud enough to get the neighbours banging the walls.

I put my ear to the door. Except for a peevish squawk, nothing. A note was partly stuck under the door. I bent and picked it up. *No answer Feb. 10, 4:30 pm. Pls. call to arrange new delivery time. Extra fee will apply.* The signature was illegible.

Had Mrs. P. been particularly unsteady in recent weeks? What if, after her bit of sleuthing, she came home exhausted and slipped in the shower? What if she'd passed out, and her cigarette lay smouldering in the depths of the leather sofa as I paced in the hallway? What then?

The doors in our apartment building are not the type the average person can open with a strong kick. Not that it hasn't happened. I did the next best thing. I ran for Doug, the super. Five minutes later, the master key turned in Mrs. Parnell's lock.

"Golly, Miss, I sure do hope Violet's all right," Doug said. "What would we do without her keeping an eye on things, eh?"

I pushed past him and into Mrs. Parnell's totally empty

apartment. Nothing in the living room. Ditto the kitchen. The bedroom door was open. Empty. I banged on the bathroom door. No answer.

What if?

I held my breath, opened the door and found nothing. Exhale. At least she wasn't dead in the bathtub. I was rattled enough to check the closets and under the bed but she wasn't there either.

Back in the living room, Lester and Pierre shrieked from their swing. A strand of millet, picked clean, lay in the bottom of their cage.

# Twenty-Eight

O kay, where could she be?

"She must be visiting friends." A shadow of doubt settled on Doug's little moon face.

Sure, and what friends would they be?

"It's funny though, because she called this morning to let me know the speakers were being delivered and to buzz the guys in if I saw them."

"And you buzzed them in?"

"Yep. It's real weird, isn't it? She's been real keen about those speakers. Not like Violet to forget the time."

"What about her family?"

"I never seen anyone visiting her except you."

"She must have dropped off to see someone. I'm sure she's fine." It was more to convince myself than him.

The shadows deepened on the moon. "She's an old lady with a walker. She could have taken a tumble easy. I'm going to check down in the storage area and recycle section and the mail room and everything, just to be sure."

"Maybe she went out," I said. "Shopping. To get cigarettes or sherry or something."

"She uses the tuck shop in the building for her smokes. I pick up her Harvey's for her. The cupboard's full."

A quick check in the liquor cabinet confirmed sherry supplies were well stockpiled.

"Maybe someone asked her to go somewhere. Maybe do a favour or something."

Doug puffed himself up. "I sure hope not. Don't make sense for her to drive in the freezing rain. Maybe we should call the police."

"Maybe we should. But first, you check the building, and I'll drive around a few places she might be, and then if she doesn't show up, you call me and I'll call them." I wrote out my cellphone number for him.

"Okey dokey." He hustled his round little body out of the apartment and to the elevator. Remarkably speedy.

I called after him, "Maybe you can get into the office and check the files. Maybe she has a relative listed there."

"Nope. No relatives, for sure. Had to check this fall for our files. She wrote 'no one' under next of kin, and for emergency contact, she put your name, Miss."

"Oh." Great.

I reached Alvin on the phone. "You heard from Mrs. Parnell?"

"No," he said, "why?"

"She seems to be missing."

"Missing?"

"Look, I sent her on a mission, and she's not back and I'm worried. I was hoping she had just dropped in to see a friend or relative, but that doesn't seem to be the case. I need to have you help me find her. I don't need you to tell me it was a bad idea to send a wobbly old lady outside in this weather to do a bit of surveillance. I'm already telling myself that. I'll go and check out the area she was in, while Doug checks the apartment. You call the hospitals. In case."

"In case of what?" The voice came from behind me.

I whirled. "Hi, Daddy," I said.

\*　　\*　　\*

How could I find her in the dark?

I made sure I wasn't distracted by the fact everyone in my family had something new to be cheesed off about. But guilt has a nasty way of preying on your concentration. I was sure guilty of letting Mrs. Parnell get into trouble. Alvin was in better emotional shape, being innocent, but he hadn't had any luck either.

For the third time, I circled the townhouse complex where Randy Cousins lived. Mrs. P's LTD was parked on the street, covered in ice, its blue and white handicapped sticker dimly visible in the front window. No sign of her.

Not for the first time, I asked myself if I should have fibbed to McCracken and Daddy. Lights from the windows shone out on the street. Was Mrs. Parnell warm and dry in one of those kitchens, sipping sherry with some software engineer who had just arrived home from a hard day?

Time to start knocking on doors. Alvin took one side, I took the other. It was straightforward. A row of townhouses, middling upscale, indistinguishable. Didn't matter which end. Randy's unit was in the middle. Something bothered me. This was the kind of neighbourhood where people would not be home in the day. But judging from the thickness of the ice on the car, Mrs. Parnell had been parked since early afternoon. My teeth chattered. The temperature hovered just below zero, making the sidewalks even more slippery.

By the third door, it was confirmed.

"This afternoon? No one here would have seen her," said the young woman who opened the door. "Everyone works. If you want to find out what's going on in the day, you'd have to talk to someone in the apartment building." She pointed across the street.

I changed tactics. "I have a friend who moved to this development. Randy Cousins. Do you know her? Number 36."

"No. We're new. We haven't met anybody." The door closed.

The apartment stood in the middle of two batches of linked units. It was on Alvin's route, but I headed over anyway. It had seen better days. I bet it got under the skin of the townhouse people. Lowered the tone.

I was prepared to like everybody in it. "Yes, she was in the neighbourhood," said the washed-out woman with the three clinging kids at the second door. "This afternoon. I came home at maybe three. She was ringing doorbells across the street."

As she spoke, the familiar aroma of Kraft Dinner drifted into the hallway. I liked it better than the whiff of diapers.

"Three? And which doorbells?"

"Didn't pay much attention. I figured she'd end up here sooner or later. Collecting for something. Had my toonie ready."

"And did she show up?"

"No. But you should be talking to Andrew. He's the one. Apartment 10. He'll be glad to talk."

Glad to talk was an understatement. I soon figured Andrew had been waiting for this particular opportunity to knock. All the bad weather must have ratcheted up the boredom factor for him. "Chronic fatigue syndrome," he told me. "Most unutterably boring thing on earth, next to being buried alive."

He'd already poured me a cup of tea when I cut in to ask him if he'd seen Mrs. Parnell.

"Yes, I saw her," Andrew said. "Across the way. Middle of the afternoon. Ringing doorbells. Alone. Didn't look like a crusading evangelical type to me. I figured collecting for something, Heart Fund maybe or Cancer Society. I would have told her to save her breath in the new houses. She'd be far more likely to get something here, even if we are all on disability or welfare."

"Did you see which units she tried?" That would be too good to be true.

"Looked like she tried all of them, except maybe not the one in the middle. Nobody answered any of them. She should have started here instead. Get a better response. A cup of tea, a sympathetic ear."

"Did she come over?"

"Never got to my place. I was waiting for her. She crossed the road and headed this way. She walked slowly because of the cane."

The cane! She didn't even have her walker.

Andrew continued. "The front door's out of my sight, so it's difficult to say. Never returned to her car though."

"It looks like she never reached the building. No one before you saw her."

"Three o'clock, would have been kids getting home. You might ask around, see if anyone saw her in the parking lot. There are always kids around the building smoking. Worth a query."

"Did you see anyone else?"

"Yes. I did see another woman. First I thought they were together, but then they never seemed to connect. The other woman went the other way. Moving fast, almost jogging."

"One of your neighbours?"

"No. I'd never seen her before. They didn't speak, the old lady and this woman. Could have been a neighbour. Some of them you never see, they leave from their garage, they go home from their garage, never set foot outside, summer, winter, never. At any rate, I didn't recognize her."

"Do you know the woman at Number 36?"

"The police officer?"

"Yes. Could it have been her?"

"Don't see her often, usually in uniform. I thought she was taller, but I could be wrong."

"Anyone else?"

"Just a young man with a Mickey Mouse scarf. Not someone from our neighbourhood."

"He's with me. Wait a minute. How could you see the mice on the scarf?"

Andrew pointed with pride to a new-looking pair of Bushnell's binoculars. "Wouldn't want to miss a sighting of Mickey."

"I'll check the parking lot." I made my way across the treacherous surface toward the back of the building, hoping to find some furtive smokers. But not a soul was stupid enough to be standing puffing in the drizzle.

Maybe they scattered when Mrs. Parnell came into view? Intimidated by a gray-haired woman with a cane? Nah, that wouldn't happen. First of all, Mrs. P. probably had her own cigarette smouldering at all times during her exploration. Second, kids aren't intimidated by authority figures any more. Third, if they are, elderly women don't represent authority. Too bad when you think about it.

But why would Mrs. P. have come over to the parking lot in the first place? I figured it out when I turned around. You had a clear view of Randy Cousins's front door from the side lot and yet, if you stood next to the big dumpster, you wouldn't be visible in turn.

Mrs. Parnell would have liked that tactic. There were plenty of butts around the dumpster, but then it was the preferred spot for junior smokers. I checked for signs of Benson and Hedges, but Mrs. P. wasn't the type who thought the world was her ashtray.

Of course, she could have stayed in her car and watched and waited. That idea hit me like a bag of wet cement. I slithered halfway down the block to the parked LTD. Of course, the doors were locked. The covering of ice was thick enough to obscure the inside. I chipped at the layer by the window with my keys and peered inside. At least she wasn't slumped over, asphyxiated.

A couple of kids in unzipped ski jackets came around the corner as I stood trying to decide what to do next.

"Hey guys," I said, "I'm looking for a gray-haired woman with a cane. Did either of you see her?"

They exchanged glances.

"I'm supposed to take her to an appointment," I said.

"Real tall lady?" a boy with bleached hair asked. "Old like?"

"That's her."

"Yeah, she was here."

Good. "Where?"

He pointed toward the parking lot of the apartment building. "There by the side."

"When?"

He shrugged. "I dunno. It was still light."

"Maybe three-thirty, four," said the other one.

"What was she doing?"

They exchanged glances. I could see they had me pegged as someone trying to hassle a little old lady.

"I mean was she heading somewhere else? Not the right kind of day for her to be out. She could get hurt."

"You're not trying to lock her up or anything?"

"Lock her up?"

"Saying it's for her own good, like she can't take care of herself any more."

"What?"

"Yeah, I heard about that on the radio. Like taking their house and their money and locking them in the nut farm and saying it's for their own good."

Great, I was the bad guy again. "No, it's nothing like that. My friend has definitely not lost it. She's pretty smart. I wouldn't want to be the person who tried to lock her up."

"Okay." I must have passed some kind of test.

"So you did see her?"

"Yes."

"And she went somewhere?"

"Nah, she stayed over by the wall and had a cigarette. She gave us a couple and we talked. She sure knows a lot about explosives."

Don't go there, I thought. "And then?"

"And then we left."

"And she waited here?"

Again with the looks.

"It's okay, guys. She was helping me with something. She's a lot tougher than she looks. So, tell me, did she ask you any questions?"

They both started to talk at once. The small, smarter one took over. "She had a picture of the lady cop across the street and she had a picture of this guy. She wanted to know did we ever see that guy bothering her."

"And had you?"

"No."

"We've seen her but we never saw him," the kid with the bleached hair said.

"And when you left where was my friend?"

They gestured to the dumpster near the side of the building. The three of us strolled toward it.

"I need to talk to anyone else who might have seen her. I'm

worried. The police won't start looking until it's too late."

"Yeah."

"Any other people around here I could talk to?"

"People kind of come and go, if you wait a bit."

"Did you see another woman approach her?"

They shook their heads like they shared a brain stem. Their joint interest appeared to have been exhausted and they headed off, shoulders hunched, hands in pockets.

I found myself pacing. The parking lot resembled one big puddle by this time and if Mrs. P. had been talking to someone else and had left with them, there'd be no footprints to show their path. To be on the safe side, I checked out the perimeter of the yard. Maybe I'd see something. Anything.

By the back fence a large wooden box stored salt for the parking lot. Just to rule out everything, I headed for it. She wouldn't have snooped over there. It would have meant heading across a wide, slippery expanse and for what?

I turned. You couldn't see Randy Cousins's place from there. The dumpster and cars blocked the view. I looked up. The windows and balconies of the apartments faced the other way. No one had a clear view of that spot.

I lifted the lid. Nothing but salt inside, nearly up to the lid.

Sometimes I get wild ideas, perhaps because bad things happen to people I know. But where was she?

Alvin loped into view. He shook his head. Another strikeout.

"She's gotta be here somewhere. People up the road saw her heading back this way a couple of hours ago."

"A guy in the apartment building spotted her around here. Couple of kids confirmed. I've hit a wall with it. We have to call the police. First, let's check the side yards of the end-units in case she slipped. She didn't have her walker, just her cane."

"Vanity, thy name is Violet," Alvin said. "You think you're in shit with the world now, Camilla. Wait until cops find out why she was in the neighbourhood."

"Doesn't matter. We have to call the police."

"Will they do a house-to-house search?"

"They'll have to. Seventy-eight-year-old woman missing? Bad weather? We'll go to the media otherwise."

"You mean P.J.?"

I nodded. "I've looked everywhere. Some kids saw her here around three. She was staking out Randy Cousins's place. And a guy saw her near a tall woman earlier. Might have been Cousins."

Alvin's teeth were rattling, but at least the Mickey Mouse scarf absorbed some of rain. I didn't want to face the spectre of his mother flying in from Sydney to preside over his deathbed.

"Everywhere?" he said.

We both stared at the dumpster by the side of the building. Since my Sorels were a lot more reliable than Alvin's pointy leather boots, I was elected to check, even though we couldn't imagine any way for her to get in there. It took a couple of minutes of slipping and clawing, but I managed to hoist myself up enough to check the inside. It had been recently emptied.

No Mrs. Parnell.

"Did you open that salt box?"

"Yep. She's not in it. Unless she's under it or behind it..."

Alvin didn't need to ask.

"No. I didn't look behind it. How could she get there? It's practically covered in snow. We couldn't climb it."

By this time we were both running. I reached it first. Alvin careened into me. When I spotted the heel of a black boot protruding from the slush behind the box, it took thirty seconds to register. Alvin grabbed my phone and dialed 911.

I was on my knees brushing off the snow, freeing her face,

checking frantically for a pulse. Feeling her icy hands.

Thinking no hand could be so cold.

\*    \*    \*

Pacing doesn't help much. And when you're pacing with others in an emergency waiting room already stuffed with stressed and exhausted pacers, sometimes people take it out on you. Edwina expressed the mood of the crowd. "That's the limit, Camilla. Is there nothing you won't do?"

I kept my mouth shut. Every couple of minutes Alexa said, "Oh, Camilla."

Edwina stayed fired up. "Poor Mrs. Parnell, what did she ever do to deserve this?"

I didn't need her to tell me off. I was doing that to myself, by myself. But Edwina seemed like an appropriate penance for my sins in this case. And she wasn't saying anything that didn't need to be said.

"Exactly. Nothing," she said, her voice attracting the rest of the waiting room. "She was minding her own business, and look what's happened. Do you ever ask yourself why you do these things to people?"

"Edwina." Daddy's voice stopped her.

Alvin jumped to his feet. "Violet insisted. She would have headed out anyway even if Camilla hadn't asked her. She loves investigating. She says it makes her feel alive."

The only other sound in the waiting room was the squeak of shoes on the polished tiles. But listening to Edwina's accusations and Alvin's surprise defence was better than returning to the clump of plastic-covered seats and meeting my father's eyes. Anything was better. He sat without speaking, while Donalda patted his hand.

I kept pacing. I didn't want to deal with one more "Oh, Camilla."

Alvin and I whipped around as a door opened and a young doctor popped in and said, "Family of Violet Parnell?" He headed toward us, shaking his head.

"Lord thundering Jesus," Alvin said. "That's always a bad sign."

I couldn't say anything. Alexa started to cry.

"It's amazing," the doctor said, still shaking his head. "I wouldn't have given two cents for her chances, but she's kicking up quite a fuss."

"Thank God," I said.

Two skinny tears rolled down Alvin's pale cheeks.

"It's too early to predict the effect on her mental abilities, but it looks like she might be okay."

"She's going to make it?" My voice was high and wobbly.

"Good chance. She's hallucinating a bit. Whenever she regains consciousness, she demands to speak to my commanding officer."

"Can we see her?" Alvin said.

"You family?"

Alvin hesitated for a smidge too long.

"Sorry, just immediate relatives. We'll keep her in ICU until we get a definite improvement in her condition."

"I am family," Alvin said.

The doctor looked at me. What the hell? Alvin was somebody's family, as long as we weren't being too specific. "Yes," I said.

My father would soon point out my need to make a good confession. I might as well chalk up a walloping list of sins. "We're all family. How long will it be until she improves? If she improves," I said.

"No way to tell. Elderly people recovering from hypothermia, a lot depends on their age, general state of health, will to live, the kind of support they get from relatives." He raised an eyebrow at Alvin. "Some of it's just plain luck."

"Right."

"The miracle is she didn't fracture any bones. But the head wound adds to the uncertainty."

"The what?"

"The injury was fairly serious. She'll need intensive care for a while."

"I didn't see a head wound," I jabbered. "What caused it?"

The doctor laid a hand on my sleeve. "Perhaps you'd better talk to the police." He looked over my shoulder, where Conn McCracken loomed.

*     *     *

There was a decided chill in McCracken's car. I sat in the back as we drove into the parking lot across from Randy Cousins's place.

"Even for you," McCracken said, "this is something, Camilla."

"The doctor was talking about a head wound? What kind?"

"We get to ask the questions," Mombourquette said. "That would be just one of many things you're unclear on."

"Did she hit her head against the box when she fell?" I asked. I answered my own question. "No, that doesn't make sense. She couldn't climb behind that box by herself. Someone dumped her. Someone strong. They must have knocked her out first."

"Maybe you didn't hear me," Mombourquette said.

"Listen," Conn said, "we're not giving you information, because you'll just use it to get into more trouble than you're already in."

"If that's possible," Mombourquette said.

"So she was hit on the head then. Look where we found her, right out of view of everyone. Someone lured her to that box, whacked her on the head, tossed her behind it out of sight and left her to die. Just like what happened to me on the canal. Hey, here's another coincidence. It happened right after a witness saw her talk to a tall woman."

Well, that torqued up the tension.

We parked in the lot. "I want you to show me exactly where you found her. Exactly how she was lying. Exactly," McCracken said.

"With pleasure. And let me mention, I don't know how yet, but it's related to Benning and you sure can't hang this one on Elaine."

"I figure those kids mugged Mrs. Parnell for her purse or her cigarettes," McCracken said.

"No. Not in this neighbourhood. In the apartment, people watch out for each other. Anyway, she still had her purse and cigarettes." I didn't mention the kids had been impressed with Mrs. P.'s knowledge of explosives. Why buy trouble?

"Anyway, Ident's on the way."

"Good. I want to know whose fault this was."

"I can tell you whose fault it was," Mombourquette said.

# Twenty-Nine

It was nearly seven-thirty when I pulled the rental car into Lindsay's driveway.

Merv was not even slightly glad to see me. "Don't you have a home?"

I pushed past him into the foyer. I tried not to elbow his gall bladder. Lindsay was curled up on the leather sofa. She smiled limply when I strode into the living room.

"This won't take long. Lindsay. You need a lawyer and I'm happy to represent you. In return, I need a favour."

I raised my hand to silence Merv. "More trouble. Mrs. Parnell was attacked this afternoon while working on this case. She's in intensive care. We have to pull together to find out who killed Benning and framed Elaine before anyone else gets hurt."

Lindsay crumpled onto the sofa and stared. "Attacked? Mrs. Parnell? But why would anyone hurt her?"

"How can you represent Lindsay when all you can think about is Elaine? You're on your own, Camilla." Merv likes to be in charge. He obviously thought the job of the guy in charge was to keep Lindsay from facing reality.

Lindsay said, "Do you think the attack on Mrs. Parnell is connected with what's been happening?"

"You bet."

"Forget it, Camilla. If she's hurt, it's because you've been sticking your nose into the wrong things again. Lindsay has been through enough. You're not getting her into any more rough situations."

I loved that, like I created the Benning nightmare. But I didn't take the bait. "Listen to yourself, Merv. Lindsay's life is on the line here. Whether you want it or not, she's involved."

Lindsay said, "She's right. What do you want me to do, Camilla?"

"You don't have to do anything," Merv said.

She gave his hand a brave little squeeze. "It's time I stood on my own two feet."

I'm glad she said it. Saved me the trouble. "Good. I want you to pay a visit to Elaine at the Regional Detention Centre. Visiting time for the public is evenings from seven to nine. You can still get there tonight if you hurry." I handed her a list of names. "Find out if she saw any of these people on her way to your place. Don't let on you're working with me. Don't show her the list. Act like it's just a regular visit. After all, you are her friend. Then make sure every name gets worked into the conversation."

Merv was ugly enough before he rolled his eyes.

Lindsay nodded. The list contained everyone I could imagine who might have spotted Elaine on her pizza run. It led off with Randy Cousins and included even unlikely candidates like Vanessa Gross-Davies, Chair of the WAVE Board of Directors, and that phony uncle, P. J. Lynch. I asked them to find out if she had seen any police officers at all.

Merv and Lindsay both lifted their eyebrows.

"And call me as soon as you find out. Leave a message if you have to. We've all had enough of this bullshit." I didn't wait for them to answer. I headed back to the hospital for the night shift.

*　*　*

As I elbowed my way through the waiting room outside the ICU, I ran into Donalda and my father. Daddy had finished his bedside duty. I'd never seen him look so tired. He leaned heavily on Donalda's arm.

"Oh, yes, um, Camilla. I've been reading to Violet." His copy of Chesterton's *St. Francis of Assisi* was still tucked under his arm. Poor Mrs. P. She was more the Winston Churchill type. Booze, smokes and rapier wit. Alvin had the right idea. Almost as soon as Mrs. P. was wheeled in, he'd draped a hot pink lei on her IV pole and left a copy of *Frank* magazine for her edification.

You can always tell when you're in an Intensive Care Unit. If you don't catch on right away, the subtle squeak of the nurses' rubber-soled shoes, the lines from intravenous drips, the half-light, the heavy hints of antiseptic and the muffled weeping will clue you in soon enough.

It was a long night. I wrapped up at daybreak, after spending hours doing paper analyses, grasping for the missing piece of insight that would clear up everything. I hadn't found it. I did slip out a couple of times to try to reach Lindsay and Merv on the pay phone. I kept getting their answering machines. And they kept getting mine. I spent the rest of the time reading the *Ottawa Citizen* to Mrs. Parnell's unconscious form. I made a point of not staring at her ashen cheeks, her cold, grey knuckles, or the lumpy skin on her hand with the needle for the intravenous feed. Since the ICU staff swore even unconscious people react well to voices, I picked out intriguing stories with military overtones. It's never hard to find some former Brigadier General belting out opinions in the paper. It made a nice change, I was sure, from my father praying or my sisters chatting about the mid-winter white sales or Alvin promising her some high-grade weed if she would just wake up.

Once an hour I left the unit to pace through the endless,

nearly deserted, hospital corridors. I needed to clear my head and to plan to let Randy Cousins get what was coming to her. I hadn't come up with a good scheme to prove she'd attacked Mrs. Parnell.

The rest of the night, I hunted for stories which might amuse her, say successful military capers involving helicopters. But I'd given up hope of hearing Mrs. Parnell's wheezy chuckle again.

"Ms. MacPhee, you'll never guess," she said suddenly around four in the morning. I dropped my newspaper when I leapt off the chair.

"What?" Not the most effusive greeting for someone who regains consciousness after a long and frightening twelve hours.

"A strange man named Eugene told me my family has been sitting with me round the clock. Isn't that amazing?"

"Eugene's your nurse this shift. Why is it amazing?"

"Everyone in my family has been dead for years. This is well beyond the call of duty, wouldn't you say?"

"Maybe they're not as dead as they look."

"What happened? You said Eugene's my nurse and this appears to be a hospital."

"You're in Intensive Care."

"Explains the appalling lack of sherry. I want to get home and get my new speakers set up. There'd better be a damned good reason for keeping me here."

"There is. You were checking out Randy Cousins and someone conked you on the head and tucked you out of sight to die of hypothermia."

"Nevertheless, apparently I didn't die. Too stubborn."

I pulled closer to the bed. "Tell me, what's the other guy look like?"

"I wish I could remember, Ms. MacPhee. Everything's blank."

"Ah." There went my hopes.

She lifted her hand to her head and massaged her temple with two bony fingers. "I'd prefer a good old-fashioned hangover any day."

"In that case, you should avoid icy, dark and deserted parking lots."

"I was in a parking lot?"

"Yes. Across the street from Randy Cousins's house. Ring any bells?"

She shook her head. "Ouch."

"Save the head-shaking for a better time. Do you recall why you checked out the parking lot?"

"Ms. MacPhee."

"What?"

"Could you welcome me back to the living before you begin the third degree?"

"Welcome back, Mrs. Parnell. You have been missed."

"By my whole family, apparently."

"Plus Lester and Pierre send their regards. As does your cat. And the guys delivering the speakers."

A throat cleared behind me. That sweet and burly guy named Eugene. "Somebody's awake. We'll get the doctor over to see you."

"Better tell him to take a number," said Mrs. P.

"We'll need to examine her now that she's conscious." Eugene pointed to the other side of the curtain, like he expected me to take the hint.

"Don't talk about me as if I'm not here," Mrs. Parnell said. "I may be old, but I'm formidable."

"Formidable's good," Eugene said.

"I hope my car hasn't been towed, Ms. MacPhee."

"Lucky I had your spare keys. Alvin drove it home for you."

"Excellent. Help yourselves to it. No good to me here."

"Time's up," Eugene said.

"I need a minute. I have a couple more questions."

"No questions. Step outside." I didn't rate a smile.

"Good-bye, Ms. MacPhee. See if you can get my friend Harvey to drop in for a visit, will you?"

*   *   *

Alvin and I were both in fairly good humour, since Mrs. Parnell had given new meaning to the phrase bounced back. Daddy and Donalda were on the job. I figured Daddy could keep Eugene in his place.

I needed to get moving because the day-to-day business of Justice for Victims had been piling up. People with problems needed to be advised, politicians needed to be badgered, funds needed to be raised, briefs needed to be barbed and bills needed to be stalled. I needed to catch the hell up, and Alvin needed to get the lead out. I did not need to sleep. A couple of hours upright on a plastic visitor's chair was plenty for anyone. I was thundering up the stairs to the hospital parking garage when the Level 3 door opened and I found myself nose to chest with Randy Cousins.

We both stood our ground.

"Well, well," she said.

I checked around. For once, not a soul crowded the metal stairway.

"I hear you're interested in my activities."

She was one scary lady. I kept quiet. Where the hell was the rest of the world when you needed it? Unless I was very wrong, this was the woman who tossed Mrs. Parnell behind a salt box and left her to die of hypothermia. Not to mention dumping me headfirst into that snowbank on the canal. I didn't feel like arguing with her at the top of a metal staircase without any witnesses.

"Let me fill you in," she said. "We're not on opposite sides."

"Right. If you're trying to find yourself alone with Mrs. Parnell, forget it. Two people are with her at all times. And she doesn't remember her assailant." I tried to deke past her and scoot through the door to the parking area. At least there'd be witnesses.

She extended her arm and blocked the way. "No wonder you piss people off."

"That's my goal in life." What the hell. She might be about to toss me down three flights of stairs, but I didn't have to snivel.

"Everyone needs a goal," she said. "We're not so different. My goal was getting that little prick Benning locked up forever."

She sounded like she meant it. That came as a surprise. I said, "I'm listening."

"I hear you think I killed him."

"Did you?"

"I hated him. I could probably have done it, but we have departmental rules."

"Maybe it was an extracurricular activity."

She chuckled. "For somebody, it probably was. I'm just as interested as you are in finding out who the somebody is."

"I'll send you monthly activity reports. How about that?"

"You're a riot. Connie and Lennie tell me your elderly friend might make it. I hear she was checking out my neighbours when she was attacked. That makes me wonder what's going on. I hope it makes you want to leave this investigation to the pros."

"What investigation? I thought the Benning case was a done deal. Elaine serves time because the cops can't believe she's innocent."

"Of course she's innocent. We're not idiots."

"Really? Maybe I'm wrong."

"You're wrong about a lot of things."

The metal door to Level 3 opened, and three people pushed into the stairwell. Randy Cousins moved sideways to let them pass.

"Oh, good. Witnesses. Courts love them." I turned and spoke to them as they clattered down the stairs. "I'm Camilla MacPhee and this is Constable Miranda Cousins. Please note the time and the fact that we're having a dispute. in case you hear that I've gone missing."

Those three certainly could scurry.

"Very funny."

"Since we're being candid, answer this. If your only involvement in this case is the pursuit of truth and justice, why was Mrs. Parnell attacked across the street from *your* house?"

Her jaw knotted. "I don't know. And I intend to find out. It will be easier without you making Connie and Lennie go ballistic every ten minutes and putting your friends and family in serious jeopardy. You know, Lennie has to swallow half a bottle of Mylanta every time he hears your name."

"Big deal. He's supposed to care about Elaine, and he's not even willing to put up with a bit of indigestion?"

"He does care about Elaine. A lot more than he should, if you ask me. Why do you think those two guys are still working on this case?"

She had me there.

"So take a bit of advice. You have strict bail conditions. Stop getting in our way, or the judge will hear about it, and you can worry about Elaine's problems from the same side of the bars." She pushed past me and headed down the stairs, shoulders squared.

My first real encounter with Randy Cousins, human being,

had been full of surprises. Two minutes of observing her up close, and I knew why McCracken and Mombourquette backed her solidly. An impressive woman. And maybe, just maybe, she was telling the truth. If so, who was lying?

To be on the safe side, I headed back into the hospital to make sure my family and all the nursing staff knew that Mrs. Parnell was not to be alone with anyone, including police officers. I gave P. J. a call too and told him what had happened to Mrs. P., in case the police didn't send out a press release on her. While I was at it, I tried once more to reach Lindsay. I left a message suggesting she leave the name or names on my voice mail if she didn't catch me the next time. I'd fill in the details later.

I felt better afterwards. I couldn't imagine any perpetrator getting past one of my sisters or even my father. Not to mention Mrs. P's day nurse, Derek, who was even bigger than Eugene.

*     *     *

I couldn't work. I paced restlessly, which isn't all that easy in a tiny office with two people in it. Eventually, I checked out the images on Alvin's painted window. After that, I decided to leave. I had plenty of time to go home, shower, shampoo and get respectable for the rehearsal.

"Or else." Edwina's words. I'd show her by turning up at the rehearsal in the little black number. I had fun anticipating her expression.

Then I remembered something I should have done much earlier. "I don't know what's the matter with me. I meant to take a look at the site along the river where Lindsay claimed she found blood and signs that Benning had been there. With all the upset about Mrs. P., I put it out of my mind," I said to Alvin.

"You can't think of everything. Lot of serious shit going down."

"Most charitable of you, Alvin, but it's important. It's probably where he was killed. I'm going to whiz by and take a quick glimpse. I'll kick myself if the rain has washed away every bit of evidence."

"It was raining before Lindsay even mentioned it. Which reminds me, she was trying to reach you."

"Damn. We're telephone tagging. Any message?"

"Just that the names you were looking for didn't come up."

In view of Alvin's good behaviour, I didn't lean on him about not mentioning Lindsay's call earlier. "I might drop in and see her after I check the river site."

Alvin jerked his head and banged his sunglasses on the lamp. "Recurring death wish, Camilla?"

"Why?"

"If you're late for this rehearsal, try to picture it. What time is Stan picking you up?"

"He's been pressed into service running errands, so I'm getting myself there. No big deal. I'm glad to go somewhere without Stan."

"He has heated seats, though, in the new car. Leather."

"Who cares? The weather's heating up. The whole city's a giant puddle. The ice on the canal is practically melted."

"I beg you, check the site another time. Don't take the chance. I'm the one who has to work with you after your sisters finish screaming. Wait a minute. Here's an idea. I have some little Valentine's chores I need to do first…"

"What kind of chores? Nothing to do with long distance calls, I hope."

He managed an expression of tremendously affronted dignity, amazing for someone with an orange tan, three Day-

Glo leis, nine earrings and a ponytail. "No. Lindsay's had such a hard time lately, I wanted to make her a card, plus get some special chocolates and drop them off for Violet in the hospital. But that won't take long. I've got the LTD. Give me the details of the location, and I'll head over and take a peek at the site. I'll let you know what I find."

I couldn't think of a good reason to say no. Even though it was Alvin, and there had to be something fishy about the proposition.

"It's a deal."

As he headed out to the Byward Market to hunt for handmade paper and Belgian chocolates, Alvin narrowed his eyes and reminded me to go straight to the rehearsal. I told him to keep me in the picture about what he saw at the river. I pressed my cellphone into his outstretched palm. "And remember, no, count them, *no* phone calls to Cape Breton."

"Okay. And on your part, get to the church on time."

"Piece of wedding cake." I closed the door behind me.

*   *   *

Lindsay had left a message on my home machine too. No joy from the RDC. Elaine knew Randy Cousins but hadn't run into her until she arrived at Lindsay's, where she recognized her as one of the officers. There was one other thing that might be useful, but probably it wasn't important. Of course, Lindsay didn't answer her phone.

Merv didn't answer her phone or his. I left messages asking that the next message have some information about the thing that was potentially useful. I fed Mrs. Parnell's cat and chucked some food at Lester and Pierre without getting bitten. Next, I took a long bath, this time with a peach bath bomb, and drifted off to sleep for a while in the tub. Afterwards, I wound my wet hair into a French roll. It was only the rehearsal. The wedding wasn't until Monday. Surely, someone would have made me a hair appointment before then.

As I anchored the hair, I noticed the message light flashing on my phone. Just like Alvin to call when I'm in the tub.

"Lord thundering Jesus, Camilla. I've been by the river. Looks like Lindsay was right. It's a great clue. Just like a Nancy Drew book. It's the break we need. Hey, it's nearly five, and I have things to do. See you later."

Well, that was useless. I dialled my cellphone number. Alvin didn't answer. Not much point in leaving a message for myself either. By this time, I had on my new rehearsal outfit and a pile of makeup. I looked fine if you care about these things. As Alexa does.

I checked the time. Five-thirty. I figured the rehearsal would start at seven. The next couple of days would be entirely given over to hair appointments, wedding, reception and all that crap. Then I could get back to the business at hand. Finding out who killed Benning. Finding out why that person would also go after Mrs. Parnell. And then fixing him or her but good.

Monday morning I'd be back on the job, with Alvin's new information making a difference. Or not. The only fly in the ointment was the unavailability of Alvin. But what the hell. Relax, stroke the cat and watch the view for the first time in weeks.

The cat sounded happy. That made one of us.

I tried Lindsay's one more time, expecting to leave another peevish message. She took me by surprise when she answered the phone.

"Camilla!"

I didn't want to beat around the bush. "So what did Elaine have to say?"

"We didn't have any luck at all. It looks like Elaine didn't see any of those people. Of course, it's hard to be sure, because I couldn't come right out and tell her what I wanted to know and why. Merv did his best, though. I think you would have been impressed with how sneaky he can be. We eliminated everyone on the list, I think."

"That's a letdown."

"I'm sorry. We did our best. And I'm ready to do anything else you can think of. Merv is, too. Seeing Elaine behind bars was so distressing. We have to get her out of that place. How can we help?"

"First, do not attempt to hang up without telling me about the potentially useful thing you mentioned."

"Oh, that. Stupid really. It wasn't easy to talk to her about this without giving you away. Elaine mentioned she saw Mia Reilly while she was waiting at the Colonnade. I think Elaine was distracted that day because she was worried about me, but maybe Mia noticed someone from your list. Why don't you ask her? Would she help you in spite of their complaint to the law society?"

"Oh, yes, she'll help, all right. And Lindsay."

"Yes?"

"Thanks. A lot."

\*   \*   \*

Anyone in the room could have heard the pieces clicking into place in my tired little brain. It took a full five minutes for my mind to process that key bit of information. And when it did, holy shit.

Mia Reilly. Of course.

Who had been in the Crown Attorney's office when so many of the charges against Benning fizzled for lack of evidence? Who would have been in a position to engineer his escape? Who knew exactly how the Crown and the police thought? Who had an insider's view of how criminals act, where drugs are available, how cars are stolen, how evidence is planted? Who was an exercise junkie, strong and flexible? Who had a legal career and a new fiancé to lose if the word oozed out she'd had a relationship with scum like Benning?

Why the hell hadn't I thought of Mia? Now all I needed was enough time to prove it.

I called my cellphone number. Alvin didn't answer. I tried again. The cellphone couldn't have been out of juice, because I'd charged it before we left the office. It couldn't have been turned off, because then I'd get the little message that the subscriber was currently not available. Alvin couldn't be talking to his mother because it would have been busy. Could Alvin have left it somewhere?

Alvin would never lose a phone. I tried one more time. He could have been in the middle of an intersection dashing across traffic on an icy road. But that would not deter our boy. Five-forty. Alvin had called before five. Where the hell was he? Somewhere where he couldn't call? Say, a hospital where you can't use cellular phones.

I was on my way.

# Thirty

"She's gone," they said, when I buzzed to get into the ICU. I felt like the breath had been knocked out of me. I toppled back onto the plastic chair in the waiting room. I didn't hear the scratchy voice of the nurse on the other side.

A pleasant-faced woman I recognized from the waiting area touched my arm. "Not that kind of gone, dear. She's moved out of ICU. That nice boy who's always with you carried her things." I was surprised at how wobbly my knees felt when I stood up. I was still shaky when I finally located Mrs. P. settled into a room with a view.

"This is a relief. I thought you were on your way to the great beyond," I said.

She was propped up in bed looking dangerous and nibbling on a Godiva truffle. "Old soldiers never die, Ms. MacPhee."

She had enough flowers to open a kiosk. I noticed roses from my father. Red. A tasteful bouquet from the girls. And a perky African violet from Doug, the building super.

"Glad to hear it. Do I conclude by that unusual heartshaped lei formation that Alvin has visited?"

"Indeed. You missed young Ferguson. Would you like one of these splendid chocolates he brought? You have to admit, he has style."

"If you want to call it that. When did he leave?"

"Quite a while ago. Couldn't wait to see you."

"Ditto. But when exactly?"

"Let me think. It was just after that snippy young woman from the Crown Attorney's office dropped in to give me a talking to about the legal fine points of stalking policewomen. Oh look, he forgot his lovely Mickey Mouse scarf."

"*Who?*"

"Alvin. He forgot his scarf."

"What snippy woman?" I gripped the side rails of her bed.

"I was taken aback too, Ms. MacPhee. The nerve of the girl. She told me I could be in just as much trouble as you if I didn't stop."

"You mean Mia Reilly was here?"

"Can't remember the name. Blonde hair. Stop jumping around, Ms. MacPhee. You'll give my roommate another heart attack."

I lowered my voice. "When? How did she know you were here?"

"Don't worry about it. Young Ferguson put her in her place. He told her the evidence he found at the river would be enough to get Elaine out of the slammer. And finger the guilty party."

"Shit."

"I don't understand. What is the problem? We have not been unduly constrained by that young woman in the past."

"That was before we knew she was a killer."

"I beg your pardon, Ms. MacPhee."

"I should have realized when McCracken confirmed that there was a hole drilled into the door of Elaine's car."

"You are mystifying me."

"I thought Randy Cousins used the drill bandit technique to get into Elaine's car. But it must have been Mia. She was prosecuting that case. She even told me that. Everything adds up. She knew how the drill bandit acted. Apparently she ran into Elaine at the pizza place when the coffee was sitting in the SUV in the parking lot, nicely out of sight. Elaine would have told her she was heading to Lindsay's. Mia would have figured, two birds with one stone."

"But why?"

"Because she'd already killed Benning."

"Killed Benning? Surely that is taking prosecution too far."

"I've been thinking about it. The failure to get Benning convicted was just as likely to result from an ally in the Office of the Crown Attorney as in the police."

"And you think this woman was his confederate?"

"Or lover. She's engaged to a partner in a big law firm. She sure wouldn't want Benning dragging her down."

"But surely, Ms. MacPhee, a professional woman like that wouldn't have been involved with Benning."

"Think of Rina Benning. Think of Lindsay. Educated, attractive, both of them. The more I think of it, the more it makes sense. She was in a position to engineer his escape. She was also in a position to frame someone else."

"That explains her determination to prosecute Ms. Ekstein. And you, for that matter."

"Elaine played right into her hands."

"But how would she know where Lindsay was? I don't think Ms. Reilly was in on that."

"She wasn't. I think she was trying to set Elaine up. And then Elaine let it slip about Lindsay and us guarding her. All she had to do was follow Elaine. That SUV is the size of a county. No trouble tracking it. She would have been prepared with the drill, some Rohypnol. She probably had it on her. I'm betting the autopsy showed Benning had taken Rohypnol too. Benning was a wild man. She couldn't have handled him conscious."

"Good grief."

"So she's aware that we found the site where he was murdered?"

Mrs. Parnell seemed to be trying to get out of bed. "Young Ferguson was heading back there to check something out and…"

"You mean she *knows* he was headed there?"

"No, she'd left before he told me about it."

Even so, Alvin's adventure seemed like a bad idea. I had no choice but to check him out. Too soon old and too late smart, my father likes to say. I learned my lesson last year about putting myself in danger. Running off alone into the park to see a possible crime scene fitted nicely into the class of stupid things.

Right. So who could help? I remained persona non grata with the police, so scratch the force. Mrs. P. was seriously out of commission.

"I'll head over and see that everything's all right."

"You don't think she'd hurt young Ferguson?"

I thought back to the scent I hadn't been able to identify just before I was shoved into the snowbank on the canal: cedar and bergamot. First Mia's cologne. Then Mia's knees in my back forcing me deeper into the snow. All that goddam exercise she bragged about had served her well.

"Yes. I think she'll hurt him."

"I'm coming with you. Don't try to stop me."

"No. You need to call for help. You're needed as communications central. Alvin has my phone, but you can reach Merv or Conn McCracken. Or Leonard Mombourquette. They'd listen to you. Merv's probably at Lindsay's. The rehearsal's not until seven. McCracken or even, God help us, Mombourquette, might still be at the station. Call everybody you can think of. See if you can get someone to meet me by the Rideau River in lower Strathcona Park. Tell them it won't take long. It's just to be on the safe side. What the hell, call P. J. Lynch too. As soon as I find Alvin and the cellphone I'll be in touch. If you don't hear from me in half an hour, call 911 and tell them one hell of a story."

"Don't forget the scarf." Mrs. Parnell handed me Alvin's hand-knit mile of mice. She was already on the phone as I raced out the door.

*　*　*

Six o'clock came and went.

Alvin, with his slippery, leather-soled shoes and light clothing, was not exactly dressed for success in the great outdoors. What if he'd slipped on the path near the river? The days might be getting longer, but with the cloud cover and driving rain, no one would spot him. All the Jimmy Buffett music in the world wouldn't keep him from freezing to death overnight.

Minutes later, the rental car fishtailed toward the Rideau River. I was dressed for the rehearsal, wearing my ankle length wool coat, the deep green silk scarf Edwina had given me for Christmas and my good knee-high black leather boots. I had the Sorels in the car, just in case, plus an umbrella and a flashlight. You never know.

By my calculations, it wouldn't take more than ten minutes from the hospital to the river. Then ten minutes to check it out and another fifteen, twenty at the outside to get to St. Jim's. Barely on time.

I took short cuts and maybe broke a few speed limits. The drizzle had turned to hard rain again. By the time I pulled into the parking lot at the end of Range Road, the wipers were working overtime and wind rocked the rental car.

Mrs. Parnell's LTD was one of five cars parked in the lot. There was no sign of Alvin. Although the way the rain sluiced down, you couldn't see anyway. I pulled off my dress boots and

*307*

jammed my feet into the Sorels. I grabbed Alvin's Mickey Mouse scarf and substituted that for the green silk. I wrapped it about eight times around my head and neck, stepped out of the car and unfurled the umbrella. The wind whipped it inside out.

Three people with four drenched dogs raced for cover out of the dog area in lower Strathcona Park and dove into their cars. I banged on their windows, one by one. None of them had seen Alvin.

I headed down through the slushy snow on the path, glad of the waterproof boots and the light standards along the way. I'd walked through that park hundreds of times when Paul and I were in law school, living in a second floor apartment on Marlborough Avenue. It's not the kind of place where you worry about your safety. Dog parks are never empty. This one has its share of joggers and cyclists in the summer, cross country skiers in the winter, and it's crawling with pooches and owners anytime. I told myself the worst that could happen to Alvin was a wet kiss from a Lab.

Two more people with dogs splashed past me on the way to the parking lot. A lone jogger, heading out of the park, followed close behind them.

By the time I hit the site, in spite of Mickey Mouse, my hair hung in wet strings, definitely not a French twist anymore. My coat was soaked, and I was damn cold, if you didn't count my feet in the trusty Sorels. I imagined Alvin's twiglike ankles snapped because of a fall on the path. That might explain it. He'd be lying helpless with the cellphone out of his agonized reach.

When I located the spot Lindsay described, I found no sign of Alvin. Nothing but slush, the sound of open water and breaking ice.

Could he have gone further into the park? But why? Because he's Alvin, that's why, I thought. What else would you need to know? I concentrated on trying to locate the little twerp. I almost missed the ringing noise.

A phone? There wasn't a building nearby. The ringing stopped briefly and started again. Four more rings and then it stopped again. Obviously, someone who used the same strategy as my sisters.

I spotted the black receiver on the far side of a scruffy bush near the river bank. I picked it up and pressed TALK.

"Camilla," someone bleated, faintly. The "battery low" sign blinked.

"Yes?"

"Where the hell are you?"

"Edwina?"

"Who else? You get yourself over to this church in the next two minutes or you may as well change your name. Got it?"

"Listen, Edwina, I need your help."

"No, you listen. Everyone's here and we're ready to go."

"What do you mean, everyone's there? It's not seven yet."

"Six-thirty. The rehearsal's at six-thirty."

"Is Leonard Mombourquette there?"

"You're breaking up. Talk loud."

"Edwina," I yelled, "I'm down at the river and…"

"Did you say down at what river? Oh, Camilla. Alexa's in tears. Stop this stupidity and get over here."

"But Alvin's…"

The line went dead. The faintest blip. Then nothing. Okay. Deal with the girls later. Now to locate Alvin mondo quicko, get help and be on my way. I figured he must have slipped with those stupid shoes and skidded off the path. So the thing to do was, check for marks, find him and drag him back to the car. Logically, the skidding would have taken place near where he dropped the phone.

"Alvin!" Yelling is always good. Ask anyone in my family.

I made my way along the path, hollering and checking the river side for sign of a long skid. No sign. The path sloped and even in the dim light, I could see the pointy tracks leading through the slush to the little clump of woods. I followed, sinking into the wet snow.

The driving rain was cold enough to chill but not to freeze. My long wool coat grew heavier. Even the wool dress underneath was getting damp, but unless I found Alvin soon, that was the least of my problems.

In the distance, I caught sight of another jogger heading out of the park. Or maybe it was the same one. They all look alike. I slid down the incline, grabbing at brush to keep me from falling. How the hell do the joggers manage in the winter, I wondered. An image of the jogger passing Lindsay's place the bitterly cold night Benning was killed flickered in my mind. That image offered answers to a couple of nagging questions. Click. Click. Could the jogger have been Mia? Had she trapped Alvin? If yes, I hoped like hell she hadn't seen me.

At the bend in the slope, I spotted it. A long track in the piled snow. Big one too. Like someone had slid right to the edge of the river bank. I left the path and waded further into the slush. Something heavy had skidded across and kept going. The track went right to the bank and then down to the edge of the river.

Lucky I had the flashlight. I shone it down toward the partly frozen shore. Even with the flashlight, I couldn't see well in the glare of the rain. There were no convenient lamp standards off the path. It takes a lot to freeze the Rideau and the weather had been mild for days. The river was noisy, strong currents moving fast under the ice. Open water frothed at the shoreline. Further out breaks showed between large plates of ice.

I was too goddam cold and wet to think straight. Not far away, a duck quacked miserably. It took a time to locate the dark, still lump near the shore.

The orange lei was a dead giveaway. It fluttered in the wind. Plastic doesn't care about the weather. Alvin lay on a small triangle of ice broken away from the shore. What the hell was he doing there? The ice plate sloped badly. I hung on to clumps of brush and half-slid, half-crawled down the bank.

"Alvin," I yelled. "Wake up!" The lump didn't move. The lei flapped in the wind.

"*Alvin.*" That was stupid. I didn't even know whether he was dead or alive. But if he moved and the ice slab tilted, he'd be dead soon. If he went under, he'd surface downstream at the locks in the Spring. Or not at all.

Maybe yelling his name wasn't the greatest idea. I could startle him and he'd roll over and then…or, typical Alvin, he'd do the opposite of what I wanted, with the same result. If I could just reach him. But first things first.

My jaw dropped as a chunk of ice flew through the air and sent the flashlight flying in a wide arc toward the river. The splash that followed was the worst sound in the world.

# Thirty-One

The jogger had descended partway down the slope. It was too late to hide.

"Surprise. I'm back." The last person I wanted to hear.

"Call 911. We have an injured person stuck on the ice." I tried to sound confident.

Mia Reilly's voice was colder than the rain. "Not dead?"

"No. But he's unconscious. We have to get him."

She moved closer. "You mean not dead yet."

"No, but if the ice separates any more and tilts, he'll be in the river."

"And you'll be right after him." Mia's usually sleek blonde bob hung dark and wet. Her makeup must have washed away, leaving her ghostlike in the fog. She wasn't showing her expensive smile tonight. Even in water-resistant black jogging gear, she must have been soaked.

"No, I think I can get him out. For God's sake, Mia, please run back and call for help. I don't know how long he's been lying there."

"His neck looks broken."

I whirled and gawked at Alvin. How many times had I threatened to break his neck? Now it didn't seem amusing. "Hurry up, then," I said.

"What's your rush?"

"Are you crazy?" On the river, a sheet of ice cracked with a bang. I whipped my head back toward Alvin. "Before it's too late, Mia. If that ice breaks off any more, he'll tilt and go under."

Nothing prepared me for her giggle.

"There's nothing funny about this." I felt angry enough to toss her and her sick little laugh into the roiling water.

"I don't know about that," she said.

"Find a long branch we could use to hook him so he doesn't go under if it does break loose."

I wanted to go for help but couldn't leave Mia with Alvin. She would smile and watch him drown. I had no tools and no way of getting him on ground without putting him at even greater risk. I was stumbling in circles and tripping on the ridiculous scarf, now stretched beyond imagination. I tramped on it as I caught my balance and realized it was strong enough to get Alvin to shore. I staggered as close as I could to the edge of the river. What was that sound? A moan?

"What?" I yelled.

The weak call was lost in the wind and rain. But it was not time for a conversation. Alvin was trying to sit up.

"Keep still. You're by the open water."

Alvin moved. The slab of ice tipped. Frantically, I unwound the scarf from my neck and tied one end to the trunk of the nearest alder.

"I'm going to toss you the scarf, then we'll go for help."

Alvin kept trying to say something.

"Can't hear you. Don't try and talk. Do you have any feeling in your hands? Can you grip the scarf if I toss it to you?"

He must have been tremendously weakened. I couldn't make out a word. The slab wobbled and tilted more.

"For Christ's sake, stop moving," I yelled.

He leaned forward.

"Shut up." I tossed the scarf.

Alvin rose to his knees. "Behind you!"

I jerked around in time to see Mia Reilly bring down a piece of broken branch. I rolled to avoid the blow and slipped from the muddy bank into the water. I plunged to my waist. I reached out to grab at the vegetation on the side. To my left, Alvin's plate of ice tipped.

"Hang on," I yelled.

The sumac held fast despite my weight. Mia Reilly kicked at my hands. Alvin moved closer. "Sorry, Camilla," he said.

I tried to say "save yourself, Alvin," but I inhaled a mouthful of icy, brown river. The wet wool coat hung like an anchor, the weight dragging me deeper into the water. If I let go of the sumac, I'd be finished. I kicked around and felt for something solid. My foot caught on a root. Mia's boot descended again.

"A tragic accident. I mean, *so* noble of you to die trying to save him."

Behind me, Alvin went quiet. Was he already beneath the water, his lungs exploding as he shot under the ice?

Mia's heel landed on my hand. I screamed and let go. My boots were flooded, too heavy to tread water. I pumped my legs to kick off the Sorels. They held fast.

I fought back panic. I kicked my feet and grabbed at the buttons of the coat. My fingers didn't want to work.

I had a dim memory that your extremities cease to function after twenty seconds in near zero water. How long had it been? Felt like weeks. Goddam boots. The current sucked me toward the muddy river bottom. The cold was so intense, I felt little else. Every instinct sent my hands flailing upwards, toward the shore, splashing. I fought the urge and forced myself to work the buttons of my coat. My fingers grew too numb to feel.

A second's a hell of a long time when you're under water fighting for your life. My lungs were aching by the time the first button opened. The second took less time. I kicked as much as I could. The boots felt like weights.

Three buttons. Four. Five.

What would they say about me? She died with her boots on? Unable to unbutton her coat? I latched on to a root near the shore. It kept me from being swept under the ice. One boot slipped off. I put my energy into freeing the other.

My lungs were burning as I bent over in the water and forced myself to take off the second boot. I used one hand and grabbed the root with the other. This time my foot came out of the Sorel, which held fast in the roots.

I couldn't do it. Too hard. I heard my father's voice. "You're a MacPhee. We are not quitters."

I fumbled until the coat opened. It slipped from my shoulders after a couple of weary shrugs. I felt the incredible lightness as the coat sank toward the river bottom.

Freed from my trap, I experienced the full pull of the current. With numb hands I clung to the root and gradually, painfully pulled myself toward the surface. Somehow now it didn't feel so cold. And, I didn't care much any more. What did it matter? Time to let go. Everything would be all right. Easy.

My father's voice again. "Not good enough. Get going."

Bad girl, in cold water again. Sorry, Daddy.

When the going gets tough, the tough get climbing.

Hand over hand, that's all, Camilla. You'll get there. Hand over hand. Don't go to sleep. Don't.

Thanks, Daddy.

I felt the rush of air as my head crested the water.

"Well, well, well, I knew there was some reason those bubbles kept coming up," said Mia Reilly. "Some people don't know when to quit. It's too bad you never learned to mind your own business."

I spat out the filthy water. "People know we're here. They know about you."

She looked around and laughed. "What people would they be? Nice bluff. Goodbye, Camilla."

I clung to the root of the tree and fought to speak. "Why are you doing this?"

"You couldn't stop digging, could you. Do you think for one minute that I'm going to let you and your idiot assistant cause me to lose everything?"

She raised her foot.

"Wait, Mia. No one suspects you."

"You couldn't just let things alone. I'm going to have a great marriage with the perfect man. He has a wonderful house, he drives a Jaguar, he's a partner in the biggest firm in town. I'll have the job I've always wanted. I didn't let Ralph wreck my career and my engagement, and I'm sure not going to let you do it. You're just not important enough to ruin everything. Don't bother looking over at that stupid kid. He's dead."

I jerked my head. Alvin had disappeared. It was over. But she wouldn't get away with it if I could save myself. My fingers were starting to lose their grip on the roots. "Forensics will put two and two together."

"They won't come up with this answer. Anyway, I'll have the perfect alibi tonight."

She was quivering, a dangerous quiver for me. Dangerous for her too because off to the side, something inched forward, out of the water and up the embankment, something dark and dangerous, clinging to a Mickey Mouse scarf. Then it stopped, just stopped. Alvin lay still, a dark lump with a flash of neon orange. We were so close to making it. He couldn't die on me.

I grasped the base of the tree and pulled myself toward the

shore, slipping and gasping. Adrenalin pumped through my system as I crawled upward and forward.

Mia was concentrating on me. She didn't notice even when the dark shape dragged itself to its feet and staggered in her direction.

"You always were a stubborn bitch, Camilla." She raised her boot. Upward and forward.

I lay in the snow on the riverbank and barely managed to gasp: "Did you kill Rina too? Did you attack Mrs. Parnell?"

"You'll never know."

"Watch me, Mia, I'm going to bring you down."

She lunged toward me. Behind her, Alvin rose like the chief ghoul in a horror movie and launched himself.

"I don't think so," she said.

Mia's knees buckled, as Alvin crashed into her. She pitched sideways and landed in the slush. I grabbed at her and caught a fist full of expensive hair. It gave me enough momentum to get onto solid ground. Mia lay still for a minute. She reared up again, just as I pulled myself to a kneeling position. Behind her, Alvin crumpled.

"I'll deal with you later," Mia yelled. With a burst of speed, she pushed me back toward the water. I wasn't going there again. She bent over, her crazy face loomed above me. "Third time lucky, Camilla." My hands were beyond feeling, my legs no longer worked. I heard my father's voice. "You're a MacPhee. MacPhees always use their heads."

With my last bit of strength, I threw myself forward and butted her chin with the top of my skull. She screamed and fell back over Alvin. The scream stopped when her head hit the rock.

I tumbled toward the ground. I probably screamed too when my leg snapped.

# Thirty-Two

L eave me alone." The wail of sirens hurt my ears. And this slapping business.

"Camilla, Camilla."

If that person didn't stop slapping me, I'd just have to open my eyes and clout him.

"She's trying to talk. Listen." Sounded a lot like Edwina.

Slap. Slap.

"I'm trying to say leave me alone."

"What is it? What's she saying."

"I don't know. She's just mumbling."

"Down here. They're down here. You better hurry." Who was that? McCracken? Wasn't he supposed to be somewhere else?

Who was crying? Alexa. I shouldn't have ruined her rehearsal.

"Sorry, Alexa."

"Oh, Camilla."

"What's she saying?" A man's voice. Whose?

"It's okay, stay quiet. Camilla. You'll be all right."

Slap me one more time and I'll tie your tail in knots, Mombourquette.

Leave me alone. Don't want to be lifted. Tired. Where is Alvin? Find Alvin. I don't want to go in there. Turn the light off. I don't need this cover on me, what is it? Heavy. I can't move my arms. Was that P. J.?

Not those goddam sirens again.

*    *    *

A hospital is not the place for a person like me. That goes double if the first furry face I see when I wrench open my eyes is Mombourquette's.

"What are you doing here?" I said, once I'd grasped the meaning of the intravenous feed, the clouds of carnations and the seasick green walls.

His nose twitched. "Just once, could you try not to be rude?"

"Not trying to be rude. I just expected something else." I didn't know what, but it sure wasn't Mombourquette.

"Sorry to let you down. Just checking to see if you were up to giving us a statement yet."

Wait a minute. If I was in the hospital, why wasn't my family crying and carrying on and reeling off rosaries to aid my recovery? "A statement? That's very sweet. Where are my sisters and my father?"

"They've been here. Keeping a vigil. But they just headed down the hall because the nurses were having a little do for Alvin."

The memories of our night at the river came flooding back. "Is he all right?"

From down the hall came the sound of a group singing "Cheeseburger in Paradise." "Never mind. I guess he is."

"He had a close call. Thanks to you. The pneumonia's starting to react to the antibiotics."

"Pneumonia? What do you mean, thanks to me? Thanks to Mia Reilly. Which reminds me, she's the one you want to talk to if you're looking for statements. She killed Benning. She admitted it. I think you'll find he'd been blackmailing her for years."

Mombourquette yawned. "Tell me something I don't know.

It's been going on since she joined the Crown Attorney's office. Benning was most likely the reason she took the job. She fiddled with enough cases to make us suspicious. That's what Randy Cousins was working on. She couldn't understand why every one of Benning's cases got tossed out or pled down. Randy already hated the SOB, and she'd figured out it had to be someone in the Crown attorney's office who was giving him the breaks. She's been watching Mia Reilly for months."

It was hard to listen to Mombourquette at the best of times. But now my head wouldn't stop spinning, and my leg throbbed. For some reason, I felt like throwing up. But I couldn't stand to let Mombourquette believe he'd solved it.

"Let me fill in the blanks for you," I said. "Benning liked to play dangerous games. He wouldn't have wanted Mia to marry, let alone marry a bigshot in the legal community. If she had solid emotional support, that would have loosened his hold on her. It was typical of Benning to turn up the blackmail burner just when things were going well for her. Only this time she had too much to lose. She's a tough little number, and she'd had enough. So she engineered his escape, slipped him a gun, and then arranged to meet him in the park. She slipped him some Rohypnol, shot him and slipped the body into the river to freeze."

"Partly right. They found traces of Rohypnol."

"Maybe Alvin and I wouldn't have risked death if you'd shared that information."

"But only partly. What makes you think he was shot?"

"What?"

"She drugged him and let him freeze. He was not shot."

For some reason I had trouble thinking straight, although that was none of Mombourquette's business. "I hope you turkeys didn't let her get away. Is she in custody?" I could hardly ask Mombourquette whose blood was at the river site without incriminating Lindsay.

"Yes. No bail either. And, by the way, we could have pulled the case together a lot faster without all your bullshit."

"Speaking of pulling, pull the other one. Who owns all these flowers? They're everywhere."

"Looks like you do. I can't imagine who sent them. Look, Conn and I and Randy Cousins just about had the case cracked."

"You mean someone sent me a prickly cactus? Was that you?"

"No. But I can sympathize with the sentiment."

"Why didn't you tell me what you were doing about Mia Reilly?"

"Gee, maybe because you're a civilian, and *we're* the police?"

"But I had evidence. Are those red roses mine?"

"You had squat, Camilla."

I kept quiet. I could feel my brain clicking. And high time too. There was only one person whose blood it could have been.

"Read my lips, Leonard. We had the answers. Alvin found Mia's fur-lined glove at the river site. I'll bet the farm the lab will find traces of Rina Benning's blood on it. I think Benning took Rina to the site and beat her seriously. When Mia joined him there, she doped him with her favourite substance, Rohypnol. She probably just did her coffee trick again. Then she bundled him up and left him to freeze. My guess is she arranged his body in that kneeling position and covered him with snow until rigour took over. Then she took Rina, who was probably dead or dying, in her car and dumped her in the country to get the search going in that area. Give herself time to play her game with Benning's body and throw suspicion on Elaine. And Lindsay too."

Mombourquette stared at the wall, which more or less confirmed my theory.

I kept talking. "One thing that really bothered me was the ice on the body. After being in that river, I realize you don't have to be frozen through to get a layer of ice on you. Since she planned the whole thing and planned to frame Elaine from the beginning, I'm betting Mia came back to the park and rolled Benning's body into the shallow part of the river. At least the outer part would freeze pretty quickly with a nice coating of ice. You should probably be checking out winch rentals. Think about it. Mia would have been able to trot through that park without anyone noticing. Even if someone did notice, how could they identify her? Everything was to muddy the waters, throw suspicion on someone else. Obviously, Mia sent you the video and made the call for you to check out Lindsay. With two strong suspects, the police were guaranteed to go down the wrong road. Who knew better how to set up evidence than an Assistant Crown Attorney? Obviously, Mia thought we had enough information to be a serious threat to her, since she tried to kill us to keep it secret." The room was whirling, but I still couldn't let Mombourquette scurry away. "So I hope you bagged that glove for evidence."

"Of course we did. But I told you…"

"Don't forget to check out winch rentals. I'm telling you. Mia and Benning were not the only people at the site. Rina Benning was there too."

"You think she was foolish enough to meet him there?"

"No, and that's been bothering me. Rina was terrified of Benning. She'd never let herself be alone with him, but why would she be afraid of a high profile Assistant Crown Attorney? Check out Mia's home, and you'll probably find the original tape. I think Benning called Mia, and she played that tape on a phone call to Rina's after she got Rina to leave. You can confirm the phone records."

"You don't need to tell us how to do our jobs."

"Good. Then you can build the case that Mia moved the dead or dying Rina to make it look like Benning was still alive. She may have killed her herself. It made Benning look like even more of a monster. Plus she would have wanted to confuse the times to establish an alibi. Just in case."

Mombourquette's nose wrinkled. "Maybe it's worth looking into. But what makes you think she was lured there and killed? Why not killed in the car?"

"Call it a hunch."

Mombourquette said, "You better not be holding out on me."

"Speaking of holding out, how come you didn't show up at the river after I called? A lot of this could have been prevented."

"Because I was at St. Jim's at six-thirty. For the rehearsal. I don't know why you bothered phoning."

"I thought the rehearsal was at seven."

"Wrong again."

"I tried to reach you. You didn't answer."

"You keep cellphones turned off in church. Which you'd know if you ever went."

"If you didn't get my message, how did you find out where Alvin and I were in time? Well, not in time, but better late than never."

"Talk about lack of gratitude. Mrs. Parnell was frantic and managed to make contact with your father at St. Jim's. I don't know how she did it, but she got through." Mombourquette looked a bit puzzled. He doesn't know Mrs. P. as well as I do.

"She wasn't exactly sure where in the park, so we all raced out to find you. It's a good thing you were near death already.

Those sisters of yours were ready to string you up."

"I don't want to talk about that. Back to Mia. You saying you have enough on her without Alvin's evidence?"

"We've located the stolen van that transported Benning's body."

"Drill hole in the door, right?"

"Yep."

"She was the one who drilled the hole in Elaine's SUV and put Rohypnol in the coffee that drugged us and the cops."

"Right. We found trace evidence supporting that in the SUV. We found the drill in her car. I'm surprised she kept it."

"She was probably hanging on to it until she got rid of all the pesky investigators. Like Alvin and Mrs. P."

"Anyway, forensics should be able to link it to the paint on the SUV and the van. I think we'll find her DNA on Elaine's clothes, now that we know what we're looking for."

"You wouldn't have even looked for the drill if I hadn't told McCracken about it."

"Hang on, Camilla. You were trying to blame it all on Randy. We were closing in on Mia anyway. Her source for the roofies blabbed. He'll testify in exchange for getting date rape charges dropped."

Now I had something else to feel sick about. "That's disgusting. You think the Crown will take him up on that offer?"

"Might not have to. We're already picking holes in her statement."

"Does the statement read like a confession?"

"No. But it's full of contradictions. She seems to have forgotten she came to at the river site and flipped out in front of plenty of witnesses, including the paramedics. Tried to fight her way out. Once it looked like you and Alvin were going to survive, she caved. That's even before the attempted murder charges for the attack on Mrs. Parnell. And you, of course, although that's more understandable."

"Funny. I'd like to know how she knew to follow Mrs. Parnell."

"She won't say anything about it. I think she was just trying to keep an eye on you and anyone connected with you. According to her office, she'd been missing time for minor medical complaints. Maybe she hung around outside your place or something. We're more interested that she's admitted to the big ticket item."

"You mean she confessed to killing Benning?"

"According to the Crown, she's going to plead down to manslaughter and interfering with a body. Rumour is her lawyer will cite battered spouse syndrome as an extenuating circumstance."

"What? Are you serious? This was completely and utterly premeditated, and you goddam well know it. What about Rina?" I shouldn't have waved my arms because it knocked the IV line loose.

This time he didn't meet my eyes. "We haven't proved that yet. She'll plead guilty to Benning, with extenuating circumstances, but not that. We're coming up empty on it. I think she'll walk on that one."

"Goddam it. She can't."

He shrugged. "We figure the Crown doesn't want a ton of media attention on this one. They'll accept a plea bargain and keep it low profile."

I figured with P. J. Lynch on the job, it would stay high-profile. I'd be happy to help with that. "Unless they get her for Rina, Leonard."

Mombourquette leaned in, uncomfortably close. "You'd better not be keeping anything from me."

"I told you. I've got a feeling. Follow up on the glove and the tape of the message Benning left for Rina. See if he called her 'Little Girl'. Don't interrupt, Leonard. And if there's blood in her car, I bet it will be Rina's."

After everything she'd been through, I didn't see any reason to hand Lindsay over.

"Time for you to stop playing detective, Camilla. You're not completely off the hook with the law society yet. Don't make me use that against you."

I snorted. "You really scare me, Leonard. What about Elaine? Did she get released yet? I imagine that will be worth an internal review."

He blushed. "Not our fault she was in there. Remember? She was making a political point. The Crown could still take action over the false confession. They could charge her with mischief or even perjury."

I struggled up to a sitting position. My head tweeted. "You'd better suggest they won't keep a low profile over Assistant Crown Attorney's Mia Reilly's crimes, if they even think about it. I'll personally see to that."

"You and me both. We found out quite a bit from Mia. She was willing to confide some stuff she didn't tell you. All it took was someone sympathetic." Was I mistaken or did a rosy blush work its way onto his face? "She claims that when Benning escaped and stole a car and chased after Alvin thinking he was you, she panicked."

"Yeah right. Use your brain, Leonard. I'm betting she had that car ready for him and she knew exactly what he was going to do. Look for the drill hole. Remember?"

"Do you have to interrupt constantly, Camilla? Then Mia called Elaine at the WAVE office and told her about Benning's escape. Mia suggested Elaine get over and protect Lindsay."

"Very strategic. Mia didn't know where Lindsay was. So all she had to do was follow. It indicates that the whole attempt to frame Elaine was premeditated and worked out before Benning's escape," I said.

"Right. Elaine mentioned she'd bring coffee and pizza from the Colonnade, and we're certain Mia used that information to modify her plan and muddy the waters. She probably couldn't believe her luck when Elaine decided to make political hay out of the whole mess. Anyway, the main thing is Elaine's out. She's getting back to normal."

"Elaine's back to normal? How long have I been in this hospital? Oh crap. Did I miss the wedding?"

"No such luck. You've been out of it for nearly two days, but it's still only Sunday. The wedding's not until tomorrow, Valentine's Day. And you'd better stay conscious."

"One more thing, Leonard. Since we're buddies again, you can tell me. Who signed that directive? The one where I was persona non grata with the police."

Mombourquette gave a rodential little chuckle. "Can't believe you fell for that one, Camilla. There was no directive. Randy and Conn and I just wanted you to keep your nose out of the case before you blew our case on Mia. Now it looks like you're out of the way for a while."

"That's what you think." I swung my legs to try to get out of bed. Nothing prepared me for the pain that shot through my thigh. I yelped and fell back on the bed, gasping.

"What the hell's wrong with my leg?"

I didn't get a chance to find out before my family hurtled through the door.

It was hours before I had the strength to call P. J. and thank him for the prickly cactus.

*       *       *

Monday, February 14, turned out to be the perfect day for a candlelight wedding, if you like that sort of thing. Soft flakes of snow, set against the indigo winter sky, made a dramatic backdrop for the wedding party's comings and goings. Alexa looked queenly in her pearl French velvet ankle length dress, with five kinds of cream flowers and quite the cleavage. Conn couldn't take his eyes off her. Even Mombourquette came across like one of the higher order vertebrates. As for me, the less said about my crutches the better.

Alexa and Conn had chosen words and music that were deep and meaningful. Alexa's boys stood tall and proud. My father wiped away a tear. The grand duchesses Donalda and Edwina wept like faucets. I was damned glad to be on drugs.

When we finally exploded from the front door of St. Jim's, into the blue winter light and headed off to Hull and the Museum of Civilization for the reception at Les Muses, just about everybody was in the mood to party.

*       *       *

"Nevertheless, don't thank me." Mrs. Parnell raised her voice to be heard above the roar of the reception. "Least I could do for my comrade-in-arms."

"It was brilliant, Violet." My father squeezed her hand. I don't remember ever seeing him quite so animated. "You are a true heroine."

"All in the line of duty." Mrs. P. swanned through the receiving line, looking swish. She sported a sweetheart rose corsage that matched her red lacquer cigarette holder. "You are her father. It seemed logical to go up the chain of command."

"It was very clever of you, Violet."

"Well. young Ferguson's the hero. He saved Camilla's bacon." She waved to Alvin without spilling a drop of her Harvey's.

Alvin beamed. No wonder. It couldn't have been easy finding a tux in any shade of orange, yet alone that one.

"Great outfit, Violet. *Totally* retro. You look surprisingly good too, Camilla. That makeup really covers your scratches," he said. "And your dress. *Love* the pink. And the slit is so up to the moment."

"Thank you, Alvin. I didn't have much choice with this cast." I smiled back at him. I felt a whole lot mellower than usual. Three days of painkillers will do that.

He pulled me away from the receiving line and whispered. "I'm so sorry."

I wasn't sure I'd heard correctly. "You're sorry? For what?"

"For blowing it like that."

I shook my head. "What are you talking about?"

"Mia at the river. Trying to kill us. She was there because I ran into her in the hospital, and I told her I'd found some information that would connect the murderer with Benning. I told her she'd regret the trouble she caused you with the Law Society, because we were just about to blow the case wide open."

"You think I didn't know that, Alvin?"

"Oh."

"But you're not to blame for Mia. If it hadn't been that, it would have been someone else, somewhere else, and maybe the ending wouldn't have been so happy."

I gave him a reassuring pat on the arm and hobbled away before my temporary niceness wore off.

I looked up the receiving line. Surrounded by hundreds of friends, colleagues and family, Alexa and Conn glowed like twin bonfires. Even I had to agree no one had ever been a more beautiful bride. You could hear Donalda chatting and Edwina issuing orders.

At a nearby table Elaine Ekstein fielded her own receiving line of well-wishers. Mombourquette, looking sleek and well-fed in a soft gray suit, stood as close as he could get without wearing her dress.

"Holy moly," Elaine screamed obligingly when Stan dropped a plastic cockroach into her peach schnapps. Randy Cousins thought that was hilarious. I steered clear of Elaine myself. I didn't feel like getting pissed off all over again.

No one mentioned Mia Reilly. It would take a hell of a long time for the police to sort out the damage she'd done. Some of it would never come to light. I was sorry she wouldn't be having much of a trial. The best I could hope for was to be in court to watch when her sentence was pronounced. If Lindsay worked up the courage to come forward, the sentence would get longer.

But this particular night, none of that mattered. The reception hall was a glittering fairyland. The flowers showed the many subtle shades of cream. The string quartet went for baroque.

I only thought about Paul once or twice during the entire evening. I had to admit, I was happy for Alexa. She deserved a new start. Maybe we all did.

Toward midnight, Alvin's slanty little eyes grew misty. He sidled closer and sniffed. "My conscience is bothering me about it."

"It's over."

"But everyone knows I saved you. No one knows you also saved me and, anyway, you wouldn't have been in danger in the first place if I hadn't told Mia about the evidence in the park."

"And no one's going to find out about it from me. End of story, Alvin."